Praise for Nancy Kress's previous b

"Kress's villains are not diabolical co. ... . .ut willfully ignorant hypocrites, shortsighted and greedy dunderheads, the well-intentioned half-baked—in short, us. But we are also the heroes whose generosity, honesty, and energy could turn our lemming tribe away from the polluted waters ahead."
—*Washington Post*

"The plotting is fast-paced, the characterization is good, and science explained in easily digestible portions."—*New Scientist*

"The kind of thriller that continually makes you want to turn the pages faster than you can read them."—*SF Site*

"That Kress remains a master is everywhere evident."—*Booklist*

"The keeness of vision to . . . see the possibilities for the future very clearly, and they are both fascinating and frightening."
—*San Francisco Examiner and Chronicle*

"Kress can reach beyond mastery of technique and generate provocative and complex art."—Gary Wolfe, *Locus*

"A glimpse into the mind of someone who is interpreting our rapidly changing world as it changes."—*SFRA Review*

"An important and unique writer."—*Denver Post*

"A new book from Nancy Kress is always a cause for celebration."—Connie Willis

"It should now be clear to all that Nancy Kress is a dominant figure in science fiction."—*Analog*

"Nancy Kress has the true storyteller's Gift—the ability to make her characters and what happens to them so vital that the reader's heart aches."—Stephen R. Donaldson

"Nancy Kress comprehends the grimy relationships among bioscience, technology, and politics; and soon we will too, if only enough of us read her. Too soon it cannot be."
—Gene Wolfe

fountain
of
age

stories

NANCY KRESS

Small Beer Press
Easthampton, MA

Fountain of Age: Stories copyright © 2012 by Nancy Kress. All rights reserved.
www.sff.net/people/nankress

Small Beer Press
150 Pleasant Street #306
Easthampton, MA 01027
www.smallbeerpress.com
www.weightlessbooks.com
info@smallbeerpress.com

Distributed to the trade by Consortium.

ISBN: 978-1-931520-45-4 (trade paper); 978-1-931520-46-1 (ebook)

Library of Congress Cataloging-in-Publication Data

Kress, Nancy.
  Fountain of age : stories / Nancy Kress. -- 1st ed.
    p. cm.
  ISBN 978-1-931520-45-4 (alk. paper) -- ISBN 978-1-931520-46-1 (ebook)
  I. Title.
  PS3561.R46F68 2012
  813'.54--dc23
                                    2012001080

First edition 1 2 3 4 5 6 7 8 9

Text set in Centaur. Titles set in Menlo.

Printed on 50# 30% PCR recycled Natures Natural paper by C-M Books in the USA.
Cover by fonografiks (fonografiks.com).

Contents

For Jack

THE ERDMANN NEXUS

"Errors, like straws, upon the surface flow,
He who would reach for pearls must dive below."
—John Dryden

The ship, which would have looked nothing like a ship to Henry Erdmann, moved between the stars, traveling in an orderly pattern of occurrences in the vacuum flux. Over several cubic light-years of space, subatomic particles appeared, existed, and winked out of existence in nanoseconds. Flop transitions tore space and then reconfigured it as the ship moved on. Henry, had he somehow been nearby in the cold of deep space, would have died from the complicated, regular, intense bursts of radiation long before he could have had time to appreciate their shimmering beauty.

All at once the "ship" stopped moving.

The radiation bursts increased, grew even more complex. Then the ship abruptly changed direction. It accelerated, altering both space and time as it sped on, healing the alterations in its wake. Urgency shot through it.

Something, far away, was struggling to be born.

ONE

Henry Erdmann stood in front of the mirror in his tiny bedroom, trying to knot his tie with one hand. The other hand gripped his walker. It was an unsteady business, and the tie ended up crooked. He yanked it out and began again. Carrie would be here soon.

He always wore a tie to the college. Let the students—and graduate students, at that!—come to class in ripped jeans and obscene T-shirts and hair tangled as if colonized by rats. Even the girls. Students were students, and Henry didn't consider their sloppiness disrespectful, the way so many did at St. Sebastian's. Sometimes he was even amused by it,

1

in a sad sort of way. Didn't these intelligent, sometimes driven, would-be physicists know how ephemeral their beauty was? Why did they go to such lengths to look unappealing, when soon enough that would be their only choice?

This time he got the tie knotted. Not perfectly—a difficult operation, one-handed—but close enough for government work. He smiled. When he and his colleagues had been doing government work, only perfection was good enough. Atomic bombs were like that. Henry could still hear Oppie's voice saying the plans for Ivy Mike were "technically sweet." Of course, that was before all the—

A knock on the door and Carrie's fresh young voice. "Dr. Erdmann? Are you ready?"

She always called him by his title, always treated him with respect. Not like some of the nurses and assistants. "How are we today, Hank?" that overweight blonde asked yesterday. When he answered stiffly, "I don't know about you, madam, but I'm fine, thank you," she'd only laughed. *Old people are so formal—it's so cute!* Henry could just see her saying it to one of her horrible colleagues. He had never been "Hank" in his entire life.

"Coming, Carrie." He put both hands on the walker and inched forward—clunk, clunk, clunk—the walker sounding loud even on the carpeted floor. His class's corrected problem sets lay on the table by the door. He'd given them some really hard problems this week, and only Haldane had succeeded in solving all of them. Haldane had promise. An inventive mind, yet rigorous, too. They could have used him in '52 on Project Ivy, developing the Teller-Ulam staged fusion H-bomb.

Halfway across the living room of his tiny apartment in the assisted living facility, something happened in Henry's mind.

He stopped, astonished. It had felt like a tentative *touch*, a ghostly finger inside his brain. Astonishment was immediately replaced by fear. Was he having a stroke? At ninety, anything was possible. But he felt fine, better in fact than for several days. Not a stroke. So what—

"Dr. Erdmann?"

"I'm here." He clunked to the door and opened it. Carrie wore a cherry red sweater, a fallen orange leaf caught on her hat, and sunglasses. Such a pretty girl, all bronze hair and bright skin and vibrant color. Outside it was drizzling. Henry reached out and gently removed the sunglasses. Carrie's left eye was swollen and discolored, the iris and pupil invisible under the outraged flesh.

"The bastard," Henry said.

That was Henry and Carrie going down the hall toward the elevator, thought Evelyn Krenchnoted. She waved from her armchair, her door wide open as always, but they were talking and didn't notice. She strained to hear, but just then another plane went overhead from the airport. Those pesky flight paths were too near St. Sebastian's! On the other hand, if they weren't, Evelyn couldn't afford to live here. Always look on the bright side!

Since this was Tuesday afternoon, Carrie and Henry were undoubtedly going to the college. So wonderful the way Henry kept busy—you'd never guess his real age, that was for sure. He even had all his hair! Although that jacket was too light for September, and not waterproof. Henry might catch cold. She would speak to Carrie about it. And why was Carrie wearing sunglasses when it was raining?

But if Evelyn didn't start her phone calls, she would be late! People were depending on her! She keyed in the first number, listened to it ring one floor below. "Bob? It's Evelyn. Now, dear, tell me—how's your blood pressure today?"

"Fine," Bob Donovan said.

"Are you sure? You sound a bit grumpy, dear."

"I'm fine, Evelyn. I'm just busy."

"Oh, that's good! With what?"

"Just *busy.*"

"Always good to keep busy! Are you coming to Current Affairs tonight?"

"Dunno."

"You should. You really should. Intellectual stimulation is so important for people our age!"

"Gotta go," Bob grunted.

"Certainly, but first, how did your granddaughter do with—"

He'd hung up. Really, very grumpy. Maybe he was having problems with irregularity. Evelyn would recommend a high colonic.

Her next call was more responsive. Gina Martinelli was, as always, thrilled with Evelyn's attention. She informed Gina minutely about the state of her arthritis, her gout, her diabetes, her son's weight problem, her other son's wife's stepdaughter's miscarriage, all interspersed with quotations from the Bible ("Take a little wine for thy stomach"—First Timothy.") She answered all Evelyn's questions and wrote down all her recommendations and—

"Evelyn?" Gina said. "Are you still there?"

"Yes, I—" Evelyn fell silent, an occurrence so shocking that Gina gasped, "Hit your panic button!"

"No, no, I'm fine, I . . . I just remembered something for a moment."

"Remembered something? What?"

But Evelyn didn't know. It hadn't been a memory, exactly, it had been a . . . what? A feeling, a vague but somehow strong sensation of . . . something.

"Evelyn?"

"I'm here!"

"The Lord decides when to call us home, and I guess it's not your time yet. Did you hear about Anna Chernov? That famous ballet dancer on Four? She fell last night and broke her leg and they had to move her to the Infirmary."

"No!"

"Yes, poor thing. They say it's only temporary, until they get her stabilized, but you know what that means."

She did. They all did. First the Infirmary, then up to Seven, where you didn't even have your own little apartment anymore, and eventually to Nursing on Eight and Nine. Better to go quick and clean, like Jed Fuller last month. But Evelyn wasn't going to let herself think like that! A positive attitude was so important!

Gina said, "Anna is doing pretty well, I hear. The Lord never sends more than a person can bear."

Evelyn wasn't so sure about that, but it never paid to argue with Gina, who was convinced that she had God on redial. Evelyn said, "I'll visit her before the Stitch 'n Bitch meeting. I'm sure she'll want company. Poor girl—you know, those dancers, they just abuse their health for years and years, so what can you expect?"

"I know!" Gina said, not without satisfaction. "They pay a terrible price for beauty. It's a little vain, actually."

"Did you hear about that necklace she has in the St. Sebastian safe?"

"No! What necklace?"

"A fabulous one! Doris Dziwalski told me. It was given to Anna by some famous Russian dancer who was given it by the czar!"

"What czar?"

"*The* czar! You know, of Russia. Doris said it's worth a fortune and that's why it's in the safe. Anna never wears it."

"Vanity," Doris said. "She probably doesn't like the way it looks now against her wrinkly neck."

"Doris said Anna's depressed."

"No, it's vanity. 'Lo, I looked and saw that all was—'"

"I'll recommend accupuncture to her," Evelyn interrupted. "Accupuncture is good for depression." But first she'd call Erin, to tell her the news.

Erin Bass let the phone ring. It was probably that tiresome bore Evelyn Krenchnoted, eager to check on Erin's blood pressure or her cholesterol or her Isles of Langerhans. Oh, Erin should answer the phone, there was no harm in the woman, Erin should be more charitable. But why? Why should one have to be more charitable just because one was old?

She let the phone ring and returned to her book, Graham Greene's *The Heart of the Matter*. Greene's world-weary despair was a silly affectation but he was a wonderful writer, and too much underrated nowadays.

The liner came in on a Saturday evening: from the bedroom window they could see its long grey form steal past the boom, beyond the—

Something was happening.

—steal past the boom, beyond the—

Erin was no longer in St. Sebastian's, she was nowhere, she was lifted away from everything, she was beyond the—

Then it was over and she sat again in her tiny apartment, the book sliding unheeded off her lap.

✹

Anna Chernov was dancing. She and Paul stood with two other couples on the stage, under the bright lights. Balanchine himself stood in the second wing, and even though Anna knew he was there to wait for Suzanne's solo, his presence inspired her. The music began. *Promenade en couronne, attitude, arabesque effacé* and into the lift, Paul's arms raising her. She was lifted out of herself and then she was soaring above the stage, over the heads of the corps de ballet, above Suzanne Farrell herself, soaring through the roof of the New York State Theater and into the night sky, spreading her arms in a *porte de bras* wide enough to take in the glittering night sky, soaring in the most perfect *jeté* in the universe, until . . .

"She's smiling," Bob Donovan said, before he knew he was going to speak at all. He looked down at the sleeping Anna, so beautiful she didn't even look real, except for the leg in its big ugly cast. In one hand, feeling like a fool but what the fuck, he held three yellow roses.

"The painkillers do that sometimes," the Infirmary nurse said. "I'm afraid you can't stay, Mr. Donovan."

Bob scowled at her. But it wasn't like he meant it or anything. This nurse wasn't so bad. Not like some. Maybe because she wasn't any spring chicken herself. *A few more years, sister, and you'll be right here with us.*

"Give her these, okay?" He thrust the roses at the nurse.

"I will, yes," she said, and he walked out of the medicine-smelling Infirmary—he hated that smell—back to the elevator. Christ, what a sorry old fart he was. Anna Chernov, that nosy old broad Evelyn Krenchnoted once told him, used to dance at some famous place in New York, Abraham Center or something. Anna had been famous. But Evelyn could be wrong, and anyway it didn't matter. From the first moment Bob Donovan laid eyes on Anna Chernov, he'd wanted to give her things. Flowers. Jewelry. Anything she wanted. Anything he had. And how stupid and fucked-up was that, at his age? Give me a break!

He took the elevator to the first floor, stalked savagely through the lobby, and went out the side door to the "remembrance garden." Stupid name, New Age-y stupid. He wanted to kick something, wanted to bellow for—

Energy punched through him, from the base of his spine up his back and into his brain, mild but definite, like a shock from a busted toaster or something. Then it was gone.

What the fuck was *that*? Was he okay? If he fell, like Anna—

He was okay. He didn't have Anna's thin delicate bones. Whatever it was, was gone now. Just one of those things.

On a Nursing floor of St. Sebastian's, a woman with just a few days to live muttered in her long, last half-sleep. An IV dripped morphine into her arm, easing the passage. No one listened to the mutterings; it had been years since they'd made sense. For a moment she stopped and her eyes, again bright in the ravaged face that had once been so lovely, grew wide. But for only a moment. Her eyes closed and the mindless muttering resumed.

In Tijuana, a vigorous old man sitting behind his son's market stall, where he sold cheap serapes to jabbering *touristos*, suddenly lifted his face to the sun. His mouth, which still had all its white flashing teeth, made a big O.

In Mumbai, a widow dressed in white looked out her window at the teeming streets, her face gone blank as her sari.

In Chengdu, a monk sitting on his cushion on the polished floor of the meditation room in the ancient Wenshu Monastery, shattered the holy silence with a shocking, startled laugh.

TWO

Carrie Vesey sat in the back of Dr. Erdmann's classroom and thought about murder.

Not that she would ever do it, of course. Murder was wrong. Taking a life filled her with horror that was only—

Ground-up castor beans were a deadly poison.

—made worse by her daily witnessing of old people's aching desire to hold onto life. Also, she—

Her stepbrother had once shown her how to disable the brakes on a car.

—knew she wasn't the kind of person who solved problems that boldly. And anyway her—

The battered-woman defense almost always earned acquittal from juries.

—lawyer said that a paper trail of restraining orders and ER documentation was by far the best way to—

If a man was passed out from a dozen beers, he'd never feel a bullet from his own service revolver.

—put Jim behind bars legally. That, the lawyer said, "would solve the problem"—as if a black eye and a broken arm and constant threats that left her scared even when Jim wasn't in the same *city* were all just a theoretical "problem," like the ones Dr. Erdmann gave his physics students.

He sat on top of a desk in the front of the room, talking about something called the "Bose-Einstein condensate." Carrie had no idea what that was, and she didn't care. She just liked being here, sitting unheeded in the back of the room. The physics students, nine boys and two girls, were none of them interested in her presence, her black eye, or her beauty. When Dr. Erdmann was around, he commanded all their geeky attention, and that was indescribably restful. Carrie tried—unsuccessfully, she knew—to hide her beauty. Her looks had brought her nothing but trouble: Gary, Eric, Jim. So now she wore baggy sweats and no makeup, and crammed her 24-carat-gold hair under a shapeless hat. Maybe if she was as smart as these students she would have learned to pick a different kind of man, but she wasn't, and she hadn't, and Dr. Erdmann's classroom was a place she felt safe. Safer, even, than St. Sebastian's, which was where Jim had blackened her eye.

He'd slipped in through the loading dock, she guessed, and caught her alone in the linens supply closet. He was gone after one punch, and when she called her exasperated lawyer and he found out she had no witnesses and St. Sebastian's had "security," he'd said there was nothing he could do. It would be her word against Jim's. She had to be able to *prove* that the restraining order had been violated.

Dr. Erdmann was talking about "proof," too: some sort of mathematical proof. Carrie had been good at math, in high school. Only Dr.

Erdmann had said once that what she'd done in high school wasn't "mathematics," only "arithmetic." "Why didn't you go to college, Carrie?" he'd asked.

"No money," she said in a tone that meant: Please don't ask anything else. She just hadn't felt up to explaining about Daddy and the alcoholism and the debts and her abusive step   brothers, and Dr. Erdmann hadn't asked. He was sensitive that way.

Looking at his tall, stooped figure sitting on the desk, his walker close to hand, Carrie sometimes let herself dream that Dr. Erdmann—Henry—was fifty years younger. Forty to her twenty-eight—that would work. She'd googled a picture of him at that age, when he'd been working at someplace called the Lawrence Radiation Laboratory. He'd been handsome, dark-haired, smiling into the camera next to his wife, Ida. She hadn't been as pretty as Carrie, but she'd gone to college, so even if Carrie had been born back then, she wouldn't have had a chance with him. Story of her life.

"—have any questions?" Dr. Erdmann finished.

The students did—they always did—clamoring to be heard, not raising their hands, interrupting each other. But when Dr. Erdmann spoke, immediately they all shut up. Someone leapt up to write equations on the board. Dr. Erdmann slowly turned his frail body to look at them. The discussion went on a long time, almost as long as the class. Carrie fell asleep.

When she woke, it was to Dr. Erdmann, leaning on his walker, gently jiggling her shoulder. "Carrie?"

"Oh! Oh, I'm sorry!"

"Don't be. We bored you to death, poor child."

"No! I loved it!"

He raised his eyebrows and she felt shamed. He thought she was telling a polite lie, and he had very little tolerance for lies. But the truth is, she always loved being here.

Outside, it was full dark. The autumn rain had stopped and the unseen ground had that mysterious, fertile smell of wet leaves. Carrie helped Dr. Erdmann into her battered Toyota and slid behind the wheel. As they started back toward St. Sebastian's, she could tell that he was exhausted. Those students asked too much of him! It was enough that he taught one advanced class a week, sharing all that physics, without them also demanding he—

"Dr. Erdmann? "

For a long terrible moment she thought he was dead. His head lolled against the seat but he wasn't asleep: His open eyes rolled back into his head. Carrie jerked the wheel to the right and slammed the Toyota alongside the curb. He was still breathing.

"Dr. Erdmann? *Henry?*"

Nothing. Carrie dove into her purse, fumbling for her cell phone. Then it occurred to her that his panic button would be faster. She tore open the buttons on his jacket; he wasn't wearing the button. She scrambled again for the purse, starting to sob.

"Carrie?"

He was sitting up now, a shadowy figure. She hit the overhead light. His face, a fissured landscape, looked dazed and pale. His pupils were huge.

"What happened? Tell me." She tried to keep her voice even, to observe everything, because it was important to be able to make as full a report as possible to Dr. Jamison. But her hand clutched at his sleeve.

He covered her fingers with his. His voice sounded dazed. "I . . . don't know. I was . . . somewhere else?"

"A stroke?" That was what they were all afraid of. Not death, but to be incapacitated, reduced to partiality. And for Dr. Erdmann, with his fine mind . . .

"No." He sounded definite. "Something else. I don't know. Did you call 911 yet?"

The cell phone lay inert in her hand. "No, not yet, there wasn't time for—"

"Then don't. Take me home."

"All right, but you're going to see the doctor as soon as we get there." She was pleased, despite everything, with her firm tone.

"It's seven-thirty. They'll all have gone home."

But they hadn't. As soon as Carrie and Dr. Erdmann walked into the lobby, she saw a man in a white coat standing by the elevators. "Wait!" she called, loud enough that several people turned to look, evening visitors and ambulatories and a nurse Carrie didn't know. She didn't know the doctor, either, but she rushed over to him, leaving Dr. Erdmann leaning on his walker by the main entrance.

"Are you a doctor? I'm Carrie Vesey and I was bringing Dr. Erdmann—a patient, Henry Erdmann, not a medical doctor—home when he had some kind of attack, he seems all right now but someone needs to look at him, he says—"

"I'm not an M.D.," the man said, and Carrie looked at him in dismay. "I'm a neurological researcher."

She rallied. "Well, you're the best we're going to get at this hour so please look at him!" She was amazed at her own audacity.

"All right." He followed her to Dr. Erdmann, who scowled because, Carrie knew, he hated this sort of fuss. The non-M.D. seemed to pick up on that right away. He said pleasantly, "Dr. Erdmann? I'm Jake DiBella. Will you come this way, sir?" Without waiting for an answer, he turned and led the way down a side corridor. Carrie and Dr. Erdmann followed, everybody's walk normal, but still people watched. *Move along, nothing to see here* . . . why were they still staring? Why were people such ghouls?

But they weren't, really. That was just her own fear talking.

You trust too much, Carrie, Dr. Erdmann had said just last week.

In a small room on the second floor, he sat heavily on one of the three metal folding chairs. The room held the chairs, a gray filing cabinet, an ugly metal desk, and nothing else. Carrie, a natural nester, pursed her lips, and Dr. DiBella caught that, too.

"I've only been here a few days," he said apologetically. "Haven't had time yet to properly move in. Dr. Erdmann, can you tell me what happened?"

"Nothing." He wore his lofty look. "I just fell asleep for a moment and Carrie became alarmed. Really, there's no need for this fuss."

"You fell asleep?"

"Yes."

"All right. Has that happened before?"

Did Dr. Erdmann hesitate, ever so briefly? "Yes, occasionally. I *am* ninety, doctor."

DiBella nodded, apparently satisfied, and turned to Carrie. "And what happened to you? Did it occur at the same time that Dr. Erdmann fell asleep?"

Her eye. That's why people had stared in the lobby. In her concern for Dr. Erdmann, she'd forgotten about her black eye, but now it immediately began to throb again. Carrie felt herself go scarlet.

Dr. Erdmann answered. "No, it didn't happen at the same time. There was no car accident, if that's what you're implying. Carrie's eye is unrelated."

"I fell," Carrie said, knew that no one believed her, and lifted her chin.

"Okay," DiBella said amiably. "But as long as you're here, Dr. Erdmann, I'd like to enlist your help. Yours, and as many other volunteers as I can enlist at St. Sebastian's. I'm here on a Gates Foundation grant in conjunction with Johns Hopkins, to map shifts in brain electrochemistry during cerebral arousal. I'm asking volunteers to donate a few hours of their time to undergo completely painless brain scans while they look at various pictures and videos. Your participation will be an aid to science."

Carrie saw that Dr. Erdmann was going to refuse, despite the magic word "science," but then he hesitated. "What kind of brain scans?"

"Asher-Peyton and functional MRI."

"All right. I'll participate."

Carrie blinked. That didn't sound like Dr. Erdmann, who considered physics and astronomy the only "true" sciences and the rest merely poor stepchildren. But this Dr. DiBella wasn't about to let his research subject get away. He said quickly, "Excellent! Tomorrow morning at eleven, Lab 6B, at the hospital. Ms. Vesey, can you bring him over? Are you a relative?"

"No, I'm an aide here. Call me Carrie. I can bring him." Wednesday wasn't one of her usual days for Dr. Erdmann, but she'd get Marie to swap schedules.

"Wonderful. Please call me Jake." He smiled at her, and something turned over in Carrie's chest. It wasn't just that he was so handsome, with his black hair and gray eyes and nice shoulders, but also that he had masculine confidence and an easy way with him and no ring on his left hand . . . *idiot*. There was no particular warmth in his smile; it was completely professional. Was she always going to assess every man she met as a possible boyfriend? Was she really that needy?

Yes. But this one wasn't interested. And anyway, he was an educated scientist and she worked a minimum-wage job. She *was* an idiot.

She got Dr. Erdmann up to his apartment and said good-night. He seemed distant, preoccupied. Going down in the elevator, a mood of desolation came over her. What she really wanted was to stay and watch Henry Erdmann's TV, sleep on his sofa, wake up to fix his coffee and have someone to talk to while she did it. Not go back to her shabby apartment, bolted securely against Jim but never secure enough that she felt really safe. She'd rather stay here, in a home for failing old people, and how perverted and sad was that?

And what *had* happened to Dr. Erdmann on the way home from the college?

THREE

Twice now. Henry lay awake, wondering what the hell was going on in his brain. He was accustomed to relying on that organ. His knees had succumbed to arthritis, his hearing aid required constant adjustment, and his prostate housed a slow-growing cancer that, the doctor said, wouldn't kill him until long after something else did—the medical profession's idea of cheerful news. But his brain remained clear, and using it well had always been his greatest pleasure. Greater even than sex, greater than food, greater than marriage to Ida, much as he had loved her.

God, the things that age let you admit.

Which were the best years? No question there: Los Alamos, working on Operation Ivy with Ulam and Teller and Carson Mark and the rest. The excitement and frustration and awe of developing the "Sausage," the first test of staged radiation implosion. The day it was detonated at Eniwetok. Henry, a junior member of the team, hadn't of course been present at the atoll, but he'd waited breathlessly for the results from Bogon. He'd cheered when Teller, picking up the shock waves on a seismometer in California, had sent his three-word telegram to Los Alamos: "It's a boy." Harry Truman himself had requested that bomb—"to see to it that our country is able to defend itself against any possible aggressor"—and Henry was proud of his work on it.

Shock waves. Yes, *that* was what today's two incidents had felt like: shock waves to the brain. A small wave in his apartment, a larger one in Carrie's car. But from what? It could only be some failure of his nervous system, the thing he dreaded most of all, far more than he dreaded death. Granted, teaching physics to graduate students was a long way from Los Alamos or Livermore, and most of the students were dolts—although not Haldane—but Henry enjoyed it. Teaching, plus reading the journals and following the online listservs, were his connection with physics. If some neurological "shock wave" disturbed his brain . . .

It was a long time before he could sleep.

"Oh my Lord, dear, what happened to *your* eye?"

Evelyn Krenchnoted sat with her friend Gina Somebody in the tiny waiting room outside Dr. O'Kane's office. Henry scowled at her. Just like Evelyn to blurt out like that, embarrassing poor Carrie. The Krenchnoted woman was the most tactless busybody Henry had ever met, and he'd known a lot of physicists, a group not noted for tact. But at least the physicists hadn't been busybodies.

"I'm fine," Carrie said, trying to smile. "I walked into a door."

"Oh, dear, how did that happen? You should tell the doctor. I'm sure he could make a few minutes to see you, even though he must be running behind, I didn't actually have an appointment today but he'd said he'd squeeze me in because something strange happened yesterday that I want to ask him about, but the time he gave me was supposed to start five minutes ago and you must be scheduled after that, he saw Gina already but she—"

Henry sat down and stopped listening. Evelyn's noise, however, went on and on, a grating whine like a dentist drill. He imagined her on Eniwetok, rising into the air on a mushroom cloud, still talking. It was a relief when the doctor's door opened and a woman came out, holding a book.

Henry had seen her before, although he didn't know her name. Unlike most of the old bats at St. Sebastian's, she was worth looking at. Not with Carrie's radiant youthful beauty, of course; this woman must be in her seventies, at least. But she stood straight and graceful; her white hair fell in simple waves to her shoulders; her cheekbones and blue eyes were still good. However, Henry didn't care for the way she was dressed. It reminded him of all those stupid childish protestors outside Los Alamos in the fifties and sixties. The woman wore a white T-shirt, a long cotton peasant skirt, a necklace of beads and shells, and several elaborate rings.

"Erin!" Evelyn cried. "How was your appointment? Everything okay?"

"Fine. Just a check-up." Erin smiled vaguely and moved away. Henry strained to see the cover of her book: *Tao Te Ching*. Disappointment lanced through him. One of *those*.

"But you weren't scheduled for a check-up, no more than I was. So what happened that—" Erin walked quickly away, her smile fixed. Evelyn said indignantly, "Well, I call that just plain rude! Did you see that, Gina? You try to be friendly to some people and they just—"

"Mrs. Krenchnoted?" the nurse said, sticking her head out the office door. "The doctor will see you now."

Evelyn lumbered up and through the door, still talking. In the blessed silence that followed, Henry said to Carrie, "How do you suppose Mr. Krenchnoted stood it?"

Carrie giggled and waved her hand toward the Krenchnoted's friend, Gina. But Gina was asleep in her chair, which at least explained how *she* stood it.

Carrie said, "I'm glad you have this appointment today, Dr. Erdmann. You *will* tell him about what happened in the car yesterday, won't you?"

"Yes."

"You promise?"

"*Yes*." Why were all women, even mild little Carrie, so insistent on regular doctor visits? Yes, doctors were useful for providing pills to keep the machine going, but Henry's view was that you only needed to see a physician if something felt wrong. In fact, he'd forgotten about this regularly scheduled check-up until this morning, when Carrie called to say how convenient it was that his appointment here was just an hour before the one with Dr. DiBella at the hospital lab. Ordinarily Henry would have refused to go at all, except that he did intend to ask Dr. Jamison about the incident in the car. Also, it was possible that fool Evelyn Krenchnoted was actually right about something for once. "Carrie, maybe you *should* ask the doctor to look at that eye."

"No. I'm fine."

"Has Jim called or come around again since—"

"No."

Clearly she didn't want to talk about it. Embarrassment, most likely. Henry could respect her reticence. Silently he organized his questions for Jamison.

But after Henry had gone into the office, leaving Carrie in the waiting room, and after he'd endured the tediums of the nurse's measuring his blood pressure, of peeing into a cup, of putting on a ridiculous paper gown, it wasn't Jamison who entered the room but a brusque, impossibly young boy in a white lab coat and officious manner.

"I'm Dr. Felton, Henry. How are we today?" He studied Henry's chart, not looking at him.

Henry gritted his teeth. "You would know better than I, I imagine."

"Feeling a bit cranky? Are your bowels moving all right?"

"My bowels are fine. They thank you for your concern."

Felton looked up then, his eyes cold. "I'm going to listen to your lungs now. Cough when I tell you to."

And Henry knew he couldn't do it. If the kid had reprimanded him—"I don't think sarcasm is appropriate here"—it would have at least been a response. But this utter dismissal, this treatment as if Henry were a child, or a moron . . . He couldn't tell this insensitive young boor about the incident in the car, about the fear for his brain. It would degrade him to cooperate with Felton. Maybe DiBella would be better, even if he wasn't an M.D.

One doctor down, one to go.

DiBella was better. What he was not, was organized.

At Redborn Memorial Hospital he said, "Ah, Dr. Erdmann, Carrie. Welcome. I'm afraid there's been a mix-up with Diagnostic Imaging. I thought I had the fMRI booked for you but they seem to have scheduled me out, or something. So we can do the Asher-Peyton scan but not the deep imaging. I'm sorry, I—" He shrugged helplessly and ran his hand through his hair.

Carrie tightened her mouth to a thin line. "Dr. Erdmann came all the way over here for your MRI, Dr. DiBella."

"'Jake,' please. I know. And we do the Asher-Peyton scan back at St. Sebastian's. I really am sorry."

Carrie's lips didn't soften. It always surprised Henry how fierce she could be in defense of her "resident-assignees." Why was usually gentle Carrie being so hard on this young man?

"I'll meet you back at St. Sebastian's," DiBella said humbly.

Once there, he affixed electrodes on Henry's skull and neck, eased a helmet over his head, and sat at a computer whose screen faced away from Henry. After the room was darkened, a series of pictures projected onto one white wall: a chocolate cake, a broom, a chair, a car, a desk, a glass: four or five dozen images. Henry had to do nothing except sit there, and he grew bored. Eventually the pictures grew more interesting, interspersing a house fire, a war scene, a father hugging a child, Rita Hayworth. Henry chuckled. "I didn't think your generation even knew who Rita Hayworth was."

"Please don't talk, Dr. Erdmann."

The session went on for twenty minutes. When it was over, DiBella removed the helmet and said, "Thank you so much. I really appreciate this." He began removing electrodes from Henry's head. Carrie stood, looking straight at Henry.

Now or never.

"Dr. DiBella," Henry said, "I'd like to ask you something. Tell you something, actually. An incident that happened yesterday. Twice." Henry liked the word "incident"; it sounded objective and explainable, like a police report.

"Sure. Go ahead."

"The first time I was standing in my apartment, the second time riding in a car with Carrie. The first incident was mild, the second more pronounced. Both times I felt something move through my mind, like a shock wave of sorts, leaving no aftereffects except perhaps a slight fatigue. No abilities seem to be impaired. I'm hoping you can tell me what happened."

DiBella paused, an electrode dangling from his hand. Henry could smell the gooey gel on its end. "I'm not an M.D., as I told you yesterday. This sounds like something you should discuss with your doctor at St. Sebastian."

Carrie, who had been upset that Henry had not done just that, said, "In the car he sort of lost consciousness and his eyes rolled back in his head."

Henry said, "My doctor wasn't available this morning, and you are. Can you just tell me if that experience sounds like a stroke?"

"Tell me about it again."

Henry did, and DiBella said, "If it had been a TIA—a mini-stroke—you wouldn't have had such a strong reaction, and if it had been a more serious stroke, either ischemic or hemorrhagic, you'd have been left with at least temporary impairment. But you could have experienced a cardiac event of some sort, Dr. Erdmann. I think you should have an EKG at once."

Heart, not brain. Well, that was better. Still, fear slid coldly down Henry's spine, and he realized how much he wanted to go on leading his current life, limited though it was. Still, he smiled and said, "All right."

He'd known for at least twenty-five years that growing old wasn't for sissies.

Carrie canceled her other resident-assignees, checking in with each on her cell, and shepherded Henry through the endless hospital rituals that followed, administrative and diagnostic and that most ubiquitous medical procedure, waiting. By the end of the day, Henry knew that his heart was fine, his brain showed no clots or hemorrhages, there was no reason for him to have fainted. That's what they were calling it now: a faint, possibly due to low blood sugar. He was scheduled for glucose-tolerance tests next week. Fools. It hadn't been any kind of faint. What had happened to him had been something else entirely, *sui generis*.

Then it happened again, the same and yet completely different.

At nearly midnight Henry lay in bed, exhausted. For once, he'd thought, sleep would come easily. It hadn't. Then, all at once, he was lifted out of his weary mind. This time there was no violet wrenching, no eyes rolling back in his head. He just suddenly wasn't in his darkened bedroom any more, not in his body, not in his mind.

He was dancing, soaring with pointed toes high above a polished stage, feeling the muscles in his back and thighs stretch as he sat cross-legged on a deep cushion he had embroidered with ball bearings rolling down a factory assembly line across from soldiers shooting at him as he ducked—

It was gone.

Henry jerked upright, sweating in the dark. He fumbled for the bed lamp, missed, sent the lamp crashing off the nightstand and onto the floor. He had never danced on a stage, embroidered a cushion, worked in a factory, or gone to war. And he'd been awake. Those were memories, not dreams—no, not even memories, they were too vivid for that. They'd been experiences, as vivid and real as if they were all happening now, and all happening simultaneously. *Experiences.* But not his.

The lamp was still glowing. Laboriously he leaned over the side of the bed and plucked it off the floor. As he set it back on the nightstand, it went out. Not, however, before he saw that the plug had been pulled from the wall socket during the fall, well before he bent over to pick it up.

The ship grew more agitated, the rents in space-time and resulting flop transitions larger. Every aspect of the entity strained forward, jumping through the vacuum flux in bursts of radiation that appeared now near one star system, now another, now in the deep black cold where no stars exerted gravity. The ship could move no quicker without destroying either nearby star systems or its own coherence. It raced as rapidly as it could, sent ahead of itself even faster tendrils of quantum-entangled information. Faster, faster . . .

It was not fast enough.

FOUR

Thursday morning, Henry's mind seemed to him as clear as ever. After an early breakfast he sat at his tiny kitchen table, correcting physics papers. The apartments at St. Sebastian's each had a small eat-in kitchen, a marginally larger living room, a bedroom and bath. Grab rails, non-skid flooring, overly cheerful colors, and intercoms reminded the residents that they were old—as if, Henry thought scornfully, any of them were likely to forget it. However, Henry didn't really mind the apartment's size or surveillance. After all, he'd flourished at Los Alamos, crowded and ramshackle and paranoid as the place had been. Most of his life went on inside his head.

For each problem set with incomplete answers—which would probably be all of them except Haldane's, although Julia Hernandez had at least come up with a novel and mathematically interesting approach—he tried to follow the student's thinking, to see where it had gone wrong. After an hour of this, he had gone over two papers. A plane screamed overhead, taking off from the airport. Henry gave it up. He couldn't concentrate.

Outside the St. Sebastian infirmary yesterday, the horrible Evelyn Krenchnoted had said that she didn't have a check-up appointment, but that the doctor was "squeezing her in" because "something strange happened yesterday." She'd also mentioned that the aging-hippie beauty, Erin Whatever-Her-Name-Was, hadn't had a scheduled appointment either.

Once, at a mandatory ambulatory-residents' meeting, Henry had seen Evelyn embroidering.

Anna Chernov, St. Sebastian's most famous resident, was a ballet dancer. Everyone knew that.

He felt stupid even thinking along these lines. What was he hypothesizing here, some sort of telepathy? No respectable scientific study had ever validated such a hypothesis. Also, during Henry's three years at St. Sebastian's—years during which Evelyn and Miss Chernov had also been in residence—he had never felt the slightest connection with, or interest in, either of them.

He tried to go back to correcting problem sets.

The difficulty was, he had two data points, his own "incidents" and the sudden rash of unscheduled doctors' appointments, and no way to either connect or eliminate either one. If he could at least satisfy himself that Evelyn's and Erin's doctor visits concerned something other than mental episodes, he would be down to one data point. One was an anomaly. Two were an indicator of . . . something.

This wasn't one of Henry's days to have Carrie's assistance. He pulled himself up on his walker, inched to the desk, and found the Resident Directory. Evelyn had no listings for either cell phone or email. That surprised him; you'd think such a yenta would want as many ways to bother people as possible. But some St. Sebastian residents were still, after all these decades, wary of any technology they hadn't grown up with. *Fools*, thought Henry, who had once driven four hundred miles to buy one of the first, primitive, put-it-together-yourself kits for a personal computer. He noted Evelyn's apartment number and hobbled toward the elevators.

"Why, Henry Erdmann! Come in, come in!" Evelyn cried. She looked astonished, as well she might. And—oh, God—behind her sat a circle of women, their chairs jammed in like molecules under hydraulic compression, all sewing on bright pieces of cloth.

"I don't want to intrude on your—"

"Oh, it's just the Christmas Elves!" Evelyn cried. "We're getting an early start on the holiday wall hanging for the lobby. The old one is getting so shabby."

Henry didn't remember a holiday wall hanging in the lobby, unless she was referring to that garish lumpy blanket with Santa Claus handing out babies to guardian angels. The angels had had tight, cotton-wool hair that made them look like Q-tips. He said, "Never mind, it's not important."

"Oh, come on in! We were just talking about—and maybe you have more information on it!—this fabulous necklace that Anna Chernov has in the office safe, the one the czar gave—"

"No, no, I have no information. I'll—"

"But if you just—"

Henry said desperately, "I'll call you later."

To his horror, Evelyn lowered her eyes and said murmured demurely, "All right, Henry," while the women behind her tittered. He backed away down the hall.

He was pondering how to discover Erin's last name when she emerged from an elevator. "Excuse me!" he called the length of the corridor. "May I speak to you a moment?"

She came toward him, another book in her hand, her face curious but reserved. "Yes?"

"My name is Henry Erdmann. I'd like to ask what will, I know, sound like a very strange question. Please forgive my intrusiveness, and believe that I have a good reason for asking. You had an unscheduled appointment with Dr. Felton yesterday?"

Something moved behind her eyes. "Yes."

"Did your reason for seeing him have to do with any sort of . . . of mental experience? A small seizure, or an episode of memory aberration, perhaps?"

Erin's ringed hand tightened on her book. He noted, numbly, that today it seemed to be a novel. She said, "Let's talk."

"I don't believe it," he said. "I'm sorry, Mrs. Bass, but it sounds like rubbish to me."

She shrugged, a slow movement of thin shoulders under her peasant blouse. Her long printed skirt, yellow flowers on black, swirled on the floor. Her apartment looked like her: bits of cloth hanging on the walls, a curtain of beads instead of a door to the bedroom, Hindu statues and crystal pyramids and Navaho blankets. Henry disliked the clutter, the childishness of the décor, even as he felt flooded by gratitude toward Erin Bass. She had released him. Her ideas about the "incidents" were so dumb that he could easily dismiss them, along with anything he might have been thinking which resembled them.

"There's an energy in the universe as a whole," she'd said. "When you stop resisting the flow of life and give up the grasping of *trishna*, you awaken to that energy. In popular terms, you have an 'out-of-body experience,' activating stored karma from past lives and fusing it into one moment of transcendent insight."

Henry had had no transcendental insight. He knew about energy in the universe—it was called electromagnetic radiation, gravity, the strong and weak nuclear forces—and none of it had karma. He didn't believe in reincarnation, and he hadn't been out of his body. Throughout all three "incidents," he'd felt his body firmly encasing him. He hadn't left; other minds had somehow seemed to come in. But it was all nonsense, an aberration of a brain whose synapses and axons, dendrites and vesicles, were simply growing old.

He grasped his walker and rose. "Thanks anyway, Mrs. Bass. Good-bye."

"Again, call me 'Erin.' Are you sure you wouldn't like some green tea before you go?"

"Quite sure. Take care."

He was at the door when she said, almost casually, "Oh, Henry? When I had my own out-of-body Tuesday evening, there were others with me in the awakened state . . . Were you ever closely connected with—I know this sounds odd—a light that somehow shone more brightly than many suns?"

He turned and stared at her.

"This will take about twenty minutes," DiBella said as Henry slid into the MRI machine. He'd had the procedure before and disliked it just as much then, the feeling of being enclosed in a tube not much larger than a coffin. Some people, he knew, couldn't tolerate it at all. But Henry'd be damned if he let a piece of machinery defeat him, and anyway the tube didn't enclose him completely; it was open at the bottom. So he pressed his lips together and closed his eyes and let the machine swallow his strapped-down body.

"You okay in there, Dr. Erdmann?"

"I'm fine."

"Good. Excellent. Just relax."

To his own surprise, he did. In the tube, everything seemed very remote. He actually dozed, waking twenty minutes later when the tube slid him out again.

"Everything look normal?" he asked DiBella, and held his breath.

"Completely," DiBella said. "Thank you, that's a good baseline for my study. Your next one, you know, will come immediately after you view a ten-minute video. I've scheduled that for a week from today."

"Fine." *Normal.* Then his brain was okay, and this weirdness was over. Relief turned him jaunty. "I'm glad to assist your project, doctor. What is its focus, again?"

"Cerebral activation patterns in senior citizens. Did you realize, Dr. Erdmann, that the over-sixty-five demographic is the fastest growing one in the world? And that globally there are now one hundred and forty million people over the age of eighty?"

Henry hadn't realized, nor did he care. The St. Sebastian aide came forward to help Henry to his feet. He was a dour young man whose name Henry hadn't caught. DiBella said, "Where's Carrie today?"

"It's not her day with me."

"Ah." DiBella didn't sound very interested; he was already prepping his screens for the next volunteer. Time on the MRI, he'd told Henry, was tight, having to be scheduled between hospital use.

The dour young man—Darryl? Darrin? Dustin?—drove Henry back to St. Sebastian's and left him to make his own way upstairs. In his apartment, Henry lowered himself laboriously to the sofa. Just a few minutes' nap, that's all he needed, even a short excursion tired him so much now—although it would be better if Carrie had been along, she always took such good care of him, such a kind and dear young woman. If he and Ida had ever had children, he'd have wanted them to be like Carrie. If that bastard Jim Peltier ever again tried to—

It shot through him like a bolt of lightning.

Henry screamed. This time the experience *hurt*, searing the inside of his skull and his spinal cord down to his tailbone. No dancing, no embroidering, no meditating—and yet others were there, not as individuals but as a collective sensation, a shared pain, making the pain worse by pooling it. He couldn't stand it, he was going to die, this was the end of—

The pain was gone. It vanished as quickly as it came, leaving him bruised inside, throbbing as if his entire brain had undergone a root canal. His gorge rose, and just in time he twisted his aching body to the side and vomited over the side of the sofa onto the carpet.

His fingers fumbled in the pocket of his trousers for the St. Sebastian panic button that Carrie insisted he wear. He found it, pressed the center, and lost consciousness.

FIVE

Carrie went home early. Thursday afternoons were assigned to Mrs. Lopez and her granddaughter had showed up unexpectedly. Carrie suspected that Vicky Lopez wanted money again since that seemed to be the only time she did turn up at St. Sebastian's, but that was not Carrie's business. Mrs. Lopez said happily that Vicky could just as easily take her to shopping instead of Carrie, and Vicky agreed, looking greedy. So Carrie went home.

If she'd been fortunate enough to have a grandmother—to have any relatives besides her no-good stepbrothers in California—she would treat that hypothetical grandmother better than did Vicky, she of the designer jeans and cashmere crew necks and massive credit-card debt. Although Carrie wouldn't want her grandmother to be like Mrs. Lopez, either, who treated Carrie like not-very-clean hired help.

Well, she *was* hired help, of course. The job as a St. Sebastian aide was the first thing she'd seen in the classifieds the day she finally walked out on Jim. She grabbed the job blindly, like a person going over a cliff who sees a fragile branch growing from crumbly rock. The weird thing was that after the first day, she knew she was going to stay. She liked old people (most of them, anyway). They were interesting and grateful (most of them anyway)—and safe. During that first terrified week at the YMCA, while she searched for a one-room apartment she could actually afford, St. Sebastian's was the one place she felt safe.

Jim had changed that, of course. He'd found out the locations of her job and apartment. Cops could find anything.

She unlocked her door after making sure the dingy corridor was empty, slipped inside, shot the deadbolt, and turned on the light. The only window faced an air shaft, and the room was dark even on the brightest day. Carrie had done what she could with bright cushions and Salvation Army lamps and dried flowers, but dark was dark.

"Hello, Carrie," Jim said.

She whirled around, stifling a scream. But the sickening thing was the rest of her reaction. Unbidden and hated—God, how hated!—but still there was the sudden thrill, the flash of excitement that energized every part of her body. *"That's not unusual,"* her counselor at the Battered Women's Help Center had said, *"because frequently an abuser and his victim are both fully engaged in the struggle to dominate each other. How triumphant do you feel when he's in the apology-and-wooing phase of the abuse cycle? Why do you think you haven't left before now?"*

It had taken Carrie so long to accept that. And here it was again. Here Jim was again.

"How did you get in?"

"Does it matter?"

"You got Kelsey to let you in, didn't you?" The building super could be bribed to almost anything with a bottle of Scotch. Although maybe Jim hadn't needed that; he had a badge. Not even the charges she'd brought against him, all of which had been dropped, had affected his job.

Nobody on the outside ever realized how common domestic violence was in cops' homes.

Jim wasn't in uniform now. He wore jeans, boots, a sports coat she'd always liked. He held a bouquet of flowers. Not supermarket carnations, either: red roses in shining gold paper. "Carrie, I'm sorry I startled you, but I wanted so bad for us to talk. Please, just let me have ten minutes. That's all. Ten minutes isn't much to give me against three years of marriage."

"We're not married. We're legally separated."

"I know. *I know.* And I deserve that you left me. I know that now. But just ten minutes. Please."

"You're not supposed to be here at all! There's a restraining order against you—and you're a cop!"

"I know. I'm risking my career to talk to you for ten minutes. Doesn't that say how much I care? Here, these are for you."

Humbly, eyes beseeching, he held out the roses. Carrie didn't take them.

"You blackened my eye the last time we 'talked,' you bastard!"

"I know. If you knew how much I've regretted that . . . If you had any idea how many nights I laid awake hating myself for that. I was out of my mind, Carrie. I really was. But it taught me something. I've changed. I'm going to A.A. now, I've got a sponsor and everything. I'm working my program."

"I've heard this all before!"

"I know. I know you have. But this time is different." He lowered his eyes, and Carrie put her hands on her hips. Then it hit her: She had said all this before, too. She had stood in this scolding, one-up stance. He had stood in his humble stance, as well. This was the apology-and-wooing stage that the counselor had talked about, just one more scene in their endless script. And she was eating it up as if it had never happened before, was reveling in the glow of righteous indignation fed by his groveling. Just like the counselor had said.

She was so sickened at herself that her knees nearly buckled.

"Get out, Jim."

"I will. I *will.* Just tell me that you heard me, that there's some chance for us still, even if it's a chance I don't deserve. Oh, Carrie—"

"Get out!" Her nauseated fury was at herself.

"If you'd just—"

"Out! Out now!"

His face changed. Humility was replaced by astonishment—this wasn't how their script went—and then by rage. He threw the flowers at her. "You won't even *listen* to me? I come here goddamn apologizing and you won't even listen? What makes you so much better than me, you fucking bitch you're nothing but a—"

Carrie whirled around and grabbed for the deadbolt. He was faster. Faster, stronger, and *that* was the old script, too, how could she forget for even a half second he—

Jim threw her to the floor. Did he have his gun? Would he—She caught a glimpse of his face, so twisted with rage that he looked like somebody else, even as she was throwing up her arms to protect her head. He kicked her in the belly. The pain was astonishing. It burned along her body she was burning she couldn't breathe she was going to die . . . His boot drew back to kick her again and Carrie tried to scream. No breath came. This was it then no no *no*—

Jim crumpled to the floor.

Between her sheltering arms, she caught sight of his face as he went down. Astonishment gaped open the mouth, widened the eyes. The image clapped onto her brain. His body fell heavily on top of hers, and didn't move.

When she could breathe again, she crawled out from under him, whimpering with short guttural sounds: *uh uh uh*. Yet a part of her brain worked clearly, coldly. She felt for a pulse, held her fingers over his mouth to find a breath, put her ear to his chest. He was dead.

She staggered to the phone and called 911.

Cops. Carrie didn't know them; this wasn't Jim's precinct. First uniforms and then detectives. An ambulance. A forensic team. Photographs, fingerprints, a search of the one-room apartment, with her consent. You have the right to remain silent. She didn't remain silent, didn't need a lawyer, told what she knew as Jim's body was replaced by a chalked outline and neighbors gathered in the hall. And when it was finally, finally over and she was told that her apartment was a crime scene until the autopsy was performed and where could she go, she said, "St. Sebastian's. I work there."

"Maybe you should call in sick for this night's shift, ma'am, it's—"

"I'm going to St. Sebastian's!"

She did, her hands shaky on the steering wheel. She went straight to Dr. Erdmann's door and knocked hard. His walker inch across the floor, inside. Inside, where it was safe.

"Carrie! What on Earth—"

"Can I come in? Please? The police—"

"Police?" he said sharply. "What police?" Peering around her as if he expected to see blue uniforms filling the hall. "Where's your coat? It's fifty degrees out!"

She had forgotten a coat. Nobody had mentioned a coat. *Pack a bag*, they said, but nobody had mentioned a coat. Dr. Erdmann always knew the temperature and barometer reading, he kept track of such things. Belatedly, and for the first time, she burst into tears.

He drew her in, made her sit on the sofa. Carrie noticed, with the cold clear part of her mind that still seemed to be functioning, that there was a very wet spot on the carpet and a strong odor, as if someone had scrubbed with disinfectant. "Could I . . . could I have a drink?" She hadn't known she was going to say that until the words were out. She seldom drank. Too much like Jim.

Jim . . .

The sherry steadied her. Sherry seemed so civilized, and so did the miniature glass he offered it in. She breathed easier, and told him her story. He listened without saying a word.

"I think I'm a suspect," Carrie said. "Well, of course I am. He just dropped dead when we were fighting . . . but I never so much as laid a hand on him. I was just trying to protect my head and . . . Dr. Erdmann, what is it? You're white as snow! I shouldn't have come, I'm sorry, I—"

"Of course you should have come!" he snapped, so harshly that she was startled. A moment later he tried to smile. "Of course you should have come. What are friends for?"

Friends. But she had other friends, younger friends. Joanne and Connie and Jennifer . . . not that she had seen any of them much in the last three months. It had been Dr. Erdmann she'd thought of, first and immediately. And now he looked so . . .

"You're not well," she said. "What is it?"

"Nothing. I ate something bad at lunch, in the dining room. Half the building started vomiting a few hours later. Evelyn Krenchnoted and Gina Martinelli and Erin Bass and Bob Donovan and Al Cosmano and Anna Chernov. More."

He watched her carefully as he recited the names, as if she should somehow react. Carrie knew some of those people, but mostly just to say hello. Only Mr. Cosmano was on her resident-assignee list. Dr. Erdmann looked stranger than she had ever seen him.

He said, "Carrie, what time did Jim . . . did he drop dead? Can you fix the exact time?"

"Well, let me see . . . I left here at two and I stopped at the bank and the gas station and the convenience store, so maybe three or thee-thirty? Why?"

Dr. Erdmann didn't answer. He was silent for so long that Carrie grew uneasy. She shouldn't have come, it was a terrible imposition, and anyway there was probably a rule against aides staying in residents' apartments, what was she *thinking*—

"Let me get blankets and pillow for the sofa," Dr. Erdmann finally said, in a voice that still sounded odd to Carrie. "It's fairly comfortable. For a sofa."

SIX

Not possible. The most ridiculous coincidence. That was all—coincidence. Simultaneity was not cause-and-effect. Even the dimmest physics undergraduate knew that.

In his mind, Henry heard Richard Feynman say about string theory, "I don't like that they're not calculating anything. I don't like that they don't check their ideas. I don't like that for anything that disagrees with an experiment, they cook up an explanation. . . . The first principle is that you must not fool yourself—and you are the easiest person to fool."

Henry hadn't liked Feynman, whom he'd met at conferences at Cal Tech.
A buffoon, with his bongo drums and his practical jokes and his lock-
picking. Undignified. But the brilliant buffoon had been right. Henry
didn't like string theory, either, and he didn't like ideas that weren't cal-
culated, checked, and verified by experimental data. Besides, the idea that
Henry had somehow killed Jim Peltier with his *thoughts* . . . preposterous.

Mere thoughts could not send a bolt of energy through a distant
man's body. But the bolt itself wasn't a "cooked-up" idea. It had happened. Henry had felt it.

DiBella had said that Henry's MRI looked completely normal.

Henry lay awake much of Thursday night, which made the second
night in a row, while Carrie slept the oblivious deep slumber of the young.
In the morning, before she was awake, he dressed quietly, left the apartment with his walker, and made his way to the St. Sebastian's Infirmary.
He expected to find the Infirmary still crammed with people who'd vomited when he had yesterday afternoon. He was wrong.

"Can I help you?" said a stout, middle-aged nurse carrying a breakfast tray. "Are you feeling ill?"

"No, no," Henry said hastily. "I'm here to visit someone. Evelyn
Krenchnoted. She was here yesterday."

"Oh, Evelyn's gone back. They've all gone back, the food poisoning
was so mild. Our only patients here now are Bill Terry and Anna Chernov."
She said the latter name the way many of the staff did, as if she'd just been
waiting for an excuse to speak it aloud. Usually this irritated Henry—what
was ballet dancing compared to, say, physics?—but now he seized on it.

"May I see Miss Chernov, then? Is she awake?"

"This is her tray. Follow me."

The nurse led the way to the end of a short corridor. Yellow cur-
tains, bedside table, monitors and IV poles; the room looked like every
other hospital room Henry had ever seen, except for the flowers. Masses
and masses of flowers, bouquets and live plants and one huge floor pot
of brass holding what looked like an entire small tree. A man, almost lost
amid all the flowers, sat in the room's one chair.

"Here's breakfast, Miss Chernov," said the nurse reverently. She
fussed with setting the tray on the table, positioning it across the bed,
removing the dish covers.

"Thank you." Anna Chernov gave her a gracious, practiced smile, and looked inquiringly at Henry. The other man, who had not risen at Henry's entrance, glared at him.

They made an odd pair. The dancer, who looked younger than whatever her actual age happened to be, was more beautiful than Henry had realized, with huge green eyes over perfect cheekbones. She wasn't hooked to any of the machinery on the wall, but a cast on her left leg bulged beneath the yellow bedcover. The man had a head shaped like a garden trowel, aggressively bristly gray crew cut, and small suspicious eyes. He wore an ill-fitting sports coat over a red T-shirt and jeans. There seemed to be grease under his fingernails—grease, in St. Sebastian's? Henry would have taken him for part of the maintenance staff except that he looked too old, although vigorous and walker-free. Henry wished him at the devil. This was going to be difficult enough without an audience.

"Miss Chernov, please forgive the intrusion, especially so early, but I think this is important. My name is Henry Erdmann, and I'm a resident on Three."

"Good morning," she said, with the same practiced, detached graciousness she'd shown the nurse. "This is Bob Donovan."

"Hi," Donovan said, not smiling.

"Are you connected in any way with the press, Mr. Erdmann? Because I do not give interviews."

"No, I'm not. I'll get right to the point, if I may. Yesterday I had an attack of nausea, just as you did, and you also, Mr. Donovan. Evelyn Krenchnoted told me."

Donovan rolled his eyes. Henry would have smiled at that if he hadn't felt so tense.

He continued, "I'm not sure the nausea *was* food poisoning. In my case, it followed a . . . a sort of attack of a quite different sort. I felt what I can only describe as a bolt of energy burning along my nerves, very powerfully and painfully. I'm here to ask if you felt anything similar."

Donovan said, "You a doctor?"

"Not an M.D. I'm a physicist."

Donovan scowled savagely, as if physics were somehow offensive. Anna Chernov said, "Yes, I did, Dr. Erdmann, although I wouldn't describe it as 'painful.' It didn't hurt. But a 'bolt of energy along the nerves'—yes. It felt like—" She stopped abruptly.

"Yes?" Henry said. His heart had started a slow, irregular thump in his chest. Someone else had also felt that energy.

But Anna declined to say what it had felt like. Instead she turned her head to the side. "Bob? Did you feel anything like that?"

"Yeah. So what?"

"I don't know what," Henry said. All at once, leaning on the walker, his knees felt wobbly. Anna noticed at once. "Bob, bring Dr. Erdmann the chair, please."

Donovan got up from the chair, dragged it effortlessly over to Henry, and stood sulkily beside a huge bouquet of autumn-colored chrysanthemums, roses, and dahlias. Henry sank onto the chair. He was at eye level with the card to the flowers, which said FROM THE ABT COMPANY. GET WELL SOON!

Anna said, "I don't understand what you're driving at, Dr. Erdmann. Are you saying we all had the same disease and it wasn't food poisoning? It was something with a . . . a surge of energy followed by nausea?"

"Yes, I guess I am." He couldn't tell her about Jim Peltier. Here, in this flower-and-antiseptic atmosphere, under Donovan's pathetic jealousy and Anna's cool courtesy, the whole idea seemed unbelievably wild. Henry Erdmann did not like wild ideas. He was, after all, a *scientist*.

But that same trait made him persist a little longer. "Had you felt anything like that ever before, Miss Chernov?"

"Anna," she said automatically. "Yes, I did. Three times before, in fact. But much more minor, and with no nausea. I think they were just passing moments of dozing off, in fact. I've been laid up with this leg for a few days now, and it's been boring enough that I sleep a lot."

It was said without self-pity, but Henry had a sudden glimpse of what being "laid up" must mean to a woman for whom the body, not the mind, had been the lifelong source of achievement, of pleasure, of occupation, of self. What, in fact, growing old must mean to such a woman. Henry had been more fortunate; his mind was his life source, not his aging body, and his mind still worked fine.

Or did it, if it could hatch that crackpot hypothesis? What would Feynman, Teller, Gell-Mann have said? Embarrassment swamped him. He struggled to rise.

"Thank you, Miss Chernov, I won't take up any more of your—"

"I felt it, too," Donovan said suddenly. "But only two times, like you said. Tuesday and yesterday afternoon. What are you after here, doc? You saying there's something going around? Is it dangerous?"

Henry, holding onto the walker, turned to stare at him. "You felt it, too?"

"I just told you I did! Now you tell me—is this some new catching, dangerous-like disease?"

The man was frightened, and covering fear with belligerence. Did he even understand what a 'physicist' was? He seemed to have taken Henry for some sort of specialized physician. What on Earth was Bob Donovan doing with Anna Chernov?

He had his answer in the way she dismissed them both. "No, Bob, there's no dangerous disease. Dr. Erdmann isn't in medicine. Now if you don't mind, I'm very tired and I must eat or the nurse will scold me. Perhaps you'd better leave now, and maybe I'll see you both around the building when I'm discharged." She smiled wearily.

Henry saw the look on Donovan's face, a look he associated with undergraduates: hopeless, helpless lovesickness. Amid those wrinkles and sags, the look was ridiculous. And yet completely sincere, poor bastard.

"Thank you again," Henry said, and left as quickly as his walker would allow. How dare she treat him like a princess dismissing a lackey? And yet . . . he'd been the intruder on her world, that feminine arena of flowers and ballet and artificial courtesy. A foreign, somehow repulsive world. Not like the rigorous masculine brawl of physics.

But he'd learned that she'd felt the "energy," too. And so had Donovan, and at the exact same times as Henry. Several more data points for . . . what?

He paused on his slow way to the elevator and closed his eyes.

When Henry reached his apartment, Carrie was awake. She sat with two strangers, who both rose as Henry entered, at the table where Henry and Ida had eaten dinner for fifty-years. The smell of coffee filled the air.

"I made coffee," Carrie said. "I hope you don't mind . . . This is Detective Geraci and Detective Washington. Dr. Erdmann, this is his apartment . . ." She trailed off, looking miserable. Her hair hung in uncombed tangles and some sort of black make-up smudged under her eyes. Or maybe just tiredness.

"Hello, Dr. Erdmann," the male detective said. He was big, heavily muscled, with beard shadow even at this hour—just the sort of thuggish looks that Henry most mistrusted. The black woman was much younger, small and neat and unsmiling. "We had a few follow-up questions for Ms. Vesey about last night."

Henry said, "Does she need a lawyer?"

"That's up to your granddaughter, of course," at the same moment that Carrie said, "I told them I don't want a lawyer," and Henry was adding, "I'll pay for it." In the confusion of sentences, the mistake about "granddaughter" went uncorrected.

Geraci said, "Were you here when Ms. Vesey arrived last night?"

"Yes," Henry said.

"And can you tell us your whereabouts yesterday afternoon, sir?"

Was the man a fool? "Certainly I can, but surely you don't suspect *me*, sir, of killing Officer Peltier?"

"We don't suspect anyone at this point. We're asking routine questions, Dr. Erdmann."

"I was in Redborn Memorial from mid-afternoon until just before Carrie arrived here. The Emergency Room, being checked for a suspected heart attack. Which," he added hastily, seeing Carrie's face, "I did not have. It was merely severe indigestion brought on by the attack of food poisoning St. Sebastian suffered yesterday afternoon."

Hah! Take that, Detective Thug!

"Thank you," Geraci said. "Are you a physician, Dr. Erdmann?"

"No. A doctor of physics."

He half-expected Geraci to be as ignorant about that as Bob Donovan had been, but Geraci surprised him. "Experimental or theoretical?"

"Theoretical. Not, however, for a long time. Now I teach."

"Good for you." Geraci rose, Officer Washington just a beat behind him. In Henry's hearing the woman had said nothing whatsoever. "Thank you both. We'll be in touch about the autopsy results."

In the elevator, Tara Washington said, "These old-people places give me the creeps."

"One day you and—"

"Spare me the lecture, Vince. I know I have to get old. I don't have to like it."

"You have a lot of time yet," he said, but his mind clearly wasn't on the rote reassurance. "Erdmann knows something."

"Yeah?" She looked at him with interest; Vince Geraci had a reputation in the Department for having a "nose." He was inevitably right about things that smelled hinkey. Truth was, she was a little in awe of him. She'd only made detective last month and was fucking lucky to be partnered with Geraci. Still, her natural skepticism led her to say, "That old guy? He sure the hell didn't do the job himself. He couldn't squash a cockroach. You talking about a hit for hire?"

"Don't know." Geraci considered. "No. Something else. Something more esoteric."

Tara didn't know what "esoteric" meant, so she kept quiet. Geraci was smart. Too smart for his own good, some uniforms said, but that was just jealousy talking, or the kind of cops that would rather smash down doors than solve crimes. Tara Washington knew she was no door-smasher. She intended to learn everything she could from Vince Geraci, even if she didn't have his vocabulary. Everything, and then some. She intended to someday be just as good as he was.

Geraci said, "Let's talk to the staff about this epidemic of food poisoning."

But the food poisoning checked out. And halfway through the morning, the autopsy report was called in. Geraci shut his cell and said, "Peltier died of 'a cardiac event.' Massive and instantaneous heart failure."

"Young cop like that? Fit and all?"

"That's what the M.E. says."

"So no foul play. Investigation closed." In a way, she was disappointed. The murder of a cop by a battered wife would have been pretty high-profile. That's why Geraci had been assigned to it.

"Investigation closed," Geraci said. "But just the same, Erdmann knows something. We're just never gonna find out what it is."

✭

SEVEN

Just before noon on Friday, Evelyn lowered her plump body onto a cot ready to slide into the strange-looking medical tube. She had dressed up for the occasion in her best suit, the polyester blue one with all the blue lace, and her good cream pumps. Dr. DiBella—such a good-looking young man, too bad she wasn't fifty years younger aha ha ha—said, "Are you comfortable, Mrs. Krenchnoted?"

"Call me Evelyn. Yes, I'm fine, I never had one of these—what did you call it?"

"A functional MRI. I'm just going to strap you in, since it's very important you lie completely still for the procedure."

"Oh, yes, I see, you don't want my brain wobbling all over the place while you take a picture of—Gina, you still there? I can't see—"

"I'm here," Gina called. "Don't be scared, Evelyn. 'Though I walk in the valley of—'"

"There's no shadows here and I'm not scared!" Really, sometimes Gina could be Too Much. Still, the MRI tube *was* a bit unsettling. "You just tell me when you're ready to slide me into that thing, doctor, and I'll brace myself. It's tight as a coffin, isn't it? Well, I'm going to be underground a long time but I don't plan on starting now, aha ha ha! But if I can keep talking to you while I go in—"

"Certainly. Just keep talking." He sounded resigned, poor man. Well, no wonder, he must get bored with doing things like this all the live-long day. She cast around for something to cheer him up.

"You're over at St. Sebastian's a lot now, aren't you, when you're not here that is, did you hear yet about Anna Chernov's necklace?"

"No, what about it? That's it, just hold your head right here."

"It's fabulous!" Evelyn said, a little desperately. He was putting some sort of vise on her head, she couldn't move it at all. Her heart sped up. "Diamonds and rubies and I don't know what all. The Russian czar gave it to some famous ballerina who—"

"Really? Which czar?"

"*The* czar! Of Russia!" Really, what did the young learn in school these days? "He gave it to some famous ballerina who was Anna Chernov's teacher and she gave it to Anna, who naturally keeps it in the St. Sebastian safe because just think if it were stolen, it wouldn't do the Home's reputation any good at all and anyway it's absolutely priceless so—oh!"

"You'll just slide in nice and slow, Evelyn. It'll be fine. Close your eyes if that helps. Now, have you seen this necklace?"

"Oh, no!" Evelyn gasped. Her heart raced as she felt the bed slide beneath her. "I'd love to, of course, but Anna isn't exactly friendly, she's pretty stuck-up, well I suppose that comes with being so famous and all but still—Doctor!"

"Do you want to come out?" he said, and she could tell that he was disappointed, she was sensitive that way, and she did want to come out but she didn't want to disappoint him, so . . . "No! I'm fine! The necklace is something I'd really like to see, though, all those diamonds and rubies and maybe even sapphires too, those are my favorite stones with that blue fire in them, I'd really really like to see it—"

She was babbling, but all at once it seemed she *could* see the necklace in her mind, just the way she'd pictured it. A string of huge glowing diamonds and hanging from them a pendant of rubies and sapphires shining like I-don't-know-what but more beautiful than anything she'd ever seen oh she'd love to touch it just once! If Anna Chernov weren't so stuck-up and selfish then maybe she'd get the necklace from the safe and show it to Evelyn let her touch it *get the necklace from the safe* it would surely be the most wonderful thing Evelyn had ever seen or imagined *get the necklace from the safe*—

Evelyn screamed. Pain spattered through her like hot oil off a stove, burning her nerves and turning her mind to a red cloud . . . So much pain! She was going to die, this was it and she hadn't even bought her cemetery plot yet oh God the pain—

Then the pain was gone and she lay sobbing as the bed slid out of the tube. Dr. DiBella was saying something but his voice was far away and growing farther . . . farther . . . farther. . . .

Gone.

Henry sat alone, eating a tuna fish sandwich at his kitchen table. Carrie had gone to work elsewhere in the building. It had been pleasant having her here, even though of course she—

Energy poured through him, like a sudden surge in household current, and all his nerves *glowed*. That was the only word. No pain this time, but something bright grew in his mind, white and red and blue but certainly not a flag, hard as stones . . . yes, stones . . . jewels . . .

It was gone. An immense lassitude took Henry. He could barely hold his head up, keep his eyes open. It took all his energy to push off from the table, stagger into the bedroom, and fall onto the bed, his mind empty as deep space.

Carrie was filling in at a pre-lunch card game in the dining room, making a fourth at euchre with Ed Rosewood, Ralph Galetta, and Al Cosmano. Mr. Cosmano was her Friday morning resident-assignee. She'd taken him to buy a birthday gift for his daughter in California, to the post office to wrap and mail it, and then to the physical therapist. Mr. Cosmano was a complainer. St. Sebastian's was too cold, the doctors didn't know nothing, they wouldn't let you smoke, the food was terrible, he missed the old neighborhood, his daughter insisted on living in California instead of making a home for her old dad, kids these days. . . . Carrie went on smiling. Even Mr. Cosmano was better than being home in the apartment where Jim had died. When her lease was up, she was going to find something else, but in the meantime she had signed up for extra hours at St. Sebastian's, just to not be home.

"Carrie, hearts led," Ed Rosewood said. He was her partner, a sweet man whose hobby was watching C-Span. He would watch anything at all on C-Span, even hearings of the House Appropriations Committee, for hours and hours. This was good for St. Sebastian's because Mr. Rosewood didn't want an aide. He had to be pried off the TV even to play cards once a week. Mike O'Kane, their usual fourth, didn't feel well enough to play today, which was why Carrie sat holding five cards as the kitchen staff clattered in the next room, preparing lunch. Outside a plane passed overhead, droned away.

"Oh, yes," Carrie said, "hearts." She had a heart, thank heavens, since she couldn't remember what was trump. She was no good at cards.

"There's the king."

"Garbage from me."

"Your lead, Ed."

"Ace of clubs."

"Clubs going around. . . . Carrie?"

"Oh, yes, I . . ." Who led? Clubs were the only things on the table. She had no clubs, so she threw a spade. Mr. Galetta laughed.

Al Cosmano said, with satisfaction, "Carrie, you really shouldn't trump your partner's ace."

"Did I do that? Oh, I'm sorry, Mr. Rosewood, I—"

Ed Rosewood slumped in his chair, eyes closed. So did Al Cosmano. Ralph Galetta stared dazedly at Carrie, then carefully laid his head on the table, eyes fixed.

"Mr. Cosmano! Help, somebody!"

The kitchen staff came running. But now all three men had their eyes open again, looking confused and sleepy.

"What happened?" demanded a cook.

"I don't know," Carrie said, "they all just got . . . tired."

The cook stared at Carrie as if she'd gone demented. "Tired?"

"Yeah . . . tired," Ed Rosewood said. "I just . . . bye, guys. I'm going to take a nap. Don't want lunch." He rose, unsteady but walking on his own power, and headed out of the dining room. The other two men followed.

"Tired," the cook said, glaring at Carrie.

"All at once! Really, really tired, like a spell of some kind!"

"A simultaneous 'spell,'" the cook said. "Right. You're new here? Well, old people get tired." She walked away.

Carrie wasn't new. The three men hadn't just had normal tiredness. But there was no way to tell this bitch that, no way to even tell *herself* in any terms that made sense. Nothing was right.

Carrie had no appetite for lunch. She fled to the ladies' room, where at least she could be alone.

Vince Geraci's cell rang as he and Tara Washington exited a convenience store on East Elm. They'd been talking to the owner, who may or may not have been involved in an insurance scam. Vince had let Tara do most of the questioning, and she'd felt herself swell like a happy balloon when he said, "Nice job, rookie."

"Geraci," he said into the cell, then listened as they walked. Just before they reached the car, he said, "Okay," and clicked off.

"What do we have?" Tara asked.

"We have a coincidence."

"A coincidence?"

"Yes." The skin on his forehead took on strange topography. "St. Sebastian's again. Somebody cracked the safe in the office."

"Anything gone?"

"Let's go find out."

Erin Bass woke on her yoga mat, the TV screen a blue blank except for CHANNEL 3 in the upper corner. She sat up, dazed but coherent. Something had happened.

She sat up carefully, her ringed hands lifting her body slowly off the mat. No broken bones, no pain anywhere. Apparently she had just collapsed onto the mat and then stayed out as the yoga tape played itself to an end. She'd been up to the fish posture, so there had been about twenty minutes left on the tape. And how long since then? The wall clock said 1:20. So about an hour.

Nothing hurt. Erin took a deep breath, rolled her head, stood up. Still no pain. And there hadn't been pain when it happened, but there had been something . . . not the calm place that yoga or meditation sometimes took her, either. That place was pale blue, like a restful vista of valleys seen at dusk from a high, still mountain. This was brightly hued, rushing, more like a river . . . a river of colors, blue and red and white.

She walked into the apartment's tiny kitchen, a slim figure in black leotard and tights. She'd missed lunch but wasn't hungry. From the cabinet she chose a chamomile tea, heated filtered water, and set the tea to steep.

That rushing river of energy was similar to what she'd felt before. Henry Erdmann had asked her about it, so perhaps he had felt it this time, as well. Although Henry hadn't seemed accepting of her explanation of *trishna*, grasping after the material moment, versus awakening. He was a typical scientist, convinced that science was the only route to knowledge, that what he could not test or measure or replicate was therefore not true even if he'd experienced it himself. Erin knew better. But there were a lot of people like Henry in this world, people who couldn't see that while rejecting "religion," they'd made a religion of science.

Sipping her tea, Erin considered what she should do next. She wasn't afraid of what had happened. Very little frightened Erin Bass. This astonished some people and confused the rest. But, really, what was there to be afraid of? Misfortune was just one turn of the wheel, illness another, death merely a transition from one state to another. What was due to come, would come, and beneath it all the great flow of cosmic energy would go on, creating the illusion that people thought was the world. She knew that the other residents of St. Sebastian's considered her nuts, pathetic, or so insulated from realty as to be both ("Trust-fund baby, you know. Never worked a day in her life.") It didn't matter. She'd made herself a life here of books and meditation and volunteering on the Nursing floors, and if her past was far different than the other residents imagined, that was their illusion. She herself never thought about the past. It would come again, or not, as *maya* chose.

Still, something should be done about these recent episodes. They had affected not just her but also Henry Erdmann and, surprisingly, Evelyn Krenchnoted. Although on second thought, Erin shouldn't be surprised. Everyone possessed karma, even Evelyn, and Erin had no business assuming she knew anything about what went on under Evelyn's loud, intrusive surface. There were many paths up the mountain. So Erin should talk to Evelyn as well as to Henry. Perhaps there were others, too. Maybe she should—

Her doorbell rang. Leaving her tea on the table, Erin fastened a wrap skirt over her leotard and went to the door. Henry Erdmann stood there, leaning on his walker, his face a rigid mask of repressed emotion. "Mrs. Bass, there's something I'd like to discuss with you. May I come in?"

A strange feeling came over Erin. Not the surge of energy from the yoga mat, nor the high blue restfulness of meditation. Something else. She'd had these moments before, in which she recognized that something significant was about to happen. They weren't mystical or deep, these occasions; probably they came from nothing more profound than a subliminal reading of body language. But, always, they presaged something life-changing.

"Of course, Dr. Erdmann. Come in."

She held the door open wider, stepping aside to make room for his walker, but he didn't budge. Had he exhausted all his strength? He was ninety, she'd heard, ten years older than Erin, who was in superb shape from a lifetime of yoga and bodily moderation. She had never smoked, drank, overeaten. All her indulgences had been emotional, and not for a very long time now.

"Do you need help? Can I—"

"No. No." He seemed to gather himself and then inched the walker forward, moving toward her table. Over his shoulder, with a forced after-thought that only emphasized his tension, he said, "Thieves broke into St. Sebastian's an hour and a half ago. They opened the safe in the office, the one with Anna Chernov's necklace."

Erin had never heard of Anna Chernov's necklace. But the image of the rushing river of bright colors came back to her with overwhelming force, and she knew that she had been right: Something had happened, and nothing was ever going to be the same again.

EIGHT

For perhaps the tenth time, Jake DiBella picked up the fMRI scans, stud-ied them yet again, and put them down. He rubbed his eyes hard with both sets of knuckles. When he took his hands away from his face, his bare little study at St. Sebastian's looked blurry but the fMRI scans hadn't changed. *This is your brain on self-destruction*, he thought, except that it wasn't his brain. It was Evelyn Krenchnoted's brain, and after she recovered consciousness, that tiresome and garrulous lady's brain had worked as well as it ever had.

But the scan was extraordinary. As Evelyn lay in the magnetic imag-ing tube, everything had changed between one moment and the next. First image: a normal pattern of blood flow and oxygenation, and the next—

"Hello?"

Startled, Jake dropped the printouts. He hadn't even heard the door open, or anyone knock. He really was losing it. "Come in, Carrie, I'm sorry, I didn't . . . You don't have to do that."

She had bent to pick up the papers that had skidded across his desk and onto the floor. With her other hand she balanced a cardboard box on one hip. As she straightened, he saw that her face was pink under the loose golden hair, so that she looked like an overdone Victorian figurine. The box held a plant, a picture frame, and various other bits and pieces.

Uh oh. Jake had been down this road before.

She said, "I brought you some things for your office. Because it looks so, well, empty. Cold."

"Thanks. I actually like it this way." Ostentatiously he busied himself with the printouts, which was also pretty cold of him, but better to cut her off now rather than after she embarrassed herself. As she set the box on a folding chair, he still ignored her, expecting her to leave.

Instead she said, "Are those MRI scans of Dr. Erdmann? What do they say?"

Jake looked up. She was eyeing the printouts, not him, and her tone was neutral with perhaps just a touch of concern for Dr. Erdmann. He remembered how fond of each other she and Henry Erdmann were. Well, didn't that make Jake just the total narcissist? Assuming every woman was interested in *him.* This would teach him some humility.

Out of his own amused embarrassment, he answered her as he would a colleague. "No, these are Evelyn Krenchnoted's. Dr. Erdmann's were unremarkable but these are quite the opposite."

"They're remarkable? How?"

All at once he found himself eager to talk, to perhaps explain away his own bafflement. He came around the desk and put the scan in her hand. "See those yellow areas of the brain? They're BOLD signals, blood-oxygen-level dependent contrasts. What that means is that at the moment the MRI image was taken, those parts of the subject's brain were active— in this case, *highly* active. And they shouldn't have been!"

"Why not?"

Carrie was background now, an excuse to put into concrete words what should never have existed concretely at all. "Because it's all wrong. Evelyn was lying still, talking to me, inside the MRI tube. Her eyes were open. She was nervous about being strapped down. The scan should show activity in the optical input area of the brain, in the motor areas connected to moving the mouth and tongue, and in the posterior parietal lobes, indicating a heightened awareness of her bodily boundaries. But instead, there's just the *opposite*. A hugely decreased blood flow in those lobes, and an almost total shut down of input to the thalamus, which relays information coming into the brain from sight and hearing and touch. Also, an enormous—really enormous—*increase* of activity in the hypothalamus and amygdalae and temporal lobes."

"What does all that increased activity mean?"

"Many possibilities. They're areas concerned with emotion and some kinds of imaginative imagery, and this much activation is characteristic of some psychotic seizures. For another possibility, parts of that profile are characteristic of monks in deep meditation, but it takes experienced meditators hours to build to that level, and even so there are differences in pain areas and—anyway, *Evelyn Krenchnoted?*"

Carrie laughed. "Not a likely monk, no. Do Dr. Erdmann's scans show any of that?"

"No. And neither did Evelyn's just before her seizure *or* just after. I'd say temporal lobe epilepsy except—"

"Epilepsy?" Her voice turned sharp. "Does that 'seizure' mean epilepsy?"

Jake looked at her then, really looked at her. He could recognize fear. He said as gently as he could, "Henry Erdmann experienced something like this, didn't he?"

They stared at each other. Even before she spoke, he knew she was going to lie to him. A golden lioness protecting her cub, except here the lioness was young and the cub a withered old man who was the smartest person Jake DiBella had ever met.

"No," she said, "Dr. Erdmann never mentioned a seizure to me."

"Carrie—"

"And you said his MRI looked completely normal."

"It did." Defeated.

"I should be going. I just wanted to bring you these things to brighten up your office."

Carrie left. The box contained a framed landscape he would never hang (a flower-covered cottage, with unicorn), a coffee cup he would never use (JAVA IS JOY IN THE MORNING), a patchwork quilted cushion, a pink African violet, and a pencil cup covered in wallpaper with yellow daisies. Despite himself, Jake smiled. The sheer wrongness of her offerings was almost funny.

Except that nothing was really funny in light of Evelyn Krenchnoted's inexplicable MRI. He needed more information from her, and another MRI. Better yet would be having her hooked to an EEG in a hospital ward for several days, to see if he could catch a definitive diagnosis of temporal-lobe epilepsy. But when he'd phoned Evelyn, she'd refused all further "doctor procedures." Ten minutes of his best persuasion hadn't budged her.

He was left with an anomaly in his study data, a cutesy coffee cup, and no idea what to do next.

"What do we do next?" asked Rodney Caldwell, the chief administrator of St. Sebastian's. Tara Washington looked at Geraci, who looked at the floor.

It was covered with papers and small, uniform, taped white boxes with names written neatly on them in block printing: M. MATTISON. H. GERHARDT. C. GARCIA. One box, however, was open, its lid placed neatly beside it, the tissue paper peeled back. On the tissue lay a necklace, a gold Coptic cross set with a single small diamond, on a thin gold chain. The lid said A. CHERNOV.

"I didn't touch anything," Caldwell said, with a touch of pride. In his fifties, he was a tall man with a long, highly colored face like an animated carrot. "That's what they say on TV, isn't it? Don't touch anything. But isn't it strange that the thief went to all the trouble to 'blow the safe'"— he looked proud of this phrase, too "—and then didn't take anything?"

"Very strange," Geraci said. Finally he looked up from the floor. The safe hadn't been "blown"; the lock was intact. Tara felt intense interest in what Geraci would do next. She was disappointed.

"Let's go over it once more," he said easily. "You were away from your office . . ."

"Yes. I went up to Nursing at 11:30. Beth Malone was on desk. Behind the front desk is the only door to the room that holds both residents' files and the safe, and Beth says she never left her post. She's very reliable. Been with us eighteen years."

Mrs. Malone, who was therefore the prime suspect and smart enough to know it, was weeping in another room. A resigned female uniform handed her tissues as she waited to be interrogated. But Tara knew that, after one look, Geraci had dismissed Malone as the perp. One of those conscientious, middle-aged, always-anxious-to-help do-gooders, she would no more have attempted robbery than alchemy. Most likely she had left her post to do something she was as yet too embarrassed to admit, which was when the thief had entered the windowless back room behind the reception desk. Tara entertained herself with the thought that Mrs. Malone had crept off to meet a lover in the linen closet. She smiled.

"A thought, Detective Washington?" Geraci said.

Damn, he missed *nothing*. Now she would have to come up with something. The best she could manage was a question. "Does that little necklace belong to the ballerina Anna Chernov?"

"Yes," Caldwell said. "Isn't it lovely?"

To Tara it didn't look like much. But Geraci had raised his head to look at her, and she realized he didn't know that a world-famous dancer had retired to St. Sebastian's. Ballet wasn't his style. It was the first time Tara could recall that she'd known something Geraci did not. Emboldened by this, and as a result of being dragged several times a year to Lincoln Center by an eccentric grandmother, Tara continued. "Is there any resident here that might have a special interest in Anna Chernov? A balletomane—" She hoped she was pronouncing the word correctly, she'd only read it in programs "—or a special friend?"

But Caldwell had stopped listening at "resident." He said stiffly, "None of our residents would have committed this crime, detective. St. Sebastian's is a private community and we screen very carefully for any—"

"May I talk to Ms. Chernov now?" Geraci asked.

Caldwell seemed flustered. "To Anna? But Beth Malone is waiting for . . . oh, all right, if that's the procedure. Anna Chernov is in the Infirmary right now, with a broken leg. I'll show you up."

Tara hoped that Geraci wasn't going to send her to do the useless questioning of Mrs. Malone. He didn't. At the Infirmary door, he said, "Tara, talk to her." Tara would have taken this as a tribute to her knowledge of ballet, except that she had seen Geraci do the same thing before. He liked to observe: the silent listener, the unknown quantity to whoever was being questioned.

As Caldwell explained the situation and made the introductions, Tara tried not to stare at Anna Chernov. She was *beautiful*. Old, yes, seventies maybe, but Tara had never seen anyone old look like that. High cheekbones, huge green eyes, white hair pinned carelessly on top of her head so that curving strands fell over the pale skin that looked not so much wrinkled (though it was) as softened by time. Her hands, long-fingered and slim-wristed, lay quiet on the bedspread, and her shoulders held straight under the white bed jacket. Only the bulging cast on one leg marred the impression of delicacy, of remoteness, and of the deepest sadness that Tara had ever seen. It was sadness for everything, Tara thought confusedly, and couldn't have said what she meant by "everything." Except that the cast was only a small part.

"Please sit down," Anna said.

"Thank you. As Mr. Caldwell said, there's been a break-in downstairs, with the office safe. The only box opened had your name on it, with a gold-and-diamond necklace inside. That is yours, isn't it?"

"Yes."

"Is it the one that Tamara Karsavina gave you? That Nicholas II gave her?"

"Yes." Anna looked at Tara more closely, but not less remotely.

"Ms. Chernov, is there anyone you can think of who might have a strong interest in that necklace? A member of the press who's been persistent in asking about it, or someone emailing you about it, or a resident?"

"I don't do email, Miss Washington."

It was Detective Washington, but Tara let it go. "Still—anyone?"

"No."

Had the dancer hesitated slightly? Tara couldn't be sure. She went on asking questions, but she could see that she wasn't getting anywhere. Anna Chernov grew politely impatient. Why wasn't Geraci stopping Tara? She had to continue until he did: "softening them up," he called it. The pointless questioning went on. Finally, just as Tara was running completely out of things to ask, Geraci said almost casually, "Do you know Dr. Erdmann, the physicist?"

"We've met once," Anna said.

"Is it your impression that he has a romantic interest in you?"

For the first time, Anna looked amused. "I think Dr. Erdmann's only romantic interest is in physics."

"I see. Thank you for your time, Ms. Chernov."

In the hall, Geraci said to Tara, "Ballet. Police work sure isn't what it used to be. You did good, Washington."

"Thank you. What now?"

"Now we find out what resident has a romantic interest in Anna Chernov. It's not Erdmann, but it's somebody."

So Anna *had* hesitated slightly when Tara asked if any resident had a special interest in her! Tara glowed inwardly as she followed Geraci down the hall. Without looking at her, he said, "Just don't let it go to your head."

She said dryly, "Not a chance."

"Good. A cop interested in *ballet* . . . Jesus H. Christ."

The ship grew agitated. Across many cubic light years between the stars, spacetime itself warped in dangerous ways. The new entity was growing in strength—and it was so far away yet!

It was not supposed to occur this way.

If the ship had become aware earlier of this new entity, this could have happened correctly, in accord with the laws of evolution. All things evolved—stars, galaxies, consciousness. If the ship had realized earlier that anywhere in this galactic backwater had existed the potential for a new entity, the ship would have been there to guide, to shape, to ease the transition. But it hadn't realized. There had been none of the usual signs.

They were happening now, however. Images, as yet dim and one-way, were reaching the ship. More critically, power was being drawn from it, power that the birthing entity had no idea how to channel. Faster, the ship must go faster . . .

It could not, not without damaging spacetime irretrievably. Spacetime could only reconfigure so much, so often. And meanwhile—

The half-formed thing so far away stirred, struggled, howled in fear.

NINE

Henry Erdmann was scared.

He could barely admit his fright to himself, let alone show it to the circle of people jammed into his small apartment on Saturday morning. They sat in a solemn circle, occupying his sofa and armchair and kitchen chairs and other chairs dragged from other apartments. Evelyn Krench-noted's chair crowded uncomfortably close to Henry's right side, her perfume sickly sweet. She had curled her hair into tiny gray sausages. Stan Dzarkis and Erin Bass, who could still manage it, sat on the floor. The folds of Erin's yellow print skirt seemed to Henry the only color amid the ashen faces. Twenty people, and maybe there were more in the building who were afflicted. Henry had called the ones he knew of, who had called the ones they knew of. Missing were Anna Chernov, still in the Infirmary, and Al Cosmano, who had refused to attend.

They all looked at him, waiting to begin.

"I think we all know why we're here," Henry said, and immediately a sense of unreality took him. He didn't understand at all why he was here. The words of Michael Faraday, inscribed on the physics building at UCLA, leapt into his mind: "Nothing is too wonderful to be true." The words seemed a mockery. What had been happening to Henry, to all of them, did not feel wonderful and was "true" in no sense he understood, although he was going to do his damnedest to relate it to physics in the only way that hours of pondering had suggested to him. Anything else— anything *less*—was unthinkable.

He continued, "Things have occurred to all of us, and a good first step is to see if we have indeed had the same experiences." *Collect data.* "So I'll go first. On five separate occasions I have felt some force seize my mind and body, as if a surge of energy was going through me, some sort of neurological shock. On one occasion it was painful, on the others not painful but very tiring. Has anyone else felt that?"

Immediately a clamor, which Henry stilled by raising his arm. "Can we start with a show of hands? Anybody else had that experience? Everybody. Okay, let's go around the circle, introducing yourself as we go, starting on my left. Please be as explicit as possible, but only descriptions at this point. No interpretations."

"Damned teacher," someone muttered, but Henry didn't see who and didn't care. His heart had speeded up, and he felt that his ears had somehow expanded around his hearing aid, so as not to miss even a syllable. He had deliberately not mentioned the times of his "seizures," or outside events concurrent with them, so as not to contaminate whatever information would be offered by the others.

"I'm John Kluge, from 4J." He was a heavy, round-faced man with a completely bald head and a pleasant voice used to making itself heard. High-school teacher, Henry guessed. History or math, plus coaching some sort of sports team. "It's pretty much like Henry here said, except I only felt the 'energy' four times. The first was around seven-thirty on Tuesday night. The second time woke me Wednesday night at eleven forty-two. I noted the time on my bedside clock. The third time I didn't note the time because I was vomiting after that food poisoning we all got on Thursday, but it was just before the vomiting started, sometime in mid-afternoon. That time the energy surge started near my heart, and I thought it was a heart attack. The last time was yesterday at eleven forty-five a.m., and in addition to the energy, I had a . . . well, a sort of—" He looked embarrassed.

"Please go on, it's important," Henry said. He could hardly breathe.

"I don't want to say a vision, but colors swirling through my mind, red and blue and white and somehow *hard*."

"Anna Chernov's necklace!" Evelyn shrieked, and the meeting fell apart.

Henry couldn't stop the frantic babble. He would have risen but his walker was in the kitchen; there was no room in the crowded living room. He was grateful when Bob Donovan put two fingers in his mouth and gave a whistle that could have deafened war dogs. "Hey! Shut up or nobody's gonna learn nothing!"

Everyone fell silent and glared resentfully at the stocky man in baggy chinos and cheap acrylic sweater. Donovan scowled and sat back down. Henry leapt into the quiet.

"Mr. Donovan is right, we won't learn anything useful this way. Let's resume going around the circle, with no interruptions, please. Mrs. Bass?"

Erin Bass described essentially the same events as John Kluge, without the Wednesday night incident but with the addition of the earlier, slight jar Henry had felt as he let Carrie into his apartment Tuesday before class. She described this as a "whisper in my mind." The next sixteen people all repeated the same experiences on Thursday and Friday, although some seemed to not have felt the "energy" on Tuesday, and some not on Tuesday or Wednesday. Henry was the only one to feel all five instances. Throughout these recitations, Evelyn Krenchnoted several times rose slightly in her chair, like a geyser about to burst. Henry did *not* want her to interrupt. He put a restraining hand on her arm, which was a mistake as she immediately covered his hand with her own and squeezed affectionately.

When it was finally Evelyn's turn, she said, "None of you had pain this last time like Henry did on Thursday—except me! I was having a medical MIT at the hospital and I was inside the machine and the pain was horrible! Horrible! And then—" she paused dramatically "—and then I saw Anna Chernov's necklace right at the time it was being stolen! And so did all of you—that was the 'hard colors,' John! Sapphires and rubies and diamonds!"

Pandemonium again. Henry, despite his growing fear, groaned inwardly. Why Evelyn Krenchnoted? Of all the unreliable witnesses . . .

"I saw it! I saw it!" Evelyn shrieked. Gina Martinelli had begun to pray in a loud voice. People jabbered to each other or sat silent, their faces gone white. A woman that Henry didn't know reached with a shaking hand into her pocket and pulled out a pill bottle. Bob Donovan raised his fingers to his lips.

Before Donovan's whistle could shatter their eardrums again, Erin Bass rose gracefully, clapped her hands, and cried surprisingly loudly, "Stop! We will get nowhere this way! Evelyn has the floor!"

Slowly the din subsided. Evelyn, who now seemed more excited than frightened by the implication of what she'd just said, launched into a long and incoherent description of her "MIT," until Henry stopped her the only way he could think of, which was to take her hand. She squeezed it again, blushed, and said, "Yes, dear."

Henry managed to get out, "Please. Everyone. There must be an explanation for all this." But before he could begin it, Erin Bass turned from aide to saboteur.

"Yes, and I think we should go around the circle in the same order and offer those explanations. But *briefly*, before too many people get too tired. John?"

Kluge said, "It could be some sort of virus affecting the brain. Contagious. Or some pollutant in the building."

Which causes every person to have the exact same hallucinations and a locked safe to open? Henry thought scornfully. The scorn steadied him. He needed steadying; every person in the room had mentioned feeling the Thursday-afternoon "energy" start in his or her heart, but no one except Henry knew that at that moment Jim Peltier was having an inexplicable heart attack as he battered Carrie.

Erin said, "What we see in this world is just *maya*, the illusion of permanence when in fact, all reality is in constant flux and change. What's happening here is beyond the world of intellectual concepts and distinctions. We're getting glimpses of the mutable nature of reality, the genuine undifferentiated 'suchness' that usually only comes with nirvana. The glimpses are imperfect, but for some reason our collective karma has afforded them to us."

Bob Donovan, next in the circle, said irritably, "That's just crap. We all got some brain virus, like Kluge here said, and some junkie cracked the office safe. The cops are investigating it. We should all see a doctor, except they can't never do anything to cure people anyway. And the people who had pain, Henry and Evelyn, they just got the disease worse."

Most people around the circle echoed the brain-disease theory, some with helpless skepticism, some with evident relief at finding any sort of explanation. A woman said slowly, "It could be the start of Alzheimer's." A man shrugged and said, "As God wills." Another just shook his head, his eyes averted.

Gina Martinelli said, "It *is* the will of God! These are the End Times, and we're being given signs, if only we would listen! 'Ye shalt have tribulations ten days: be thou faithful unto death, and I will give thee a crown of life.' Also—"

"It might be the will of God, Gina," interrupted Evelyn, unable to restrain herself any longer, "but it's mighty strange anyway! Why, I saw that necklace in my mind plain as day, and at just that moment it was being stolen from the safe! To my mind, that's not God, and not the devil neither or the robbery would have been successful, you see what I mean? The devil knows what he's doing. No, this was a message, all right, but from those who have gone before us. My Uncle Ned could see spirits all the time, they trusted him, I remember one time we all came down to breakfast and the cups had all been turned upside down when nobody was in the room and Uncle Ned, he said—"

Henry stopped listening. Ghosts. God. Eastern mysticism. Viruses. Alzheimer's. Nothing that fit the facts, that adhered even vaguely to the laws of the universe. These people had the reasoning power of termites.

Evelyn went on for a while, but eventually even she noticed that her audience was inattentive, dispirited, or actually asleep. Irene Bromley snored softly in Henry's leather armchair. Erin Bass said, "Henry?"

He looked at them hopelessly. He'd been going to describe the two-slit experiments on photons, to explain that once you added detectors to measure the paths of proton beams, the path became predetermined, even if you switched on the detector *after* the particle had been fired. He'd planned on detailing how that astonishing series of experiments changed physics forever, putting the observer into basic measurements of reality. Consciousness was woven into the very fabric of the universe itself, and consciousness seemed to him the only way to link these incredibly disparate people and the incredible events that had happened to them.

Even to himself, this "explanation" sounded lame. How Teller or Feynman would have sneered at it! Still, although it was better than anything he'd heard here this morning, he hated to set it out in front of these irrational people, half ignoramuses and the other half nutcases. They would all just reject it, and what would be gained?

But he had called this meeting. And he had nothing else to offer.

Henry stumbled through his explanation, trying to make the physics as clear as possible. Most of the faces showed perfect incomprehension. He finished with, "I'm not saying there's some sort of affecting of reality going on, through group consciousness." But wasn't that exactly what he *was* saying? "I don't believe in telekinesis or any of that garbage. The truth is, I don't know what's happening. But something is."

He felt a complete fool.

Bob Donovan snapped, "None of you know nothing. I been listening to all of you, and you haven't even got the facts right. I *seen* Anna Chernov's necklace. The cops showed it to me yesterday when they was asking me some questions. It don't got no sapphires or rubies, and just one tiny diamond. You're full of it, Evelyn, to think your seizure had anything to do with anything—and how do we know you even felt any pain at the 'very second' the safe was being cracked? All we got's your word."

"Are you saying I'm a liar?" Evelyn cried. "Henry, tell him!"

Tell him what? Startled, Henry just stared at her. John Kluge said harshly, "I don't believe Henry Erdmann is lying about his pain," and Evelyn turned from Donovan to Kluge.

"You mean you think *I* am? Who the hell do you think you are?"

Kluge started to tell her who he was: among other things, a former notary public. Other people began to argue. Evelyn started to cry, and Gina Martinelli prayed loudly. Erin Bass rose and slipped out the front door. Others followed. Those that remained disputed fiercely, the arguments growing more intense as they were unable to convince their neighbors of their own theories. Somewhere among the anger and contempt, Carrie Vesey appeared by Henry's side, her pretty face creased with bewildered concern, her voice high and strained.

"Henry? What on Earth is going on in here? I could hear the noise all the way down the hall . . . What is this all about?"

"Nothing," he said, which was the stupidest answer possible. Usually the young regarded the old as a separate species, as distant from their own concerns as trilobites. But Carrie had been different. She had always treated Henry as inhabiting the same world as herself, with the same passions and quirks and aims and defeats. This was the first time he had ever seen Carrie look at him as both alien and unsound, and it set the final seal on this disastrous meeting.

"But, Henry—"

"I said it's nothing!" he shouted at her. "Nothing at all! Now just leave me the hell alone!"

TEN

Carrie stood in the ladies' room off the lobby, pulling herself together. She was *not* going to cry. Even if Dr. Erdmann had never spoken to her like that before, even if ever since Jim's death she had felt as if she might shatter, even if . . . everything, she was *not going to cry*. It would be ridiculous. She

was a professional—well, a professional aide anyway—and Henry Erdmann was an old man. Old people were irritable sometimes. This whole
incident meant nothing.

Except that she knew it did. She had stood outside Dr. Erdmann's door
for a long time as people slipped out, smiling at her vaguely, and Evelyn
Krenchnoted babbled on inside. The unprecedented meeting had first piqued
her curiosity—Henry Erdmann, hosting a party at ten o'clock on a Saturday morning? Then, as she realized what Evelyn was saying, disbelief took
Carrie. Evelyn meant . . . Evelyn thought . . . and even Dr. Erdmann believed
that "something" had been happening, something weird and unexplainable
and supernatural, at the moment that Evelyn was under the MRI . . . *Henry!*

But Jake DiBella had been upset by Evelyn's scans.

The door of the ladies' opened and the first of the Saturday visitors entered, a middle-aged woman and a sulky teenage girl. "Honestly,
Hannah," the woman said, "it's only an hour out of your precious day and
it won't kill you to sit with your grandmother and concentrate on someone
else besides yourself for a change. If you'd just—"

Carrie went to DiBella's office. He was there, working at his desk.
No sign of her picture, cushion, coffee cup; she couldn't help her inevitable, stupid pang. He didn't want them. Or her. Another failure.

"Dr. DiBella—"

"'Jake.' Remember?" And then, "Carrie, what is it?"

"I just came from Dr. Erdmann's apartment. They were having a
meeting, about twenty people, all of them who've felt these 'seizures' or
whatever they are, all at the same time. Like the one you captured on
Evelyn's MRI scan."

He stared at her. "What do you mean, 'at the same time'?"

"Just what I said." She marveled at her own tone—none of her shaki-
ness showed. "They said that at the exact same time that Evelyn was showing all that weird activity under the MRI, each of them was feeling it, too,
only not so strong. And it was the exact same time that Anna Chernov's
necklace was being stolen. And they all saw the necklace in their minds."
Only—hadn't Mr. Donovan said that the necklace looked different from
what Evelyn said? Confusion took Carrie.

Jake looked down at whatever he was writing, back at Carrie, down
again at his notes. He came around the desk and closed his office door.

Taking her arm, he sat her gently in the visitor's chair, unadorned by her cushion. Despite herself, she felt a tingle where his hand touched her.

"Dr. Erdmann was involved in this? Tell me again. Slowly, Carrie. Don't leave anything out."

Evelyn Krenchnoted made her way to Gina Martinelli's apartment on Five. Really, Henry had been unbearably rude—to that poor young girl, to everybody at the meeting, and especially to Evelyn herself. He hadn't comforted her when that awful Donovan man called her a liar, he hadn't put his hand on hers again, he'd just yelled and yelled—and just when things between them had been going so well!

Evelyn needed to talk to Gina. Not that Gina had been any help at the meeting, not with all that praying. Gina was really a lot smarter than she looked, she'd been a part-time tax preparer once, but hardly anybody knew it because Gina never opened her mouth except to pray. Not that there was anything wrong with praying, of course! Evelyn certainly believed in God. But you had to help Him along a little if you really wanted something. You couldn't expect the Lord to do everything.

Evelyn had even curled her hair for Henry.

"Gina? Sweetie? Can I come in?"

"You're already in," Gina said. She had to speak loud because she had Frank Sinatra on the record player. Gina loved Frank Sinatra. For once she wasn't reading her Bible, which Evelyn thought was a good sign. She lowered her bulk onto Gina's sofa.

"So what did you think of that meeting?" Evelyn said. She was looking forward to a good two-three hours of rehashing, sympathy, and gossip. It would make her feel a lot better. Less creepy. Less afraid.

But instead, Gina said, "There was a message on the machine when I got back here. Ray is coming next week."

Oh, God, Gina's son. Who was only after her money. Ray hadn't visited in over a year, and now that Gina had told him she was leaving everything to the daughter . . . and there was a lot of everything to leave. Gina's late husband had made major money in construction.

"Oh, sweetie," Evelyn said, a little perfunctorily. Ordinarily she would have adored discussing Gina's anguish; for one thing, it made Evelyn glad she had never had kids. But now, with so much else going on—Henry and the attempted robbery and Evelyn's seizure and the strange comments at the meeting—

Frank Sinatra sang about ants and rubber tree plants. Gina burst into tears.

"Oh, sweetie," Evelyn repeated, got up to put her arms around Gina, and resigned herself to hearing about Ray Martinelli's selfishness.

Bob Donovan sat beside Anna Chernov's bed in the Infirmary. The man simply could not take a hint. She would either have to snub him outright or tell him in so many words to stop visiting her. Even the sight of him, squat and toad-faced and clumsy, made her shudder. Unfair, but there it was.

She had danced with so many beautiful men.

Which had been the best? Frederico, partnering her in *LaValse*—never had she been lifted so effortlessly. Jean, in *Scotch Symphony*, had been equally breathtaking, But the one she always returned to was Bennet. After she'd left the New York City Ballet for American Ballet Theater and her career had really taken off, they'd always danced together. Bennet, so dazzling as Albrecht in *Giselle*. . . . Guesting at a gala at the Paris Opera, they'd had seventeen curtain calls and—

Her attention was reclaimed by something Bob Donovan said.

"Could you repeat that, please, Bob?"

"What? Old Henry's crackpot theory? Science gibberish!"

"Nonetheless, would you repeat it?" She managed a smile.

He responded to the smile with pathetic eagerness. "Okay, yeah, if you want. Erdmann said, lemme think . . ." He screwed up his already crevassed face in an effort to remember. Although she was being unkind again. He probably wasn't all that bad looking, among his own class. And was she any better? These days she couldn't bear to look in a mirror. And the sight of the ugly cast on her leg filled her with despair.

"Erdmann said there was some experiments in physics, something with two slips, where people's consciences changed the path of some little . . . particles . . . by just thinking about them. Or maybe it was watching them. And that was the link between everybody who had so-called 'energy' at the same time. Group conscience. A new thing."

Consciousness, Anna translated. Group consciousness. Well, was that so strange? She had felt it more than once on stage, when a group of dancers had transcended what they were individually, had become a unity moving to the music in the creation of beauty. Such moments had, for her, taken the place of religion.

Bob was going on now about what other people at the meeting had said, offering up ungrammatical accounts in a desperate bid to please her, but even as she recognized this, Anna had stopped listening. She thought instead about Bennet, with whom she'd had such fantastic chemistry on and off stage, Bennet lifting her in the *grand pas de deux* of Act II, rosin from the raked stage rising around her like an angelic cloud, herself soaring and almost flying . . .

"Tell me again," Jake said.

"Again?" This was the third time! Not that Carrie really minded. She hadn't had his total attention—anybody's total attention—like this since Jim died. Not that she wanted Jim back . . . She shuddered even as she went through it all again. By the end, she was belligerent.

"Why? Are you saying you believe all this stuff about a group consciousness?"

"No. Of course not. Not without confirmation . . . but Erdmann is a scientist. What other data does he have that he isn't telling you?"

"I don't know what you mean." And she didn't; this conversation was beyond her. Photon detectors, double-slit experiments, observational predetermination . . . Her memory was good, but she knew she lacked the background to interpret the terms. Her own ignorance made her angry.

"Henry had two other experiences of 'energy' when he was with you, you said. Were there others when he was away from you?"

"How should I know? You better ask him!"

"I will. I'll ask them all."

"It sounds stupid to me." Immediately she was frightened by her own tone. But Jake just looked at her thoughtfully.

"Well, it sounds stupid to me, too. But Henry is right about one thing—*something* is happening. There's hard data in the form of Evelyn's MRI, in the fact that the safe was opened without the lock being either tampered with or moved to the right combination—"

"It *did?*"

"The detective told me, when he was asking questions yesterday. Also, I got the physician here to let me look at the lab results for everybody admitted to the Infirmary Thursday afternoon. Professional courtesy. There was no food poisoning."

"There wasn't?" All at once Carrie felt scared.

"No." DiBella sat thinking a long while. She scarcely dared breathe. Finally he said slowly, as if against his own will or better judgment—and that much she understood, anyway—"Carrie, have you ever heard of the principle of emergent complexity?"

"I did *everything* for that boy," Gina sobbed. "Just everything!"

"Yes, you did," said Evelyn, who thought Gina had done too much for Ray. Always lending him money after he lost each job, always letting him move back home and trash the place. What that kid had needed— and bad—was a good hiding, that's what.

"Angela didn't turn out this way!"

"No." Gina's daughter was a sweetie. Go figure.

"And now I just get it settled in my mind that he's out of my life, I come to grips with it, and he says he's flying back here to see 'his old ma' and he loves me! He'll just stir everything up again like he did when he got home from the Army, and when he divorced Judy, and when I had to find that lawyer for him in New York . . . Evelyn, nobody, but *nobody*, can rip you up inside like your child!"

"I know," said Evelyn, who didn't. She went on making little clucking noises while Gina sobbed. A plane roared overhead, and Frank Sinatra sang about it having been a very good year when he was twenty-one.

Bob Donovan took Anna's hand. Gently she pulled it away. The gentleness was for her, not him—she didn't want a scene. His touch repelled her. But oh, Bennet's touch . . . or Frederico's . . . Still, it was the dancing she missed. And now she would never dance again. She might, the doctors said, not even walk without a limp.

Never dance. Never feel her legs spring into a *ballotté* or soar in the exuberance of a *flick jeté*, back arched and arms thrown back, an arrow in ecstatic flight.

"Carrie, have you ever heard of the principle of emergent complexity?"

"No." Jake DiBella was going to make her feel dumb again. But he didn't mean to do that, and as long as she could sit here in his office with him, she would listen. Maybe he needed someone to listen. Maybe he needed her. And maybe he would say something that would help her make it all right with Dr. Erdmann.

Jake licked his lips. His face was still paper white. "'Emergent complexity' means that as an evolving organism grows more complex, it develops processes that wouldn't seem implied by the processes it had in simpler form. In other words, the whole becomes greater than the sum of the parts. Somewhere along the line, our primitive human ancestors developed self-awareness. Higher consciousness. That was a new thing in evolution."

Old knowledge stirred in Carrie's mind. "There was a pope—I was raised Catholic—some pope, one of the John-Pauls maybe, said there was a point where God infused a soul into an animal heritage. So evolution wasn't really anti-Catholic."

Jake seemed to be looking through her, at something only he could see. "Exactly. God or evolution or some guy named Fred—however it happened, consciousness did emerge. And if, now, the next step in complexity is emerging . . . if that . . ."

Carrie was angered, either by his line of thought or by his ignoring her; she wasn't sure which. She said sharply, "But why now? Why *here*?"

His question brought his gaze back to her. He took a long time to answer, while a plane droned overhead on the flight path out of the airport. Carrie held her breath.

But all he said was, "I don't know."

Gina had worked herself up to such a pitch that she wasn't even praying. Ray, Ray, Ray—This wasn't what Evelyn wanted to talk about. But she had never seen Gina like this. All at once Gina cried passionately, drowning out Sinatra singing, *Fly Me to the Moon*, "I wish he weren't coming! I wish his plane would just go on to another city or something, just not land here! I don't want him here!"

Never dance again. And the only love available from men like Bob Dono-van . . . No. *No.* Anna would rather be dead.

"Well, I don't believe it!" Carrie said. "Emerging complexity—I just don't believe it's happening at St. Sebastian's!"

"Neither do I," said Jake. For the first time since she'd entered his office, he smiled at her.

Outside the building, a boom sounded.

Carrie and Jake both looked toward the door. Carrie thought first of terrorism, a car bomb or something, because everybody thought first of terrorism these days. But terrorism at an assisted living facility was ridiculous. It was a gas main exploding, or a bus crash just outside, or . . .

Henry Erdmann appeared in the open doorway to the study. He didn't have his walker with him. He sagged against the doorjamb, his sunken eyes huge and his mouth open. Before Carrie could leap up to help him and just before he slumped to the floor, he croaked, "Call the police. We just brought down a plane."

Anguish ripped through the ship. Not its own agony, but the Other's. No guidance, no leading, it was raging wild and undisciplined. If this went on, it might weaken the ship too much for the ship to ever help it.

If this went on, the Other could damage spacetime itself.

The ship could not let that happen.

ELEVEN

When Henry Erdmann collapsed, DiBella moved swiftly to the old man. Carrie stood frozen—stupid! Stupid! "Get the doctor," Jake cried. And then, "*Go,* Carrie. He's alive."

She ran out of Jake's office, nearly tripping over the walker Henry had left in the hallway. He must have been coming to see Jake when it happened—when *what* happened? She raced to the lobby and the call phone, her mind so disordered that only as she shoved open the double doors did she realize that of course it would have been faster to hit Henry's panic button—Jake would do that—but Henry seldom wore his panic button, he—

She stopped cold, staring.

The lobby was full of screaming people, mostly visitors. Among them, old people lay fallen to the floor or slumped in wheel chairs. It was Saturday morning and on Saturday morning relatives arrived to take their mothers and grandfathers and great-grandmothers for brunch, for a drive, for a visit home . . . Bundled in sweaters and jackets and shawls, the seniors had all collapsed like so many bundles of dropped laundry. St. Sebastian nurses, aides, and even desk volunteers bent ineffectually over the victims.

Fear roiled Carrie's stomach, but it also preternaturally heightened her perceptions.

Mr. Aberstein, a St. Sebastian resident even though he was only sixty-seven, stood unaffected by the elevators. Mrs. Kelly sat alert in her wheelchair, her mouth a wide pink O. She was seventy-one. Mr. Schur . . .

"Nurse! Come quick, please, it's Dr. Erdmann!" Carrie caught at the sleeve of a passing nurse in purple scrubs, but he shook her off and raced to an old woman lying on the floor. Everyone here was too busy to help Carrie. She ran back to Jake's office.

Henry lay quietly on the floor. Jake had turned him face up and put a cushion—her cushion, Carrie thought numbly, the patchwork one she'd brought Jake—under Henry's feet. Henry wasn't wearing his panic button. She gasped, "No one can come, it's happened to all of them—"

"All who?" Jake said sharply.

She answered without thinking. "All of them over eighty. Is Henry—"

"He's breathing normally. his color's good, and he's not clammy. I don't think he's in shock. He's just . . . out. *All of them over eighty?*"

"Yes. No. I don't know, I mean, about the age, but all the older ones in the lobby just collapsed and the younger residents seem fine . . . Jake, what *is it?*"

"I don't know. Carrie, do this now: Go to one of the common rooms and turn the TV to the local news channel. See if there's been a . . . a plane crash—"

He stopped. Both of them heard the sirens.

Henry did not wake. All of Redborn Memorial Hospital's ambulances had gone to the crash site. The St. Sebastian staff moved afflicted residents to the dining room, which looked like a very peaceful war hospital. The residents didn't wake, moan, or need emergency treatment with the exception of one woman who had broken a hip falling to the floor. She was sent over to Memorial. Monitors couldn't be spared from the Nursing floor, where nearly everyone had fallen into the coma, but a few spare monitors were carried down from the Infirmary. They showed no anomalies in heart rate or blood pressure.

Relatives summoned family doctors, sat by cots, screamed at St. Sebastian staff, who kept repeating, "Redborn Memorial is aware of the situation and they'll get the St. Sebastian residents over there as soon as they can. *Please*, sir, if you'd just—"

Just be patient. Just believe that we're doing our best. Just be reassured by your mother's peaceful face. Just accept that we don't know any more than you do. Just leave me alone!

Carrie checked on her resident-assignees, one by one. They were all affected, most collapsed in their apartments. They were all moved into the Infirmary. They were all over eighty.

She was hurrying from Al Cosmano's apartment—empty, he must have been elsewhere when it happened—back to the Infirmary when a man caught at her arm. "Hey! Ms. Vesey!"

One of the detectives who'd investigated Jim's death. Carrie's belly clenched. "Yes?"

"Where do I find the hospital administrator? Caldwell?"

"He's not here, he went out of town for the weekend, they sent for him—why?"

"I need to see him. Who's in charge? And what the hell happened here?"

So not about Jim's death. Still—a cop. Some part of her mind shuddered—Jim had been a cop—but at the same time, she seized on this. Official authority. Someone who investigated and found answers. Security. There was a reason she'd married Jim in the first place.

She said as calmly as she could manage, "We've had an . . . an epidemic of collapses among the very old. All at the same time. About a half hour ago."

"Disease?"

"No." She heard how positive she sounded. Well, she was positive. "When the plane went down."

He looked baffled, as well he might. She said, "I'll take you to Dr. Jamison. He's the St. Sebastian's physician."

Jamison wasn't in the dining room. Carrie, leading Detective Geraci, found the doctor in the kitchen, in a shouting match with Jake DiBella. "No, damn it! You're not going to further upset the relatives for some stupid, half-baked theory—No!" Jamison stalked off.

Carrie said, "Dr. Jamison, this is—" He pushed past her, heading back to his patients. She expected the detective to follow him, but instead Geraci said to Jake, "Who are you?"

"Who wants to know?"

She had never seen Jake so rude. But he was angry and frustrated and scared—they were all scared.

"Detective Geraci, RPD. You work here?"

Carrie said quickly, before the two men could get really nasty, "This is Dr. DiBella. He's doing a medical research project at St. Sebastian's, on . . . on brain waves."

Geraci said, "I received an anonymous call. Me, not the Department, on my cell, from the St. Sebastian front desk. The caller said there was information here about the plane crash. You know anything about that, doctor?"

Carrie saw that Vince Geraci believed Jake did have information. How did she know that? How did *he* know that? But it was there in every line of the detective's alert body: He knew that Jake knew something.

Jake didn't answer, just stared at Geraci. Finally Geraci said, "The plane went down half a mile from here. A U.S. Air commuter plane carrying forty-nine passengers, including thirty-one members of the Aces High Senior Citizen Club. They were on a three-day trip to the casinos at Atlantic City. Everyone on board is dead."

Jake said, "I can't talk to you now. I have to take some brain scans while these people are unconscious. After that idiot Jamison realizes what I'm doing and throws me out, we can talk. Carrie, I'll need your help. Go to my office and put all the equipment in the corner onto the dolly, throw a blanket over it, and bring it the back way into the kitchen. Quickly!"

She nodded and hurried off, so fast that she didn't realize Geraci was behind her until they reached Jake's office.

"Let me get that, it's heavy," he said.

"No, it's not." She lugged the console onto its dolly. "Shouldn't you be asking people questions?"

"I am. Does DiBella always order you around like that?"

Did he? She hadn't noticed. "No." She added the helmet and box of peripherals on top of the console, then looked around for a blanket. There wasn't one.

"Do you work for DiBella or for St. Sebastian's?"

"St. Sebastian's. I have to go to the linen closet."

When she returned with a blanket, Geraci was reading the papers on Jake's desk. Wasn't that illegal? Carrie threw the blanket over the equipment. Geraci grabbed the handle of the dolly before she could.

"You need me," he said. "Anybody stops you, I'll just flash my badge."

"Okay," she said ungraciously. She could have done this, for Jake, by herself.

They brought the equipment into the kitchen. Jake set it up on the counter, ignoring the cook who said helplessly, "So nobody's having lunch, then?" All at once she ripped off her apron, flung it onto the floor, and walked out.

Jake said to Carrie, "Hold the door." He slipped through to the dining room and, a moment later, wheeled in a gurney with an elderly woman lying peacefully on it. "Who is she, Carrie?"

"Ellen Parminter." After a moment she added, "Eighty-three." Jake grunted and began attaching electrodes to Mrs. Parminter's unconscious head.

Geraci said, "Come with me, Carrie."

"No." Where did she get the *nerve?* But, somehow, he brought that out in her.

He only smiled. "Yes. This is an official police investigation, as of this minute."

She went, then, following him back to Jake's office. Carrie was shaking, but she didn't want him to see that. He did, though; he seemed to see everything. "Sit down," he said gently. "There, behind the desk—you didn't like me reading DiBella's papers before, did you? It's legal if they're in plain sight. You seem like a really good observer, Carrie. Now, please tell me everything that's been happening here. From the very beginning, and without leaving anything out. Start with why you told DiBella that woman's age. Does her age matter to what he's doing?"

Did it? She didn't know. How could it . . . people aged at such different rates! Absolute years meant very little, except that—

"Carrie?"

All at once it seemed a relief to be able to pour it all out. Yes, he was trained to get people to talk, she knew that, and she didn't really trust his sudden gentleness. It was merely a professional trick. But if she told it all, that might help order her chaotic thoughts. And maybe, somehow, it might help the larger situation, too. All those people dead on the plane—

She said slowly, "You won't believe it."

"Try me anyway."

"*I* don't believe it."

This time he just waited, looking expectant. And it all poured out of her, starting with Henry's "seizure" on the way home from the university. The vomiting epidemic among seven or so patients, that wasn't the food poisoning that St. Sebastian's said it was. Evelyn Krenchnoted's functional MRI. Anna Chernov's necklace, what Evelyn thought the necklace looked like and what Bob Donovan said it really was. The secret meeting this morning in Henry's apartment. What Carrie had overheard: Henry's words about photons and how human observation, affected the paths of fundamental particles. Jake's lecture on 'emergent complexity.' Henry's appearance at Jake's office, saying just before he collapsed, "Call the police. We just brought down a plane." The mass collapse of everyone over eighty and of no one younger than that. The brain scans Jake was taking now, undoubtedly to see if they looked normal or like Evelyn's. The more Carrie talked, the more improbable everything sounded.

When she finished, Geraci's face was unreadable.

"That's it," she said miserably. "I have to go see how Henry is."

"Thank you, Carrie." His tone was unreadable. "I'm going to find Dr. Jamison now."

He left, but she stayed. It suddenly took too much energy to move. Carrie put her head in her hands. When she straightened again, her gaze fell on Jake's desk.

He'd been writing when she'd burst in with the news of the meeting in Henry's apartment. Writing on paper, not on a computer: thick pale green paper with a faint watermark. The ink was dark blue. "My dearest James, I can't tell you how much I regret the things I said to you on the phone last night, but, love, please remember—"

Carrie gave a short, helpless bark of laughter. *My dearest James . . .* God, she was such a fool!

She shook her head like a dog spraying off water, and went to look for Henry.

The new being was quiet now. That made this a good time to try to reach it. That was always best done through its own culture's symbols. But ship had had so little time to prepare . . . This should have been done slowly, over a long time, a gradual interaction as the new entity was guided, shaped, made ready. And ship was still so far away.

But it tried, extending itself as much as possible, searching for the collective symbols and images that would have eased a normal transition—

—and roiled in horror.

TWELVE

Evelyn Krenchnoted lay on a cot jammed against the dining room window. She lay dreaming, unaware of the cool air seeping through the glass, or the leaves falling gold and orange in the tiny courtyard beyond. In her dream she walked on a path of light. Her feet made no sound. She moved toward more light, and somewhere in that light was a figure. She couldn't see it or hear it, but she knew it was there. And she knew who it was.

It was someone who really, truly, finally would listen to her.

✪

Al Cosmano squirmed in his sleep. "He's waking," a nurse said.

"No, he's not." Dr. Jamison, passing yet again among the rows of cots and gurneys and pallets on the floor, his face weary. "Some of them have been doing that for hours. As soon as the ambulances return, move this row next to the hospital."

"Yes, doctor."

Al heard them and didn't hear them. He was a child again, running along twilight streets toward home. His mother was there, waiting. Home . . .

The stage was so bright! The stage manager must have turned up the lights, turned them up yet again—the whole stage was light. Anna Chernov couldn't see, couldn't find her partner. She had to stop dancing.

Had to stop dancing.

She stood lost on the stage, lost in the light. The audience was out there somewhere in all that brightness, but she couldn't see them any more than she could see Bennet or the corps de ballet. She felt the audience, though. They were there, as bright as the stage, and they were old. Very, very old, as old as she was, and like her, beyond dancing.

She put her hands over her face and sobbed.

Erin Bass saw the path, and it led exactly where she knew it would: deeper into herself. That was where the buddha was, had always been, would always be. Along this path of light, curving and spiraling deeper into her own being, which was all being. All around her were the joyful others, who were her just as she was them—

A jolt, and she woke in an ambulance, her arms and legs and chest strapped down, a young man leaning over her saying, "Ma'am?" The path was gone, the others gone, the heavy world of *maya* back again around her, and a stale taste in her dehydrated mouth.

Lights and tunnels—where the hell was he? An A-test bunker, maybe, except no bunker was ever this brightly lit, and where was Teller or Mark or Oppie? But, no, Oppie hadn't ever worked on this project, Henry was confused, that was it, he was just confused—

And then he wasn't.

He woke all at once, a wrenching transition from sleep-that-wasn't-really sleep to full alertness. In fact, his senses seemed preternaturally sharp. He felt the hard cot underneath his back, the slime of drool on his cheek, the flatness of the dining-room fluorescent lights. He heard the roll of rubber gurney wheels on the low-pile carpet and the clatter of cutlery in the kitchen dishwashers. He smelled Carrie's scent, wool and vanilla and young skin, and he could have described every ligament of her body as she sat on the chair next to his cot in the dining room of St. Sebastian's, Detective Geraci beside her.

"Henry?" Carrie whispered.

He said, "It's coming. It's almost here."

Ship withdrew all contact. It had never encountered anything like this before. The pre-being did not **coalesce.**

Its components were not uniform, but scattered among undisciplined and varied matter-specks who were wildly heterozygotic. Unlike the components of every other pre-being that ship had detected, had guided, had become. All the other pre-ships had existed as one on the matter plane, because they were alike in all ways. These, too, were alike, built of the same physical particles and performing the same physical processes, but somewhere something had gone very wrong, and from that uniform matter they had not evolved uniform consciousness. They had no harmony. They used violence against each other.

Possibly they could, if taken in, use that violence against ship.

Yet ship couldn't go away and leave them. Already they were changing spacetime in their local vicinity. When their melding had advanced farther, the new being could be a dangerous and powerful entity. What might it do?

Ship pondered, and feared, and recoiled from what might be necessary: the destruction of what should have been an integral part of itself.

THIRTEEN

Jake DiBella clutched the printouts so hard that the stiff paper crumpled in his hand. Lying on the sofa, Henry Erdmann frowned at the tiny destruction. Carrie had pulled her chair close enough to hold Henry's hand, while that RPD detective, Geraci, stood at the foot of the couch. What was he doing here, anyway? DiBella didn't know, but he was too agitated to care for more than a fleeting second.

Carrie said to Henry, "I still think you should go to the hospital!"

"I'm not going, so forget it." The old man struggled to sit up. She would have stopped him, but Geraci put a hand on her shoulder and gently restrained her. *Throwing around his authority*, DiBella thought.

Henry said, "Why at St. Sebastian's?"

The same question that Carrie had asked. DiBella said, "I have a theory." His voice sounded strange to himself. "It's based on Carrie's observation that nobody under eighty has been . . . affected by this. If it is some sort of uber-consciousness that's . . . that's approaching Earth . . ." He couldn't go on. It was too silly.

It was too real.

Henry Erdmann was apparently not afraid of either silliness or reality—which seemed to have become the same thing. Henry said, "You mean it's coming here because 'uber-consciousness' emerges only among the old, and nowadays there's more old than ever before."

"For the first time in history, you over-eighties exceed one percent of the population. A hundred forty million people world-wide."

"But that still doesn't explain why here. Or why us."

"For God's sake, Henry, everything has to start somewhere!"

Geraci said, surprising DiBella, "All bifurcation is local. One lungfish starts to breathe more air than water. One caveman invents an axe. There's always a nexus. Maybe that nexus is you, Dr. Erdmann."

Carrie tilted her head to look up at Geraci.

Henry said heavily, "Maybe so. But I'm not the only one. I wasn't the main switch for the energy that brought down that airplane. I was just one of the batteries linked in parallel."

The science analogies comfort Erdmann, DiBella thought. He wished something would comfort him.

Carrie said, "I think Evelyn was the switch to open the safe for Anna Chernov's necklace."

Geraci's face sharpened. But he said, "That doesn't really make sense. I can't go that far."

Henry's sunken eyes grew hard. "You haven't had to travel as far as *I* have in order to get to this point, young man. Believe me about that. But

I *experienced* the . . . the consciousness. That data is anecdotal but real. And those brain scans that Dr. DiBella is mangling there aren't even anecdotal. They're hard data."

True enough. The brain scans DiBella had taken of the unconscious oldsters, before that irate idiot Jamison had discovered him at work and thrown him out, were cruder versions of Evelyn Krenchnoted's under the fMRI. An almost total shut-down of the thalamus, the relay station for sensory information flowing into the brain. Ditto for the body-defining posterior parietal lobes. Massive activity in the back of the brain, especially in the temporoparietal regions, amygdalae, and hippocampus. The brain scan of an epileptic mystical state on speed. And as unlike the usual scan for the coma-state as a turtle was to a rocketship to the stars.

DiBella put his hands to his face and pulled at his skin, as if that might rearrange his thoughts. When he'd dropped his hands, he said slowly, "A single neuron isn't smart, isn't even a very impressive entity. All it really does is convert one type of electrical or chemical signal into another. That's it. But neurons connected together in the brain can generate incredibly complex states. You just need enough of them to make consciousness possible."

"Or enough old people for this 'group consciousness'?" Carrie said. "But why only old people?"

"How the hell should I know?" DiBella said. "Maybe the brain needs to have stored enough experience, enough sheer *time.*"

Geraci said, "Do you read Dostoievski?"

"No," DiBella said. He didn't like Geraci. "Do *you?*"

"Yes. He said there were moments when he felt a 'frightful' clarity and rapture, and that he would give his whole life for five seconds of that and not feel he was paying too much. Dostoievski was an epileptic."

"I know he was an epileptic!" DiBella snapped.

Carrie said, "Henry, can you sense it now? That thing that's coming?"

"No. Not at all. Obviously it's not quantum-entangled in any classical sense."

"Then maybe it's gone away."

Henry tried to smile at her. "Maybe. But I don't think so. I think it's coming for us."

"What do you mean, 'coming for you'?" Geraci said skeptically. "It's not a button man."

"I don't know what I mean," Henry said irritably. "But it's coming, and soon. It can't afford to wait long. Look what we did . . . that plane . . ."

Carrie's hand tightened on Henry's fingers. "What will it do when it gets here?"

"I don't know. How could I know?"

"Henry—" Jake began.

"I'm more worried about what *we* may do before it arrives."

Geraci said, "Turn on CNN."

DiBella said pointedly, "Don't you have someplace you should be, Detective?"

"No. Not if this really is happening."

To which there was no answer.

At 9:43 p.m., the power grid went down in a city two hundred miles away. "No evident reason," said the talking head on CNN, "given the calm weather and no sign of any—"

"Henry?" Carrie said.

"I . . . I'm all right. But I felt it."

Jake said, "It's happening farther away now. That is, if it was . . . if that was . . ."

"It was," Henry said simply. Still stretched full-length on the sofa, he closed his eyes. Geraci stared at the TV. None of them had wanted any food.

At 9:51, Henry's body jerked violently and he cried out. Carrie whimpered, but in a moment Henry said, "I'm . . . conscious." No one dared comment on his choice of word. Seven minutes later, the CNN anchor announced breaking news: a bridge over the Hudson River had collapsed, plunging an Amtrak train into the dark water.

Over the next few minutes, Henry's face showed a rapid change of expression: fear, rapture, anger, surprise. The expressions were so pronounced, so distorted, that at times Henry Erdmann almost looked like someone else. Jake wondered wildly if he should record this on his cell camera, but he didn't move. Carrie knelt beside the sofa and put both arms around the old man, as if to hold him here with her.

"We . . . can't help it," Henry got out. "If one person thinks strongly enough about—ah, God!"

The lights and TV went off. Alarms sounded, followed by sirens. Then a thin beam of light shone on Henry's face; Geraci had a pocket flashlight. Henry's entire body convulsed in seizure, but he opened his eyes. DiBella could barely hear his whispered words.

"It's a *choice.*"

The only way was a choice. Ship didn't understand the necessity—how could any single unit choose other than to become part of its whole? That had never happened before. Birthing entities came happily to join themselves. The direction of evolution was toward greater complexity, always. But choice must be the last possible action here, for this misbegotten and unguided being. If it did **not** *choose to merge—*

Destruction. To preserve the essence of consciousness itself, which meant the essence of all.

FOURTEEN

Evelyn, who feared hospitals, had refused to go to Redborn Memorial to be "checked over" after the afternoon's fainting spell. That's all it was, just fainting, nothing to get your blood in a boil about, just a—

She stopped halfway between her microwave and kitchen table. The casserole in her hand fell to the floor and shattered.

The light was back, the one she'd dreamed about in her faint. Only it wasn't a light and this wasn't a dream. It was there in her mind, and it was her mind, and she was it . . . had always been it. How could that be? But the presence filled her and Evelyn knew, beyond any doubt, that if she joined it, she would never, ever be alone again. Why, she didn't need words, had never needed words, all she had to do was choose to go where she belonged anyway . . .

Who knew?

Happily, the former Evelyn Krench noted became part of those waiting for her, even as her body dropped to the linguini-spattered floor.

✹

In a shack in the slums of Karachi, a man lay on a pile of clean rags. His toothless gums worked up and down, but he made no sound. All night he had been waiting alone to die, but now it seemed his wait had truly been for something else, something larger than even death, and very old.

Old. It sought the old, and only the old, and the toothless man knew why. Only the old had earned this, had paid for this in the only coin that really mattered: the accumulation of sufficient sorrow.

With relief he slipped away from his pain-wracked body and into the ancient largeness.

No. He wasn't moving, Bob thought. The presence in his mind terrified him, and terror turned him furious. Let them—whoever—try all their cheap tricks, they were as bad as union negotiators. Offering concessions that would never materialize. Trying to fool him. He wasn't going anywhere, wasn't becoming anything, not until he knew exactly what the deal was, what the bastards wanted.

They weren't going to get him.

But then he felt something else happen. He knew what it was. Sitting in the Redborn Memorial ER, Bob Donovan cried out, "No! Anna—you can't!" even as his mind tightened and resisted until, abruptly, the presence withdrew and he was alone.

In a luxurious townhouse in San José, a man sat up abruptly in bed. For a long moment he sat completely still in the dark, not even noticing that the clock and digital-cable box lights were out. He was too filled with wonder.

Of course—why hadn't he seen this before? He, who had spent long joyful nights debugging computers when they still used vacuum tubes— how could he have missed this? He wasn't the whole program, but rather just one line of code! And it was when you put all the code together, not before, that the program could actually run. He'd been only a fragment, and now the whole was here . . .

He joined it.

✪

Erin Bass experienced *sartori*.

Tears filled her eyes. All her adult life she had wanted this, longed for it, practiced meditation for hours each day, and had not even come close to the mystical intoxication she felt now. She hadn't known, hadn't dreamed it could be this oneness with all reality. All her previous striving had been wrong. There was no striving, there was no Erin. She had never been created; she was the creation and the cosmos; no individual existed. Her existence was not her own, and when that last illusion vanished so did she, into the all.

Gina Martinelli felt it, the grace that was the glory of God. Only . . . only where was Jesus Christ, the savior and Lord? She couldn't feel him, couldn't find Him in the oneness . . .

If Christ was not there, then this wasn't Heaven. It was a trick of the Cunning One, of Satan who knows a million disguises and sends his demons to mislead the faithful. She wasn't going to be tricked!

She folded her arms and began to pray aloud. Gina Martinelli was a faithful Christian. She wasn't going anywhere; she was staying right here, waiting for the one true God.

A tiny woman in Shanghai sat at her window, watching her great-grand-children play in the courtyard. How fast they were! Ai, once she had been so fast . . .

She felt it come over her all at once, the gods entering her soul. So it was her time! Almost she felt young again, felt strong . . . that was good. But even if had not been good, when the gods came for you, you went.

One last look at the children, and she was taken to the gods.

Anna Chernov, wide awake in the St. Sebastian Infirmary that had become her prison, gave a small gasp. She felt power flow through her, and for a wild moment she thought it was the same force that had powered a life-time of arabesques and jetés, a lifetime ago.

It was not.

This was something outside of herself, separate . . . but it didn't have to be. She could take it in herself, become it, even as it became her. But she held back.

Will there be dancing?

No. Not as she knew it, not the glorious stretch of muscle and thrust of limb and arch of back. Not the creation of beauty through the physical body. No. No dancing.

But there was power here, and she could use that power for another kind of escape, from her useless body and this Infirmary and a life without dance. From somewhere distant she head someone cry, "Anna—you can't!" But she could. Anna seized the power, both refusing to join it or to leave it, and bent it onto herself. She was dead before her next breath.

Henry's whole body shuddered. It was here. It was him.

Or not. "It's a choice," he whispered.

On the one hand, everything. All consciousness, woven into the very fabric of space-time itself, just as Wheeler and the rest had glimpsed nearly a hundred years ago. Consciousness at the quantum level, the probability-wave level, the co-evolvee with the universe itself.

On the other hand, the individual Henry Martin Erdmann. If he merged with the uber-consciousness, he would cease to exist as himself, his separate mind. And his mind was everything to Henry.

He hung suspended for nanoseconds, years, eons. Time itself took on a different character. Half here, half not, Henry knew the power, and what it was, and what humanity was not. He saw the outcome. He had his answer.

"No," he said.

Then he lay again on his sofa with Carrie's arms around him, the other two men illuminated dimly by a thin beam of yellow light, and he was once more mortal and alone.

And himself.

Enough merged. The danger is past. The being is born, and is ship, and is enough.

FIFTEEN

Months to identify all the dead. Years to fully repair all the damage to the world's infrastructure: bridges, buildings, information systems. Decades yet to come, DiBella knew, of speculation about what had actually happened. Not that there weren't theories already. Massive EMP, solar radiation, extrasolar radiation, extrastellar radiation, extraterrestrial attack, global terrorism, Armageddon, tectonic plate activity, genetically engineered viruses. Stupid ideas, all easily disproved, but of course that stopped no one from believing them. The few old people left said almost nothing. Those that did, were scarcely believed.

Jake scarcely believed it himself.

He did nothing with the brain scans of Evelyn Krenchnoted and the three others, because there was nothing plausible he could do. They were all dead, anyway. "Only their bodies," Carrie always added. She believed everything Henry Erdmann told her.

Did DiBella believe Henry's ideas? On Tuesdays he did, on Wednesdays not, on Thursdays belief again. There was no replicable proof. It wasn't science. It was . . . something else.

DiBella lived his life. He broke up with James. He visited Henry, long after the study of senior attention patterns was over. He went to dinner with Carrie and Vince Geraci. He was best man at their wedding.

He attended his mother's sixty-fifth birthday party, a lavish shindig organized by his sister in the ballroom of a glitzy downtown hotel. The birthday girl laughed, and kissed the relatives who'd flown in from Chicago, and opened her gifts. As she gyrated on the dance floor with his Uncle Sam, DiBella wondered if she would live long enough to reach eighty.

Wondered how many others in the world would reach eighty.

"It was only because enough of them chose to go that the rest of us lost the emerging power," Henry had said, and DiBella noted that *them* instead of *we*. "If you have only a few atoms of uranium left, you can't reach critical mass."

DiBella would have put it differently: If you have only a few neurons, you don't have a conscious brain. But it came to the same thing in the end.

"If so many hadn't merged, then the consciousness would have had to . . ." Henry didn't finish his sentence, then or ever. But DiBella could guess.

"Come on, boy," Uncle Sam called, "get yourself a partner and dance!"

DiBella shook his head and smiled. He didn't have a partner just now and he didn't want to dance. All the same, old Sam was right. Dancing had a limited shelf life. The sell-by date was already stamped on most human activity. Someday his mother's generation, the largest demographic bulge in history, would turn eighty. And Henry's choice would have to be made yet again.

How would it go next time?

THE KINDNESS OF STRANGERS

When morning finally dawns, Rochester isn't there anymore.

Jenny stands beside Eric, gazing south from the rising ground that yesterday was a fallow field. Maybe the whole city hasn't vanished. Certainly the tall buildings are gone, Xerox Square and Lincoln Tower and the few others that just last night poked above the horizon, touched by the red fire of the setting September sun. But, unlike Denver or Tokyo or Seattle, Rochester, New York sits—sat—on flat ground and there's no point from which the whole city could be seen at once. And it was such a *small* city.

"Maybe they only took downtown," Jenny says to Eric, "and Penfield is still there or Gates or Brighton . . ."

Eric just looks at her and pulls out his cell yet again. Most of the others—other what? refugees?—are still asleep in their cars or tents or sleeping bags on the dew-soaked weeds. There aren't nearly as many refugees as Jenny expected. Faced with the choice of staying in the city—and such a small city!—or leaving it, most had stayed. Devil you know and all that.

She thinks she might be a little hysterical.

Eric walks around the car, cell pressed to his ear. Deirdre will not answer, will never answer again, but that won't stop him from trying. He tried even as he and Jenny hastily packed up her Dodge Caravan yesterday afternoon, even as she drove frantically south, even as they were stopped. When the battery in Eric's cell runs down, he will take hers. Jenny, sure of this if of nothing else, presses her hands to her temple, trying to stop the blood pounding there. It doesn't work.

"Good morning," says an alien, coming up behind her. "Breakfast is ready now."

Jenny whirls around and stumbles backward, falling against the hood of her van. This one is female, a tall Scandinavian-looking blonde. Her

79

pink skin glows with health; her blue eyes shine warmly; her teeth are small and regular. She is dressed like last night's alien, in a ground-length, long-sleeved brown garment. Loose, modest, cultureless, suitable for dissolving cities on any part of the globe.

Definitely a little hysterical.

"No, thank you," Jenny manages.

"Are you sure?" the alien asks. She gestures toward the low, pale buildings at the far end of the sloping meadow. "The coffee is excellent today."

"No, thank you."

The alien smiles and moves on to the next car. Eric turns on Jenny. "Why are you so *polite* to them?"

She doesn't answer. To say anything—anything at all—will be to unleash the rage he's been battling for fourteen hours. So far, Eric has held that rage in check. She can't risk it.

"Here," he says, thrusting a Quaker Oats breakfast bar at her. She isn't hungry but takes it anyway.

"Some of us are going to dig a latrine," he says, not looking at her, and strides off.

Two cars over, a woman with crazy eyes fires a nine-millimeter at the alien. The bullet ricochets off her, striking another car's hubcap. People wake and cry out. The alien smiles at the crazed human.

"Good morning. Breakfast is ready now."

Probably the aliens aren't even present. If you touch one—or hit it or shotgun it or hurl a Molotov cocktail at it, all of which were tried last night—you encounter a tough, impenetrable shell that doesn't even wobble under impact. *Personal force field*, someone said. *Holographic projection*, said another, *protected by a force field*. Jenny has no idea who's right, and it hardly matters. The same maybe-force-field was what stopped her and Eric's mad drive south last night. Another transparent wall prevented her from retracing her route. A hundred or so cars were thus invisibly herded into this empty field, their drivers leaping out to compare sketchy information, children crying in the back seat and wives hunched over car radios, their faces in white shock.

Mumbai and Karachi had been first, vanishing at 2:16 p.m. No explosion, no dust, no blinding light. One moment, reported dazed observers by satellite, the great cities and their vast suburbs had existed and the next they were gone, leaving bare ground that ended in roads sheared off as neatly as if by a very sharp knife, in halves of temples on the shear line, in bisected holy cows. The ground was not even scorched. People standing beyond the vanishing point saw nothing happen.

Fifteen minutes later it was Delhi, Shanghai, and Moscow.

Fifteen minutes after that, Seoul, Sao Paolo, Istanbul, Lima, and Mexico City.

Then Jakarta, New York, Tokyo, Beijing, Cairo, Tehran, and Riyad.

By this time the hysterical media had figured out that cities were vanishing in order of size, and by a progression of prime numbers. At 3:16 p.m. (London, Bogotá, Lagos, Baghdad, Bangkok, Lahore, Dacca, Rio de Janeiro, Bangalore, Wuhan, and Tientsin), the panicked evacuations began. Most people were vaporized (except that no vapor remained) long before they reached the end of the murderous city traffic jams.

Canton, Toronto, Jiddah, Abidjan, Chongqing, Santiago, Calcutta, Singapore, Chennai, St. Petersburg, Shenyang, Los Angeles, Ahmadabad.

As soon as he heard, Eric called Deirdre in Chicago, over and over, even as he and Jenny had been packing her car. He hadn't been able to get through by either cell or land line: ALL CIRCUITS BUSY. PLEASE TRY YOUR CALL AGAIN LATER.

Pusan, Alexandria, Hyderabad, Ankara, Pyongyang, Yokohama, Montreal, Casablanca, Ho Chi Minh City, Berlin, Nanjing, Addis Ababa, Poona, Medellin, Kano.

Only two United States cities so far. Jenny lived in Henrietta, Rochester's southernmost suburb. The roads were crowded but not impassable. She inched through traffic, the radio turned on, while Eric tried Deirdre over and over again. ALL CIRCUITS BUSY.

At 4:01, Chicago vanished along with Omdurman, Surat, Madrid, Sian, Kanpur, Havana, Jaipur, Nairobi, Harbin, Buenos Aires, Incheon, Surabaya, Kiev, Hangchou, Salvador, Taipei, Hai Phong, and Dar es Salaam. Eric kept calling. He said, "Maybe she was visiting someone out of the city, shopping at a mall someplace rural. . . . She doesn't always have her cell turned on!"

Jenny knew better than to answer. She concentrated on the road, on the traffic, on the panicky radio announcer relaying by satellite a report from where Houston used to be.

"Can I have that?"

A small voice at her elbow. Jenny realizes she is still holding the unopened Quaker Oats bar. The little boy is maybe five or six, dirty and snot-nosed, but with wide dark eyes that hold soft depths, like ash. He stares hungrily at the breakfast bar.

"Sure, take it." Her voice is thick. "What's your name?"

"Ricky." He tears off the wrapping and drops it on the grass. Jenny picks it up.

"Where's your mom, Ricky?"

"Over there." He gobbles the bar in three bites. His mother, a voluptuous redhead in pink stretch pants, sits on the ground with her back against an old green SUV. She nurses an infant from one large breast and watches Jenny. All at once she bawls, "Ricky! Get your ass over here!"

Ricky ignores this. "Do you got any more food?"

"No," Jenny lies. Apparently not everyone thought to pack their cars with food. Those that have, will run out before long. The low, pale buildings still sit unvisited.

"Ricky!" his mother screams, and this time he leaves.

Jenny pulls off her sweater; the morning sun is turning the day hot. She opens her cell to key in her brother Bob's number. Bob lives with his family in Dundee, a small town fifty miles away; his and Jenny's mother lives with them. Jenny's sister and her family are nearby. "Bob? You all okay? . . . No, nothing changed since last night. . . . Jane? You talk to her? . . . Okay, look, I don't want to run down the phone too much . . . Love you, too. . . ." When she closes the case, Eric is back.

They stare at each other. *Now it will come,* Jenny thinks. She feels as if she's carrying a teacup of nitroglycerin across a tightrope; the fall is only a matter of time. But all Eric says is, "There's a man here who's good at organization. We divided into sections and checked out the whole wall. No breaks, and it extends as far up as anyone can throw a stone and as far underground as we had time to dig. The force field surrounds the buildings, too. Anything new on the radio?"

"No," Jenny says, not telling him that she hasn't been listening. But he knows; his question was not inquisitive but hostile. He can't help that, Jenny knows as much, but she recoils as if he'd struck her. She's always been too sensitive to rejection.

Eric says, "I'm going back to help the tunnel crew."

"Okay." And then she can't stand it anymore. "Eric, I'm so sorry, but it's not my fault that my family is alive and Deirdre and Mary—"

"*Don't*," he says, so low and dangerous that Jenny is shocked into silence. Eric is not ordinarily a dangerous man. One thing she loved about him was his light-hearted exuberance.

He walks away, his back toward her, and Jenny covers her face with her hands. It is her fault, will always be her fault. Not that Eric's wife and daughter are dead, of course, but that Eric was with Jenny, in bed with Jenny in another city, pumping away on top of Jenny, when it happened. He will never forgive either of them for that.

They met a year ago, at the American Library Association annual conference, in Kansas City. Jenny's attraction to him was instantaneous, and so was her glance at the wedding ring on Eric's left hand. But he was so handsome and so charming, and she was so thrilled by the almost unprecedented masculine attention. They drifted together at the luncheon held between "Reference Tools for the Online Generation" and "Collaborative Approaches to Information Literacy." They had a drink in the bar after the obligatory inedible banquet, laughing at the dullness of the speakers. One drink became many. They spent the last night of the conference in Jenny's room, and the next day she'd flown back to Rochester, suspended somewhere between euphoria and dread. Two days later she'd emailed him. Eric had replied, and things had gone on from there.

Sometimes, if she hadn't had an email or phone call from him in several days, Jenny let herself imagine that he'd told his wife about the affair. He'd told her, and then he'd moved out of their Evanston home, and he was just waiting to hear from his lawyer before he told Jenny the great news. She let herself imagine all this in exquisite detail—the scene with Deirdre, Eric's complicated emotions, the phone call to Jenny and how understanding she would be—even while she knew it was not going to happen. Very few married men actually left their wives for their mistresses. Eric adored his six-year-old daughter. He had never even said that he loved Jenny.

But she loved him, and she knew it was turning her desperate, which in turn was driving him away. She waited, helpless and all but hopeless, by the phone. She turned up the volume on her computer ("You've got mail!") so that anywhere in the apartment she would know the instant his email came through. She wrote long, eloquent letters giving him tender ultimatums, and never sent the letters because she knew he would not choose her. It took all her strength to never ask him the Fatal Questions: Do we have a future? Are you tired of me? Is there somebody else? Somebody besides Deirdre, she meant. She tried not to think about Deirdre, and the effort further exhausted her. Finally she googled Deirdre and got over a thousand hits; Deirdre was a successful real estate agent in Evanston. She was slim, tanned, smiling, dressed more stylishly than Jenny had ever managed. She grew roses and played golf. Jenny mailed one of the eloquent ultimatums.

"I think we'd better end this, Jenny," Eric said gently on the phone. "I'm sorry, but this isn't what I'd thought it was. I don't want you to get any more hurt than it seems you already are."

Seems? More hurt? Not "what he thought it was?" What was that? She found a steeliness she didn't know she possessed. "I want to discuss this in person, Eric. I think you owe me that!" And he agreed, from guilt or compassion or fair play or who-knew-what. He flew to Rochester on a Friday morning, a return flight scheduled for that evening, six hours in which to end what had become the center of her life. She lured him— there really was no other word—into a farewell fuck, thinking desperately, stupidly, *Maybe if it's really good, better than Deirdre* . . . But Friday afternoon Mumbai and Karachi disappeared, and a few hours later Chicago took Deirdre (maybe) and little Mary along with three million other people, and now Rochester is gone and Eric can barely look at Jenny.

She gets into the minivan, but even with the passenger door open, the September sun starts to heat up the car. For something to do, she straightens the blankets on top of the mattress that fills the back of the van; she and Eric, not touching, slept here last night. She checks their boxes of food, bottles of water, two flashlights and small hoard of extra batteries. Jenny, no camper, didn't own the tent, Coleman lanterns, propane stoves she sees blossoming over the field like mushrooms. Communities are forming. Ricky and two other little boys have started a soccer game in the middle of the semicircle of cars. Somebody's dog, barking wildly, chases the boys. In front of the green SUV, three women gossip over coffee bubbling on a campfire. One of them is Ricky's slatternly mother, and the other two look enough like her to be her sisters or cousins. Out of desperation—she will go mad if she just sits here—Jenny fights off her innate shyness and walks over.

The oldest of the women, overweight and sweet-faced in a Red-wings T-shirt, says, "Hi, honey. Want some coffee?"

"Yes, please." The small kindness almost brings tears. "Thank you so much. I'm Jenny."

"Carleen, and this here's Sue and Cheri." Carleen hands Jenny coffee in a thick white mug. "I figure we're all in this together, so we better stick together, right?"

"Right," Jenny says unconvincingly. Cheri, Ricky's mother, is study-ing Jenny as if planning to dissect her. The coffee is hot and wonderful.

Sue is as talkative as Carleen. "Your husband at the big pow-wow?"

How to answer that? Cheri's gaze sharpens. Jenny finally says, "They investigated the . . . the wall this morning and found no breaks. Now they're trying to tunnel underneath."

"That's what my Ted said," Sue says. "But he told me he thinks an assault on the ETs' building is gonna have to happen sooner or later."

Jenny nods. "ET" conjures up for her the cuddly and benevolent creature from the old movie, not the beautiful alien megaterrorist who offered her breakfast and who may or may not even be bodily present. And "assault" is an alarming word all by itself. These look like gun people, which Jenny and Eric emphatically are not.

Carleen says, "If the assholes really do have food in there and— Ricky! Be careful!"

The soccer ball has nearly gone into the campfire. Cheri grabs for her son, who wriggles away with the agility of long practice. She bellows, "Ricky!" The child darts behind Carleen and grabs her ample waist.

"There now, he didn't mean nothing, Cheri—don't get your blood in a boil. Ricky, you be good now, you hear?"

Ricky nods and darts off. Desultory chatter reveals that Carleen is Cheri and Sue's mother, the grandmother of Ricky and the now-sleeping infant, Daniella. Carleen does not, to Jenny's eyes, look anywhere near old enough to be a grandmother. Sue is the mother of the other two little boys, non-identical twins. Neither Carleen nor Cheri mentions husbands, either present or vaporized in Rochester. Carleen is casually maternal to anyone who enters her radar, including Jenny. Cheri asks fake-nonchalant questions about Eric, which Jenny avoids answering. After a half hour of this, the coffee is gone, the fire is out, and Jenny is emotionally exhausted.

She excuses herself, crawls onto the mattress in the hot van, and falls fitfully asleep. When she wakes, sweaty and unrefreshed, Eric still hasn't returned. She stumbles out of the car into a mid-afternoon chaos of cooking, unleashed pets, gossiping, worrying, grieving. Radios yammer, although it's clear that groups have pooled electronic resources to save batteries. Women cry. Children either race frantically around or sit in frightened huddles against parents' knees. There are no aliens visible.

Carleen comes over, evidently a response to Jenny's dazed look. "You need the latrine, honey? Over there." She points. "And your husband said to tell you to go ahead and eat without him, he's gonna work on the tunnel and he'll get something later. You got to make sure he eats, Jenny. Some of these men are mad enough to just burn themselves out."

Jenny nods. She finds the latrine, efficiently and deeply dug behind the field's only line of scrub bushes, divided by a blanket on poles into separate pits for males and females. Many of these people, she realizes, are far better at basic survival than she. Not that that's hard. On the way back to the van, she notices a prayer service of some sort under a tarp strung between two cars, a card game around a collapsible table, and a woman reading a book to a toddler on her lap. All the adults wear the resolute, pinched look of people going through funeral rites and determined to do them correctly despite whatever they might be feeling. This should, Jenny thinks, be an inspiring model for her own behavior, but instead it makes her feel even more inadequate.

How long will Eric stay away from her?

The rest of the day, it turns out. Jenny calls her brother Bob on the cell and then sits in the van, waiting. The early September dusk falls and a few cars, chosen by lottery, train their headlights on the low, pale buildings across the meadow. This hardly seems necessary, since the buildings glow with their own subtle light. People put on sweaters and jackets and the smell of canned stew fills the air. Three aliens begin to circulate among the cars.

"Good evening. Dinner is ready now."

People turn their backs or glare menacingly. Sue spits, a glob of sputum that slides off the alien's protective shell. This one is a man, tall and brown-skinned, handsome as an African-American movie star. Sue's husband, Ted, snarls, "Get your ass out of here!"

"Are you sure? The chicken Marengo is excellent."

Cheri appears with a shotgun. The alien smiles at her. Carleen says sharply, "Don't you fire that thing with all these people around—what the hell's wrong with you? Jenny, honey, you want some coffee?"

Cheri returns the shotgun to the green SUV. Ricky sits beside Carleen's fire, eating Chef Boy-Ar-Dee ravioli from a plastic bowl, his baby sister asleep in an infant seat on the grass beside him. Cheri has changed from the pink pants and tee dotted with baby spit to tight jeans and a spangled red sweater cut very low. She has spectacular breasts. Jenny accepts the coffee but no ravioli; she's still not hungry and anyway she doesn't want to deplete their food supply.

"Honey, you got to eat," Carleen says. "Even a bitty thing like you gotta eat."

"I had something in the van," Jenny lies.

Cheri says, "Not into sharing?"

Jenny faces her. "Would you like some organic yogurt? I have some in the cooler."

Carleen laughs and says, "That's telling her!" Cheri smiles, too, but it's a nasty secret smile, as though Jenny has revealed dirty underwear. Cheri says, "No, thanks." Ricky demands more ravioli and Cheri gives it to him, then turns to her mother.

"Will you watch the kids a bit? I'm going to go find Ralph."

Carleen snaps, "You'd do better to stay away from that no-good."

Cheri doesn't answer, just strolls off into the darkness. Carleen says to Jenny, as if Jenny were her own age and not Cheri's, "Kids. Soon as they get tits you can't tell them nothing."

Jenny, whose own tits are negligible, has no idea what to say to this.

"That Ralph'll just break her heart, same as the daddies of these two." She picks up Daniella, who's starting to fuss in her infant seat.

The information that Cheri, too, is having her heart broken by someone should make Jenny feel more kinship with her. It doesn't. She crawls onto the mattress in the van, trying to read Dickens by flashlight while she waits for Eric to come back for dinner. She's fixed him a sandwich from the best of everything thrown hastily into her cooler. Two bottles of beer are as chilled as the melting ice will get them. Jenny knows it's a pathetic offering, but as the hours pass and he doesn't appear to witness her pathos, anger sets in. What right has he to treat her this way? None of this is her fault. Somewhere deep in her bruised and frightened mind she knows that Eric is staying away because he's afraid of what he'll say if he comes back to her, but she doesn't want to look at this. Looking at it would finish her off.

He doesn't come back all night.

In the very early morning, anger replaced by frenzied anxiety, Jenny looks for him. Eric is asleep near the half-dug tunnel, rolled up in somebody's extra sleeping bag. He lies on his back, his dark hair flopping to one side, and in sleep all the anger and guilt and fear have smoothed out. Through the grime on his face snake tear trails. Jenny's heart melts and she crouches beside him. "Eric . . ."

He wakes, stares at her, and tightens his mouth to a thin, straight line. That's all she sees; all she can bear. She gets up and walks away, making herself put one sneaker in front of the next, moving blindly through the damp weeds. It's over. He will never forgive her, never forgive himself, possibly never even approach the van again. The frenzy of tunnel digging, which will do no good, will eventually be replaced by frenzies of another sort, any other sort, anything to blot our everything he's lost. And she will not be able to change his mind. Eric is not strong enough to fight off his own passions, including the passion for self-destruction. If he were, he wouldn't have become involved with her—or with his other women—in the first place.

All this comes to Jenny in an instant, like a blow. It's all she can do to remain upright, walking. Her cell rings. It will be her brother but, even knowing how cruel she's being, she can't bring herself to answer. As the field comes alive around her, she sits alone in her van, wishing she had died in Rochester.

✱

Another two days and most of the food and water have run out. Except for a few dour loners, mostly armed, people have been remarkably generous with their supplies. There have been no fights, no looting, no theft. Jenny, who hasn't been able to eat, gave most of her food to Carleen, who made it last as long as possible among her small matriarchal band, which now apparently includes Jenny. Jenny doesn't care, not about anything.

Outside help, it's learned through numerous phone calls, was stopped by a second invisible wall about a mile from the camp. Not even a helicopter was able to rise high enough to surmount the barrier. Relatives, cops, and the Red Cross remain parked just outside in case something, unspecified, lets them drive closer. Most cell phones, including Jenny's, have exhausted their batteries, although a few people have the equipment to recharge phones from car cigarette lighters. Jenny doesn't find out if hers can be recharged. Bob knows that Jenny's still alive, and there is nothing else to report. The car radios now pick up only two small-town stations, but these report that cities have stopped disappearing. A schedule has been organized and a track cleared to drive cars around the field, so that the batteries will not run down and both radio and heat will still be available. It's a nice balance between using up gas and preserving batteries. Jenny does not participate.

Three times a day aliens circulate around the field, offering breakfast, lunch, dinner. No one accepts. The aliens are cursed, spat on, attacked, and once—although this is looked on with disfavor—publicly prayed over.

Tunnels of varying depths now ring the field beside the invisible wall. None of them go deeper than the barrier, but digging them has given many people something physical to drain off rage and grief.

Every once in a while Jenny glimpses Eric in the distance, working on yet another futile tunnel, or huddled in desperate conference with other men, or with Cheri. Each of these sightings turns her inside out like a sock, all her vulnerable organs battered by the smallest sound, breeze, photon of light.

"My Cheri never was no good around men," Carleen says, handing Jenny yet another cup of boiled coffee, not meeting her eyes. It's the first time Carleen has mentioned the situation. Jenny doesn't reply. Carleen's kindness is like air, ubiquitous and necessary and equally available to everyone, but even air hurts Jenny now.

"Honey," Carleen adds, "you gotta *eat*."

"Later," Jenny says, the syllable scraping her throat like gritty vomit.

Carleen goes away, but half an hour later Ricky appears beside the van, holding a book. He is incredibly dirty, smells bad, and clearly does not want to be there. "You spozed to read me this."

It's *Treasure Island* in the original, a book whose flowery language and slow pace Ricky will neither understand nor enjoy. Where on Earth did Carleen get it? She must have asked every last person in the camp, must have remembered that Jenny is—was—a librarian, must have cudgeled her slow wits to think of something that might make Jenny feel better. Jenny starts to cry. An old song title fills her head: "Roses From The Wrong Man." Carleen is not a man and this filthy child with his reluctant offering is about as far from roses as it's possible to get, but Jenny is in too much pain to appreciate the incongruity. She only knows that if it had been Eric who'd arranged this perverse kindness on her behalf, she could have borne anything. But it is not Eric.

Ricky looks at her tears with the same alarm as would any grown man. "Hey! You . . . you gonna read me that book?"

"No. You'd hate it. Go play."

Released, Ricky gives a whoop and races away, running backward, maybe to fulfill some small-boy notion of paying attention to the adult he's been told to pay attention to. No one else is in the center of the field; the cars are doing their daily promenade to charge up batteries. The red Taurus is not going very fast and the driver slams on her brakes, but not soon enough. Ricky is hit.

He starts shrieking to wake the dead. Carleen and Cheri both scream and dart from beside their SUV, Cheri with Daniella clamped to one naked breast. Sue's husband, Ted, leaps from his car and reaches Ricky just as Jenny does. Ted says, "Ricky! Buddy!"

The child is wailing and writhing on the flattened weeds. His left arm hangs at a strange angle. Ted gently holds down Ricky's shoulders. "Lie still, buddy, till we see what's broken." Cheri thrusts Daniella at Carleen, yells something anguished, and throws herself practically on top of Ricky. Ted shoves her off. "For Chrissake, let me see how bad he's hurt! Don't crush him, Cheri!"

"Ted's an EMT," Sue says at Jenny's elbow. "What happened?"

Jenny shakes her head. She can't speak. Cheri says shakily, "He was just racing around like always and—fuck it, why does everything always happen to me!"

Jenny just stares at her. The statement is so selfish, so inadequate, so stupid, that no response is possible. A thought forms in Jenny's mind: *If this is what Eric prefers to me, the hell with him.* The next second she's ashamed of this thought; it's as self-absorbed as Cheri's. She turns her attention to Ricky.

His arm is broken. There are no doctors or professional nurses among the refugees. Ted sets the arm, using as a splint a piece of wood torn from a chair leg. Ted is obviously no expert at this but he's resourceful, gentle, and willing to accept responsibility. Everything, Jenny thinks coldly, that Eric is not. Ricky screams like an animal in a steel-toothed trap. The driver of the red Taurus blubbers apologies; no one blames her. The accident is thoroughly discussed at every campfire, in every tent, on every mattress in the back of every van. Ricky is given a hoarded candy bar, a precious comic book, and a hefty slug of cough syrup mixed with whiskey to make him sleep.

Jenny can't sleep. Lying alone on her mattress, she tries to think coldly about her and Eric, about the destroyed cities, about what will happen now. She can't quite manage enough coldness, but it's better than the hell of the last four days. Somewhere in the deep dark there's a tap at the window.

Eric. . . . Hope burns so sudden, so hot, that Jenny feels scorched inside. She nearly cries out as she fumbles for the door, the flashlight.

Carleen stands there, her meaty arms limp by her side. In the upward-slanting glow from the flashlight, she says despairingly, "Ricky."

Jenny stumbles from the van, follows Carleen. Stars shine in a clear, cold sky. Jenny's lighted watch face says 4:18 a.m. The SUV tailgate gapes open and Jenny sees the usual mattress, a double in this monster vehicle, on which Ricky lies, glassy-eyed. Daniella whimpers softly in her infant seat. Cheri is not here. With Eric?

"He been like this for a coupla hours now," Carleen says in a low, steady voice. "He won't drink or eat or talk. And his arm's swelling up and turning all dark." She trains the flashlight on Ricky's arm.

Jenny bends over the child, who smells as if he's shit his pants. Gangrene—could it set in that fast? She doesn't know, but clearly something is radically wrong.

Carleen goes on in that strange, even voice. "I can't leave Daniella. And Ted don't know enough to deal with this."

"I don't know anything about medical matters, either—certainly not as much as Ted!"

Carleen continues as if Jenny hadn't spoken. "Anyway Sue's got some kind of diarrhea now and Ted can't leave his kids. Not for good. Can't take the risk. And I got Daniella. Can't count on Cheri."

Jenny straightens and turns. The two women stare at each other. For a long moment, it seems to Jenny, her universe hangs in the balance, all of it: Eric and vaporized Rochester, Deirdre and Jenny's job at the vanished public library, the running-down cell phones and Jenny's mother waiting for her in Dundee, the stars far overhead and the trodden-down weeds underfoot in this desperate refugee camp no one planned on.

Jenny nods.

Together they pick up Ricky and situate him in Jenny's arms. Ricky moans, but softly. He's heavy, reeking, only half conscious. There is nobody else up, or at least nobody that Jenny sees. In the dark she carries Ricky the entire length of the field, trying not to shift him even as he grows heavier and heavier, navigating by the pale glow from the alien buildings.

Up close, they present rough, cream-colored walls like stucco, but no stucco ever shone with its own light. The buildings all seem interconnected but Jenny sees only one entry, itself filled with light instead of any tangible door. She walks through the light and into a wide space—surely wider than the whole building appears from the outside?—that is absolutely empty.

"Hello," Jenny calls, inadequately, and suddenly she can hold Ricky no longer. She sinks with her burden to the stucco floor. This is as hopeless as everything else in her stupid life. She doesn't even like this kid.

"Hello," an alien says. It's the tall blonde woman in the standard brown robe; she materializes from empty air. "Is this little person hurt?"

Anger rises in Jenny at the cloying pseudo-friendliness of *"this little person"*—these beings have murdered nine-tenths of the Earth's population!—but for Ricky's sake she holds the anger in check. "Yes. He's hurt. His arm is broken and some kind of infection has set in."

"What's his name?" the alien asks. Her eyes are blue and warm as the Mediterranean.

"Ricky."

"And what's your name?"

What can that possibly matter? "Jenny."

"Jenny, close your eyes, please."

Should she do it? It makes no more sense than anything else, so why not. She has no idea what she's doing here. She closes her eyes.

"You may open them now."

Even before Jenny can do that, Ricky says, "What the fuck!"

He jumps up and gazes wildly around. His arm is whole, the clumsy splint and darkened swelling both gone. His clothes are clean. He shrieks in fear and jumps into Jenny's lap, hiding his face against her neck. His hair smells of sweet grass.

Jenny struggles to stand while holding Ricky, who mercifully is too scared to scream. She must stand; she can't face this terrible being from a sitting position on the ground. A table stands beside the alien, an ordinary picnic table with benches, the surface laden with scrambled eggs, toast, sweet rolls, orange juice, fragrant hot coffee. The plastic plates have a pattern of daisies. Jenny goes weak in the knees. She dumps Ricky onto a bench. He clutches her around the waist but then sees the sweet rolls and looks up at Jenny.

"Eat," she manages to get out. And to the alien, "Why?"

The smiling blue eyes widen slightly. "Didn't you want me to repair him?"

"I mean, why did you kill all those cities? *All those people?*"

The alien nods. "I see. Sit down, Jenny."

"No."

"All right. But the coffee is excellent today."

"Why did you do it?" Mumbai, Karachi, Delhi, Shanghai, Moscow . . . all in strict order of size. The meticulousness alone is monstrous.

The alien says, "Why did that man hurt Ricky when he tried to pull his arm bones back into the correct line?"

For a minute Jenny can't think what the creature means. Then she gets it. "Are you saying you committed massive genocide *for our own good?*"

"There were too many of you," the alien says. She sits gracefully on the picnic bench across from Ricky, who is gobbling eggs and sweet rolls with one hand, the other fastened firmly on Jenny's jacket. "In one more generation you would have had irreversible climate change, starvation, war, and suffering beyond belief. We spared you all that."

Jenny can barely speak. "You did . . . it was . . ."

"It was an act of kindness," the alien says, "and I know it seems hard now, but we've spared your species an incredible amount of suffering. In two more generations, your altered world will seem normal to its inhabitants. Two generations after that, you will thank us for our intervention. And you will have learned, and you will do much better this time. We've seen this before, you know."

Jenny doesn't know. She doesn't know anything. The worst is that, with her book-nourished imagination, she can actually see how that monstrous prophecy might come about. The gratitude of the masses in countries where most people never, ever had enough to eat until the cites disappeared. . . . Religion would help. Saviors from the stars, revered and deified and carrying out the will of God, of Allah, of Shiva in the endless dance of destruction in order for there to be room for creation.

The alien says, as if reading her thoughts, "You humans have a talent for self-destruction, you know. You cause a lot of your own suffering. It's unfortunate."

Jenny picks up a butter knife and hurls it at the woman's eyes.

It doesn't connect, of course. The knife bounces off the alien's face and the only response is from Ricky, scared all over again, and also full enough with good food to have the energy for response. He wails and wraps himself around the still standing Jenny.

The alien stands, too. "Don't think we're not sympathetic, Jenny. But we look at things differently than you do. Good-bye."

"Wait!" Jenny cries over Ricky's screams. "One more question! Why keep us here inside this invisible cage? What did you hope to learn?"

The alien answers without hesitation. "Whether you were different in small enough groups. And you are. A few hundred of you outside Rochester and Bogotá and Nantes and Chengdu—you're much better beings in smaller groups. It's chaotic out there just now, but you *will* cooperate better on survival, even if you're no happier. We're very glad to know this. It justifies our decision. Good-bye, Jenny."

The alien vanishes. Then the building vanishes. It's not yet dawn outside, but Jenny hears a siren in the distance, drawing closer. Somewhere in the field a car door slams. She sets Ricky down and tugs at him to walk toward Carleen's camp. The siren comes closer still; Eric and his work crew won't need those tunnels now. Jenny can go to Dundee as soon as Bob arrives for her. He may be on his way now.

Ricky tries to break free but Jenny holds him firmly. He isn't going to get hit by another car, not while he's with her. She has no idea what the future holds for Ricky, for any of them. But now—finally!—hatred of the self-righteous aliens, blithely playing Old Testament God, burns stronger in her than does despair over Eric. *"It justifies our decision"* . . . The hell it does! All those innocent lives, all the grief tearing apart the survivors . . .

Hatred is a great heartener. Hatred, and the knowledge that she is going to be needed (*"It's chaotic out there just now . . ."*), as Carleen and Ricky had needed her. These things, hatred and usefulness, aren't much (*"—even if you're no happier—"*) but they're something. And both are easier than love.

She brings the child back to his grandmother as the camp wakes and the cars drive in.

BY FOOLS LIKE ME

Hope creeps quietly into my bedroom without knocking, peering around the corner of the rough doorjamb. I'm awake; sleep eludes me so easily now. I know from the awful smell that she has been to the beach.

"Come in, child, I'm not asleep."

"Grandma, where's Mama and Papa?"

"Aren't they in the field?" The rains are late this year and water for the crops must be carried in ancient buckets from the spring in the dell.

"Maybe. I didn't see them. Grandma, I found something."

"What, child?"

She gazes at me and bites her lip. I see that this mysterious find bothers her. Such a sensitive child, though sturdy and healthy enough, God knows how.

"I went to the beach," she confesses in a rush. "Don't tell Mama! I wanted to dig you some trunter roots because you like them so much, but my shovel went clunk on something hard and I . . . I dug it up."

"Hope," I reprimand, because the beach is full of dangerous bits of metal and plastic, washed up through the miles of dead algae on the dead water. And if a soot cloud blows in from the west, it will hit the beach first.

"I'm sorry," she says, clearly lying, "but, Grandma, it was a metal box and the lock was all rusted and there was something inside and I brought it here."

"The box?"

"No, that was too heavy. The . . . just wait!"

No one can recognize most of the bits of rusted metal and twisted plastic from before the Crash. Anything found in a broken metal box should be decayed beyond recognition. I call "Hope! Don't touch anything slimy—" but she is already out of earshot, running from my tiny bedroom with its narrow cot, which is just blankets and pallet on a rope

96

frame to keep me off the hard floor. It doesn't; the old ropes sag too much, just as the thick clay walls don't keep out the heat. But that's my fault. I close the window shutters only when I absolutely have to. Insects and heat are preferable to dark. But I have a door, made of precious and rotting wood, which is more than Hope or her parents have on their sleeping alcoves off the house's only other room. I expect to die in this room.

Hope returns, carrying a bubble of sleek white plastic that fills her bare arms. The bubble has no seams. No mold sticks to it, no sand. Carefully she lays the thing on my cot.

Despite myself, I say, "Bring me the big knife and be very careful, it's sharp."

She gets the knife, carrying it as gingerly as an offering for the altar. The plastic slits more readily than I expected. I peel it back, and we both gasp.

I am the oldest person on Island by two decades, and I have seen much. Not of the world my father told me about, from before the Crash, but in our world now. I have buried two husbands and five children, survived three great sandstorms and two years where the rains didn't come at all, planted and first-nursed a sacred tree, served six times at the altar. I have seen much, but I have never seen so much preserved sin in one place.

"What . . . Grandma . . . what is that?"

"A book, child. They're all books."

"Books?" Her voice holds titillated horror. "You mean . . . like they made before the Crash? Like they cut down *trees* to make?"

"Yes."

"Trees? Real *trees*?"

"Yes." I lift the top one from the white plastic bubble. Firm thick red cover, like . . . dear God, it's made from the skin of some animal. My gorge rises. Hope musn't know that. The edges of the sin are gold. My father told me about books, but not that they could look like this. I open it.

"Oh!" Hope cries. "Oh, Grandma!"

The first slate—no, first *page*, the word floating up from some childhood conversation—is a picture of trees, but nothing like the pictures children draw on their slates. This picture shows dozens of richly colored trees, crowded together, each with *hundreds* of healthy, beautifully detailed green leaves. The trees shade a path bordered with glorious flowers. Along the path runs a child wearing far too many wraps, following a large white animal dressed in a wrap and hat and carrying a small metal machine. At the top of the picture, words float on golden clouds: ALICE IN WONDERLAND.

"Grandma! Look at the—Mama's coming!"

Before I can say anything, Hope grabs the book, shoves it into the white bubble, and thrusts the whole thing under my cot. I feel it slide under my bony ass, past the sag that is my body, and hit the wall. Hope is standing up by the time Gloria crowds into my tiny room.

"Hope, have you fed the chickens yet?"

"No, Mama, I—"

Gloria reaches out and slaps her daughter. "Can't I trust you to do anything?"

"Please, Gloria, it's my fault. I sent her to see if there's any more mint growing in the dell."

Gloria scowls. My daughter-in-law is perpetually angry, perpetually exhausted. Before my legs gave out and I could still do a full day's work, I used to fight back. The Island is no more arid, the see-oh-too no higher, for Gloria than for anyone else. She has borne no more stillborn children than have other women, has endured no fewer soot clouds. But now that she and my son must feed my nearly useless body, I try to not anger her too much, to not be a burden. I weave all day. I twist rope, when there are enough vines to spare for rope. I pretend to be healthier than I am.

Gloria says, "We don't need mint, we need fed chickens. Go, Hope." She turns.

"Gloria—"

"What?" Her tone is unbearable. I wonder, for the thousandth time, why Bill married her, and for the thousandth time I answer my own question.

"Nothing," I say. I don't tell her about the sin under the bed. I could have, and ended it right there. But I do not.

God forgive me.

✸

Gloria stands behind the altar, dressed in the tattered green robe we all wear during our year of service. I sit on a chair in front of the standing villagers; no one may miss services, no matter how old or sick or in need of help to hobble to the Grove. Bill half carried me here, afraid no doubt of being late and further angering his wife. It's hard to have so little respect for my son.

It is the brief time between the dying of the unholy wind that blows all day and the fall of night. Today the clouds are light gray, not too sooty, but not bearing rain, either.

The altar stands at the bottom of the dell, beside the spring that makes our village possible. A large flat slab of slate, it is supported by boulders painstakingly chiseled with the words of God. It took four generations to carve that tiny writing, and three generations of children have learned to read by copying the sacred texts onto their slates. I was among the first. The altar is shaded by the six trees of the Grove and from my uncomfortable seat, I can gaze up at their branches against the pale sky.

How beautiful they are! Ours are the tallest, straightest, healthiest trees of any village on Island. I planted and first-nursed one of them myself, the honor of my life. Even now I feel a thickness in my shriveled chest as I gaze up at the green leaves, each one wiped free of dust every day by those in service. Next year, Hope will be one of them. There is nothing on Earth lovelier than the shifting pattern of trees against the sky. Nothing.

Gloria raises her arms and intones, "'Then God said, "I give you every plant and every tree on the whole Earth. They will be food for you.""'

"Amen," call out two or three people.

"'Wail, oh pine tree,'" Gloria cries, "'for the cedar has fallen, the stately trees are ruined! Wail, oaks—'"

"Wail! Wail!"

I have never understood why people can't just worship in silence. This lot is sometimes as bad as a flock of starlings.

"—oaks of Bashan, the—"

Hope whispers, "Who's Bashan?"

Bill whispers back, "A person at the Crash."

"'—dense forest has been cut down! And they were told—told!— not to harm the grass of Earth or any plant or tree.'"

Revelation 9:4, I think automatically, although I never did find out what the words or numbers mean.

"'The vine is dried up!'" Gloria cries, "'the fig tree is withered! The pomegranate and the palm and the apple tree, all the trees of the field, are dried up! Surely the joy of mankind is withered away!'"

"Withered! Oh, amen, withered!"

Joel 1:12.

"'Offer sacrifices and burn incense on the high places, under any spreading tree!'"

Amy Martin, one of the wailers, comes forward with the first sacrifice, an unrecognizable piece of rusted metal dug up from the soil or washed up on the beach. She lays it on the altar. Beside me Hope leans forward, her mouth open and her eyes wide. I can read her young thoughts as easily as if they, too, are chiseled in stone: *That metal might have been part of a "car" that threw see-oh-two and soot into the air, might have been part of a "factory" that poisoned the air, might have even been part of a "saw" that cut down the forests!* Hope shudders, but I glance away from the intensity on her face. Sometimes she looks too much like Gloria.

Two more sacrifices are offered. Gloria takes an ember from the banked fire under the altar—the only fire allowed in the village—and touches it briefly to the sacrifices. "'Instead of the thornbush will grow the pine tree, and instead of briars the myrtle will grow. This will be for the Lord's glory, for an everlasting sign which—'"

I stop listening. Instead I watch the leaves move against the sky. What is "myrtle"—what did it look like, why was it such a desirable plant? The leaves blur. I have dozed off, but I realize this only when the whole Village shouts together, "We will never forget!" and services are over.

Bill carries me back through the quickening darkness without stars or moon. Without the longed-for rain. Without the candles I remember from my childhood on Island, or the dimly remembered (dreamed?) fireless lights from before that. There are no lights after dark on Island, nothing that might release soot into the air.

We will never forget.

It's just too bad that services are so boring.

✺

Alice in Wonderland.

> *Pride and Prejudice*
> *Birds of India and Asia*
> *Moby Dick*
> *Morning Light*
> *Jane Eyre*
> *The Sun Also Rises*

I sit on my cot, slowly sounding out the strange words. Of course the sun rises—what else could it do? It's rising now outside my window, which lets in pale light, insects, and the everlasting hot wind.

"Can I see, Grandma?" Hope, naked in the doorway. I didn't hear the door open. She could have been Gloria. And is it right for a child to see this much sin?

But already she's snuggled beside me, smelling of sweat and grime and young life. Even her slight body makes the room hotter. All at once a memory comes to me, a voice from early childhood: *Here, Anna, put ice on that bruise. Listen, that's a—*

What bruise? What was I to listen to? The memory is gone.

"M—m—m—oh—bee—-Grandma, what's a 'moby'?"

"I don't know, child."

She picks up a different one. "J—j—aye—n . . . Jane! That's Miss Anderson's name! Is this book about her?"

"No. Another Jane, I think." I open *Moby Dick.* Tiny, dense writing, pages and pages of it, whole burned forests of it.

"Read the sin with the picture of trees!" She roots among the books until she finds *Alice in Wonderland* and opens it to that impossible vision of tens, maybe hundreds, of glorious trees. Hope studies the child blessed enough to walk that flower-bordered path.

"What's her name, Grandma?"

"Alice." I don't really know.

"Why is she wearing so many wraps? Isn't she *hot?* And how many days did her poor mother have to work to weave so many? "

I recognize Gloria's scolding tone. The pages of the book are crisp, bright and clear, as if the white plastic bubble had some magic to keep sin fresh. Turning the page, I begin to read aloud. "'Alice was beginning to get very tired of sitting by her sister on the bank—'"

"She has a *sister*," Hope breathes. Nearly no one does now; so few children are carried to term and born whole.

"'—and tired of having nothing to do: once—'"

"How could she have nothing to do? Why doesn't she carry water or weed crops or hunt trunter roots or—"

"Hope, are you going to let me read this to you or not?"

"Yes, Grandma. I'm sorry."

I shouldn't be reading to her at all. *Trees* were cut down to make this book; my father told me so. As a young man, not long after the Crash, he himself was in service as a book sacrificer, proudly. Unlike many of his generation, my father was a moral man.

"'—or twice she had peeped into the book her sister was reading, but it had no pictures or conversation in it, "and what is the use of a book," thought Alice, "without pictures or conversation?" So she was considering—'"

We read while the sun clears the horizon, a burning merciless ball, and our sweat drips onto the gold-edged page. Then Gloria and Bill stir in the next room and Hope is on the floor in a flash, shoving the books under my sagging cot, running out the door to feed the chickens and hunt for their rare, precious eggs.

The rains are very late this year. Every day Gloria, scowling, scans the sky. Every day at sunset she and Bill drag themselves home, bone-weary and smeared with dust, after carrying water from the spring to the crops. The spring is in the dell, and water will not flow uphill. Gloria is also in service this year and must nurse one of the trees, wiping the poisonous dust from her share of the leaves, checking for dangerous insects. More work, more time. Some places on Earth, I was told once, have too much water, too many plants from the see-oh-too. I can't imagine it. Island has heard from no other place since I was a young woman and the last radio failed. Now a radio would be sin.

I sit at the loom, weaving. I'm even clumsier than usual, my fingers stiff and eyes stinging. From too much secret reading, or from a high see-oh-too day? Oh, let it be from the reading!

"Grandma," Hope says, coming in from tending the chickens. "My throat hurts." Her voice is small; she knows.

Dear God, not *now*, not when the rains are already so late . . . But I look out the window and yes, I can see it on the western horizon, thick and brown.

"Bring in the chickens, Hope. Quick!"

She runs back outside while I hobble to the heavy shutters and wrestle them closed. Hope brings in the first protesting chicken, dumps it in her sleeping alcove, and fastens the rope fence. She races back for the next chicken as Bill and Gloria run over the fields toward the house.

Not *now*, when everything is so dry . . .

They get the chickens in, the food covered, as much water inside as can be carried. At the last moment Bill swings closed the final shutter, and we're plunged into darkness and even greater heat. We huddle against the west wall. The dust storm hits.

Despite the shutters, the holy protection of wood, dust drifts through cracks, under the door, maybe even through chinks in the walls. The dust clogs our throats, noses, eyes. The wind rages: *oooeeeeeeeeoooooeeeee.* Shrinking beside me, Hope gasps, "It's trying to get in!"

Gloria snaps, "Don't talk!" and slaps Hope. Gloria is right, of course; the soot carries poisons that Island can't name and doesn't remember. Only I remember my father saying, "Methane and bio-weapons . . ."

Here, Anna, put ice on that bruise. Listen, that's a—

A what? What was that memory?

Then Gloria, despite her slap, begins to talk. She has no choice; it's her service year and she must pray aloud. "'Wail, oh pine tree, for the cedar has fallen, the stately trees are ruined! Wail, oaks of Bashan, the dense forest has been cut down!'"

I want Gloria to recite a different scripture. I want, God forgive me, Gloria to shut up. Her anger burns worse than the dust, worse than the heat.

"'The vine is dried up and the fig is withered; the pomegranate—'"

I stop listening.

Listen, that's a—

Hope trembles beside me, a sweaty mass of fear.

The dust storm proves mercifully brief, but the see-oh-too cloud pulled behind it lasts for days. Everyone's breathing grows harsh. Gloria and

Bill, carrying water, get fierce headaches. Gloria makes Hope stay inside, telling her to sit still. I see in Gloria's eyes the concern for her only living child, a concern that Hope is too young to see. Hope sees only her mother's anger.

Left alone, Hope and I sin.

All the long day, while her parents work frantically to keep us alive, we sit by the light of a cracked shutter and follow Alice down the rabbit hole, through the pool of tears, inside the White Rabbit's house, to the Duchess's peppery kitchen. Hope stops asking questions, since I know none of the answers. What is pepper, a crocodile, a caucus race, marmalade? We just read steadily on, wishing there were more pictures, until the book is done and Alice has woken. We begin *Jane Eyre*: "'There was no possibility of taking a walk that day . . .'"

Birds of India and Asia has gorgeous pictures, but the writing is so small and difficult that I can't read most of it. Nonetheless, this is the book I turn to when Hope is asleep. So many birds! And so many colors on wings and backs and breasts and rising from the tops of heads like fantastic feathered trees. I wish I knew if these birds were ever real, or if they are as imaginary as Alice, as the white Rabbit, as marmalade. I wish—

"Grandma!" Hope cries, suddenly awake. "It's raining outside!"

Joy, laughter, dancing. The whole village gathers at the altar under the trees. Bill carries me there, half running, and I smell his strong male sweat mingled with the sweet rain. Hope dances in her drenched wrap like some wild thing and chases after the other children.

Then Gloria strides into the Grove, grabs Hope, and throws her onto the altar. "You've sinned! My own daughter!"

Immediately everyone falls silent. The village, shocked, looks from Gloria to Hope, back to Gloria. Gloria's face is twisted with fury. From a fold of her wrap she pulls out *Alice in Wonderland*.

"This was in the chicken coop! This! A sin, trees *destroyed* . . . you had this in our very house!" Gloria's voice rises to a shriek.

Hope shrinks against the wide flat stone and she puts her hands over her face. Rain streams down on her, flattening her hair against her small skull. The book in Gloria's hand sheds droplets off its skin cover. Gloria tears out pages and throws them to the ground, where they go sodden and pulpy as maggots.

"Because of you, God might not have sent any rains at all this year! We're just lucky that in His infinite mercy—you risked—you—"

Gloria drops the mutilated book, pulls back her arm, and with all her force strikes Hope on the shoulder. Hope screams and draws into a ball, covering her head and neck. Gloria lashes out again, a sickening thud of hand on tender flesh. I cry, "Stop! No, Gloria, stop—Bill—let me go!"

He doesn't. No one else moves to help Hope, either. I can feel Bill's anguish, but he chokes out, "It's right, Mama." And then, invoking the most sacred scripture of all, he whispers, "We will never forget."

I cry out again, but nothing can keep Hope from justice, not even when I scream that it is my fault, my book, my sin. They know I couldn't have found this pre-Crash sin alone. They know that, but no one except me knows when Gloria passes beyond beating Hope for justice, for Godly retribution, into beating her from Gloria's own fury, her withered fig tree, her sin. No one sees but me. And I, an old woman, can do nothing.

Hope lies on her cot, moaning. I crouch beside her in her alcove, its small window unshuttered to the rain. Bill bound her broken arm with the unfinished cloth off my loom, then went into the storm in search of his wife.

"Hope . . . dear heart . . ."

She moans again.

If I could, I would kill Gloria with my own hands.

A sudden lone crack of lightning brightens the alcove. Already the skin on Hope's wet arms and swollen face has started to darken. One eye swells.

Here, Anna, put ice on that bruise. Listen, that's a——

"Grandma . . ."

"Don't talk, Hope."

"Water," Hope gasps and I hold the glass for her. Another flash of lightning and for a moment Gloria stands framed in the window. We stare at each other. With a kind of horror I feel my lips slide back, baring my teeth. Gloria sees, and cold slides down my spine.

Then the lightning is gone, and I lay my hand on Hope's battered body.

The rain lasts no more than a few hours. It's replaced by day after day of black clouds that thunder and roil but shed no water. Day after day. Gloria and Bill let half the field die in their attempt to save the other half. The rest of the village does much the same.

Hope heals quickly; the young are resilient. I sit beside her, weaving, until she can work again. Her bruises turn all the colors of the angry earth: black and dun and dead-algae green. Gloria never looks at or speaks to her daughter. My son smiles weakly at us all, and brings Hope her meal, and follows Gloria out the door to the fields.

"Grandma, we sinned."

Did we? I don't know anymore. To cut down *trees* in order to make a book . . . my gorge rises at just the thought. Yes, that's wrong, as wrong as anything could ever be. Trees are the life of the Earth, are God's gift to us. Even my father's generation, still so selfish and sinful, said so. Trees absorb the see-oh-too, clean the air, hold the soil, cool the world. Yes.

But, against that, the look of rapture on Hope's face as Alice chased the White Rabbit, the pictures of *Birds of India and Asia,* Jane Eyre battling Mrs. Reed . . . Hope and I destroyed nothing ourselves. Is it so wrong, then, to enjoy another's sin?

"We sinned," Hope repeats, mourning, and it is her tone that hardens my heart. "No, child. We didn't."

"We didn't?" Her eyes, one still swollen, grow wide.

"We didn't make the books. They already *were.* We just read them. Reading isn't sinful."

"Nooooo," she says reluctantly. "Not reading the altar scriptures. But Alice is—"

Gloria enters the house. She says to me, "Services tonight."

I say, "I'm not going."

Gloria stops dead halfway to the wash bucket, her field hat suspended in her hand. For the briefest moment I see something like panic on her face, before it vanishes into her usual anger. "Not going? To services?"

"No."

Hope, frightened, looks from her mother to me. Bill comes in.

Gloria snaps, with distinct emphasis, "*Your* mother says she's not going to services tonight."

Bill says, "Mama?"

"No," I say, and watch his face go from puzzlement to the dread of a weak man who will do anything to avoid argument. I hobble to my alcove and close the door. Later, from my window, I watch them leave for the Grove, Hope holding her father's hand.

Gloria must have given him silent permission to do that.

My son.

Painfully I lower myself to the floor, reach under my cot, and pull out the white plastic bubble. For a while I gaze at the pictures of the gorgeous birds of India and Asia. Then I read *Jane Eyre*. When my family returns at dusk, I keep reading as long as the light holds, not bothering to hide any of the books, knowing that no one will come in.

One heavy afternoon, when the clouds steadily darken and I can no longer see enough to make out words, a huge bolt of lightning shrieks through the sky—*crack!* For a long moment my head vibrates. Then silence, followed by a shout: "Fire!"

I haul myself to my knees and grasp the bottom of the window. The lightning hit one of the trees in the Grove. As I watch, numb, the fire leaps on the ceaseless wind to a second tree.

People scream and run, throwing buckets of muddy water from the spring. I can see that it will do no good—too much dry timber, too much wind. A third tree catches, a fourth, and then the grass too is on fire. Smoke and ash rise into the sky.

I sink back onto my cot. I planted one of those trees, nursed it as I'd once nursed Bill. But there is nothing I can do. Nothing.

By the light of the terrible flames I pick up *Jane Eyre* and, desperately, I read.

And then Hope bursts in, smeared with ash, sweat and tears on her face.

"Hope—no! Don't!"

"Give it to me!"

"No!"

We struggle, but she is stronger. Hope yanks *Jane Eyre* out of my hands and hurls it to the floor. She drops on top of it and crawls under my cot. Frantically I try to press down the sagging ropes so that she can't get past them, but I don't weigh enough. Hope backs out with the other books in their plastic bubble. She scrambles to her feet.

"We did this! You and me! Our sin made God burn the trees!"

"No! Hope—"

"Yes! We did this, just like the people before the Crash!"

We will never forget.

I reach for her, for the books, for everything I've lost or am about to lose. But Hope is already gone. From my window I see her silhouetted against the flames, running toward the grass. The village beats the grass with water-soaked cloths. I let go of the sill and fall back onto the cot before I can see Hope throw the books onto the fire.

Gloria beats Hope again, harder and longer this time. She and Bill might have put me out of the house, except that I have no place to go. So they settle for keeping me away from Hope, so that I cannot lead her further into sin.

Bill speaks to me only once about what happened. Bringing me my meal—meager, so meager—he averts his eyes from my face and says haltingly, "Mama . . . I . . ."

"Don't," I say.

"I have to . . . you . . . Gloria . . ." All at once he finds words. "A little bit of sin is just as bad a big sin. That's what *you* taught me. What all those people thought before the Crash—that their cars and machines and books each only destroyed a little air so it didn't matter. And look what happened! The Crash was—"

"Do you really think you're telling me something I don't know? Telling *me*?"

Bill turns away. But as he closes the door behind him, he mumbles over his shoulder, "A little bit of sin is as bad as a big sin."

I sit in my room, alone.

Bill is not right. Nor is Gloria, who told him what to say. Nor is

Hope, who is after all a child, with a child's uncompromising, black-and-white faith. They are all wrong, but I can't find the arguments to tell them so. I'm too ignorant. The arguments must exist, they *must*—but I can't find them. And my family wouldn't listen anyway.

Listen, Anna, that's a—

A nightingale.

The whole memory flashes like lightning in my head: my father, bending over me in a walled garden, laughing, trying to distract me from some childish fall. *Here, Anna, put ice on that bruise. Listen, that's a nightingale!* A cube of frozen water pulled with strong fingers from his amber drink. Flowers everywhere, flowers of scarcely believable colors, crimson and gold and blue and emerald. And a burst of glorious unseen music, high and sweet. A bird, maybe one from *Birds of India and Asia.*

But I don't know, can't remember, what a nightingale looks like. And now I never will.

FIRST RITES

One: Haihong

She sat rigid on the narrow seat of the plane, as if her slightest movement might bring the Boeing 777 down over the Pacific. No one noticed. Pregnant women often sat still, and this one was very pregnant. Only the flight attendant, motherly and inquisitive, bent over the motionless figure.

"Can I bring you anything, ma'am?"

The girl's head jerked up as if shot. "No . . . no." And then, in nearly unaccented English, "Wait. Yes. A Scotch and soda."

The flight attendant's mouth narrowed, but she brought the drink. These girls today—you'd think this one would know better. Although maybe she came from some backward area of China without prenatal care. In her plain brown maternity smock and sandals, it was hard to tell. The girl wasn't pretty and wore no wedding ring. Well, maybe that was why the poor thing was so nervous. An uneducated provincial going home to face the music. Still, she shouldn't drink. In fact, at this late stage, she shouldn't even be flying. What if she went into labor on the plane?

Deng Haihong, one chapter short of her Ph.D. thesis at U.C. San Diego, gulped the Scotch and closed her eyes, waiting for its warmth to reach her brain. Another three hours to Shanghai, two-and-a-half to Chengdu, and perhaps two hours on the bus to Auntie's. If no one questioned her at the airports. If she wasn't yet on any official radar. If she could find Auntie.

If . . .

Eyes still closed, Haihong laid both hands on her bulging belly, and shuddered.

✺

Shuangliu Airport in Chengdu had changed in four years. When Haihong had left, it had been the glossy, bustling gateway to the prosperous southwest and then on to Tibet, and Chengdu had been China's fifth largest city. Now, since half of Sichuan province had been under quarantine, only seven people deplaned from an aircraft so old that it had no live TV-feed. Five of the seven already wore pathogen masks. Haihong pulled on hers, not because she thought any deadly pathogens from the war still lingered here—she knew better—but because it made her more inconspicuous. Her stomach roiled as she approached Immigration.

Let it be just one more bored official . . .

It was not. "Passport and Declaration Card?"

Haihong handed them over, inserted her finger into the reader, and tried to smile. The woman took forever to scrutinize her papers and biological results. The screen at her elbow scrolled but Haihong couldn't see what it said . . . For a long terrible moment she thought she might faint.

Then the woman smiled. "Welcome home. You have come home to have your child here, in the province of your ancestors?"

"Yes," Haihong managed.

"Congratulations."

"Thank you." Emily's curious American phrase jumped into her mind: *I would give my soul for a drink right now.*

Too bad Haihong had already sold her soul.

Chengdu had finished the Metro just before the quarantine, and it was still operating. Everyone wore the useless paper pathogen masks. In California, Emily had laughed at the idea that the flimsy things would protect against any pathogens that had mutated around their terminator genes, and she and Haihong had had their one and only fight. "The people are just trying to survive!" Haihong had yelled, and Emily had gone all round-eyed and as red as only those blonde Americans could, and said apologetically, "I suppose that whatever makes them feel better . . ." Haihong had stormed out of the crummy apartment she shared with Emily and Tess only because it saved money.

It had been Emily who told her about the clinic in the first place.

As Haihong pulled her rolling suitcase toward Customs, her belly lurched hard. She stopped, terror washing through her: *Not here, not here!*

But after that one hard kick, the baby calmed down. Haihong made it though Customs, the pills intact in the lining of her dress. She made it onto the Metro, off at the bus station.

The terror abated. Not departed—it would never do that, she realized bleakly. But at least the chance of detection was over. In the bus station, crowded as Shuangliu had not been, she was just one more Chinese girl in inexpensive cotton clothing that had probably been made in Guangdong province before being exported to the U.S. Only the poorest Chinese remained in Sichuan; everyone who could afford to had gone through bio-decon and fled. Chengdu had been the place that North Korea chose to bio-attack to bring the huge Chinese dragon to its knees. Sichuan had been the sacrifice, and rather than have the attack continued on Guangdong's export factories or Bejing's government or Shanghai's soaring foreign tourism, China had not retaliated toward its ancient enemy, at least not with weapons. Politics had been more effective, aided by the world's outrage. Now North Korea was castrated, full of U.N. peace-keeping forces and bio-inspectors and very angry Chinese administrators. Both of Haihong's parents had died in the brief war.

"Be careful, Little Sister." An ancient man, gnarled as an old tree, took Haihong's elbow to help her onto the bus. The small kindness nearly made her cry. Pregnant women cried so easily. The trip had been so long, so draining . . . she wanted a drink.

"*Shie-shie*," she said, and watched his face to see if he frowned at her accent. She had spoken only English for so long. But his expression didn't change.

The bus, nearly as ancient as the kind grandfather, smelled of unwashed bodies and urine. Haihong fell asleep, mercifully without dreams. When she woke, it was night in the mountains and the baby was kicking hard. Her stomach growled with hunger. A different passenger sat beside her, a boy of maybe six or seven, with his mother snoring across the aisle. He ducked his head and said shyly, "Do you wish for a boy or a girl?"

The baby was a boy. Ben, shaken, had analyzed with Haihong the entire genome from amnio tissue. Haihong knew the baby's eye and hair color, prospective height, blood type, probable IQ, degree of far future baldness. She knew the father was Mexican. She knew the fetus's poly-morphic alleles.

She smiled at the boy and said softly, "Whatever Heaven sends."

Haihong's screams shattered the night. The midwife, back in prominence after the doctor left and the village clinic closed, murmured gently from her position beside the squatting Haihong. The smell of burning incense didn't mask the earthy odor of her spilt waters. Auntie held a kerosene lamp above the midwife's waiting hands. Auntie's face had not unclenched, not once, since Haihong had finally found her living in a hut at the edge of a vast vineyard in which she, like everyone else, toiled endlessly. The workers' huts had running water but no electricity. Outside, more women had gathered to wait.

Haihong cried, "I will die!"

"You will not die," the midwife soothed. Through the haze of pain, Haihong realized that the woman thought she feared death. If only it were that simple . . . But Haihong had done all she could. Had explained to Auntie, who was not her aunt but her old amah and therefore much harder to trace directly to Haihong, about the pills. She had explained, but would the old woman understand? O, to have come this far and not succeed, not save her son . . .

Her body split in two, and the child was born. His wail filled the hut. Haihong, battered from within, gasped, "Give . . . me!"

They laid the bloody infant in her arms. Auntie remembered what had been rehearsed, drilled into her, for the past nine days. Her obedience had made her an ideal amah when Haihong had been young. Her obe-dience, and her instinctive love. Her eyes never left the crying baby, but wordlessly she held out to Haihong the prepared dish holding pulverized green powder.

With the last of her strength, Haihong transferred three grains of powder to her fingertip and touched the baby's tongue. The grains dis-solved. The baby went on wailing and all at once Haihong was sick of him, sick of the chance she had taken and the sacrifice she had made, sick of it all, necessary as it had been. She said, "Take him," and Auntie greedily grabbed the baby from her arms. Haihong tried to shut her ears against his crying. She wanted nothing now but sleep. Sleep, and the drink that, surrounded as they were by vineyards, would be possible soon, today, tomorrow, all the days left in her utterly ruined life.

Two: Cixin

Deng Cixin was in love with the mountains. Unlike anything else, they made him feel calm inside, like still water.

"Sit still, *bow bei'r*," Auntie said many times each day. "Be calm!" But Cixin could not sit still. He raced out the door, scattering the chickens, through the neat rows of grapes tied to their stakes, into the village. He scooped up handfuls of pebbles and hurled them at the other children, provoking cries of, "*Fen noon an hi!*" Angry boy. He was always angry, never knowing at what, always running, always wanting to be someplace else. Except when he was in the mountains.

His mother took him there once every week. She put him into his seat on her bicycle, sometimes pedaling hard with sweat coming out in interesting little globes on the back of her neck, and sometimes walking the bicycle. They covered several miles. After he turned four, Cixin walked part of the way. He liked to run in circles around his mother until he got too tired and she scooped him back onto the bicycle seat. The ride back down was thrilling, too: a headlong dash like the wind. Cixin urged her on: *Faster! Faster!* If he could just go fast enough, they might leave the ground forever and he would never have to go back to the village.

The best part, however, was in the mountains. Mama brought a *picnic*—that was a word from the secret language, the one he and his mother always used when not even Auntie was around. Nobody else knew about the secret language. It was for the two of them alone. The picnic had all the things Cixin liked best: congee with chicken and sweetened bean curd and orange juice. Although the orange juice was only for him; Mama had wine or beer.

As they ascended higher and higher, Cixin would feel his shoulders and knees and stomach loosen. He didn't run around up here; he didn't *have* to run around. The air grew sharp and clean. The mountains stood, firm and tall and strong—and how long they stood there! Millions of years, Mama said. Cixin liked thinking about that. You couldn't be angry at something so strong and old. You could rest in it.

"Tell me again," Cixin would say, sitting on the edge of Mama's blanket. "Where do the mountains go?"

"All the way to Tibet, *bow bei'r.*"

"And Tibet is the highest place in the world."

"The very highest."

After a while Mama would fall asleep, thin and pale on her blanket, her short dark hair flopping sideways. Even then Cixin didn't feel the need to run around. He sat and looked at the mountains, and his mind seemed to drift among the clouds, until sometimes he couldn't tell which was clouds and which was himself. Sometimes a small animal or bird would sit on the ground only meters away, and Cixin would let it rest, too.

When Mama awoke, it was time for the *once-a-week.* That was a word from the secret language, too.

The once-a-week was tiny little green specks that Mama counted carefully. They melted on Cixin's tongue and tasted faintly sour. Mama always said the same words, every time, and he had to answer the same words, every time.

"You must swallow the once-a-week, Cixin."

"I must swallow the once-a-week."

"*Every* week."

"Every week."

"If you do not swallow it, you will die."

"I will die." Dead birds, dead rats, a mangy dog dead in the road. Cixin could picture himself like that. The picture terrified him.

"And you must not tell anyone except Auntie about the once-a-week. Ever."

"I must not tell anyone except Auntie about the once-a-week ever."

"Promise me, *bow bei'r.*"

"I promise." And then, for the first time, "Where does the once-a-week come from?"

"Ah." Mama looked sad. "From very far away."

"From Tibet?"

"No. Not Tibet."

"Where?" He had a sudden idea, fueled by the stories Auntie told him of dragons and ghost warriors. "From a land of magic?"

"There is no magic." Mama's voice sounded even sadder. "Only science."

"Is science a kind of magic?"

She laughed, but it was not a happy sound. "Yes, I suppose it is. Black magic, sometimes. Now fold the blanket; we must go back."

Cixin forgot about science and magic and the once-a-week at the exciting thought of the wild bicycle dash down the mountain.

Twice a year Mama took the bus to Chengdu, another far away land of black magic. For days before she left, Auntie spent extra time kneeling at the household shrine. Cixin, five, eight, nine years old, raced around even more than usual. Mama snapped at him.

"Sit still!"

"Ah, he's wild today, that one," Auntie said, but unlike Mama, she was smiling. Auntie was very old. She didn't work in the vineyards any more, but Mama did. Some nights Mama didn't come home. Some nights she came home very late, falling down and either giggling or crying. Then she and Auntie argued when they thought Cixin could not hear.

"I said sit still!" Mama slapped him.

Cixin raced out the door, tried to kick the neighbor's dog, did not connect. He kept running in circles until he was exhausted and his heart was too tired to hurt so much and he saw Xiao sitting by the irrigation ditch with her ancient iPod. Cixin, panting, dropped down beside her.

"Let me see, Xiao."

She handed over the iPod. A year younger than Cixin and the daughter of the vineyard foreman, Xiao had possessions that the other village children could only dream of. Sweet-natured and docile, she always shared.

Cixin put the iPod to his ear but was too restless to listen to the music. But instead of hurling it into the ditch, as he might have done with anybody else, he handed it carefully back to Xiao. With her, he always tried to be careful.

"My mother is going to a magic land. To Chengdu."

Xiao laughed. She was the only person that Cixin allowed to laugh at him. Her laugh reminded him of flowers. She said, "Chengdu isn't a magic land. It's a city. I went there."

"You *went* there? When?"

"Last year. My father took me on the bus. Look, there's your mother waiting for the bus. She—" Xiao dropped her eyes.

Cixin spat. "She's drunk."

"I know." Xiao was always truthful.

"I don't care!" Cixin shouted. He wanted to leap up and race around again, he wanted to sit beside Xiao and ask about Chengdu, he didn't know what he wanted. The bus stopped and Mama lurched on. "I hope she never comes back!"

"You don't mean that," Xiao said. She took his hand. Cixin jerked his whole body to face her.

"Kiss me!"

"No!" Shocked, she dropped his hand and got to her feet.

He jumped up. "Don't go, Xiao! You don't have to kiss me!" Just saying the words desolated him. "You don't ever have to kiss me. Nobody ever has to kiss me."

She studied him from her beautiful dark eyes. "You're very strange, Cixin."

"I am not." But he knew he was.

A band of boys emerged from between the rows of grapes. When they saw Cixin, they began to yell. "*Fen noon an hi! Ben dan!*"

Cixin knew he was an angry boy but not a stupid one. He grabbed a rock from the irrigation ditch and hurled it at the boys. It fell short but they swarmed around him, careful not to touch Xiao.

Cixin broke free and raced off. They shouted after him: "Half breed! Son of a whore!" He was faster than all of them, even among the trees that began on the other side of the village, even when the ground began to slope upward toward the mountains. He and his mother never went there anymore. So now Cixin would go by himself. He would run higher and higher, all the way to Tibet, and maybe he would go live with the monks and maybe he would die on the way and it didn't matter which. No one would care. His mother was a drunk and a whore, his Auntie was old and would die soon anyway, Xiao was so rich and she had an iPod and she would never ever kiss him.

He leaned against a tree until his breath was strong again. Then he again started up the mountain, walking to Tibet.

Three: Ben

Ben Malloy brought his coffee to the farthest booth of the San Diego cybershop and closed the door. The booth smelled of urine and semen. Public booths, used only by the desperately poor or desperately criminal or deeply paranoid, were always unsavory. He shouldn't have brought coffee but he'd been up all night, working when the lab was quiet and deserted, and he needed the caffeine.

He accessed the untraceable account, encrypted through remixers in Finland and God-knew-where-else, and her email was there.

> B—
> *Your package arrived. Thank you. Still no breakthrough. Symptoms unchanged. I suspect elevated CRF and cortisol, serotonin fluctuations, maybe neuron damage. Akathesia, short REM latency. Sichuan quarantine may lift soon—rumors.*
> H
> *I cannot do this anymore. I just cannot.*

Akathesia. Short REM latency. Ben had taught her those terms, so far from her own field. Haihong had always been a quick study.

He closed his eyes and let the guilt wash over him. She'd made the choices—both of them—so why was the guilt his? All he'd done was break several laws and risk his professional future to try to save her.

The guilt was because he'd failed.

Also because he'd misunderstood so much. He had thought of Haihong as an American. Taking her California Ph.D. in English literature, going out for hamburgers at Burger King and dancing to pellet rock and loving strappy high-heeled shoes. A girl with more brains than sense, to whom he'd attributed American attitudes and expediencies. And he'd been wrong. Underneath the California-casual-cum-grad-student-intensity-cum-sexually-liberated woman, Haihong had been foreign to him in ways he had not understood. Ben Jinkang Molloy's grandmother and father had both married Americans; his father and Ben himself had been born here. He didn't even speak Chinese.

His father had called him, all those years ago, from Florida. "Ben, your second cousin is coming from China to study in San Diego."

"My second cousin? What second cousin?"

"Her name is Deng Haihong. She's my cousin Deng Song's daughter, from near Chengdu. You need to look out for her."

Ben, busy with his first post-doc, had been faintly irritated with this intrusion into his life. "Does she even speak English?"

"Well, I should hope so. She's studying for a doctorate in English literature. Listen, buddy, she's an orphan. Both parents were casualties of that stupid savagery in Sichuan. She has nobody."

His father knew how to push Ben's buttons. Solitary by nature, Ben was nonetheless a sucker for stray kittens, homeless beggars, lost causes. He could picture his father, tanned and relaxed in the retirement condo in West Palm Beach, counting on this trait in Ben.

He said resignedly, "When does she arrive?"

"Tuesday. You'll meet her plane, won't you?"

"Yes," Ben had said, not realizing that the single syllable would commit him to four years of mentorship, of playing big brother, of pleasure and exasperation, all culminating in the disastrous conversation that had been the beginning of the end.

He and Haihong had sat across from each other in a dark booth at a favorite campus bar, Fillion's.

"I'm pregnant," Haihong said abruptly. "No beer for me tonight."

He had stiffened. Oh God, that arrogant bastard Scott, he'd warned her the guy was no good, *why* did women always go for the bad-boy jerks . . .

Haihong laughed. "No, it's not Scott's. You're always so suspicious, Ben."

"Then who—"

"It's nobody's. I'm a surrogate."

He peered at her, struggling to take it in, and saw the bravado behind her smile. She was defiant, and scared, and determined, all at once. Haihong's determination could crack granite. It had to be, for her to have come this far from where she'd been born. He said stupidly, "A surrogate?"

Again that brittle laugh. "You sound as if you never heard the word before. What kind of geneticist are you?"

"Haihong, if you needed money . . ."

"It's not that. I just want to help some infertile couple."

She was lying, and not well. Haihong, he'd learned, lied often, usually to cover up what she perceived as her own inadequacies. And she was fiercely proud. Look at the way she always leapt to the defense of her two friends and roommates, slutty Tess and brainless Emily. If Ben castigated Haihong now, if he was anything other than supportive, she would never trust him again.

But something here didn't smell right.

He said carefully, "I know another woman who acted as a surrogate, and it took a year for her to complete the medical surveillance and background checks. Have you been planning this for a whole year?"

"No, this is different. The clinic is in Mexico. American restrictions don't apply."

Alarms sounded in Ben's head. Haihong, despite her intelligence, could be very naïve. She'd grown up in some backwater village that was decades behind the gloss and snap of Shanghai or Beijing. Ben was not naïve. His post-doc had been at a cutting-edge big-pharm; he was now a promising researcher at the San Diego Neuroscience Institute. A lot of companies found it convenient to have easy access to Mexico for drug testing. FDA approval required endless and elaborate clinical trials, but the starving Mexican provinces allowed a lot more latitude as long as there was "full disclosure to all participants." As if an ignorant and desperate day laborer could, or would, understand the medical jargon thrown at him in return for use of his body. Congress had been conducting hearings on the issue for years, with no effect whatsoever. Any procedure or drug experimented within Mexico would, of course, then have to be retested in the U.S. But ninety percent of all new drugs failed. Mexico made a cheap winnowing ground.

And, of course, there were always rumors of totally banned procedures available there for a price. But no big pharm or rogue genetics outfit would actually use a legitimate fertility clinic for experimentation . . . would they?

"Haihong, what's the name of the clinic?"

"Why?"

Their drinks came, Dos Equis for him and Diet Coke for her. After the waitress left, Ben said casually, "I may be able to find out stuff for you. Their usual pay rate for surrogates, for instance. Make sure you're not getting ripped off." Unlike Haihong, Ben was a good liar.

Haihong nodded. So it was the money. "Okay. The clinic is called Dispensario de las Colinas Verdes."

He'd never heard of it. "How did you learn about this place?"

"Emily." She was watching him warily now, ready to resent any criticism of her friend. He said only, "Okay, I'll get on it. How did your meeting with your thesis advisor go yesterday?"

He saw her relax. She launched into a technical discussion of semiotics that he didn't even try to follow. Instead he tried to find traces of his family's faces in hers. Around the eyes, maybe, and the nose . . . but he and his brothers stood six feet, his hair was red, and he had the spare tire of most sedentary Americans. She was tiny, fragilely made. And fragile in other ways, too, capable of an hysterical emotionalism kept in check only by her relentless drive to accomplishment. Ben had seen her drunk once, it was not pretty, and she'd never let him see her that way again. Haihong was a mass of contradictions, this cousin of his, and he groped through his emotions to find one that fit how he felt about her. He didn't find it.

Abruptly he said, interrupting something about F. Scott Fitzgerald, "Is the egg yours or a donor's?"

Anger darkened her delicate features. "None of your business!"

So the egg was hers, and she was more uneasy about the whole business than she pretended. All at once he remembered a stray statistic: Twenty-one percent of surrogate mothers changed their mind about giving up their babies.

"Sorry," he said. "Now what was that again about Fitzgerald?"

She was eight months along before he cracked Dispensario de las Colinas Verdes.

His work at the Neuroscience Institute was with genetically modi-
fied proteins that packaged different monoamines into secretory vesicles,
the biological storage and delivery system for signal molecules. Ben specialized in brain neurotransmitters. This allowed him access to work-in-
progress by the Institute's commercial and academic partners. Colinas
Verdes was not among them.

However, months of digging—most of it not within the scope of
his grant and some of it blatant favor-trading—finally turned up that one
of the Institute's partners had a partner. That small company, which had
already been fined twice by the FDA, had buried in its restricted online
sites a single reference to the Mexican clinic. It was enough. Ben was good
at follow-through.

Haihong was huge. She waddled around campus, looking as if
she'd swallowed a basketball, her stick legs in their little sandals looking
unable to support her belly. The final chapter of her dissertation had been
approved in draft form by her advisor. The date for her oral defense had
been set. She beamed at strangers; she fell into periods of vegetable lassitude; she snapped at friends; she applied feverishly for teaching posts.
Sometimes she cried and then, ten minutes later, laughed hysterically. Ben
watched her take her vitamins, do her exercises, resolutely avoid alcohol.
He couldn't bring himself to tell her anything.

The day in her fourth month that she said to him, awe in her voice,
"Right now he's growing eyelashes," Ben was sure. She was going to keep
the baby.

Twenty-one percent.

He went himself to Mexico, presenting his passport at the border,
driving his Saab through the dusty countryside. Two hours from Tijuana
he reached the windowless brick building that was not the bright and convenient clinic Haihong had gone to. This was the clinic's research head-
quarters, its controlling brain. Ben went in armed with the names and
forged references of the partner company, with his formidable knowledge
of curing-edge genetics, with pretty good Spanish, with American status
and bluster. He spent an hour with the Mexican researchers on site, and
left before he was exposed. He obtained names and then checked them
out in the closed deebees at the Institute. Previous publications, conference appearances, chatter on the e-lists that post-docs, in self-defense,
create to swap information that might impact their collective futures. It

took all his knowledge to fill in the gaps, complete the big picture.

Then he sat with his head in his hands, anxiety battering him in waves, and wondered how he was ever going to tell Haihong.

He waited another week, working eighteen hours a day, sleeping in his lab on a cot, neglecting the job he was paid to do and cutting off both his technicians and his superiors. The latter decided to indulge him; they all thought he was brilliant. Every few hours Ben picked up the phone to call the FBI, the FDA, the USBP, anyone in the alphabet soup of law enforcement who could have shut it all down. But each time he put down the phone. Not until he had the inhibitor, which no one would have permitted him to cobble together had they known. Let alone permit giving it to Haihong.

A lot had been known about neurotransmitters for over seventy years, ever since the first classes of antidepressants. Only the link with genetics was new, and in the last five years, that field—Ben's field—had exploded. He had the fetus's genome. The genetics were new, but the countermeasures for the manifested behaviors were not. Ben knew enough about brain chemistry and cerebral structures.

What he hadn't known enough about was Haihong.

"An inhibitor," she said at the end of his long, lurching explanation, and her calm should have alerted him. An eerie, dangerous calm, like the absence of ocean sucked away from the beach just before the tsunami rolls in. He should have recognized it. But he'd been awake for twenty-two hours straight. He was so tired.

"Yes, an inhibitor," he echoed. "And it will work."

"You're sure."

Nothing like this was ever sure, but he said, "Yes. As sure as I can be." He tried to put an arm around her but she pushed him away.

"An inhibitor calibrated to body weight."

"Yes. Increasing in direct proportion."

"For his entire life."

"Yes. I think so. Haihong—"

"Side effects?" Still that eerie calm.

Ben ran his hand through his red hair, making it all stand up. "I don't know. How can I know?" He wanted to be reassuring, but the brain contained a hundred billion neurons, each with a thousand or so branches. That was ten-to-the-hundred-trillionth power of possible neural connections. He was pretty sure what neurotransmitters the genemods on the baby would increase production of, and pretty sure he could inhibit it. But the side effects? Anybody's guess. Even aspirin affected different people differently.

Haihong said, "A six-month shelf life and a one-week half-life in the body."

She echoed his terminology perfectly, still in that quiet, mechanical voice. Ben put out his hand to touch her again, drew it back. "Yes. Haihong, we need to call the FDA, now that I have something to use as an emergency drug, and let them take over the—"

"Give me the first batch."

He did. This was why he'd made it, because he'd known months ago what she had never told him in words. Twenty-one percent.

He agreed to put off calling the authorities for one more day. "Just give me time to assimilate it all, Ben. A little time. Okay?"

He'd agreed. It was her life, her child. Not his.

The next day she'd been gone.

In the foul public cyberbooth, nine years later, Ben deleted Haihong's email. *Rumors,* she'd written, *Sichuan quarantine may lift soon.* Interred in her remote village, which the most modern of technologies had forced back into the near primitive, she hadn't even heard the news. The quarantine had always been as much political as anything else, or it wouldn't have been in force so long. It was to be lifted today and even now, right there in Chengdu from which she must have sent her email, she still seemed oblivious. *I cannot do this anymore. I just cannot.*

What exactly did that mean?

He left his coffee untouched in the filthy booth. Outside, in the fresh air under California's blue sky, he pulled out his handheld and booked a flight to China.

Four: Haihong

She left the People's Internet Building at dusk. Usually she spent several hours online, as long as she could afford, in an orgy of catching up on news, on the academic world, on anything outside the quarantine. She only had the opportunity every six months.

This time, she left as soon as she'd emailed Ben, uploading onto him her bi-annual report, her gratitude, her despair. Unfair, of course, but how could it matter? Ben, in California, had everything; he could add a little despair to his riches. To Haihong nothing mattered any longer, nothing except Cixin, the unruly child who did not love her and for whom she'd given her future. A fruitless sacrifice, since Cixin had no future, either. Everything barren, everything a waste.

She clutched the package in her hand, the precious six-month supply of inhibitor of proteins in the posterior superior parietal lobes. The pills were sewn inside a gift for Cixin, a stuffed toy he was too old for. Ben had not done any further work on the side-effects. Maybe he had no way to measure them, eight thousand miles away from his research subject. Maybe he had lost interest. So Cixin would go on being irritable, restless, underweight, over-stressed. He would—

Outside, Haihong blinked. The sparse and rotting skeleton left of Chengdu seemed to have gone mad! Gongs sounded, sirens blared, people poured out of the dilapidated buildings, more people than she had known were left in the city. They were shouting something, something about the quarantine . . .

Starting forward, she didn't even see the pedicab speeding around the corner, racing along the nearly trafficless street. The driver, a strong and large man, saw her too late. He yelled and braked, but Haihong had already gone flying. Her tiny and malnourished body struck the ground head first. Bleeding from her mouth, unable to feel any of her body below the neck, her last thought was a wordless prayer for her son.

Five: Cixin

By afternoon Cixin was exhausted from walking away from the village, up into the mountains. His legs ached and his empty stomach moaned. Worse, he was afraid he was lost.

He had been careful to follow the path where Mama used to ride her bicycle, and it had led him to their old picnic place. Cixin had stopped and rested there, but the usual calm had not come over him. Should he try to worship, like Auntie did when she bowed in front of her little shrine? Mama said, in the secret language, that worship was nonsense. But nothing Mama said could be trusted. She was a drunk and a whore.

Cixin swiped a tear from his dusty cheek. It was stupid to cry. And he wasn't really lost. After the picnic place, the path had become narrower and harder to see, and maybe—*maybe*—he had lost it, but he was still climbing uphill. Tibet was uphill, at the top of the mountains. He was all right.

But so thirsty! If he just had some water . . .

An hour later he came to a stream. It was shallow and muddy, but he lay on his belly and lapped at the water. That helped a little. Cixin staggered up on his aching legs and resumed climbing.

An hour after that, it began to get dark.

Now fear took him. He'd been sure he would reach Tibet before nightfall . . . after all, look how far he'd come! There should be monks coming out to greet him, taking him into a warm place with water and beancurd and congee . . . Nothing was right.

"Stupid monks!" he screamed as loud as he could, but then stopped because what if the monks were on their way to get him and they heard him and turned back? So he yelled, "I didn't mean it!"

But still no monks came.

Darkness fell swiftly. Cixin huddled at the base of a pine tree, arms wrapped around his body and legs drawn up for warmth. It didn't help. He didn't want to race around, not on his hurting legs and not in the dark, and yet it was hard to sit still and do nothing. Every noise terrified him—what if a tiger came? Mama said the tigers were all gone from China but Mama was a drunk and a whore.

Shivering, he eventually slept.

In the morning the sun returned, warming him, but everything else was even worse. His belly ached more than his legs. Somehow his tongue had swollen so that it seemed to fill his entire dry mouth. Should he go back to the place where the water had been? But he didn't remember how to get there. All the pine trees, all the larches, all the gray boulders, looked the same.

Cixin whimpered and started climbing. Surely Tibet couldn't be much farther. There'd been a map of China in the village school he'd attended until his inability to sit still made him leave, and on the map Tibet looked very close to Sichuan. He was almost there.

The second nightfall found him no longer able to move. He collapsed beside a boulder, too exhausted even to cry. The picture of the dead dog in the road filled his mind, filled his fitful dreams. When he woke, he was covered with small, stinging bites from something. His cry came out as a hoarse, frustrated whimper. The rising sun filled his eyes, blinding him, and he turned away and tried to sit up.

Then it happened.

Cixin *knew*.

He was lifted out of his body. Thirst and hunger and insect bites vanished. He was not Cixin, and everything—the whole universe—was Cixin. He was woven into the universe, breathed with it, was one with it, and it spoke to him wordlessly and sang to him without music. Everything was him, and he was everything. He was the gray boulder and the yellow sun rising and the rustling pine trees and the hard ground. He was *them* and he felt them, it, all, and the mountains reverberated with surprise and with his name: *Cixin*.

Come.

Cixin.

The child sat on the parched ground, expressionless, and was still and calm.

"Cixin!"

A sour, familiar taste melting on his tongue, a big hand in his mouth. Then, after a measureless time that was not time, water forced down his throat.

"Cixin!"

Cixin blinked. Then he cried out and would have toppled over had not the big man—how big he was! How pale!—steadied him. More water touched Cixin's lips.

"Not too much, buddy, not at first," the big man said, and he spoke the secret language that only Cixin and Mama knew. How could that be?

All at once everything on Cixin hurt, his belly and neck and swollen legs and most of all his head. And the big man had red hair standing up all over his head like an attacking rooster. Cixin started to cry.

The big man lifted him in his arms and put him over his shoulder. Cixin just glimpsed the two other men, one from his village and one a stranger, their faces rigid with something that Cixin didn't understand. Then he fainted.

When he came to, he lay on his bed at Auntie's house. The big man was there, and the stranger, but the village man was not. The big man was saying, very slowly, some words in the secret language to the stranger, and he was repeating them in real words to Auntie. Cixin tried to say something—he didn't even know what—but only a croak came out.

Auntie rushed over to him. She had been crying. Auntie never cried, and fear of this made Cixin wail. Something terrible had happened, and it had happened to Mama. How did Cixin know this? He knew.

And underneath: that other knowing, half memory and half dream, already faded and yet somehow more real even than Auntie's tears or the big man's strange red hair:

Cixin. Come. Cixin.

The big man was Cousin Benjamin Jinkang Molloy. Cixin tasted the ridiculous name on his tongue. Despite the red hair, Cousin Ben sometimes looked Chinese, but mostly he did not. That made no sense, but then neither did anything else.

Auntie didn't like Cousin Ben. She didn't say so, but she wouldn't look at him, didn't offer him tea, frowned when his back was turned and she wasn't crying or at her shrine. Ben visited every day, at first with his "translator" and then, when he saw how well Cixin spoke the secret language, alone. He paid money to Xiao's father to sleep at Xiao's house. Xiao was not allowed to visit Cixin at his bed.

He said, "Why can you talk Mama's secret words?"

"It's English. Where I live, everybody speaks English."

"Do you live in Tibet?" That would be exciting!

"No. I live in America."

Cixin considered this. America might be exciting, too—Xiao's iPod came from there. Sudden tears pricked Cixin's eyes. He wanted to see

Xiao. He wanted Mama, who was as dead as the dog in the road. He
wanted an iPod. He wanted to get out of bed and race around but his
body hurt and anyway Auntie wouldn't let him get up.

Ben said carefully, "Cixin, what happened to you up on the
mountain?"

"I got lost."

"I know. I found you, remember? But what happened before that?"

"Nothing." Cixin closed his lips tight. He didn't actually remember what had happened on the mountain, only that something had. But
whatever it was, he wasn't going to share it with some strange red-headed
cousin who wasn't even from Tibet. It was *his*. Maybe if Mama hadn't got
dead . . .

The tears came then and Cixin, ashamed, turned his face toward the
wall. Gently Ben turned it back.

"I know you miss your mother, buddy. But my time here is short and
I need you to pay attention."

That was just stupid. People needed food and water and clothes and
iPods—they didn't "need" Cixin's attention. He scowled.

Ben said, "Listen to me. It's very important that you go on taking
the pills your mother was giving you."

"You mean the once-a-week?"

"Yes. I'm going to show you exactly how much to take, and you must
do it *every single week*."

"I know. Or I will die."

Ben shut his eyes, then opened them again. "Is that what she told
you?"

"Yes." Something inside him trembled, like a tremor deep in the
earth. "Is it true?"

"Yes. It's true. In a very important way."

"Okay." All at once Cixin liked speaking the secret language again.
It made Mama seem closer, and it made Cixin special. Suddenly he had
a thought that made him jerk upright in bed, rattling his head. "Are you
really from America?"

"Yes."

"And Mama was, too?"

"She lived there for a while, yes."

"She liked it there?"

"Yes, I think she did."

"Take me to America with you!"

Ben didn't look surprised—why not? Cixin himself was surprised by his thought: surprised, delighted, frightened. In America he would be away from the village boys, away from the school that threw him out. In America he could have an iPod. "Please, Cousin Ben, please please please!"

"Cixin, I can't. Auntie is your closest relative and she—"

"She's not really my Auntie! She was Mama's amah, is all! You're my elder cousin!"

Ben said gently, "She loves you."

Cixin fell back on his bed, hurting his head even more. *Love.* Mama loved him and she died and left him. Auntie loved him and she was keeping him from going to America. Cousin Ben didn't love him or he would take him away from this evil village. Love was terrible and ugly. Cixin glared savagely at this horrible cousin. "Then after you go I won't take my once-a-week and I will die!"

Ben stood. "I will not be blackmailed by a nine-year-old."

Cixin didn't know what "blackmail" was, but it sounded evil. Everywhere he was surrounded by evil. Better to die. Again he turned his face to the wall.

Later, he would always think that had made the difference. His silence, his turning away. If he had fought back, Ben would have said more about blackmail and gone away, angry. But instead he ran his hand through his red hair until it stood up like bristly grass—Cixin could just see this out of the corner of his eye—and then put his hand over his face.

"All right, Cixin. I'll take you to America. But I warn you, it may take a long, long time to arrange."

Six: BEN

It took nearly two years.

If Ben hadn't had family contacts at the State Department, it would have been even longer, might have been impossible. The Chinese were discouraging foreign adoptions; Cixin was from within formerly quarantined Sichuan; the death certificate for Haihong needed to be obtained from a glacially slow bureaucracy and presented in triplicate. But on the other hand, Chinese-American relations were in a positive phase. Ben could prove Haihong had been his second cousin. Ben had received a Citizens' Commendation from the FBI for exposing the surrogate-ring of American girls exploited by a sleazy Mexican fertility clinic. And Uncle James was on the State desk for East Asia.

During those two years, Ben sent Auntie money and Cixin presents. An iPod, which seemed to be a critical object. Jeans and sneakers. Later, a laptop, to be used at the vineyard foreman's house to communicate with Ben. They exchanged email, and Cixin's troubled Ben. Fluent in spoken English, Cixin was barely literate in any language, and he didn't seem to be learning much from the school software Ben supplied.

> *Cuzin Ben this is Cixin. Wen r yu comin 4 me. Anty is sik agen. Evrybuddy hates me. I hate it hear. Com soon or I wil die.*
> *Cixin*

> *Cixin—*
> *I am making plans to bring you here as fast as I can. Please be patient.*

Could Cixin read that word? Maybe not. The backward connection at the foreman's house didn't permit even such a basic tool as a camlink.

> *Please wait without fuss.*

> *Haihong saying during her pregnancy, "Ben, please don't fuss at me!"*

> *Take your once-a-week, use your school software, and be good.*

What else? How did you write to a child you'd barely met?

> *You will like America. Soon, I hope.*
> *Ben*

Soon, I hope. But did he? Cixin would be an enormous responsibility, and Ben would bear it mostly alone. His parents, old when Ben had been born, lived in failing health in Florida, his sisters in Des Moines and Buffalo. Ben worked long hours in his lab. What was he going to do with a illegally genemod, barely literate, ADH adolescent who shared less than three percent of Ben's genetic heritage and nothing of his cultural one?

And then, because complications always attracted more complications, he met Renata.

A group from his department at the Institute went out for Friday Happy Hour. Ordinarily Ben avoided these gatherings. People drank too much, barriers were lowered that might better have stayed raised, flirtations started that proved embarrassing on Monday morning. But Ben knew he was getting a reputation as standoffish, if not downright snobbish, and he had to work with these people. So he went to Happy Hour.

They settled into a long table, scientists and technicians and secretaries. Dan Silverstein, a capable researcher fifteen years Ben's senior, talked about his work with envelope proteins. Susie, the intern whom somebody really should do something about, shot Ben smoldering glances across the table. Ben spotted Renata at the bar.

She sat alone. Tall, a mop of dirty blonde curls, glasses. Pretty enough but nothing remarkable about her except the intensity with which she was both consuming beer and marking on a sheaf of papers. At Grogan's during a Friday Happy Hour? Then she looked up, pure delight on her face, and laughed out loud at something on the papers.

Ben excused himself to go to the men's room. Taking the long way back, he peered over her shoulders. School tests of some kind—

"Do I know you?" She'd caught him. Her tone was cool but not belligerent, looking for neither a fight nor a connection. Self-sufficient.

"No, we've never met." And then, because she was turning back to her papers, dismissing him, "Are you a teacher? What was so funny?"

She turned back, considering. The set of her mouth said, *This better not be a stupid pick-up line,* but there was a small smile in her eyes. "I teach physics at a community college."

"And physics is funny?"

"Are you at all familiar with John Wheeler's experiments?"

She flung the question at him like a challenge, and all at once Ben was enjoying himself. "The nineteen-eighty delayed-choice experiment?"

The smile reached her mouth, giving him full marks. "Yes. Listen to this. The question is, '*Describe what Wheeler found when he used particle detectors with photon beams.*' And the answer should be . . ." She looked at Ben, the challenge more friendly now.

"That the presence or absence of a detector, no matter how far down the photon's path, and even if the detector is switched on *after* the photon passes the beam splitter, affects the outcome. The detector's presence or absence determines whether the photon registers as a wave or a particle."

"Correct. This kid wrote, 'Wheeler's particles and his detectors acted weird. I think both were actually broken. Either that or it was a miracle.'" She laughed again.

"And it's funny when your students don't learn anything?"

"Oh, he's learned something. He's learned that when you haven't got the vaguest idea, give it a stab anyway." She looked fondly at the paper. "I like this kid. I'm going to fail him, but I like him."

Something turned over in Ben's chest. It was her laugh, or her cheerful pragmatism, or . . . He didn't know what. He stuck out his hand. "I'm Ben Molloy. I work at the Neuroscience Institute."

"Renata Williams." She shook hands, her head tipped slightly to one side, the bar light glinting on her glasses. "I've always had a thing for scientists. All that arcane knowledge."

"Not so arcane."

"Says you. Sit down, Ben."

They talked until long after his department had left Grogan's. Ben found himself telling her things he'd never told anyone else, incidents from his childhood that were scary or funny or puzzling, dreams from his adolescence. She listened intently, her glasses on top of her head, her chin tilted to one side. Renata was more reticent about her own past ("Not much to tell—I was a goody-goody grind"), but she loved teaching and became enthusiastic about her students. They were carrying out some elaborate science project involving the data from solar flares; this was an active sun-spot year. Renata pulled out her students' sunspot charts and explained them in the dim light from the bar. Eventually the weary bartender stopped shooting them meaningful glances and flatly told them, "Leave, already!"

Ben drove to her apartment. They left her car in the parking lot of the bar until the next day. In bed she was different: more vulnerable, less sure of herself. Softer. She slept with one hand all night on Ben's hip, as if to make sure he was still actually there. Ben lay awake and felt, irrationally but definitely, that he had come home.

Renata worked long hours, teaching five courses ("Community colleges are the sweatshops of academe"), but with a difference. When she wasn't working, she had a life. She saw friends, she kick-boxed, she played in a chess league, she went to movies. Ben, who did none of these things, felt both envious and left-out. Renata just laughed at him.

"If you really wanted to kick-box, you'd take a class in it. People generally end up doing what they want to do, if they can. My hermit." She kissed him on the nose.

If they can. Ben didn't tell Renata about Cixin. The first month, he assured himself, they were just getting to know each other. (A lie: he'd known her, *recognized* her, that first night at Grogan's.) Then, as each month passed—three, four, six—it got harder to explain why he'd delayed. How would Renata react? She was kind but she was also honest, valuing openness and sincerity, and she had a temper.

I'm adopting a Chinese boy for whom I've broken several laws that could still send me to jail, including practicing medicine without a license and administering untested drugs that induce socially disabling side-effects. Perfect. Nothing added to romance like felony charges. Unless it was medical experimentation on a child.

Sometimes Ben looked at Renata, sleepy after sex or squinting at her computer, glasses on top of her curly head, and thought, *It will be all right.* Renata would understand. She came from a large family, and although she didn't want kids herself, she would accept Cixin. Look at how much effort she put into her students, how many endless extra hours working with them on the sunspot project. And Cixin was eleven; in seven more years he'd be off onto his own life.

Other times he knew that he'd lied to Renata, that Cixin was not an easy-to-accept or lovable child, and that his arrival would make Ben's world fall apart. At such times, his desperation made him moody. Renata usually laughed him out of it. But still he didn't tell her.

Then, in August, Uncle James called from Washington. His voice was jubilant.

"I just got the final approval, Ben. You can go get your cousin any time now. You're a daddy! And send me a big cigar—it's a boy!"

Ben clutched his cell so tight that all blood left his fingers. "Thanks," he said.

"Tell me how it works," Renata said. They were the first words she'd spoken in fifteen long minutes, all of which Ben had spent talking. Her dangerous calm reminded him of Haihong, all those years ago.

They were in his apartment, which had effectively if not officially become hers as well. His half-packed suitcase lay open on the bed. Ben stood helplessly beside the suitcase, a pair of rolled-up socks in his hand. Renata sat in a green brocade chair that had been a gift from his mother and Ben knew that if he approached that chair, she would explode.

He took refuge in science. "It's an alteration in the genes that create functional transporter proteins. Those are the amines that get neurotransmitters across synapses to the appropriate brain-cell receptors. The mechanisms are well understood—in fact, there are polymorphic alleles. If you have one gene, your body makes more transporters; with the other version, you get less."

"What difference does that make?"

"It affects mood and behavior. Less serotonin, for example, is connected to depression, irritability, aggression, inflexibility."

"And this alleged genemod in your cousin gave him less serotonin?"

"No." *Alleged genemod.* Ben dragged his hand through his hair. "He probably does have less serotonin, but that's a side effect. The genemod affected other proteins that in turn affected others . . . it's a cascade. Everything's interconnected in the brain. But the functional result in Cixin would be a flood of transporters and neurotransmitters in two brain regions, the superior parietal lobes and the temporoparietal region."

"I don't want jargon, Ben. I want explanations."

"I'm trying to give them to you. I'm doing the best I can to—"

"Then do better! Six months we've been together and you never mention that you're adopting a child . . . what is the *effect* of the extra transporters on those parts of the brain?"

"Without the inhibiting drug I designed for him, near-total catatonia."

"That doesn't make sense! Nobody would deliberately design genes to do that!"

"They didn't." Suddenly tired, he sat on the edge of the bed. His flight to Shanghai left in six hours. "Those brain areas orient the body in space and differentiate between self and others. The research company was trying to develop heightened awareness, perception of others' movements, and reactions to muscular shifting."

She got it. "Better fighting machines."

"Yes."

"Then why—"

"They were rogue geneticists, Renata. They didn't have access to all the most recent research. They screwed up. They're all in jail now."

"And the Neuroscience Institute—"

His patience gave way. "Of course the Institute wasn't involved! I told you—we helped shut the whole thing down."

"Except for your little part in supplying this kid with homemade inhibitors. His other problems you mentioned, the restlessness and aggression—"

"Most likely side-effects of the inhibitor," Ben said wearily. "You can't alter the ratio of neurotransmitters in the brain without a lot of side effects. Cixin's body is under huge stress and his behavior is consistent with fluctuating neurotransmitters and high concentrations of cortisol and other stress hormones."

She said nothing.

"Renata, I promise you—"

"Yeah, well, I've seen what your words are worth." She got up from the green chair and walked around him, toward the door. He knew better than to try to stop her. "If you'd told me about Cixin from the beginning—even only that he was coming here to live with you—that would be one thing. I could have accepted it. I mean—that poor kid. It's not his fault, and I understand family ties as well as you Chinese, or part-Chinese, or whatever you're calling yourself now. But, Ben, I *asked* you. I said after our first week or so, 'Do you see yourself ever wanting children in your life?' And you said no. And now you tell me—" She broke off.

All this time he'd been holding the socks. Carefully, as if they were made of glass, he laid them into his suitcase. A small part of his chaotic mind registered that, like most socks nowadays, they had probably been exported from China. He said, "Will you still be here when I get back?"

"I don't know."

They looked at each other.

"I don't know, Ben," she repeated. "I don't know who you really are."

It was the rainy season in Sichuan and over ninety degrees. Ben's clothing stuck to his body as he waited in the bus station in Chengdu; Cixin's village still had no maglev service. The station looked cleaner and more prosperous than when he'd come to China two years ago. Children in blue-and-white school uniforms marched past, carrying pictures of giant pandas. Ben had emailed Cixin to ask Auntie to bring him to Chengdu, but Cixin got off the bus alone.

He hadn't grown much. At eleven—almost twelve—he was a small, weedy boy with suspicious dark eyes, thin cheeks, and an unruly shock of black hair falling over his forehead. A large greenish bruise on one cheek. He carried a small backpack, nothing else. He didn't smile.

Ben locked his knees against a tide of conflicting emotions. Apprehension. Pity. Resentment. Longing for Renata. But he tried. He said, "Hey, buddy" and put a hand on Cixin's shoulder. Cixin flinched and Ben removed the hand.

He tried again. "Hello, Cixin. It's good to see you. Now let's go to America."

Seven: Cixin

He didn't know who he really was.

Not now, in these strange and bewildering places. Cixin had never been out of his village. He'd assumed the videos on his laptop had been made-up lies, like Mama telling him about Tibet. But here was Chengdu, full of cars and pedicabs and scooters and huge buildings like mountains and buildings partly fallen down and signs that sprang up from the ground but dissolved when you walked through them and flashing lights and millions of people and men with big guns. . . . Cixin, who just last week had beaten up three village boys at once and thought of himself secretly as "The Tiger," clutched Ben's hand and didn't know what this world was, what he himself was anymore.

"It's all right, buddy," Ben said and Cixin glared at him and dropped the hand, angry because Ben wasn't afraid.

They sat together in the back of the plane to Shanghai. For a while Cixin was content to stare out the window as the ground fell away and they rose into clouds—up into *clouds!* But eventually he couldn't stay still.

"I'm getting up," he told Ben.

"Toilet's just behind us," Ben said.

Cixin didn't need a toilet, he needed to run. Space between the rows of seat was narrow but he barreled down it, waving his arms. A boy a few years older walked in the opposite direction—on Cixin's aisle! The boy didn't step aside. Cixin shoved him away and kept running. The boy staggered up and started after Cixin but was stopped by a shout in Chinese from a man seated nearby. Cixin ran the length of the aisle, cut across the plane, ran back down a different aisle, where Ben grabbed him by the arm.

"Sit, Cixin. *Sit.* You can't run in here."

"Why? Will they throw me off?" This was funny—they were on a plane!—and Cixin laughed. Once he started, he couldn't seem to stop. A man in a blue uniform moved purposefully toward them. Cixin stopped laughing—what if it was a soldier with a hidden gun? He cowered into his seat and tried to make himself very small.

The maybe-soldier and Cousin Ben talked softly. Ben sat down and shook a yellow pill from a plastic bottle. "Take this with your bottled water."

"That's not my once-a-week!" The once-a-week, for reasons Cixin didn't understand, had to be left behind at Auntie's. *Too risky for Customs,* Ben said, *especially for me.* Which made no sense because Ben didn't take the once-a-week, only Cixin did.

"No, it's not your once-a-week," Ben said, "but take it anyway. Now!"

Cixin recognized anger. Ben might have a gun, too. In the videos, all Americans had guns. He took the pill, tapped on the window, kicked the back of the seat until the woman in it turned around and said something sharply in Chinese.

Cixin wasn't clear on what it was. A slow languor had fallen over the plane. Then sleep slid into him as softly as the fog by the river, as calmly

as something . . . something right at the edge of memory . . . a pine tree
and a gray boulder and . . .

He slept.

Another airport. Stumbling through it half awake. Shouting, people
surging, a wait in a locked room . . . maybe it was a dream. Ben's face tired
and white as old snow. Then another plane, or maybe not . . . yes. Another
plane. More sleep. When he woke truly and for real, he lay in a small
room with blue walls and red cloth at the windows, four stacked houses
up into the sky, in San Diego, America.

Cixin ran. Waves pounded the shore, the wind whistled hard—*whoosh!
whoosh!*—and sand blew against his bare legs, his pumping arms, his face.
He laughed and swallowed sand. He ran.

Ben waited where the deserted beach met the parking lot, the hood
of his jacket pulled up, his face red and angry. "Cixin! Get in the car!"

Cixin, exhausted and dripping and happy—as happy as he ever got
here—climbed into the front seat of Ben's Saab. Rain pounded the wind-
shield. Ben shouted, "You ran away from your tutor again!"

Cixin nodded. His tutor was stupid. The man had been telling him
that rainstorms like this were rare and due to the Earth getting hotter. But
with his own body Cixin had experienced many rainstorms, every summer
of his life, and they all were hot. So he ran away from the stupid tutor,
and from the even stupider girl who was supposed to come take care of
him after the tutor left and before Ben came home from work. He ran the
seven streets from Ben's house-in-the-sky to the beach because the beach
was the only place in America that he liked. And because he wanted to
run in the rain.

"You can't just leave the condo by yourself," Ben said. "And I pay
that tutor to bring you up to speed before school starts in September,
even though—you can't just go down to the beach during a typhoon! And
I had to leave the lab in the middle of—"

There was more, but Cixin didn't listen. He'd only been in America
ten days but already he knew that Ben wouldn't beat him. Still, Ben was
very angry, and Ben was good to him, and Ben had showed him the wonderful beach in the first place. So Cixin hung his head and studied the

sand stuck to his knees, but he didn't actually listen. That much was not necessary.

"—adjust your dosage," Ben finished. Cixin said nothing, respectfully. Ben sighed and started the car, his silly red hair stuck to his head.

When they were nearly back at the houses-stacked-in-the-sky, Cixin said, "You look sick, Cousin Ben."

"I'm fine," Ben said shortly.

"You don't eat."

"I eat enough. But, Cixin, you're driving me crazy."

"Yes." It seemed polite to agree. "But you don't eat and you look sick and sad. Are you sad?"

Ben glanced over, rain dripping off his collar. "You surprise me sometimes, buddy."

That was *not* a polite answer. Cixin scowled and stared out the window at the "typhoon" and tapped his sandy sneaker on the sodden floor of the car. He wanted to run again.

And Ben was too sad.

In the "condo," instead of the stupid tutor, a woman sat on the sofa. How did she get in? A robber! Cixin rushed to the phone, shouting, "911! 911!" Ben had taught him that. Robbers—how exciting!

But Ben called, "It's all right, Cixin." His voice sounded so strange that Cixin stopped his mad dash and, curious, looked at him.

"Renata," Ben said thickly.

"I couldn't stay away after all," the woman said, and then they were hugging. Cixin turned away, embarrassed. Chinese people did not behave like that. And the woman was ugly, too tall and too pale, like a slug. Not pretty like Xiao. The way Ben was holding her . . . Cixin hated the woman already. She was evil. She was not necessary.

He rushed into his room and slammed the door.

But at dinnertime the woman was still there. She tried to talk to Cixin, who refused to talk back.

"Answer Renata," Ben said, his voice dangerously quiet.

"What did you say?" Cixin made his voice high and silly, to insult her.

"I asked if you found any sand dollars on the beach."

He looked at her then. "Dollars made of sand?"

"No. They're the shells of ocean creatures. Here." She put something on the table beside his plate. "I found this one last week. I'll bet you can't find one bigger than this."

"Yes! I can!" Cixin shouted. "I'm going now!"

"No, you're not," Ben said, pulling him back into his chair. But Ben was smiling. "Tomorrow's Saturday. We'll all go."

"And if we go in the evening and if the clouds have lifted, there should be something interesting to see in the sky," Renata said. "But I won't tell you what, Cixin. It's a surprise."

Cixin couldn't wait until Saturday evening. He woke very early. Ben and Renata were still asleep in Ben's bed—she must be a whore even if she wasn't as ugly as he thought at first—and here it was *morning*. A little morning, pale gray in a corner of the sky. The rainstorm was all gone.

He dressed, slipped out of the house-in-the-sky, and ran to the beach. No one was there. The air was calm now and the water had stopped pounding and something strange was happening to the sky over the water. Ribbons of color—green, white, green—waved in the sky like ghosts. Maybe they were ghosts! Frightened, Cixin turned his back, facing the part of the sky where the sun would come up and chase the ghosts away. But then he couldn't see the water. He turned back and ran and ran along the cool sand. To his left, in San Diego, sirens started to sound. Cixin ignored them.

Finally, exhausted, he plopped down. The sun was up now and the sky ghosts gone. Nobody else came out on the beach. Cixin watched the nearest tiny waves kissing the sand.

Something happened.

A soft, calm feeling stole through him, calm as the water. He didn't even want to run anymore. He sat cross-legged, half hidden by a sand drift, dreamily watching the ocean, and all at once he *was* the ocean. Was the sand, was the sky, was the whole universe and they were him.

Cixin. Come. Cixin.

Voices, everywhere and nowhere, but Cixin didn't have to answer because they already knew the answer. They were him and he was them.

Peace. Belonging. Everything. Time and no time.

And then Ben was forcing open his mouth, putting in something that melted on his tongue, and it all went away.

But this time memory lingered. It had happened. It was real.

Eight: Ben

"I'd dropped the dosage to try to mitigate the side effects," Ben said. He ran his hand through his filthy hair. Cixin lay asleep in his room, sunburned and exhausted. God only knew how long he'd been gone before Ben found his empty bed.

Renata pulled her eyes from CNN. The solar flare, the largest ever recorded and much more powerful than anticipated, had played havoc with radio communications from Denver to Beijing. Two planes had crashed. The aurora borealis was visible as far south as Cuba. Renata said, "Ben, you can't go on fiddling with his dosage and giving him sleeping pills when you get it wrong. You're not even an M.D., and yet you're playing God with that child's life!"

"And what do you think I should do?" Ben shouted. It was a relief to shout, even as he feared driving her away again. "Should I let him go catatonic? You didn't see him two years ago in China—I did! He'd been in a vegetative state for two days and he would have died if I hadn't found him! Is that what you think should happen?"

"No. You should get him medical help. You wouldn't have to say anything about the genemods or—"

"The hell I wouldn't! What happens when they ask me what meds Cixin takes? If I didn't tell them, he could die. If I do, I go to jail. And how long do you think it would take a medical team to find drug traces in his body? Inhibitors have a long half-life. And even if I explain everything, and if I'm believed, what happens to Cixin then? He's not even on my medical insurance until the adoption is final! So he'd be warehoused, catatonic, in some horrifying state hospital, and I'd be standing trial. Is that what you want?"

"No. Wait. I don't know." She wasn't yelling at him now; her voice held sorrow and compassion. CNN announced that a total of 312 people had died in the two air disasters. "But, sweetheart, the situation as it stands isn't good for you or Cixin, either. What are you going to do?"

"What can I do? He just isn't anything like a normal—Cixin!"

The boy stood in the doorway, his shock of black hair stiff from salt air, his eyes puffy from sleep. He suddenly looked much older.

"Ben—what does the once-a-week do to me?"

Renata drew a long breath.

"It's complicated," Ben said finally.

"I need to know."

Cixin wasn't fidgeting, or yelling, or running. Something had happened on the beach, something besides sunburn and dehydration. Ben's tired mind stabbed around for a way to explain things to a nearly illiterate eleven-year-old. Nothing occurred to him.

Renata switched off the television and said quietly, "Tell him, Ben. Or I will."

"Butt out, Renata!"

"No. And don't you ever try to bully me. You'll lose."

He had already lost. Shooting a single furious glance at her, Ben turned to Cixin. "You have a . . . a sickness. A rare disease. If you don't take the once-a-week, you will die like your mother said, but first you go all stiff and empty. Like this." Ben, feeling like a fool, sat on the rug and made his body rigid and his face blank.

"Empty?"

"Yes. No thoughts, nothing. No *Cixin*. That's how you were on the beach, like that for a long time, which is why you're so sunburned." And maybe more than sunburned. A big solar flare came with a proton storm, and those could cause long-term biochemical damage. Ben couldn't cope with that just now, not on top of everything else. "Do you understand, Cixin? You went empty. Like a . . . a Coke can all drunk up."

"Empty," Cixin repeated. All at once he smiled, a smile so enigmatic and complicated that Ben was startled. Then the boy went back into his room and closed the door.

"Spooky," Ben said inadequately. He struggled up from the rug. "How do you think he took it?"

"I don't know." Renata seemed as disconcerted as Ben. "I only know what I would be thinking if I were him."

"What would you be thinking?" All at once he desperately wanted to know.

"I would be wondering who I really was. Wondering where the pills ended and I, Cixin, began."

"He's eleven," Ben said scornfully. Scorn was a relief. "He doesn't have sophisticated thoughts like that."

September. Cixin started school, the oldest kid in the fourth grade. Fortunately, he was small enough to sort of fit in and large enough to not be picked on by his classmates. He could not read at grade level, could not concentrate on his worksheets, could not sit still during lessons. After one week, his teacher called Ben to school for an "instructional team meeting." The team recommended Special Ed.

After two weeks, Cixin had another episode of catatonia. Again Ben found him at the beach, sitting half in the water, motionless amid frolicking children and splashing teens and sunbathing adults. A small boy with a sand pail said conversationally, "That kid dead."

"He's not dead," Ben snapped. Wearily he forced a dose of inhibitor onto Cixin's tongue. It melted, and he came to and stared at Ben from dark, enigmatic eyes that slowly turned resentful.

"Go away, Ben."

"I can't, damn it!"

Cixin said, "You don't understand."

In his khakis and loafers—the school had called him at work to report Cixin's absence—Ben lowered himself to sit on the wet sand. The blue Pacific rolled in, frothy at the whitecaps and serene beyond. The sun shone brightly. Ben said, "Make me understand."

"I can't."

"Try. Why do you do it, Cixin? What happens when you go empty?"

"It's not empty."

"Then what is it?" He willed himself to patience. This was a child, after all.

Cixin took a long time answering. Finally he said, "I see. Everything."

"What kind of everything?"

"*Everything.* And it talks to me."

Ben went as still as Cixin had been. He hadn't even realized . . . hadn't even *thought* of that. He'd thought of neurotransmitter ratios, neural architecture plasticity, blood flow changes, synaptic miscues. And somehow he'd missed this. *It talks to me.*

Cixin leapt up. "I'm not going back to Special Ed!" he yelled and raced away down the sand, his school papers streaming out of the unzipped backpack flapping on his skinny shoulders.

"Temporal lobe epilepsy?" Renata said doubtfully. "But . . . he doesn't have seizures?"

"It's not *grand mal*," Ben said. They sat in Grogan's. Ben had drugged Cixin again with Dozarin, hating himself for doing it but needing, beyond all reason, to escape his apartment for a few hours. "With *petit mal*, seizures can go completely unnoticed. And obviously it's not the only aberration going on in his brain, but I think it's a factor."

"But . . . if he's hearing voices, isn't that more likely to be schizophrenia or something like that?"

"I'm no doctor, as you're constantly telling me, but temporal-lobe epilepsy is a very well documented source of religious transports. Joan of Arc, Hildegaard of Bingen, maybe even Saul on the road to Damascus."

"But why does your inhibitor work on him at all? Isn't epilepsy a thing about electrical firing of—"

"I don't know why it works!" Ben said. He drained his gin and tonic and set the glass, harder than necessary, onto the table between them. "Don't you get it, Renata? I don't know anything except that I'm reaching the end of my rope!"

"I can see that," Renata said. "Have you considered that Cixin might be telling the truth?'

"Of course he's 'telling the truth,' as he experiences it. Temporal-lobe seizures can produce visual and auditory hallucinations that seem completely real."

"That's not what I meant."

"What did you mean?"

Renata fiddled with the rim of her glass. "Maybe the voices Cixin hears *are* real."

Ben stared at her. *You think you know someone* . . . "Renata, you teach science. Since when do you dabble in mysticism?"

"Since always. I just don't advertise it to everybody."

That hurt. "I'm hardly 'everybody.' Or at least I thought I wasn't."

"You're taking it wrong. I just meant that I haven't closed the door on the possibility of other worlds besides this one, other levels of being. Spirits, aliens, gods and angels, parallel universes that bleed through . . . I don't know. But there's never been a human society, ever, that didn't believe in some sort of mystery beyond the veil."

He didn't know anymore who she was. Ben motioned to the waiter for another gin and tonic. When his thoughts were at least partly collected, he said, "You can't—"

"What I can or cannot do doesn't matter. The point is, what are *you* going to do now?"

"I'm going to have an implant inserted under Cixin's skin that will deliver the correct dose of inhibitor automatically."

"Really." Her tone was dangerous. "And who will perform this surgery? You?"

"Of course not. It can be done in Mexico."

"Do you know what you're saying, Ben? You're piling one criminal offense on top of another, and you're treating that boy like a lab rat."

"He's sick and I'm trying to make him better!" God, why wouldn't she understand?

"Are you going to at least explain all that to him?"

"No. He wouldn't understand."

She finished her wine, stood, and looked down at him with the fearlessness he both admired and disliked in her. The light from behind the bar glinted on her glasses. "Tell Cixin what you're going to do. Or I will."

"It's none of your business! I'm his guardian!"

"You've made it my business. And even if you were fully his legal guardian—which you're not, yet—you're not being his friend. Not until you can consider his mind as well as his brain."

"There's no difference, Renata,"

"The hell there isn't. Tell him, Ben. Or I will."

✸

He took a day to think about it, a day during which he was furious with Renata, and longed for her, and addressed angry arguments to her in his mind. Then, reluctantly, he left work in the middle of the afternoon (his boss was beginning to grumble about all the absences) to pick up Cixin at school.

Cixin wasn't there.

Nine: Cixin

The voices came to him as he colored a map of the neighborhood around his school. All week they'd been working on maps, which wasn't as stupid as the other schoolwork. Cixin sat at his desk and vigorously wielded crayons. Playground, 7-Eleven, houses, maglev stop, school building. North, west, legend to tell what the little drawings were. Blue, red, green . . .

Cixin.

He froze, his hand holding the green crayon suspended above his desk.

Cixin.

The voice was faint—but it was there. He looked wildly around the room. He knew the room was there, the other kids were there, he was there. In this school room, not on the beach, and not in that other place where even the beach disappeared and he could feel the Earth and sky breathe. So how could he be hearing . . .

Cix . . . in . . .

"Where are you?" he cried.

"I'm right here," the teacher's aide said. She hurried to Cixin's desk and put a hand on his shoulder.

Cixin . . .

"Come back!" He jumped up, scattering the crayons and knocking away the teacher's hand.

"I haven't gone anywhere," she said soothingly. "I'm right here, dear. What do you need?"

Standing, he could see out the classroom window to the parking lot. Ben's white car pulled in and parked.

Ben was coming for him. Cixin didn't know how he knew that, but he knew. Ben didn't like the voices. Ben was very smart and very American and he knew how to do things, get things, make things happen. Ben was coming for Cixin and Ben was going to make the voices go away forever.

Cixin's mind raced. Ben would have to pass front-door security, go to the school office, get a pass, come down the hall. . . . Cixin didn't hesitate. He ran.

"Cixin!" his teacher called. The other children began shouting. The aide tried to grab Cixin but he twisted away, ran out of the room and down the hall, zigged left, dashed toward the door to the playground. The school doors were locked from the outside but not the inside; Cixin burst through and kept running. Across the playground, over the fence, behind houses to the street . . . *run, fen noon nan hi* . . .

Eventually he had to stop, panting hard, leaning over with his hands on his knees. The houses here were small and didn't go up into the sky like Ben's house. Beyond were stores and eating houses and a gas station. Cixin walked behind a place with the good smell of pizza coming from it. Except for the beach, pizza was the best thing about America. Back here no one in a white car could see him. There was a big metal box with an opening high up.

Climbing on a broken chair, Cixin peered inside the big metal box. Some garbage, not much, and a bad smell, not too bad. He hauled himself up and tumbled inside. The garbage included a lot of pizza boxes, some with half-eaten pizzas inside. And no one could find him.

Many things were clear to him now. Ben saying to Renata, "I'll have to adjust the dosage. He's growing." The way to hear the voices, to go to that other place where he saw everything and breathed with the sky, was by having no once-a-week, and by waiting until the one he took before wasn't in his head anymore. Ben had made him swallow the last once-a-week last Wednesday. This was Tuesday, and already the voices, faint, were there.

He curled up in a corner of the Dumpster to wait.

Ten: Ben

He looked everywhere, the beach first. The day was warm and the sands choked with people who didn't have to be at work, as well as teenagers who probably should have been in school, but no Cixin. Ben raced back to the apartment: nothing. He called the school again, which advised him to call the police. Instead he called Renata's cell; she had no classes Tuesday afternoon.

"I'm very worried about—"

"How did you hear so *fast?*" she demanded.

"What?"

"You're inside, aren't you? Was the TV on at the lab? If there's a basement in your building go there but stay away from the power connections and make sure you can get out easily if there's a fire. We put the bulletin out on campus, but who knows how many won't hear it—twenty minutes! God!"

"What are you talking about?"

"The flare! The solar flare!" And then, "What are *you* talking about?"

"Cixin's missing. He ran away."

"Shit!" And then, very rapidly, "Listen, Ben, another solar flare's been detected, a huge one, I mean *really* huge. Word just came down from the *Hinode*. It's bigger than the 1859 superflare and that one—just *listen*. There's an associated proton storm and nobody knows exactly when it will hit but the one in 2005 accelerated to almost a third of light speed. Best estimate is twenty minutes. There's going to be fires and power outages and communication disruptions but also proton storms that have biological consequences to living tissue that—you can't go down to the beach to look for him now!"

"I've already been. He's not there."

"Then where—"

"I don't know!" Ben shouted. "But I've got to look!"

"Where?" she asked, and her practicality only enraged him more.

"I don't know! But he's out there alone and if there are fires—" The phone went dead.

He stood holding it, this dead and useless piece of technology, listening to the sirens start outside and mount to a frenzied wail. Where could Cixin have gone? Ben knew no place else to look, no place else that Cixin ever went. Although he had liked that V-R arcade Ben had once taken him to . . .

He tore out of the apartment, raced down the stairs, and stopped, frozen.

In the bright sunlight, lights were going out. Traffic lights, the neon window sign at Rosella's Café. They sparked in a glowing electrical arc and went dead. Smoke poured from the windows of a gas station a block over. People stopped, stared, and turned to their cell phones. Ben saw their faces when they realized the cells were all dead.

The sirens grew louder, then all at once stopped.

"What is it?" a young Hispanic woman asked him, clutching his arm. She wore shorts and a green halter top and she wheeled a pram with a fat, gurgling baby.

Ben shook off her hand. "A solar flare, get inside and stay away from windows and appliances!" She let out a great cry of horrified non-understanding but he was already gone, running the several blocks to the V-R arcade.

It took him ten minutes. Cixin wasn't there. The doors yawned crazily open, and a machines in one of the cubicles had shorted and begun to burn.

The city couldn't survive this. The country couldn't survive this. Panic, no communications, fires, the grid gone . . . and the radiation of a proton storm. Ten more minutes.

He found a corner of the arcade farthest from the booths, near the refreshment counter, and crawled under the largest table. It wouldn't help, of course, and it didn't make him feel better. But it was all he could do: wait for the beginning of the end under a wooden picnic table whose underside was stuck with wads of gum from children that might or might not be alive by tomorrow.

Eleven: Cixin

Cixin.

"I'm here," he said aloud, to the empty pizza boxes in the Dumpster. That was kind of funny because the voices didn't speak out loud; they didn't really have words at all. Just a feeling inside his head, and the feeling was him, Cixin. And then a picture:

The whole world, out in space, but covered with such a big gray fog that he couldn't even see the planet. But Cixin knew it was under the fog, and knew too that the voices hadn't known it. Not before. But now they did, because they knew Cixin was here. He was them and they were him and both were everything. It was all the way it should be, and he was calm and safe—he would always be safe now.

Hi, he said and it might have been out loud or not, it was all the same thing.

Twelve: Ben

No other V-R booth shorted and caught fire, although the first one was still smoking. Ben crawled out from under the table. He'd been there half an hour—how long did a proton storm last? He had no idea.

In his pocket, his cell rang.

Ben pulled it out and stared at it incredulously. How . . . After a moment he had the wits to answer.

"Ben! Are you all right?"

Renata. "Yes. No. I don't know, I didn't find Cixin . . . How come this thing works?"

"I don't know." She sounded bewildered. "Mine came on, so I called you . . . Some communications are back. Not where the grid is out or the satellites destroyed, of course, but the radio stations that didn't get hit are coming through clear now and—it isn't possible!"

For the first and only time ever, he heard hysteria in her voice. In *Renata's* voice. "The solar radiation. It . . . it isn't reaching Earth anymore."

"It missed us?"

"No! I mean, yes, apparently . . . before the *Hinode* burned out, it— that's the Japanese spacecraft designed especially to monitor the sun, I told you about it—the data shows—the coronal mass ejection—"

"Renata, you're not making sense." Perversely, her panic steadied him. "Where are you?"

"I'm home. I have a radio. I'm not—it isn't—"

"Stay there. I'll get to you somehow. How much of the city is on fire?"

"Not enough!" she cried, which made no sense. "Did you find Cixin?"

"No." He'd told her that already. Pain scorched his heart. "Stay where you are. I'll call the cops about Cixin and then come."

"You won't get through to the police," she said, her voice still high with that un-Renata-like hysteria.

"I know," he said.

It took him over an hour to walk to her place. He kept trying the cops on his cell until the battery went dead. He skirted fires, looting, police cars, crying people in knots on the sidewalk, but Renata was right: This was not enough damage compared to what he had seen starting in the first few minutes of the solar storm. What the fuck had happened?

"It was deflected," Renata said when he finally got to her apartment. She'd calmed down. The power was off but bright sunlight poured into the window; the battery-powered radio was turned to the federal emergency station; beside the radio lay a gun that Ben had no idea Renata even owned. He stared at the gun while she said, "Cixin?"

"Still no idea."

She locked the door and put her arms around him. "You're bleeding."

"It's nothing, a fuss with some homeless guy that—what does the radio say?"

"Not much." She let him go and turned the volume lower. "The satellites are mostly knocked out, but not all because a few were in high orbit nightside and didn't get here until it . . . stopped."

"*What* stopped?"

"All of it," she said simply. "The radiation, including the proton storm, just curved around the Van Allen Belt and was deflected off into space."

He was no physicist. "That's good, right? Isn't that what the Van Allen is supposed to do? Only . . . only why did the radiation start for a while and *then* stop?"

"Bingo." Abruptly she sat down hard on the sofa. Ben joined her, surprised at how much his legs hurt. "What happened can't happen, Ben. Radiation just doesn't deflect that way by itself. And the magnetic fields contained in the coronal mass ejection were not only really intense, they were in direct opposition with Earth's magnetic field. We should have take a hit like . . . like nothing ever before. Far, far worse than the superstorm of 1859. And we didn't. In fact, protons should still be entering the atmosphere. And they aren't."

He tried to understand, despite the anxiety swamping him for Cixin. "Why isn't that all happening?"

"Nobody knows."

"Well, what does the radio say?"

She flung out her hands. "Unknown quantum forces. Angels. Aliens. God. Secret government shields. Don't you understand . . . *nobody knows*. This just can't be happening."

But it was. Ben said wearily, "Where do you think I should look next for Cixin?"

They found him two days later. It took that long for basic city services to begin to resume and for anyone to approach the Dumpster. Cixin was catatonic, dehydrated, bitten by rats. He was taken to the overburdened hospital. Ben was called when a nurse discovered Cixin's name and phone number sewn into the waistband of his jeans—Renata's idea. He found Cixin rigid on a gurney parked in a hallway jammed with more patients. He had an IV, a catheter, and multiple bandages. His eyes were empty.

Ben put the inhibitor on Cixin's tongue. Slowly Cixin woke up, his dark eyes over sunken cheeks turning reproachful. Ben yelled for a doctor, but no one came.

"Cixin."

"They . . . didn't . . . know," he croaked.

"It's okay, buddy, I'm here now, it's okay . . . Who didn't know what?"

But painfully Cixin turned his face to the wall and would say no more.

The staff wanted to do a psych evaluation. Ben argued. They turned stubborn. Eventually he said they could get a court order if they wanted to but for right now he was taking his boy home as soon as the treatment for dehydration was completed. The harassed hospital official said several harsh things and promised legal action. A day later Ben signed out Cixin AMA, against medical advice, and drove him home through streets returning to normal much faster than anyone had thought possible.

There was a dreary familiarity to the scene: Cixin asleep in his room, Ben and Renata with drinks in the living room, talking about him. How many times in the last few months had they done this? How many more to come?

Renata had just come from the small bedroom. She'd asked to talk to Cixin alone. "He won't tell you anything," Ben had warned, but she'd gone in anyway. Now she sat, pale and purse-lipped, on Ben's sofa, holding her drink as if it were an alien object.

"Did he tell you anything?" Ben said tiredly. He stood by the window, facing her.

"Yes. No. Just what he told you—'They didn't know' and 'Let me go back.' Plus one other thing."

"What?" Jealousy, perverse and ridiculous, prodded him: Cixin had talked more freely to her than to him.

"He said there was a big explosion, a long time ago."

"A big explosion?"

"A long time ago."

That hardly seemed useful. Ben said, "I don't know what to do. I just don't."

Renata hesitated. "Ben . . . do you remember when we met? At Grogan's?"

"Yes, of course—why wouldn't I? Why bring that up now?"

"I was correcting papers, remember? My students were supposed to answer questions about Wheeler's two-slit experiments."

Ben stared at her. She was very pale and her expression was strange, both hesitant and wide-eyed, completely unlike Renata. "I remember," he said. "So?"

"The original 1927 two-slit experiment showed that a photon could be seen as both a wave and a particle that—"

"Don't insult my intelligence," Ben snapped, and wondered at whom his nasty tone was aimed. He tried again. "Of course I know that. And your students were writing about Wheeler's demonstration that observation determines the outcome of which one a photon registers as."

"The presence or absence of observation also determines the results of a whole slew of other physics experiments," she said. "All right, you know all that. But *why*?"

"Feynman's probability wave equations—"

"Explain exactly nothing! They describe the phenomenon, they quantify it, but they don't explain why *observation*, which essentially means human consciousness, should be so woven into the very fabric of the universe at its most basic level. Until humans observe anything fundamental, in a very real sense it doesn't exist. It's only a smear of unresolved probability. So why does consciousness give form to the entire universe?"

"I don't know. Why?"

"I don't know either. But I think Cixin does."

Ben stared at her.

Renata looked down at the drink in her hand. Her shoulders trembled. "The explosion Cixin said he saw in his mind—he said, 'It made everything.' I think he was talking about the Big Bang. I think he feels a presence of some kind when he's in his catatonic state. That whatever genemods he has, they've somehow opened up parts of his mind that in the rest of us are closed."

Ben put his glass down carefully on the coffee table and sat beside her on the sofa. "Renata, he does feel a presence. He's experiencing decreased blood flow in the posterior superior parietal lobes, which define body borders. He loses those borders when he goes into his trance. And very rapid firing in the tempoparietal region can lead to the sense of an 'other' or presence in the brain. Cixin's consciousness gets caught in neural feedback loops in both those areas—which are, incidentally, the same areas of the brain that SPECT images highlight in Buddhist monks who are meditating. What Cixin feels is real to him—but that doesn't make it real in the cosmos. Doesn't make it a . . . a . . . ."

"Overmind," she said. "Cosmic consciousness. I don't know what to call it. But I think it's there, and I think it's woven into the universe at some deeply fundamental level, and I think Cixin was accidentally given a heightened ability to be in contact with it."

Ben said, "I don't know what to say."

"Don't say anything. Just think about it. I'm going home now, Ben. I can't take anymore tonight."

Neither could he. He was flabbergasted, dismayed, even horrified by what she'd said. How could she believe such mystical bullshit? He didn't know who she was anymore.

It wasn't until hours later that, unable to sleep, he realized that Renata also thought her "cosmic consciousness" had diverted the solar flare radiation away from Earth in order to protect Cixin.

Thirteen: Cixin

Cixin sat in his bedroom, cross-legged on the bed. His iPod lay beside him, but he wasn't listening to it, hadn't listened to it for the past week. Nor had he gone to school, played video games, or sent email to Xiao. He was just waiting.

Xiao—he would miss her. Ben had been very good to him, and so had Renata, but he knew he wouldn't miss them. That was bad, maybe, but it was true.

Maybe Xiao would come one day, too. After all, if the voices were everything, and they were him, then they should be Xiao, too, right? But Xiao couldn't hear them. Ben couldn't hear them. Renata couldn't hear them. Only Cixin could, and probably not until tomorrow. And this time . . .

The nurse hired to watch him while he was "sick" looked up from her magazine, smiled, and turned another page. Cixin didn't hate her. He was surprised he didn't hate her, but she couldn't help being stupid. Anymore than Ben could help it, or Renata, or Xiao. They didn't know.

Cixin knew.

And when he felt the calm steal over him, felt himself expand outward, he knew the voices would be early and that was so good!

Cixin.

Yes, he said, but only inside his mind, where the nurse couldn't hear.

Come.

Yes, he thought, because that was right, that was where he belonged. With the voices. But there was something to do first.

He made a picture in his mind, the same picture he'd seen once before, the whole Earth wrapped in a gray fog. He made the sun shining brightly, and a ray gun shooting from the sun to the Earth, the way

Renata had described it to him. The picture said POW!! Like a video game. Then he made the ray gun go away.

Yes, formed in his mind. *We'll watch over them.*

Cixin sighed happily. Then he became everything and went home, to where he knew, beyond any need to race around or yell at people or be *fen noon nan hi,* who he really was.

He never heard the nurse cry out.

Fourteen: Ben

She came to him through the bright sunshine, hurrying down the cement path, her dirty blond curls hidden by a black hat. The black dress made her look out of place. This was Southern California; people wore black only for gala parties, not for funerals. But Renata, his numb and weary mind irrelevantly remembered, came originally from Ohio.

Ben turned his back on her.

She wasn't fooled. Somehow she knew that he hadn't turned away from not wanting her there, but from wanting her there too much. No one else stood beside the grave. Ben hadn't told his family about Cixin's death, and he'd discouraged his few friends from attending. And they, bewildered to learn only after the death that anti-social Ben had been adopting a child, nodded and murmured empty consolations. And then, of course, there were the sunspots. A second coronal mass ejection had occurred just yesterday, and everyone was jumpy.

"Ben, I just heard and I'm so sorry," Renata said. From her, the words didn't sound so empty. Her eyes held tears, and the hand she put on his arm held a tenderness he badly needed but wouldn't allow himself to take.

"Thank you," he said stiffly. If she even alluded to all that other nonsense. . . . And of course, being Renata, she did. "I know you loved him. And you did the best you could for him—I know that, too. But maybe he's where he wanted to be."

"Can it, Renata."

"All right. Will you come have coffee with me now?"

He looked down. So small a coffin. Two cemetery employees waited, trying not to look impatient, to lower the coffin into its hole, cover it up, and get back inside. To their eyes, this was a non-funeral: no mourners, no minister or priest or rabbi, only this one dour man reading from a book that wasn't even holy.

"Please," Renata said. "You shouldn't stay here, love."

He let himself be led away. Behind him the men began to work with feverish speed.

"They're afraid," he said. "Idiots."

"Not everybody can understand science, Ben." Then, shockingly, she laughed. He knew why, but she clapped one hand over her mouth. "I'm so sorry!"

"Forget it."

Not everybody could understand science, no. In Ben's experience, almost nobody even tried. Half the population still equated evolution with the devil. But the president had made a speech on TV last night and another one this morning: *The new solar flare presents no danger. There will be no repeat of last week's crisis. The radiation is not reaching Earth.* Wisely, she had not tried to say why the radiation was not reaching Earth. Nor why the astronauts on *Hope of Heaven*, the Chinese space shuttle, had not been fried in orbit. *No danger* was as far as the president could go. It was already like crossing into Wonderland.

Ben and Renata walked to his Saab. If she'd parked her own car somewhere in the cemetery, as she must have, she seemed willing to leave it. Gently she took the book from his hands and studied the cover.

"I'm not giving in," he said, too harshly.

"I know."

"If there really were . . . 'more,' were really something that could be reached, contacted, by more or different brain connections—then what evolutionary gain could have made humanity lose it? Was it too distracting, interfering with survival? Too calming? Too *what*?"

"I don't know."

"It doesn't make sense," Ben said. "And if it really were genetic, really were that the rest of us aren't making enough of some chemicals or connective tissues or . . . I just can't believe it, Renata."

"I know."

He wished she would stop saying that. She handed back to him James Behren's *Quantum Physics and Consciousness*, but he knew she'd already seen the page he'd dog-eared and underlined. She already knew that over the grave of Cixin, who could barely decipher any language, Ben had read aloud about two-slit and delayed-choice and particle-detector experiments. Renata knew, always, everything.

"Maybe," she said after a long silence, "if they know now that the rest of us possess consciousness, however rudimentary, not just Cixin . . . if they know that, then maybe someday . . ."

She could never just leave anything alone. That's who she was. Ben shifted the book to his other hand and put an arm around her.

"No," he said. "Not possible."

This time she didn't answer. But she leaned against him and they walked out of the cemetery together, under the bright blue empty sky.

END GAME

Allen Dodson was sitting in seventh-grade math class, staring at the back of Peggy Corcoran's head, when he had the insight that changed the world. First his own world and then, eventually, like dominos toppling in predestined rhythm, everybody else's, until nothing could ever be the same again. Although we didn't, of course, know that back then.

The source of the insight was Peggy Corcoran. Allen had sat behind her since third grade (Anderson, Blake, Corcoran, Dodson, DuQuesne . . .) and never thought her remarkable. Nor was she. It was 1982 and Peggy wore a David Bowie T-shirt and straggly brown braids. But now, staring at the back of her mousy hair, Allen suddenly realized that Peggy's head must be a sloppy mess of skittering thoughts and contradictory feelings and half-buried longings—*just as his was*. Nobody was what they seemed to be!

The realization actually made his stomach roil. In books and movies, characters had one thought at a time: *"Elementary, my dear Watson." "An offer he couldn't refuse." "Beam me up, Scotty!"* But Allen's own mind, when he tried to watch it, was different. *Ten more minutes of class I'm hungry gotta pee the answer is x+6 you moron what would it be like to kiss Linda Wilson M*A*S*H on tonight really gotta pee locker stuck today Linda eight more minutes do the first sixteen problems baseball after school—*

No. Not even close. He would have to include his mind watching those thoughts and then his thoughts about the watching thoughts and then—

And Peggy Corcoran was doing all that, too.

And Linda Wilson.

And Jeff Gallagher.

And Mr. Henderson, standing at the front of math class.

And everyone in the world, all with thoughts zooming through their heads fast as electricity, thoughts bumping into each other and fighting

160

each other and blotting each other out, a mess inside every mind on the whole Earth, nothing sensible or orderly or predictable . . . Why, right this minute Mr. Henderson could be thinking terrible things even as he assigned the first sixteen problems on page 145, terrible things about Allen even or Mr. Henderson could be thinking about his lunch or hating teaching or planning a murder . . . *You could never know.* No one was settled or simple, nothing could be *counted on* . . .

Allen had to be carried, screaming, from math class.

I didn't learn any of this until decades later, of course. Allen and I weren't friends, even though we sat across the aisle from each other (Edwards, Farr, Fitzgerald, Gallagher . . .). And after the screaming fit, I thought he was just as weird as everyone else thought. I never taunted Allen like some of the boys, or laughed at him like the girls, and a part of me was actually interested in the strange things he sometimes said in class, always looking as if he had no idea how peculiar he sounded. But I wasn't strong enough to go against the herd and make friends with such a loser.

The summer before Allen went off to Harvard, we did become—if not friends—then chess companions. "You play rotten, Jeff," Allen said to me with his characteristic, oblivious candor, "but nobody else plays at all." So two or three times a week we sat on his parents' screened porch and battled it out on the chess board. I never won. Time after time I slammed out of the house in frustration and shame, vowing not to return. After all, unlike wimpy Allen, I had better things to do with my time: girls, cars, James Bond movies. But I always went back.

Allen's parents were, I thought even back then, a little frightened by their son's intensity. Mild, hard-working people fond of golf, they pretty much left Allen alone from his fifteenth birthday on. As we moved rooks and knights around the chess board in the gathering darkness of the porch, Allen's mother would timidly offer a pitcher of lemonade and a plate of cookies. She treated both of us with an uneasy respect that, in turn, made me uneasy. That wasn't how parents were supposed to behave.

Harvard was a close thing for Allen, despite his astronomical SATs. His grades were spotty because he only did the work in courses he was interested in, and his medical history was even spottier: bouts of depression when he didn't attend school, two brief hospitalizations in a psychiatric ward. Allen would get absorbed by something—chess, quantum physics, Buddhism—to the point where he couldn't stop, until all at once his interest vanished as if it had never existed. Harvard had, I thought in my eighteen-year-old wisdom, every reason to be wary. But Allen was a National Merit scholar, and when he won the Westinghouse science competition for his work on cranial structures in voles, Harvard took him.

The night before he left, we had our last chess match. Allen opened with the conservative Italian game, which told me he was slightly distracted. Twelve moves in, he suddenly said, "Jeff, what if you could tidy up your thoughts, the way you tidy up your room every night?"

"Do what?" My mother "tidied up" my room, and what kind of weirdo used words like that, anyway?

He ignored me. "It's sort of like static, isn't it? All those stray thoughts in a mind, interfering with a clear broadcast. Yeah, that's the right analogy. Without the static, we could all think clearer. Cleaner. We could see farther before the signal gets lost in uncontrolled noise."

In the gloom of the porch, I could barely see his pale, broad-cheeked face. But I had a sudden insight, rare for me that summer. "Allen—is that what happened to you that time in seventh grade? Too much . . . static?"

"Yeah." He didn't seem embarrassed, unlike anybody normal. It was as if embarrassment was too insignificant for this subject. "That was the first time I saw it. For a long time I thought if I could learn to meditate—you know, like Buddhist monks—I could get rid of the static. But meditation doesn't go far enough. The static is still there, you're just not paying attention to it anymore. But it's still there." He moved his bishop.

"What exactly happened in the seventh grade?" I found myself intensely curious, which I covered by staring at the board and making a move.

He told me, still unembarrassed, in exhaustive detail. Then he added, "It should be possible to adjust brain chemicals to eliminate the static. To unclutter the mind. It should!"

"Well," I said, dropping from insight to my more usual sarcasm, "maybe you'll do it at Harvard, if you don't get sidetracked by some weird shit like ballet or model railroads."

"Checkmate," Allen said.

I lost track of him after that summer, except for the lengthy Bakersville High School Alumni Notes faithfully mailed out every single year by Linda Wilson, who must have had some obsessive/compulsiveness of her own. Allen went on to Harvard Medical School. After graduation he was hired by a prestigious pharmaceutical company and published a lot of scientific articles about topics I couldn't pronounce. He married, divorced, married again, divorced again. Peggy Corcoran, who married my cousin Joe and who knew Allen's second wife, told me at my father's funeral that both ex-wives said the same thing about Allen: He was never emotionally present.

I saw him for myself at our twentieth-fifth reunion. He looked surprisingly the same: thin, broad-faced, pale. He stood alone in a corner, looking so pathetic that I dragged Karen over to him. "Hey, Allen. Jeff Gallagher."

"I know."

"This is my wife, Karen."

He smiled at her but said nothing. Karen, both outgoing and compassionate, started a flow of small talk, but Allen shut her off in midsentence. "Jeff, you still play chess?"

"Neither *Karen* nor I play now," I said pointedly.

"Oh. There's someone I want you to see, Jeff. Can you come to the lab tomorrow?"

The "lab" was sixty miles away, in the city, and I had to work the next day. But something about the situation had captured my wife's eclectic and sharply intelligent interest. She said, "What is it, Allen, if you don't mind my asking?"

"I don't mind. It's a chess player. I think she might change the world."

"You mean the big important chess world?" I said. Near Allen, all my teenage sarcasm had returned.

"No. The whole world. Please come, Jeff."

"What time?" Karen said.

"Karen—I have a job."

"Your hours are flexible," she said, which was true. I was a real estate agent, working from home. She smiled at me with all her wicked sparkle. "I'm sure it will be fascinating."

Lucy Hartwick, twenty-five years old, was tall, slender, and very pretty. I saw Karen, who unfortunately inclined to jealousy, glance at me. But I wasn't attracted to Lucy. There was something cold about her beauty. She barely glanced up at us from a computer in Allen's lab, and her gaze was indifferent. The screen displayed a chess game.

"Lucy's rating, as measured by computer games anyway, is 2670," Allen said.

"So?" Two thousand six hundred and seventy was extremely high; only twenty or so players in the world held ratings above 2700. But I was still in sarcastic mode, even as I castigated myself for childishness.

Allen said, "Six months ago her rating was 1400."

"So six months since she first leaned to play, right?" We were talking about Lucy, bent motionless above the chess board, as if she weren't even present.

"No, she had played twice a week for five years."

That kind of ratings jump for someone with mediocre talent who hadn't studied chess several hours a day for years—it just didn't happen. Karen said, "Good for you, Lucy!" Lucy glanced up blankly, then returned to her board.

I said, "And so just how is this supposed to change the world?"

"Come look at this," Allen said. Without looking back, he strode toward the door.

I was getting tired of his games, but Karen followed him, so I followed her. Eccentricity has always intrigued Karen, perhaps because she's so balanced, so sane, herself. It was one reason I fell in love with her.

Allen held out a mass of graphs, charts, and medical scans as if he expected me to read them. "See, Jeff, these are all Lucy, taken when she's playing chess. The caudate nucleus, which aids the mind in switching gears from one thought to another, shows low activity. So does the thalamus, which processes sensory input. And here, in the—"

"I'm a Realtor, Allen," I said, more harshly than I intended. "What does all this garbage *mean?*"

Allen looked at me and said simply, "She's done it. Lucy has. She's learned to eliminate the static."

"What static?" I said, even though I remembered perfectly our conversation of twenty-five years ago.

"You mean," said Karen, always a quick study, "that Lucy can concentrate on one thing at a time without getting distracted?"

"I just said so, didn't I?" Allen said. "Lucy Hartwick has control of her own mind. When she plays chess, that's *all* she's doing. As a result, she's now equal to the top echelons of the chess world."

"But she hasn't actually played any of those top players, has she?" I argued. "This is just your estimate based on her play against some computer."

"Same thing," Allen said.

"It is not!"

Karen peered in surprise at my outrage. "Jeff—"

Allen said, "Yes, Jeff, listen to Carol. Don't—"

"'Karen'!"

"—you understand? Lucy's somehow achieved *total* concentration. That lets her just . . . just soar ahead in understanding of the thing she chooses to focus on. Don't you understand what this could mean for medical research? For . . . for any field at all? We could solve global warming and cancer and toxic waste and . . . and everything!"

As far as I knew, Allen had never been interested in global warming, and a sarcastic reply rose to my lips. But either Allen's face or Karen's hand on my arm stopped me. She said gently, "That could be wonderful, Allen."

"It will be!" he said with all the fervor of his seventh-grade fit. "It will be!"

"What was that all about?" Karen said in the car on our way home.

"Oh, that was just Allen being—"

"Not Allen. You."

"Me?" I said, but even I knew my innocence didn't ring true.

"I've never seen you like that. You positively sneered at him, and for what might actually be an enormous break-through in brain chemistry."

"It's just a theory, Karen! Ninety percent of theories collapse as soon as anyone runs controlled experiments."

"But you, Jeff . . . you *want* this one to collapse."

I twisted in the driver's seat to look at her face. Karen stared straight ahead, her pretty lips set as concrete. My first instinct was to bluster . . . but not with Karen.

"I don't know," I said quietly. "Allen has always brought out the worst in me, for some reason. Maybe . . . maybe I'm jealous."

A long pause, while I concentrated as hard as I could on the road ahead. Yellow divider, do not pass, 35 mph, pothole ahead . . .

Then Karen's hand rested lightly on my shoulder, and the world was all right again.

After that I kept in sporadic touch with Allen. Two or three times a year I'd phone and we'd talk for fifteen minutes. Or, rather, Allen would talk and I'd listen, struggling with irritability. He never asked about me or Karen. He talked exclusively about his research into various aspects of Lucy Hartwick: her spinal and cranial fluid, her neural firing patterns, her blood and tissue cultures. He spoke of her as if she were no more than a collection of biological puzzles he was determined to solve, and I couldn't imagine what their day-to-day interactions were like. For some reason I didn't understand, I didn't tell Karen about these conversations.

That was the first year. The following June, things changed. Allen's reports—because that's what they were, reports and not conversations—became non-stop complaints.

"The FDA is taking forever to pass my IND application. Forever!"

I figured out that "IND" meant "initial new drug," and that it must be a green light for his Lucy research.

"And Lucy has become impossible. She's hardly ever available when I need her, trotting off to chess tournaments around the world. As if chess mattered as much as my work on her!"

I remembered the long-ago summer when chess mattered to Allen himself more than anything else in the world.

"I'm just frustrated by the selfishness and the bureaucracy and the politics."

"Yes," I said.

"And doesn't Lucy understand how important this could be? The incredible potential for improving the world?"

"Evidently not," I said, with mean satisfaction that I disliked myself for. To compensate I said, "Allen, why don't you take a break and come out here for dinner some night. Doesn't a break help with scientific thinking? Lead sometimes to real insights?"

I could feel, even over the phone line, that he'd been on the point of refusal, but my last two sentences stopped him. After a moment he said, "Oh, all right, if you want me to," so ungraciously that it seemed he was granting me an inconvenient favor. Right then, I knew that the dinner was going to be a disaster.

And it was, but not as much as it would have been without Karen. She didn't take offense when Allen refused to tour her beloved garden. She said nothing when he tasted things and put them down on the tablecloth, dropped bits of food as he chewed, slobbered on the rim of his glass. She listened patiently to Allen's two-hour monologue, nodding and making encouraging little noises. Toward the end her eyes did glaze a bit, but she never lost her poise and wouldn't let me lose mine, either.

"It's a disgrace" Allen ranted, "the FDA is hobbling all productive research with excessive caution for—do you know what would happen if Jenner had needed FDA approval for his vaccines? We'd all still have smallpox, that's what! If Louis Pasteur—"

"Why don't you play chess with Jeff?" Karen said when the meal finally finished. "While I clear away here."

I exhaled in relief. Chess was played in silence. Moreover, Karen would be stuck with cleaning up after Allen's appalling table manners.

"I'm not interested in chess anymore," Allen said. "Anyway, I have to get back to the lab. Not that Lucy kept her appointment for tests on . . . she's wasting my time in Turkistan or someplace. Bye. Thanks for dinner."

"Don't invite him again, Jeff," Karen said to me after Allen left. "Please."

"I won't. You were great, sweetheart."

Later, in bed, I did that thing she likes and I don't, by way of saying thank you. Halfway through, however, Karen pushed me away. "I only like it when you're really *here*," she said. "Tonight you're just not focusing on us at all."

After she went to sleep, I crept out of bed and turned on the computer in my study. The heavy fragrance of Karen's roses drifted through the window screen. Lucy Hartwick was in Turkmenistan, playing in the Chess Olympiad in Ashgabat. Various websites detailed her rocketing rise to the top of the chess world. Articles about her all mentioned that she never socialized with her own or any other team, preferred to eat all her meals alone in her hotel room, and never smiled. I studied the accompanying pictures, trying to see what had happened to Lucy's beauty.

She was still slender and long-legged. The lovely features were still there, although obscured by her habitual pose while studying a chess board: hunched over from the neck like a turtle, with two fingers in her slightly open mouth. I had seen that pose somewhere before, but I couldn't remember where. It wasn't appealing, but the loss of Lucy's good looks came from something else. Even for a chess player, the concentration on her face was formidable. It wiped out any hint of any other emotion whatsoever. Good poker players do that, too, but not in quite this way. Lucy looked not quite human.

Or maybe I just thought that because of my complicated feelings about Allen.

At 2:00 a.m. I sneaked back into bed, glad that Karen hadn't woken while I was gone.

"She's gone!" Allen cried over the phone, a year later. "She's just gone!"

"Who?" I said, although of course I knew. "Allen, I can't talk now, I have a client coming into the office two minutes from now."

"You have to come down here!"

"Why?" I had ducked all of Allen's calls ever since that awful dinner, changing my home phone to an unlisted number and letting my secretary turn him away at work. I'd only answered now because I was expecting a call from Karen about the time for our next marriage counseling session. Things weren't as good as they used to be. Not really bad, just clouds blocking what used to be steady marital sunshine. I wanted to dispel those clouds before they turned into major thunderstorms.

"You have to come," Allen repeated, and he started to sob.

Embarrassed, I held the phone away from my ear. Grown men didn't cry like that, not to other men. All at once I realized why Allen wanted me to come to the lab: because he had no other human contact at all.

"Please, Jeff," Allen whispered, and I snapped, "Okay!"

"Mr. Gallagher, your clients are here," Brittany said at the doorway, and I tried to compose a smile and a good lie.

And after all that, Lucy Hartwick wasn't even gone. She sat in Allen's lab, hunched over a chess board with two fingers in her mouth, just as I had seen her a year ago on the Web.

"What the hell—Allen, you *said*—"

Unpredictable as ever, he had calmed down since calling me. Now he handed me a sheaf of printouts and medical photos. I flashed back suddenly to the first time I'd come to this lab, when Allen had also thrust on me documents I couldn't read. He just didn't learn.

"Her white matter has shrunk another seventy-five percent since I saw her last," Allen said, as though that were supposed to convey something to me.

"You said Lucy was gone!"

"She is."

"She's sitting right there!"

Allen looked at me. I had the impression that the simple act required enormous effort on his part, like a man trying to drag himself free of a concrete block to which he was chained. He said, "I was always jealous of you, you know."

It staggered me. My mouth opened but Allen had already moved back to the concrete block. "Just look at these brain scans, seventy-five percent less white matter in six months! And these neurotransmitter levels, they—"

"Allen," I said. Sudden cold had seized my heart. "Stop." But he babbled on about the caudate nucleus and antibodies attacking the basal ganglia and bi-directional rerouting.

I walked over to Lucy and lifted her chessboard off the table.

Immediately she rose and continued playing variations on the board in my arms. I took several steps backward; she followed me, still playing. I hurled the board into the hall, slammed the door, and stood with my back to it. I was six-one and 190 pounds; Lucy wasn't even half that. In fact, she appeared to have lost weight, so that her slimness had turned gaunt.

She didn't try to fight me. Instead she returned to her table, sat down, and stuck two fingers in her mouth.

"She's playing in her head, isn't she," I said to Allen.

"Yes."

"What does 'white matter' do?"

"It contains axons which connect neurons in the cerebral cortex to neurons in other parts of the brain, thereby facilitating intercranial communication." Allen sounded like a textbook.

"You mean, it lets some parts of the brain talk to other parts?"

"Well, that's only a crude analogy, but—"

"It lets different thoughts from different parts of the brain reach each other," I said, still staring at Lucy. "It makes you aware of more than one thought at a time."

Static.

Allen began a long technical explanation, but I wasn't listening. I remembered now where I'd seen that pose of Lucy's, head pushed forward and two fingers in her mouth, drooling. It had been in an artist's rendering of Queen Elizabeth I in her final days, immobile and unreachable, her mind already gone in advance of her dying body.

"*Lucy's gone,*" Allen had said. He knew.

"Allen, what baseball team did Babe Ruth play for?"

He babbled on about neurotransmitters.

"What was Bobby Fisher's favorite opening move?" Silently I begged him, *Say e4, damn it.*

He talked about the brain waves of concentrated meditation.

"Did you know that a tsunami will hit Manhattan tomorrow?"

He urged overhaul of FDA clinical-trial design.

I said, as quietly as I could manage, "You have it, too, don't you. You injected yourself with whatever concoction the FDA wouldn't approve, or you took it as a pill, or something. You wanted Lucy's static-free state, like some fucking *dryer sheet*, and so you gave this to yourself from her. And now neither one of you can switch focus at all." The call to me had been Allen's last, desperate foray out of his perfect concentration on this project. No—that hadn't been the last.

I took him firmly by the shoulders. "Allen, what did you mean when you said 'I was always jealous of you'?"

He blathered on about MRI results.

"Allen—please tell me what you meant!"

But he couldn't. And now I would never know.

I called the front desk of the research building. I called 911. Then I called Karen, needing to hear her voice, needing to connect with her. But she didn't answer her cell, and the office said she'd left her desk to go home early.

Both Allen and Lucy were hospitalized briefly, then released. I never heard the diagnosis, although I suspect it involved an "inability to perceive and relate to social interactions" or some such psychobabble. Doesn't play well with others. Runs with scissors. Lucy and Allen demonstrated they could physically care for themselves by doing it, so the hospital let them go. Business professionals, I hear, mind their money for them, order their physical lives. Allen has just published another brilliant paper, and Lucy Hartwick is the first female World Chess Champion.

Karen said, "They're happy, in their own way. If their single-minded focus on their passions makes them oblivious to anything else—well, so what. Maybe that's the price for genius."

"Maybe," I said, glad that she was talking to me at all. There hadn't been much conversation lately. Karen had refused any more marriage counseling and had turned silent, escaping me by working in the garden. Our roses are the envy of the neighborhood. We have Tuscan Sun, Ruffled Cloud, Mister Lincoln, Crown Princess, Golden Zest. English roses, hybrid teas, floribunda, groundcover roses, climbers, shrubs. They glow scarlet, pink, antique apricot, deep gold, delicate coral. Their combined scent nauseates me.

I remember the exact moment that happened. We were in the garden, Karen kneeling beside a flower bed, a wide hat shading her face from the sun so that I couldn't see her eyes.

"Karen," I said, trying to mask my desperation, "Do you still love me?"

"Hand me that trowel, will you, Jeff?"

"Karen! Please! Can we talk about what's happening to us?"

"The Tahitian Sunsets are going to be glorious this year."

I stared at her, at the beads of sweat on her upper lip, the graceful arc of her neck, her happy smile.

Karen clearing away Allen's dinner dishes, picking up his sloppily dropped food. Lucy with two fingers in her mouth, studying her chess board and then touching the pieces.

No. Not possible.

Karen reached for the trowel herself, as if she'd forgotten I was there.

Lucy Hartwick lost her championship to a Russian named Dmitri Chertov. A geneticist at Stamford made a breakthrough in cancer research so important that it grabbed all headlines for nearly a week. By a coincidence that amused the media, his young daughter won the Scripps Spelling Bee. I looked up the geneticist on the Internet; a year ago he'd attended a scientific conference with Allen. A woman in Oregon, some New Age type, developed the ability to completely control her brain waves through profound meditation. Her husband is a chess grandmaster.

I walk a lot now, when I'm not cleaning or cooking or shopping. Karen quit her job; she barely leaves the garden even to sleep. I kept my job, although I take fewer clients. As I walk, I think about the ones I do have, mulling over various houses they might like. I watch the August trees begin to tinge with early yellow, ponder overheard snatches of conversation, talk to dogs. My walks get longer and longer, and I notice that I've started to time my speed, to become interested in running shoes, to investigate transcontinental walking routes.

But I try not to think about walking too much. I observe children at frenetic play during the last of their summer vacation, recall movies I once liked, wonder at the intricacies of quantum physics, anticipate what I'll cook for lunch. Sometimes I sing. I recite the few snatches of poetry I learned as a child, relive great football games, chat with old ladies on their porches, add up how many calories I had for breakfast. Sometimes I even mentally rehearse basic chess openings: the Vienna Game or the Petroff Defense. I let whatever thoughts come that will, accepting them all.

Listening to the static, because I don't know how much longer I've got.

IMAGES OF ANNA

The morning was turning out to be a bust. The first client wanted to pay with a personal check, which I've learned to not accept. She had no cash, credit card, or ID. The second client had cash but turned out to be a thirteen-year-old kid who wanted a "really sexy picture" for her boyfriend. No way: session cancelled. The third client was late.

"The electric bill is overdue," Carol said conversationally. She rearranged her table of cosmetics, hair extensions, and earrings, none of which needed rearranging. Carol was easily bored. I was easily panicked. Not a good business combination, and Glamorous You was barely hanging on. In Boston even the rent for a small, third-floor walk-up is expensive.

Carol riffled idly through the hanging rack of negligees, gowns, and filmy scarves for clients that don't bring their own stuff. Glamorous You doesn't do cheesecake: no nude, bra-and-panties, or implied-masturbation shots. The costumes are fun but not raunchy; the negligees are opaque. I'm good with lighting, and Carol is a whiz at makeup and hair. We make our customers look more desirable than they'll ever look in real life, but still decent. That's why the electric bill was overdue.

"What's this client's name again?" I said.

Carol consulted her booking calendar, which featured a lot of white space. "Anna Somebody—here she comes now." The door opened.

"Hello," the client said. "I'm sorry I'm late."

I blinked. We get a lot of older women, although not usually this old. Maybe fifty, fifty-five, she had a brown pageboy considerably darker than her gray eyebrows, twenty extra pounds, and a sagging neck. But that wasn't it. She just wasn't a Glamorous You type. Brown slacks, baggy white blouse, brown tweed blazer, all worn with gumball-pink lipstick and small pearl earrings. She looked like she should be heading up a grant-writing committee somewhere.

173

"Anna O'Connor," she said, holding out her hand. "Are you Ben Preston?"

"Yes. Nice to meet you. My assistant, Carol."

"Hi, Carol."

She had a nice smile. Looking closer, I could see the regular features under the wrinkles, the good cheekbones, the nice teeth. This woman had been attractive once, in a bland girl-next-door way. Didn't she realize how much time had passed?

She did. "Let me tell you what I'm after here, Ben. I'm not young or gorgeous, and I don't want to pretend I am. I just want to look as good as a fifty-seven-year-old can without looking like beef dressed as veal. Or sending your camera into mechanical heart failure." She laughed, light and self-mocking, without strain. I liked her.

"I think we can do that, Anna—may I call you Anna?"

"Please."

"We offer three settings: a bed, arm chair, or wind machine against an outdoor backdrop. Which would you prefer?"

"The armchair, please."

No surprise there. While I set up the shot, Carol did prep and they picked out a costume. When Anna emerged from the dressing room, I was agreeably surprised. Carol had darkened Anna's eyebrows, shadowed her eyes, exchanged the kiddie-pink lipstick for a rich brown-red. Her hair had lost its helmet look and had some volume and swing. Anna had chosen not the Victorian gown I'd expected but rather a floor-length, emerald-green robe that skimmed over waist and hips but revealed her still-good cleavage. She looked terrific. Not like a model, of course, nor youthful, but still feminine and appealing.

"You look great," I said, glad to mean it for once.

"I think that's mostly due to Carol," Anna said, with that same light self-mockery. She seemed at ease in her own ageing skin. No rings on her hand, and I wondered whom the negligee photo was intended for.

"All right, if you'll just sit in or stand by the arm chair . . . however you feel comfortable. You just—hold it!"

She was a natural. All her poses were sexy without being parodies, and her refusal to take herself seriously came through in her body language. The result was sensuality as light-hearted fun. As I shot her from several different angles, I enjoyed myself more than I had photographing younger, prettier women. We bantered and laughed. When the shoot was done and Anna had changed back into her own clothes—but had not, I was glad to see, washed off Carol's makeup—I broke my own rule and asked her.

"And the picture will be for . . ."

"Boyfriend," she said, embarrassed. "That's such a silly word at my age, but all the other words are even sillier. Beau? Main squeeze? Gentleman caller?" She pantomimed an Edwardian curtsey and laughed.

"Well, he's a lucky guy," I said. Carol stared at me. I never got personal with clients—too much chance for misinterpretation. But Anna was old enough to be my mother, for Chrissake. "Will he come with you to choose the shot? Or is the photo a surprise?"

"A surprise. Besides, he lives in Montana. We met online."

My good mood collapsed. I'd wanted this to be something positive. But she was just one more older woman being strung along by some Internet Lothario getting his rocks off by feeding on attention from lonely and desperate women. Best case scenario: He hadn't asked her for money. Yet.

"Ben, it's not like that," Anna said, looking at my face. "I've met him in person. He's visited here twice. You're sweet to be concerned, but I can take care of myself."

"Right," I said. "So you'll come back Thursday to see the proofs."

"See you then."

When she'd paid me and left, Carol said, "Lighten up, Ben. Not every woman is as stupid as Laurie was."

I turned away. Since we had no more clients booked for today, Carol left. I went into the darkroom and developed Anna's pictures.

And just like that, reality fell apart.

Film is not digital. There's no chance to lose bytes in the bowels of a computer, to merge files, to have information corrupted by malfunctions or cosmic rays or viruses. Film is physically contained on a discrete roll. The images may be blurry, overexposed, underexposed, red-eyed, unflattering, partial, or missing, but there's no way they can be of someone else entirely.

Anna's twenty-four pictures included three women about her own age, ten children, two teenage boys, and nine shots of the same older man. He was gray-haired, lean, and handsome, a brown-eyed Paul Newman.

I stared at the photos in baffled shock. What the hell had happened? I had never seen any of these people before, had no idea how they had turned up in my camera. Nothing made sense.

Fear slid down my spine, viscous and greasy as oil.

In the end I hid the photos, called Anna, and told both her and Carol that I'd screwed up and ruined the shoot. Carol ragged on me without mercy. Anna agreed to another session, no extra charge, a week from Saturday morning.

In between, I shot a trashy-looking woman—teased red hair, black leather bustier—who was a happily married mother of two, and a patrician blonde beauty who, I suspected, was a hooker. I shot two giggly eighteen-year-olds who said they wanted to be models and who hadn't the remotest chance of succeeding. I shot a pretty, sad-eyed young woman who wanted a glamorous picture to send to her soldier husband deployed in Afghanistan.

A hundred times I pulled out the Anna-photos-with-no-Anna, and never came close to solving the mystery or mentioning it to anyone. What was I going to say? "Your pictures seem to be of several other people— are you a multiple personality? A witch? A mirage?" Give me a break.

When Anna arrived for her second shoot, she seemed subdued. The shots in the green negligee still looked good through my lens, but they lacked the fresh zest of the first session. That's the difference between professional models and amateurs: The pros can fake freshness. Off camera, that's not always a desirable quality.

I wasn't as light-hearted, either. In fact, I could barely keep my mind on the raw shots, so tense I was about what they might develop into. After Anna and Carol left, I went straight to the darkroom.

Twelve shots of the older man, eight children, two pictures each of one of the teenage boys and one of the middle-aged women. Some of the children were seated at a table, drawing with crayons. The teenager scowled ferociously. All the backgrounds were out of focus. No shots of Anna.

I stared at the negatives until I couldn't see anything at all.

I followed her. Her phone number was on the client-contact sheet. I fed it into an online reverse directory and turned up an address in Framingham, one of those peculiar Boston suburbs that's upper-middle-class along bodies of water and working class everywhere else. Anna lived in a modest, well-kept bungalow on a maple-shaded street. Saturday afternoon she spent at a local community center. Saturday night she met two women—not those in the pictures—for dinner and a movie. Sunday she took the MTA into Boston and viewed an exhibit of art deco jewelry at the Museum of Fine Arts. Monday she went to work at the Framingham Public Library. I photographed her parking her car, entering the restaurant, leaving the movie theater, buying a ticket at the museum, even standing behind the reference desk helping an after-school gaggle of noisy teenagers. Each time I developed the pictures right away. None of them were of Anna.

Increasingly, the *settings* weren't even there. Her house was blurry, and so was the restaurant. The theater marquee was a blur. The museum had become a vague outline, and the library picture showed only the faint suggestion of the reference desk, behind which stood the scowling teenage boy. Each subsequent set of photos showed increasing haze, a pearly incandescent glow, although the people recurred sharply. If anything, they were too sharp, as if over time they were taking on knife-edged properties, almost able to slice right through the photographic paper. Yet at the same time, parts of their bodies—a shoulder, a back, the top of a head—seemed weirdly obscured, as if receding into deep and inexplicable shadow.

None of it made any sense. All of it scared me.

It finally occurred to me to google Anna, who had a surprisingly large online presence without actually posting anything herself. She turned up in other people's blogs, in small-town newspaper articles over two decades, in the proceedings of ALA conferences, in the Alumni Notes of her college. She ran childrens' programs at the community center. She organized disaster-relief drives. A show of her paintings had hung on the walls of a local bank. She was the person that friends turned to in times of trouble. Why had such a woman—gregarious, kind, pretty, bright— never married, never had kids? One blogger wrote: *Dinner last night with Anna O'Connor. If she can't find the right guy, what hope is there for the rest of us?* To which someone had added the comment: *Some people are just too picky. Deluded overage romantics, still hoping for a soulmate.*

Bitch. But correct? I could see in Anna the outlines of a life both brave and sad: filled with useful activities but still feeling itself some- how displaced. Not a skilled enough painter for a commercial art gallery. More intelligent than most people—she'd graduated magna cum laude from Northwestern—but not ambitious enough for big-time academe or for a corporate career. Lots of friends but with no one really close, and thus lonely underneath. I knew many people like that, including me.

Until she met this Montana guy online, who turned her into the hopeful, sexy woman who'd come to be photographed at Glamorous You.

I gazed again at the baffling, terrifying photos that couldn't exist, and then I drove back out to Framingham.

"Ben! What are you doing here—did you come to bring me the replace- ment pictures? You didn't have to do that."

She came down the stone steps of the library, the last person to leave. Eight o'clock on a warm September night and sunset was long over. In the bright floodlights from the library, Anna looked both tired and tense, like a person who'd spent the day carrying loads of bricks up flimsy ladders. She wore another librarian outfit, brown pantsuit and sensible shoes, and her pink lipstick had been mostly chewed off.

"No, I didn't bring the proofs. I have to talk to you about them. Will you come have a drink with me?"

"I don't think that would . . . Oh, why not. Is something wrong? Do you need to talk?"

"No. Yes. Is there a bar close by?"

She didn't know. Not a party girl. I found a fake Irish pub on Route 9, called her on my cell, and she joined me in a booth in the back. I'd already downed a double Scotch on the rocks. Another sat waiting for

Anna. She took a sip and made the face of someone used to white wine. In the gloom of the pub, she looked old and strained.

"Okay, Ben, what's this about?"

How do you blurt out that existing photographs—tangible, physical objects—can't possibly exist? I was going to sound like a psychotic. Or a fraud. Can't take flattering pictures of a client? Pretend she's not there.

I said, "The pictures of you are coming out . . . odd."

She flushed. "I know I'm not very photogenic—"

"No, it's not that." She had absolutely no inkling. I would have bet my eyes on it.

"Then what is it?"

"The photos are . . . blurry."

"Blurry?"

"Yes." I couldn't do it, I just couldn't. "Very blurry. It's my fault. I'm here to refund your deposit."

"But . . . you have a terrific reputation as a photographer. I checked."

I shrugged. Her mouth tightened. "Oh, I see. I look ridiculous, don't I? A woman in her fifties posing for a glamour shot. And you don't want to embarrass me by saying so."

"No, it's not that at all. I just—"

"Anything else here?" the waitress said. She wore a silly white apron with green shamrocks on it. I ordered more doubles. When mine came, I seized the glass as if it were a tree in a tsunami.

We sat in a heavy, unpleasant silence that stretched on and on. And on. Anna finished her first drink and made strong inroads on the second. Nothing I could think of to say seemed right, or even possible. Finally Anna made a sudden movement. I thought she was getting up to leave, but instead she said, "How much do you think a person should change herself for love?"

My answer was instantaneous and violent. "Not at all! Nothing!"

She peered at me, eyes a little unfocused, and I realized that Anna O'Connor could not hold her liquor. But if her inhibitions were in decline, her perceptiveness wasn't.

"Who was she, Ben? Your wife?"

"Ex-wife."

If it had been anyone else in the world, I wouldn't mention Laurie. I hated to talk about her, even with Carol, although Carol knows the whole story because she and Laurie were friends. But I was desperate to keep Anna talking until I heard something—anything!—that would make sense out of those photos. And I don't hold my liquor all that well, either.

"Tell me," Anna said.

Pain always turned me angry. "Not much to tell. My wife and I had some problems. Nothing big, or so I thought. Then she met a guy in a chat room. She had an affair, she left me, and he left her. She wanted to come back to our marriage, and I said no way. It was good and she broke it. The pity-me note she mailed me said she was tired of trying to be somebody she couldn't. Well, I can't be somebody I'm not, either. I couldn't ever trust her again. End of story."

"I'm so sorry." From Anna it didn't sound perfunctory or condescending or phony. "You said 'It was good' but your marriage must have been troubled before she even met the other man."

Laurie had always said it was troubled; I'd thought it was mostly fine. She said I was "never emotionally present," but didn't all women say that? All the ones I'd known said it. *I feel like I'm always pursuing you, Ben, and never the other way around, and I don't like it.* I scowled at Anna and tried to push away all memories of Laurie. As usual, it didn't work.

Anna said gently, "Why didn't you let her come back? It looks to me like you still love her."

I snorted. "I told you, I won't change who I am. And I don't take sloppy seconds."

"That's a *terrible* thing to say, Ben! She's not a whore, just somebody who made a mistake. Maybe somebody who needs you."

"I'm not the Salvation Army, Anna." I knew how my comments sounded. I also knew how much I needed to sound that way, especially to myself. Tough. Beyond caring.

Anna said, "My guess is that maybe you need her, too."

"You don't know anything about either of us!"

"No, I don't. I'm sorry to pry."

"Then don't!"

I thought she'd leave then. Instead she said, "What really happened to my photos?"

I stared across the table. The original set of proofs were in my messenger bag. Pissed at her now, I took them out.

The weird thing was that after the first shock, she didn't seem surprised, or at least not surprised enough. Her forehead crinkled like a topographical map but her eyes didn't register all that much disbelief. She studied the kids, the teenagers, the adults, the handsome older man. I saw that she knew them.

"That's him, isn't it?" I said. "Your boyfriend."

"Yes."

"How did he—"

"I don't know. I was thinking about him, about all of them. . . . I don't know."

"Are you saying that I shot a *picture* of what was in your mind instead of—"

"I don't know!"

She stood, so quickly that she knocked into her second empty glass, sending it skidding across the table. She didn't pick it up. "It's late I have to go to work tomorrow thanks for the drink don't worry about the—"

"You can't drive, Anna. You're drunk." Apparently that didn't take much.

She made a despairing little noise and lurched toward the ladies'. When she returned, her face was wet and a cab waited outside.

That was the last time I ever spoke to her.

But I went on shooting her, whenever I could get away from Glamorous You. I photographed Anna outside her house, outside the library, with friends, on the playground at the community center. Maybe she saw me, maybe not. Certainly she never acknowledged me.

Anna hurrying across the street to her parked car—but the negative showed another woman, younger and in tears.

Anna blinking in sunlight on the library steps—but it became the graying older man and the library was a dark blur.

Anna on her porch, both porch and house a swirl of black, Anna replaced by three small children.

I studied the photographs in my darkroom, in the kitchenette of my unkempt condo, in the middle of the night. *Let it go,* Laurie used to say, about so many things. But I couldn't let this go. I kept looking for clues, trying to put it all together, shooting yet more film. I spent time—a lot of time—online, delving into Anna's public life, looking for photos. I found them.

Then Anna disappeared.

I don't know when he told her the truth, no more than I know anything else that transpired between them. The first chat-room encounter, the first emails, the first phone calls. Probably he told her how isolated he felt in Montana. Probably he told her how isolated he felt in this world, and at first she had no idea that the hackneyed phrase could have a double meaning. Maybe he told her why he was in Montana, of all places. Or not.

And she told him about her own version of loneliness, because that's what all lovers tell each other. Just as all lovers say that finding each other is a miracle, an unlooked-for gift from what maybe isn't such an indifferent universe after all. They each say that they would give up so very much to be with the other. Cheat on a marriage, leave a spouse, then regret bitterly their own stupid actions and promise the moon and stars for another chance.

How much do you think a person should change for love? The answer in all the self-help books is: Don't. The lover is supposed to accept you just the way you are, unconditionally. But when Anna asked me that, she didn't yet know the full truth. She suspected something, that was clear not only from the anxiety and tension on her face, but from the photographs themselves. In each set of shots, the people got sharper. I found most of those people in jpg files, in blurry newspaper photos, in blog postings, in yearbook shots. The teenage boys were her troubled nephews; Anna had gotten one an after-school job at the library. The women were her newly widowed younger sister plus two of Anna's friends. One had been laid off from her job but was now rehired. The other had broken her leg. The children were all from the community center, disadvantaged kids for whom Anna volunteered her time. Only Montana Man had no online photos.

What was he? Why was he alone in Montana, without others of his kind? By choice, or as the result of some unimaginable catastrophe? I would never know. The only image I would ever have of him was from Anna's mind, as he somehow changed her from the inside out, changed her fundamental relationship to the world as I understood it. While she let him do it.

The pictures tell the story—but *not* the pictures of the people. It's actually the backgrounds that matter. In the first one, my studio is only slightly blurred. With each subsequent shoot, the backgrounds—how Anna saw this world—got hazier, became nothing but shadows. Then the shadows turned into black miasma, as Anna struggled with her decision. The last several roles of film are like that.

Except for the very last photograph.

She saw me, that time. It was early morning. Dressed in the dreary brown pantsuit, she came out of her house, stood on her porch, and smiled at me where I waited in my car, camera raised. She even posed a little, as she had done that first day in the studio. Her smile was luminous, suffused with joy. Then she went back inside and closed the door.

The developed shot shows a woman dressed in some sort of gauzy robe, wings spread wide from her shoulders, skin lit from within. Her tiny silver horns catch the dawn light. Her tail wraps loosely around her body. She is beautiful.

But, then, she always was. What makes me unable to stop looking at the picture, what makes me so glad for her, is not her beauty. It is that, finally, the images in Anna's mind are not of all those other people she can help but of herself, happy. He did that for her. He—whatever the hell he really is—gave her herself. That's what Anna wanted me to see, on her porch that last day: What can happen when you change for someone else.

"Can" happen. Not "will." No guarantees.

I frame the photo but I never hang it. I redouble my efforts to pick up clients, which makes both Carol and the electric company happy. I spend too much time at the fake Irish pub, sipping and thinking, and then thinking some more.

And eventually I pick up the phone and call Laurie.

LAWS OF SURVIVAL

My name is Jill. I am somewhere you can't imagine, going somewhere even more unimaginable. If you think I like what I did to get here, you're crazy.

Actually, I'm the one who's crazy. You—any "you"—will never read this. But I have paper now, and a sort of pencil, and time. Lots and lots of time. So I will write what happened, all of it, as carefully as I can.

After all—why the hell not?

I went out very early one morning to look for food. Before dawn was safest for a woman alone. The boy-gangs had gone to bed, tired of attacking each other. The trucks from the city hadn't arrived yet. That meant the garbage was pretty picked over, but it also meant most of the refugee camp wasn't out scavenging. Most days I could find enough: a carrot stolen from somebody's garden patch, my arm bloody from reaching through the barbed wire. Overlooked potato peelings under a pile of rags and glass. A can of stew thrown away by one of the soldiers on the base, but still half full. Soldiers on duty by the Dome were often careless. They got bored, with nothing to do.

That morning was cool but fair, with a pearly haze that the sun would burn off later. I wore all my clothing, for warmth, and my boots. Yesterday's garbage load, I'd heard somebody say, was huge, so I had hopes. I hiked to my favorite spot, where garbage spills almost to the Dome wall. Maybe I'd find bread, or even fruit that wasn't too rotten.

Instead I found the puppy.

Its eyes weren't open yet and it squirmed along the bare ground, a scrawny brown-and-white mass with a tiny fluffy tail. Nearby was a fluid-soaked towel. Some sentimental fool had left the puppy there, hoping . . . what? It didn't matter. Scrawny or not, there was some meat on the thing. I scooped it up.

184

The sun pushed above the horizon, flooding the haze with golden light.

I hate it when grief seizes me. I hate it and it's dangerous, a violation of one of Jill's Laws of Survival. I can go for weeks, months without thinking of my life before the War. Without remembering or feeling. Then something will strike me—a flower growing in the dump, a burst of birdsong, the stars on a clear night—and grief will hit me like the maglevs that no longer exist, a grief all the sharper because it contains the memory of joy. I can't afford joy, which always comes with an astronomical price tag. I can't even afford the grief that comes from the memory of living things, which is why it is only the flower, the birdsong, the morning sunlight that starts it. My grief was not for that puppy. I still intended to eat it.

But I heard a noise behind me and turned. The Dome wall was opening.

Who knew why the aliens put their Domes by garbage dumps, by waste pits, by radioactive cities? Who knew why aliens did anything?

There was a widespread belief in the camp that the aliens started the War. I'm old enough to know better. That was us, just like the global warming and the bio-crobes were us. The aliens didn't even show up until the War was over and Raleigh was the northernmost city left on the East Coast and refugees poured south like mudslides. Including me. That's when the ships landed and then turned into the huge gray Domes like upended bowls. I heard there were many Domes, some in other countries. The Army, what was left of it, threw tanks and bombs at ours. When they gave up, the refugees threw bullets and Molotov cocktails and prayers and graffiti and candle-light vigils and rain dances. Everything slid off and the Domes just sat there. And sat. And sat. Three years later, they were still sitting, silent and closed, although of course there were rumors to the contrary. There are always rumors. Personally, I'd never gotten over a slight disbelief that the Dome was there at all. Who would want to visit us?

The opening was small, no larger than a porthole, and about six feet above the ground. All I could see inside was a fog the same color as the Dome. Something came out, gliding quickly toward me. It took me a moment to realize it was a robot, a blue metal sphere above a hanging basket. It stopped a foot from my face and said, "This food for this dog."

I could have run, or screamed, or at the least—the very least—looked around for a witness. I didn't. The basket held a pile of fresh produce, green lettuce and deep purple eggplant and apples so shiny red they looked lacquered. And *peaches* . . . My mouth filled with sweet water. I couldn't move.

The puppy whimpered.

My mother used to make fresh peach pie.

I scooped the food into my scavenger bag, laid the puppy in the basket, and backed away. The robot floated back into the Dome, which closed immediately. I sped back to my corrugated-tin and windowless hut and ate until I couldn't hold any more. I slept, woke, and ate the rest, crouching in the dark so nobody else would see. All that fruit and vegetables gave me the runs, but it was worth it.

Peaches.

Two weeks later, I brought another puppy to the Dome, the only survivor of a litter deep in the dump. I never knew what happened to the mother. I had to wait a long time outside the Dome before the blue sphere took the puppy in exchange for produce. Apparently the Dome would only open when there was no one else around to see. What were they afraid of? It's not like PETA was going to show up.

The next day I traded three of the peaches to an old man in exchange for a small, mangy poodle. We didn't look each other in the eye, but I nonetheless knew that his held tears. He limped hurriedly away. I kept the dog, which clearly wanted nothing to do with me, in my shack until very early morning and then took it to the Dome. It tried to escape but I'd tied a bit of rope onto its frayed collar. We sat outside the Dome in mutual dislike, waiting, as the sky paled slightly in the east. Gunshots sounded in the distance.

I have never owned a dog.

When the Dome finally opened, I gripped the dog's rope and spoke to the robot. "Not fruit. Not vegetables. I want eggs and bread."

The robot floated back inside.

Instantly I cursed myself. Eggs? Bread? I was crazy not to take what I could get. That was Law of Survival #1. Now there would be nothing. Eggs, bread . . . *crazy*. I glared at the dog and kicked it. It yelped, looked indignant, and tried to bite my boot.

The Dome opened again and the robot glided toward me. In the gloom I couldn't see what was in the basket. In fact, I couldn't see the basket. It wasn't there. Mechanical tentacles shot out from the sphere and seized both me and the poodle. I cried out and the tentacles squeezed harder. Then I was flying through the air, the stupid dog suddenly howling beneath me, and we were carried through the Dome wall and inside.

Then nothing.

A nightmare room made of nightmare sound: barking, yelping, whimpering, snapping. I jerked awake, sat up, and discovered myself on a floating platform above a mass of dogs. Big dogs, small dogs, old dogs, puppies, sick dogs, dogs that looked all too healthy, flashing their forty-two teeth at me—why did I remember that number? From where? The largest and strongest dogs couldn't quite reach me with their snaps, but they were trying.

"You are operative," the blue metal sphere said, floating beside me. "Now we must begin. Here."

Its basket held eggs and bread.

"Get them away!"

Obediently it floated off.

"Not the food! The dogs!"

"What to do with these dogs?"

"Put them in cages!" A large black animal—German shepherd or Boxer or something—had nearly closed its jaws on my ankle. The next bite might do it.

"Cages," the metal sphere said in its uninflected mechanical voice. "Yes."

"Son of a bitch!" The shepherd leaping high, had grazed my thigh; its spittle slimed my pants. "Raise the goddamn platform!"

"Yes."

The platform floated so high, so that I had to duck my head to avoid hitting the ceiling. I peered over the edge and . . . no, that wasn't possible. But it was happening. The floor was growing upright sticks, and the sticks were growing cross bars, and the crossbars were extending themselves into mesh tops . . . Within minutes, each dog was encased in a cage just large enough to hold its protesting body.

"What to do now?" the metal sphere asked.

I stared at it. I was, as far as I knew, the first human being to ever enter an alien Dome, I was trapped in a small room with feral caged dogs and a robot . . . *what to do now?*

"Why . . . why am I here?" I hated myself for the brief stammer and vowed it would not happen again. Law of Survival #2: Show no fear.

Would a metal sphere even recognize fear?

It said, "These dogs do not behave correctly."

"Not behave correctly?"

"No."

I looked down again at the slavering and snarling mass of dogs; how strong was that mesh on the cage tops? "What do you want them to do?"

"You want to see the presentation?"

"Not yet." Law #3: Never volunteer for anything.

"What to do now?"

How the hell should I know? But the smell of the bread reached me and my stomach flopped. "Now to eat," I said. "Give me the things in your basket."

It did, and I tore into the bread like a wolf into deer. The real wolves below me increased their howling. When I'd eaten an entire loaf, I looked back at the metal sphere. "Have those dogs eaten?"

"Yes."

"What did you give them?"

"Garbage."

"*Garbage?* Why?"

"In hell they eat garbage."

So even the robot thought this was Hell. Panic surged through me; I pushed it back. Surviving this would depend on staying steady. "Show me what you fed the dogs."

"Yes." A section of wall melted and garbage cascaded into the room, flowing greasily between the cages. I recognized it: It was exactly like the garbage I picked through every day, trucked out from a city I could no longer imagine and from the Army base I could not approach without being shot. Bloody rags, tin cans from before the War, shit, plastic bags, dead flowers, dead animals, dead electronics, cardboard, eggshells, paper, hair, bone, scraps of decaying food, glass shards, potato peelings, foam rubber, roaches, sneakers with holes, sagging furniture, corn cobs. The smell hit my stomach, newly distended with bread.

"You fed the dogs *that?*"

"Yes. They eat it in hell."

Outside. Hell was outside, and of course that's what the feral dogs ate, that's all there was. But the metal sphere had produced fruit and lettuce and bread for me.

"You must give them better food. They eat that in . . . in hell because they can't get anything else."

"What to do now?"

It finally dawned on me—slow, I was too slow for this, only the quick survive—that the metal sphere had limited initiative along with its limited vocabulary. But it had made cages, made bread, made fruit—hadn't it? Or was this stuff grown in some imaginable secret garden inside the Dome? "You must give the dogs meat."

"Flesh?"

"Yes."

"No."

No change in that mechanical voice, but the "no" was definite and quick. Law of Survival #4: Notice everything. So—no flesh-eating allowed here. Also no time to ask why not; I had to keep issuing orders so that the robot didn't start issuing them. "Give them bread mixed with . . . with soy protein."

"Yes."

"And take away the garbage."

"Yes."

The garbage began to dissolve. I saw nothing poured on it, nothing rise from the floor. But all that stinking mass fell into powder and vanished. Nothing replaced it.

I said, "Are you getting bread mixed with soy powder?" *Getting* seemed the safest verb I could think of.

"Yes."

The stuff came then, tumbling through the same melted hole in the wall, loaves of bread with, presumably, soy powder in them. The dogs, barking insanely, reached paws and snouts and tongues through the bars of their cages. They couldn't get at the food.

"Metal sphere—do you have a name?"

No answer.

"Okay. Blue, how strong are those cages? Can the dogs break them? Any of the dogs?"

"No."

"Lower the platform to the floor."

My safe perch floated down. The aisles between the cages were irregular, some wide and some so narrow the dogs could reach through to touch each other, since each cage had "grown" wherever the dog was at the time. Gingerly I picked my way to a clearing and sat down. Tearing a loaf of bread into chunks, I pushed the pieces through the bars of the least dangerous-looking dogs, which made the bruisers howl even more. For them, I put chunks at a distance they could just reach with a paw through the front bars of their prisons.

The puppy I had first brought to the Dome lay in a tiny cage. Dead.

The second one was alive but just barely.

The old man's mangy poodle looked more mangy than ever, but otherwise alert. It tried to bite me when I fed it.

"What to do now?"

"They need water."

"Yes."

Water flowed through the wall. When it had reached an inch or so, it stopped. The dogs lapped whatever came into their cages. I stood with wet feet—a hole in my boot after all, I hadn't known—and a stomach roiling from the stench of the dogs, which only worsened as they got wet. The dead puppy smelled especially horrible. I climbed back onto my platform.

"What to do now?"

"You tell me," I said.

"These dogs do not behave correctly."

"Not behave correctly?"

"No."

"What do you want them to do?"

"Do you want to see the presentation?"

We had been here before. On second thought, a "presentation" sounded more like acquiring information ("Notice everything") than like undertaking action ("Never volunteer"). So I sat cross-legged on the platform, which was easier on my uncushioned bones, breathed through my mouth instead of my nose, and said "Why the hell not?"

Blue repeated, "Do you want to see the presentation?"

"Yes." A one-syllable answer.

I didn't know what to expect. Aliens, spaceships, war, strange places barely comprehensible to humans. What I got was scenes from the dump.

A beam of light shot out from Blue and resolved into a three-dimensional holo, not too different from one I'd seen in a science museum on a school field trip once (*no. push memory away*), only this was far sharper and detailed. A ragged and unsmiling toddler, one of thousands, staggered toward a cesspool. A big dog with patchy coat dashed up, seized the kid's dress, and pulled her back just before she fell into the waste.

A medium-sized brown dog in a guide-dog harness led around someone tapping a white-headed cane.

An Army dog, this one sleek and well-fed, sniffed at a pile of garbage, found something, pointed stiffly at attention.

A group of teenagers tortured a puppy. It writhed in pain, but in a long lingering close-up, tried to lick the torturer's hand.

A thin, small dog dodged rocks, dashed inside a corrugated tin hut, and laid a piece of carrion beside an old lady lying on the ground.

The holo went on and on like that, but the strange thing was that the people were barely seen. The toddler's bare and filthy feet and chubby knees, the old lady's withered cheek, a flash of a camouflage uniform above a brown boot, the hands of the torturers. Never a whole person, never a focus on people. Just on the dogs.

The "presentation" ended.

"These dogs do not behave correctly," Blue said.

"These dogs? In the presentation?"

"These dogs here do not behave correctly."

"These dogs *here.*" I pointed to the wet, stinking dogs in their cages. Some, fed now, had quieted. Others still snarled and barked, trying their hellish best to get out and kill me.

"These dogs here. Yes. What to do now?"

"You want these dogs to behave like the dogs in the presentation."

"These dogs here must behave correctly. Yes."

"You want them to . . . do what? Rescue people? Sniff out ammunition dumps? Guide the blind and feed the hungry and love their torturers?"

Blue said nothing. Again I had the impression I had exceeded its thought processes, or its vocabulary, or its something. A strange feeling gathered in my gut.

"Blue, you yourself didn't build this Dome, or the starship that it was before, did you? You're just a . . . a computer."

Nothing.

"Blue, who tells you what to do?"

"What to do now? These dogs do not behave correctly."

"Who wants these dogs to behave correctly?" I said, and found I was holding my breath.

"The masters."

The masters. I knew all about them. Masters were the people who started wars, ran the corporations that ruined the Earth, manufactured the bioweapons that killed billions, and now holed up in the cities to send their garbage out to us in the refugee camps. Masters were something else I didn't think about, but not because grief would take me. Rage would.

Law of Survival #5: Feel nothing that doesn't aid survival.

"Are the masters here? In this . . . inside here?"

"No."

"Who is here inside?"

"These dogs here are inside."

Clearly. "The masters want these dogs here to behave like the dogs in the presentation."

"Yes."

"The masters want these dogs here to provide them with loyalty and protection and service."

No response.

"The masters aren't interested in human beings, are they? That's why they haven't communicated at all with any government."

Nothing. But I didn't need a response; the masters' thinking was already clear to me. Humans were unimportant—maybe because we had, after all, destroyed each other and our own world. We weren't worth contact. But dogs: companion animals capable of selfless service and great unconditional love, even in the face of abuse. For all I knew, dogs were unique in the universe. For all I know.

Blue said, "What to do now?"

I stared at the mangy, reeking, howling mass of animals. Some feral, some tamed once, some sick, at least one dead. I chose my words to be as simple as possible, relying on phrases Blue knew. "The masters want these dogs here to behave correctly."

"Yes."

"The masters want *me* to make these dogs behave correctly."

"Yes."

"The masters will make me food, and keep me inside, for to make these dogs behave correctly."

Long pause; my sentence had a lot of grammatical elements. But finally Blue said, "Yes."

"If these dogs do not behave correctly, the masters—what to do then?"

Another long pause. "Find another human."

"And *this* human here?"

"Kill it."

I gripped the edges of my floating platform hard. My hands still trembled. "Put me outside now."

"No."

"I must stay inside."

"These dogs do not behave correctly."

"I must make these dogs behave correctly."

"Yes."

"And the masters want these dogs to display . . ." I had stopped talking to Blue. I was talking to myself, to steady myself, but even that I couldn't manage. The words caromed around in my mind—loyalty, service, protection—but none came out of my mouth. I couldn't do this. I was going to die. The aliens had come from God-knew-where to treat the dying Earth like a giant pet store, intrigued only by a canine domestication that had happened ten thousand years ago and by nothing else on the planet, nothing else humanity had or might accomplish. Only dogs. *The masters want these dogs to display—*

Blue surprised me with a new word. "Love," it said.

Law #4: Notice everything. I needed to learn all I could, starting with Blue. He'd made garbage appear, and food and water and cages. What else could he do?

"Blue, make the water go away." And it did, just sank into the floor, which dried instantly. I was fucking Moses, commanding the Red Sea. I climbed off the platform, inched among the dog cages, and studied them individually.

"You called the refugee camp and the dump 'hell.' Where did you get that word?"

Nothing.

"Who said 'hell'?"

"Humans."

Blue had cameras outside the Dome. Of course he did; he'd seen me find that first puppy in the garbage. Maybe Blue had been waiting for someone like me, alone and non-threatening, to come close with a dog. But it had watched before that, and it had learned the word "hell," and maybe it had recorded the incidents in the "presentation." I filed this information for future use.

"This dog is dead." The first puppy, decaying into stinking pulp. "It is killed. Non-operative."

"What to do now?"

"Make the dead dog go away."

A long pause: thinking it over? Accessing data banks? Communicating with aliens? And what kind of moron couldn't figure out by itself that a dead dog was never going to behave correctly? So much for artificial intelligence.

"Yes," Blue finally said, and the little corpse dissolved as if it had never been.

I found one more dead dog and one close to death. Blue disappeared the first, said no to the second. Apparently we had to just let it suffer until it died. I wondered how much the idea of "death" even meant to a robot. There were twenty-three live dogs, of which I had delivered only three to the Dome.

"Blue—did another human, before you brought me here, try to train the dogs?"

"These dogs do not behave correctly."

"Yes. But did a human *not me* be inside? To make these dogs behave correctly?"

"Yes."

"What happened to him or her?"

No response.

"What to do now with the other human?"

"Kill it."

I put a hand against the wall and leaned on it. The wall felt smooth and slick, with a faint and unpleasant tingle. I removed my hand.

All computers could count. "How many humans did you kill?"

"Two."

Three's the charm. But there were no charms. No spells, no magic wards, no cavalry coming over the hill to ride to the rescue; I'd known that ever since the War. There was just survival. And, now, dogs.

I chose the mangy little poodle. It hadn't bit me when the old man had surrendered it, or when I'd kept it overnight. That was at least a start. "Blue, make this dog's cage go away. But *only* this one cage!"

The cage dissolved. The poodle stared at me distrustfully. Was I supposed to stare back, or would that get us into some kind of canine pissing contest? The thing was small but it had teeth.

I had a sudden idea. "Blue, show me how this dog does not behave correctly." If I could see what it wasn't doing, that would at least be a start.

Blue floated to within a foot of the dog's face. The dog growled and backed away. Blue floated away and the dog quieted but it still stood in what would be a menacing stance if it weighed more than nine or ten pounds: ears raised, legs braced, neck hair bristling. Blue said, "Come." The dog did nothing. Blue repeated the entire sequence and so did Mangy.

I said, "You want the dog to follow you. Like the dogs in the presentation."

"Yes."

"You want the dog to come when you say 'Come.'"

"Love," Blue said.

"What is 'love,' Blue?"

No response.

The robot didn't know. Its masters must have had some concept of "love," but fuck-all knew what it was. And I wasn't sure I knew anymore, either. That left Mangy, who would never "love" Blue or follow him or lick his hand because dogs operated on smell—even I knew that about them—and Blue, a machine, didn't smell like either a person or another dog. Couldn't the aliens who sent him here figure that out? Were they watching this whole farce, or had they just dropped a half-sentient computer under an upturned bowl on Earth and told it, "Bring us some loving dogs"? Who knew how aliens thought?

I didn't even know how dogs thought. There were much better people for this job—professional trainers, or that guy on TV who made tigers jump through burning hoops. But they weren't here, and I was. I squatted on my haunches a respectful distance from Mangy and said, "Come."

It growled at me.

"Blue, raise the platform this high." I held my hand at shoulder height. The platform rose.

"Now make some cookies on the platform."

Nothing.

"Make some . . . cheese on the platform."

Nothing. You don't see much cheese in a dump.

"Make some bread on the platform."

Nothing. Maybe the platform wasn't user-friendly.

"Make some bread."

After a moment, loaves tumbled out of the wall. "Enough! Stop!"

Mangy had rushed over to the bread, tearing at it, and the other dogs were going wild. I picked up one loaf, put it on the platform, and said, "Make the rest of the bread go away."

It all dissolved. No wonder the dogs were wary; I felt a little dizzy myself. A sentence from so long-ago child's book rose in my mind: *Things come and go so quickly here!*

I had no idea how much Blue could, or would, do on my orders. "Blue, make another room for me and this one dog. Away from the other dogs."

"No."

"Make this room bigger."

The room expanded evenly on all sides. "Stop." It did. "Make only this end of the room bigger."

Nothing.

"Okay, make the whole room bigger."

When the room stopped expanding, I had a space about forty feet square, with the dog cages huddled in the middle. After half an hour of experimenting, I got the platform moved to one corner, not far enough to escape the dog stench but better than nothing. (Law #1: Take what you can get.) I got a depression in the floor filled with warm water. I got food, drinking water, soap, and some clean cloth, and a lot of rope. By distracting Mangy with bits of bread, I got rope onto her frayed collar. After I got into the warm water and scrubbed myself, I pulled the poodle in. She bit me. But somehow I got her washed, too. Afterwards she shook herself, glared at me, and went to sleep on the hard floor. I asked Blue for a soft rug.

He said, "The other humans did this."

And Blue killed them anyway.

"Shut up," I said.

The big windowless room had no day, no night, no sanity. I slept and ate when I needed to, and otherwise I worked. Blue never left. He was an oversized, all-seeing eye in the corner. Big Brother, or God.

Within a few weeks—maybe—I had Mangy trained to come when called, to sit, and to follow me on command. I did this by dispensing bits of bread and other goodies. Mangy got fatter. I didn't care if she ended up the Fat Fiona of dogs. Her mange didn't improve, since I couldn't get Blue to wrap his digital mind around the concept of medicines, and even if he had I wouldn't have known what to ask for. The sick puppy died in its cage.

I kept the others fed and watered and flooded the shit out of their cages every day, but that was all. Mangy took all my time. She still regarded me warily, never curled up next to me, and occasionally growled. Love was not happening here.

Nonetheless, Blue left his corner and spoke for the first time in a week, scaring the hell out of me. "This dog behaves correctly."

"Well, thanks. I tried to . . . no, Blue . . ."

Blue floated to within a foot of Mangy's face, said, "Follow," and floated away. Mangy sat down and began to lick one paw. Blue rose and floated toward me.

"This dog does not behave correctly."

I was going to die.

"No, listen to me—listen! The dog can't smell you! It behaves for humans because of humans' smell! Do you understand?"

"No. This dog does not behave correctly."

"Listen! How the hell can you learn anything if you don't listen? You have to have a smell! Then the dog will follow you!"

Blue stopped. We stood frozen, a bizarre tableau, while the robot considered. Even Mangy stopped licking her paw and watched, still. They say dogs can smell fear.

Finally Blue said, "What is smell?"

It isn't possible to explain smell. Can't be done. Instead I pulled down my pants, tore the cloth I was using as underwear from between my legs, and rubbed it all over Blue, who did not react. I hoped he wasn't made of the same stuff as the Dome, which even spray paint had just slid off of. But, of course, he was. So I tied the strip of cloth around him with a piece of rope, my fingers trembling. "Now try the dog, Blue."

"Follow," Blue said, and floated away from Mangy.

She looked at him, then at me, then back at the floating metal sphere. I held my breath from some insane idea that I would thereby diminish my own smell. Mangy didn't move.

"This dog does not be—"

"She will if I'm gone!" I said desperately. "She smells me *and* you . . . and we smell the same so it's confusing her! But she'll follow you fine if I'm gone, do you understand?"

"No."

"Blue . . . I'm going to get on the platform. See, I'm doing it. Raise the platform *very high*, Blue. Very high."

A moment later my head and ass both pushed against the ceiling, squishing me. I couldn't see what was happening below. I heard Blue say, "Follow," and I squeezed my eyes shut, waiting. My life depended on a scrofulous poodle with a gloomy disposition.

Blue said, "This dog behaves correctly."

He lowered my platform to a few yards above the floor, and I swear that—eyeless as he is and with part of his sphere obscured by my underwear—he looked right at me.

"This dog does behave correctly. This dog is ready."

"Ready? For . . . for what?"

Blue didn't answer. The next minute the floor opened and Mangy, yelping, tumbled into it. The floor closed. At the same time, one of the cages across the room dissolved and a German shepherd hurtled towards me. I shrieked and yelled, "Raise the platform!" It rose just before the monster grabbed me.

Blue said, "What to do now? This dog does not behave correctly."

"For God's sakes, Blue—"

"This dog must love."

The shepherd leapt and snarled, teeth bared.

I couldn't talk Blue out of the shepherd, which was as feral and vicious and unrelenting as anything in a horror movie. Or as Blue himself, in his own mechanical way. So I followed the First Law: Take what you can get.

"Blue, make garbage again. A lot of garbage, right here." I pointed to the wall beside my platform.

"No."

Garbage, like everything else, apparently was made—or released, or whatever—from the opposite wall. I resigned myself to this. "Make a lot of garbage, Blue."

Mountains of stinking debris cascaded from the wall, spilling over until it reached the dog cages.

"Now stop. Move my platform above the garbage."

The platform moved. The caged dogs howled. Uncaged, the shepherd poked eagerly in the refuse, too distracted to pay much attention to me. I had Blue lower the platform and I poked among it, too, keeping one eye on Vicious. If Blue was creating the garbage and not just trucking it in, he was doing a damn fine job of duplication. Xerox should have made such good copies.

I got smeared with shit and rot, but I found what I was looking for. The box was nearly a quarter full. I stuffed bread into it, coated the bread thoroughly, and discarded the box back onto the pile.

"Blue, make the garbage go away."

It did. Vicious glared at me and snarled. "Nice doggie," I said, "have some bread." I threw pieces and Vicious gobbled them.

Listening to the results was terrible. Not, however, as terrible as having Vicious tear me apart or Blue vaporize me. The rat poison took all "night" to kill the dog, which thrashed and howled. Throughout, Blue stayed silent. He had picked up some words from me, but he apparently didn't have enough brain power to connect what I'd done with Vicious's death. Or maybe he just didn't have enough experience with humans. What does a machine know about survival?

"This dog is dead," Blue said in the "morning."

"Yes. Make it go away." And then, before Blue could get there first, I jumped off my platform and pointed to a cage. "This dog will behave correctly next."

"No."

"Why not this dog?"

"Not big."

"Big. You want big." Frantically I scanned the cages, before Blue could choose another one like Vicious. "This one, then."

"Why the hell not?" Blue said.

It was young. Not a puppy but still frisky, a mongrel of some sort with short hair of dirty white speckled with dirty brown. The dog looked liked something I could handle: big but not too big, not too aggressive, not too old, not too male. "Hey, Not-Too," I said, without enthusiasm, as Blue dissolved her cage. The mutt dashed over to me and tried to lick my boot.

A natural-born slave.

I had found a piece of rotten, moldy cheese in the garbage, so Blue could now make cheese, which Not-Too went crazy for. Not-Too and I stuck with the same routine I used with Mangy, and it worked pretty well. Or the cheese did. Within a few "days" the dog could sit, stay, and follow on command.

Then Blue threw me a curve. "What to do now? The presentation."

"We had the presentation," I said. "I don't need to see it again."

"What to do now? The presentation."

"Fine," I said, because it was clear I had no choice. "Let's have the presentation. Roll 'em."

I was sitting on my elevated platform, combing my hair. A lot of it had fallen out during the malnourished years in the camp, but now it was growing again. Not-Too had given up trying to jump up there with me and gone to sleep on her pillow below. Blue shot the beam out of his sphere and the holo played in front of me.

Only not the whole thing. This time he played only the brief scene where the big, patchy dog pulled the toddler back from falling into the cesspool. Blue played it once, twice, three times. Cold slid along my spine.

"You want Not-Too . . . you want this dog here to be trained to save children."

"This dog here does not behave correctly."

"Blue . . . How can I train a dog to save a child?"

"This dog here does not behave correctly."

"Maybe you haven't noticed, but we haven't got any fucking children for the dog to practice on!"

Long pause. "Do you want a child?"

"No!" Christ, he would kidnap one or buy one from the camp and I would be responsible for a kid along with nineteen semi-feral dogs. No.

"This dog here does not behave correctly. What to do now? The presentation."

"No, not the presentation. I saw it, *I saw it.* Blue . . . the other two humans who did not make the dogs behave correctly . . ."

"Killed."

"Yes. So you said. But they did get one dog to behave correctly, didn't they? Or maybe more than one. And then you just kept raising the bar higher. Water rescues, guiding the blind, finding lost people. Higher and higher."

But to all this, of course, Blue made no answer.

I wracked my brains to remember what I had ever heard, read, or seen about dog training. Not much. However, there's a problem with opening the door to memory: you can't control what strolls through. For the first time in years, my sleep was shattered by dreams.

I walked through a tiny garden, picking zinnias. From an open window came music, full and strong, an orchestra on CD. A cat paced beside me, purring. And there was someone else in the window, someone who called my name and I turned and—

I screamed. Clawed my way upright. The dogs started barking and howling. Blue floated from his corner, saying something. And Not-Too made a mighty leap, landed on my platform, and began licking my face.

"Stop it! Don't do that! I won't remember!" I shoved her so hard she fell off the platform onto the floor and began yelping. I put my head in my hands.

Blue said, "Are you not operative?"

"Leave me the fuck alone!"

Not-Too still yelped, shrill cries of pain. When I stopped shaking, I crawled off the platform and picked her up. Nothing seemed to be broken—although how would I know? Gradually she quieted. I gave her some cheese and put her back on her pillow. She wanted to stay with me but I wouldn't let her.

I would not remember. *I would not.* Law #5: Feel nothing.

We made a cesspool, or at least a pool. Blue depressed part of the floor to a depth of three feet and filled it with water. Not-Too considered this a swimming pool and loved to be in it, which was not what Blue wanted ("This water does not behave correctly"). I tried having the robot dump various substances into it until I found one that she disliked and I could tolerate: light-grade motor oil. A few small cans of oil like those in the dump created a polluted pool, not unlike Charleston Harbor. After every practice session I needed a bath.

But not Not-Too, because she wouldn't go into the "cesspool." I curled myself as small as possible, crouched at the side of the pool, and thrashed. After a few days, the dog would pull me back by my shirt. I moved into the pool. As long as she could reach me without getting any liquid on her, Not-Too happily played that game. As soon as I moved far enough out that I might actually need saving, she sat on her skinny haunches and looked away.

"This dog does not behave correctly."

I increased the cheese. I withheld the cheese. I pleaded and ordered and shunned and petted and yelled. Nothing worked. Meanwhile, the dream continued. The same dream, each time not greater in length but increasing in intensity. *I walked through a tiny garden, picking zinnias. From an open window came music, full and strong, an orchestra on CD. A cat paced beside me, purring. And there was someone else in the window, someone who called my name and I turned and—*

And woke screaming.

A cat. I had had a cat, before the War. Before everything. I had always had cats, my whole life. Independent cats, aloof and self-sufficient, admirably disdainful. Cats—

The dog below me whimpered, trying to get onto my platform to offer comfort I did not want.

I would not remember.

"This dog does not behave correctly," day after day.

I had Blue remove the oil from the pool. But by now Not-Too had been conditioned. She wouldn't go into even the clear water that she'd reveled in before.

"This dog does not behave correctly."

Then one day Blue stopped his annoying mantra, which scared me even more. Would I have any warning that I'd failed, or would I just die?

The only thing I could think of was to kill Blue first.

Blue was a computer. You disabled computers by turning them off, or cutting the power supply, or melting them in a fire, or dumping acid on them, or crushing them. But a careful search of the whole room revealed no switches or wires or anything that looked like a wireless control. A fire in this closed room, assuming I could start one, would kill me, too. Every kind of liquid or solid slid off Blue. And what would I crush him with, if that was even possible? A piece of cheese?

Blue was also—sort of—an intelligence. You could kill those by trapping them somewhere. My prison-or-sanctuary (depending on my

mood) had no real "somewheres." And Blue would just dissolve any structure he found himself in.

What to do now?

I lay awake, thinking, all night, which at least kept me from dreaming, I came up with two ideas, both bad. Plan A depended on discussion,
never Blue's strong suit.

"Blue, this dog does not behave correctly."

"No."

"This dog is not operative. I must make another dog behave correctly. Not this dog."

Blue floated close to Not-Too. She tried to bat at him. He circled
her slowly, then returned to his position three feet above the ground.
"This dog is operative."

"No. This dog *looks* operative. But this dog is not operative inside
its head. I cannot make this dog behave correctly. I need a different dog."

A very long pause. "This dog is not operative inside its head."

"*Yes.*"

"You can make another dog behave correctly. Like the presentation."

"Yes." It would at least buy me time. Blue must have seen "not
operative" dogs and humans in the dump; God knows there were enough
of them out there. Madmen, rabid animals, druggies raving just before
they died, or were shot. And next time I would add something besides oil
to the pool; there must be something that Blue would consider noxious
enough to simulate a cesspool but that a dog would enter. If I had to, I'd
use my own shit.

"This dog is not operative inside its head," Blue repeated, getting
used to the idea. "You will make a different dog behave correctly."

"Yes!"

"Why the hell not?" And then, "I kill this dog."

"No!" The word was torn from me before I knew I was going to say
anything. My hand, of its own volition, clutched at Not-Too. She jumped
but didn't bite. Instead, maybe sensing my fear, she cowered behind me,
and I started to yell.

"You can't just kill everything that doesn't behave like you want!
People, dogs . . . you can't just kill everything! You can't just . . . I had a cat
. . . I never wanted a dog but this dog . . . she's behaving correctly for her!

For a fucking traumatized dog and you can't just—I had a dog I mean a cat I had. . . . I had. . . ."

—*from an open window came music, full and strong, an orchestra on CD. A cat paced beside me, purring. And there was someone else in the window, someone who called my name and I turned and*—

"I had a child!"

Oh, God no no no . . . It all came out then, the memories and the grief and the pain I had pushed away for three solid years in order to survive . . . *Feel nothing* . . . Zack Zack *Zack* shot down by soldiers like a dog *Look, Mommy, here I am Mommy look* . . .

I curled in a ball on the floor and screamed and wanted to die. Grief had been postponed so long that it was a tsunami. I sobbed and screamed; I don't know for how long. I think I wasn't quite sane. No human should ever have to experience that much pain. But of course they do.

However, it can't last too long, that height of pain, and when the flood passed and my head was bruised from banging it on the hard floor, I was still alive, still inside the Dome, still surrounded by barking dogs. Zack was still dead. Blue floated nearby, unchanged, a casually murderous robot who would not supply flesh to dogs as food but who would kill anything he was programmed to destroy. And he had no reason not to murder me.

Not-Too sat on her haunches, regarding me from sad brown eyes, and I did the one thing I told myself I never would do again. I reached for her warmth. I put my arms around her and hung on. She let me.

Maybe that was the decision point. I don't know.

When I could manage it, I staggered to my feet. Taking hold of the rope that was Not-Too's leash, I wrapped it firmly around my hand. "Blue," I said, forcing the words past the grief clogging my throat, "make garbage."

He did. That was the basis of Plan B; that Blue made most things I asked of him. Not release, or mercy, but at least rooms and platforms and pools and garbage. I walked toward the garbage spilling from the usual place in the wall.

"More garbage! Bigger garbage! I need garbage to make this dog behave correctly!"

The reeking flow increased. Tires, appliances, diapers, rags, cans, furniture. The dogs' howling rose to an insane, deafening pitch. Not-Too pressed close to me.

"Bigger garbage!"

The chassis of a motorcycle, twisted beyond repair in some unimaginable accident, crashed into the room. The place on the wall from which the garbage spewed was misty gray, the same fog that the Dome had become when I had been taken inside it. Half a sofa clattered through. I grabbed Not-Too, dodged behind the sofa, and hurled both of us through the onrushing garbage and into the wall.

A broken keyboard struck me in the head, and the gray went black.

Chill. Cold with a spot of heat, which turned out to be Not-Too lying on top of me. I pushed her off and tried to sit up. Pain lanced through my head and when I put a hand to my forehead, it came away covered with blood. The same blood streamed into my eyes, making it hard to see. I wiped the blood away with the front of my shirt, pressed my hand hard on my forehead, and looked around.

Not that there was much to see. The dog and I sat at the end of what appeared to be a corridor. Above me loomed a large machine of some type, with a chute pointed at the now-solid wall. The machine was silent. Not-Too quivered and pressed her furry side into mine, but she, too, stayed silent. I couldn't hear the nineteen dogs on the other side of the wall, couldn't see Blue, couldn't smell anything except Not-Too, who had made a small yellow puddle on the floor.

There was no room to stand upright under the machine, so I moved away from it. Strips ripped from the bottom of my shirt made a bandage that at least kept blood out of my eyes. Slowly Not-Too and I walked along the corridor.

No doors. No openings or alcoves or machinery. Nothing until we reached the end, which was the same uniform material as everything else. Gray, glossy, hard. Dead.

Blue did not appear. Nothing appeared, or disappeared, or lived. We walked back and studied the overhead bulk of the machine. It had no dials or keys or features of any kind.

I sat on the floor, largely because I couldn't think what else to do, and Not-Too climbed into my lap. She was too big for this and I pushed her away. She pressed against me, trembling.

"Hey," I said, but not to her. Zack in the window *Look, Mommy, here I am Mommy look. . . .* But if I started down that mental road, I would be lost. Anger was better than memory. Anything was better than memory. "Hey!" I screamed. "Hey, you bastard Blue, what to do now? What to do now, you Dome shits, whoever you are?"

Nothing except, very faint, an echo of my own useless words.

I lurched to my feet, reaching for the anger, cloaking myself in it. Not-Too sprang to her feet and backed away from me.

"What to do now? What bloody fucking hell to do *now*?"

Still nothing, but Not-Too started back down the empty corridor. I was glad to transfer my anger to something visible, real, living. "There's nothing there, Not-Too. *Nothing*, you stupid dog!"

She stopped halfway down the corridor and began to scratch at the wall.

I stumbled along behind her, one hand clamped to my head. What the hell was she doing? This piece of wall was identical to every other piece of wall. Kneeling slowly—it hurt my head to move fast—I studied Not-Too. Her scratching increased in frenzy and her nose twitched, as if she smelled something. The wall, of course, didn't respond; nothing in this place responded to anything. Except—

Blue had learned words from me, had followed my commands. Or had he just transferred my command to the Dome's unimaginable machinery, instructing it to do anything I said that fell within permissible limits? Feeling like an idiot, I said to the wall, "Make garbage." Maybe if it complied and the garbage contained food . . .

The wall made no garbage. Instead it dissolved into the familiar gray fog, and Not-Too immediately jumped through, barking frantically.

Every time I had gone through a Dome wall, my situation had gotten worse. But what other choices were there? Wait for Blue to find and kill me, starve to death, curl up and die in the heart of a mechanical alien mini-world I didn't understand. Not-Too's barking increased in pitch and volume. She was terrified or excited or thrilled . . . How would I know? I pushed through the gray fog.

Another gray metal room, smaller than Blue had made my prison but with the same kind of cages against the far wall. Not-Too saw me and raced from the cages to me. Blue floated toward me . . . No, not Blue. This metal sphere was dull green, the color of shady moss. It said, "No human comes into this area."

"Guess again," I said and grabbed the trailing end of Not-Too's rope. She'd jumped up on me once and then had turned to dash back to the cages.

"No human comes into this area," Green repeated. I waited to see what the robot would do about it. Nothing.

Not-Too tugged on her rope, yowling. From across the room came answering barks, weirdly off. Too uneven in pitch, with a strange undertone. Blood, having saturated my makeshift bandage, once again streamed into my eyes. I swiped at it with one hand, turned to keep my gaze on Green, and let Not-Too pull me across the floor. Only when she stopped did I turn to look at the mesh-topped cages. Vertigo swooped over me.

Mangy was the source of the weird barks, a Mangy altered not beyond recognition but certainly beyond anything I could have imagined. Her mange was gone, along with all her fur. The skin beneath was now gray, the same gunmetal gray as everything else in the Dome. Her ears, the floppy poodle ears, were so long they trailed on the floor of her cage, and so was her tail. Holding on to the tail was a gray grub.

Not a grub. Not anything Earthly. Smooth and pulpy, it was about the size of a human head and vaguely oval. I saw no openings on the thing but Mangy's elongated tail disappeared into the doughy mass, so there must have been at least one orifice. As Mangy jumped at the bars, trying to get at Not-Too, the grub was whipped back and forth across the cage floor. It left a slimy trail. The dog seemed oblivious.

"*This dog is ready,*" Blue had said.

Behind me Green said, "No human comes into this area."

"Up yours."

"The human does not behave correctly."

That got my attention. I whirled around to face Green, expecting to be vaporized like the dead puppy, the dead Vicious. I thought I was already dead—and then I welcomed the thought. *Look, Mommy, here I am*

Mommy look . . . The laws of survival that had protected me for so long couldn't protect me against memory, not anymore. I was ready to die.

Instead Mangy's cage dissolved, she bounded out, and she launched herself at me.

Poodles are not natural killers, and this one was small. However, Mangy was doing her level best to destroy me. Her teeth closed on my arm. I screamed and shook her off, but the next moment she was biting my leg above my boot, darting hysterically toward and away from me, biting my legs at each lunge. The grub, or whatever it was, lashed around at the end of her new tail. As I flailed at the dog with both hands, my bandage fell off. Fresh blood from my head wound blinded me. I stumbled and fell and she was at my face.

Then she was pulled off, yelping and snapping and howling.

Not-Too had Mangy in her jaws. Twice as big as the poodle, she shook Mangy violently and then dropped her. Mangy whimpered and rolled over on her belly. Not-Too sprinted over to me and stood in front of me, skinny legs braced and scrawny hackles raised, growling protectively.

Dazed, I got to my feet. Blood, mine and the dogs', slimed everything. The floor wasn't trying to reabsorb it. Mangy, who'd never really liked me, stayed down with her belly exposed in submission, but she didn't seem to be badly hurt. The grub was still latched onto the end of her tail like a gray tumor. After a moment she rolled onto her feet and began to nuzzle the grub, one baleful eye on Not-Too: *Don't you come near this thing!* Not-Too stayed in position, guarding me.

Green said—and I swear its mechanical voice held satisfaction, no one will ever be able to tell me any different—"These dogs behave correctly."

The other cages held grubs, one per cage. I reached through the front bars and gingerly touched one. Moist, firm, repulsive. It didn't respond to my touch, but Green did. He was beside me in a flash. "No!"

"Sorry." His tone was dog-disciplining. "Are these the masters?"

No answer.

"What to do now? One dog for one . . ." I waved at the cages.

"Yes. When these dogs are ready."

This dog is ready, Blue had said of Mangy just before she was tumbled into the floor. Ready to be a pet, a guardian, a companion, a service animal to alien . . . what? The most logical answer was "children." Lassie, Rin Tin Tin, Benji, Little Guy. A boy and his dog. The aliens found humans dangerous or repulsive or uncaring or whatever, but dogs . . . You could count on dogs for your kids. Almost, and for the first time, I could see the point of the Domes.

"Are the big masters here? The adults?"

No answer.

"The masters are not here," I said. "They just set up the Domes as . . . as nurseries-slash-obedience schools." And to that statement I didn't even expect an answer. If the adults had been present, surely one or more would have come running when an alien blew into its nursery wing via a garbage delivery. There would have been alarms or something. Instead there was only Blue and Green and whatever 'bots inhabited whatever place held the operating room. Mangy's skin and ears and tail had been altered to fit the needs of these grubs. And maybe her voice-box, too, since her barks now had that weird undertone, like the scrape of metal across rock. Somewhere there was an OR.

I didn't want to be in that somewhere.

Green seemed to have no orders to kill me, which made sense because he wasn't programmed to have me here. I wasn't on his radar, which raised other problems.

"Green, make bread."

Nothing.

"Make water."

Nothing.

But two indentations in a corner of the floor, close to a section of wall, held water and dog-food pellets. I tasted both, to the interest of Not-Too and the growling of Mangy. Not too bad. I scooped all the rest of the dog food out of the trough. As soon as the last piece was out, the wall filled it up again. If I died, it wasn't going to be of starvation.

A few minutes ago, I had wanted to die. *Zack* . . .

No. Push the memory away. Life was shit, but I didn't want death, either. The realization was visceral, gripping my stomach as if that organ had been laid in a vise, or . . . There is no way to describe it. The feeling just was, its own justification. I wanted to live.

Not-Too lay a short distance away, watching me. Mangy was back in her cage with the grub on her tail. I sat up and looked around. "Green, this dog is not ready."

"No. What to do now?"

Well, that answered one question. Green was programmed to deal with dogs, and you didn't ask dogs "what to do now." So Green must be in some sort of communication with Blue, but the communication didn't seem to include orders about me. For a star-faring advanced race, the aliens certainly weren't very good at LANs. Or maybe they just didn't care—how would I know how an alien thinks?

I said, "I make this dog behave correctly." The all-purpose answer.

"Yes."

Did Green know details—that Not-Too refused to pull me from oily pools and thus was an obedience-school failure? It didn't seem like it. I could pretend to train Not-Too—I could actually train her, only not for water rescue—and stay here, away from the killer Blue, until . . . until what? As a survival plan, this one was shit. Still, it followed Laws #1 and #3: Take what you can get and never volunteer. And I couldn't think of anything else.

"Not-Too," I said wearily, still shaky from my crying jag, "Sit."

"Days" went by, then weeks. Not-Too learned to beg, roll over, bring me a piece of dog food, retrieve my thrown boot, lie down, and balance a pellet of dog food on her nose. I had no idea if any of these activities would be useful to an alien, but as long as Not-Too and I were "working," Green left us alone. No threats, no presentations, no objections. We were behaving correctly. I still hadn't thought of any additional plan. At night I dreamed of Zack and woke in tears, but not with the raging insanity of my first day of memory. Maybe you can only go through that once.

Mangy's grub continued to grow, still fastened onto her tail. The other grubs looked exactly the same as before. Mangy growled if I came too close to her, so I didn't. Her grub seemed to be drying out as it got bigger. Mangy licked it and slept curled around it and generally acted like some mythical dragon guarding a treasure box. Had the aliens bonded those two with some kind of pheromones I couldn't detect? I had no way of knowing.

Mangy and her grub emerged from their cage only to eat, drink, or shit, which she did in a far corner. Not-Too and I used the same corner, and all of our shit and piss dissolved odorlessly into the floor. Eat your heart out, Thomas Crapper.

As days turned into weeks, flesh returned to my bones. Not-Too also lost her starved look. I talked to her more and more, her watchful silence preferable to Green's silence or, worse, his inane and limited repertoires of answers. *"Green, I had a child named Zack. He was shot in the war. He was five." "This dog is not ready."*

Well, none of us ever are.

Not-Too started to sleep curled against my left side. This was a problem because I thrashed in my sleep, which woke her, so she growled, which woke me. Both of us became sleep-deprived and irritable. In the camp, I had slept twelve hours a day. Not much else to do, and sleep both conserved energy and kept me out of sight. But the camp was becoming distant in my mind. Zack was shatteringly vivid, with my life before the war, and the Dome was vivid, with Mangy and Not-Too and a bunch of alien grubs. Everything in between was fading.

Then one "day"—after how much time? I had no idea—Green said, "This dog is ready."

My heart stopped. Green was going to take Not-Too to the hidden OR, was going to—"No!"

Green ignored me. But he also ignored Not-Too. The robot floated over to Mangy's cage and dissolved it. I stood and craned my neck for a better look.

The grub was hatching.

Its "skin" had become very dry, a papery gray shell. Now it cracked along the top, parallel to Mangy's tail. She turned and regarded it quizzically, this thing wriggling at the end of her very long tail, but didn't attack or even growl. Those must have been some pheromones.

Was I really going to be the first and only human to see a Dome alien?

I was not. The papery covering cracked more and dropped free of the dog's tail. The thing inside wiggled forward, crawling out like a snake shedding its skin. It wasn't a grub but it clearly wasn't a sentient being, either. A larva? I'm no zoologist. This creature was as gray as everything else in the Dome but it had legs, six, and heads, two. At least, they might have been heads. Both had various indentations. One "head" crept forward, opened an orifice, and fastened itself back onto Mangy's tail. She continued to gaze at it. Beside me, Not-Too growled.

I whirled to grab frantically for her rope. Not-Too had no alterations to make her accept this . . . thing as anything other than a small animal to attack. If she did—

I turned just in time to see the floor open and swallow Not-Too. Green said again, "This dog is ready," and the floor closed.

"No! Bring her back!" I tried to pound on Green with my fists. He bobbed in the air under my blows. "Bring her back! Don't hurt her! Don't . . ." do what?

Don't turn her into a nursemaid for a grub, oblivious to me.

Green moved off. I followed, yelling and pounding. Neither one, of course, did the slightest good. Finally I got it together enough to say, "When will Not-Too come back?"

"This human does not behave correctly."

I looked despairingly at Mangy. She lay curled on her side, like a mother dog nursing puppies. The larva wasn't nursing, however. A shallow trough had appeared in the floor and filled with some viscous glop, which the larva was scarfing up with its other head. It looked repulsive.

Law #4: Notice everything.

"Green . . . okay. Just . . . okay. When will Not-Too come back here?"

No answer; what does time mean to a machine?

"Does the other dog return here?"

"Yes."

"Does the other dog get a . . ." A what? I pointed at Mangy's larva.

No response. I would have to wait.

But not, apparently, alone. Across the room another dog tumbled, snarling, from the same section of wall I had once come through. I recognized it as one of the nineteen left in the other room, a big black beast with powerful looking jaws. It righted itself and charged at me. There was no platform, no place to hide.

"No! Green, no, it will hurt me! This dog does not behave—"

Green didn't seem to do anything. But even as the black dog leapt toward me, it faltered in mid-air. The next moment, it lay dead on the floor.

The moment after that, the body disappeared, vaporized.

My legs collapsed under me. That was what would happen to me if I failed in my training task, was what had presumably happened to the previous two human failures. And yet it wasn't fear that made me sit so abruptly on the gray floor. It was relief, and a weird kind of gratitude. Green had protected me, which was more than Blue had ever done. Maybe Green was brighter, or I had proved my worth more, or in this room as opposed to the other room, all dog-training equipment was protected. I was dog-training equipment. It was stupid to feel grateful.

I felt grateful.

Green said, "This dog does not—"

"I know, I know. Listen, Green, what to do now? Bring another dog here?"

"Yes."

"I choose the dog. I am the . . . the dog leader. Some dogs behave correctly, some dogs do not behave correctly. I choose. Me."

I held my breath. Green considered, or conferred with Blue, or consulted its alien and inadequate programming. Who the hell knows? The robot had been created by a race that preferred Earth dogs to whatever species usually nurtured their young, if any did. Maybe Mangy and Not-Too would replace parental care on the home planet, thus introducing the idea of babysitters. All I wanted was to not be eaten by some canine nanny-trainee.

"Yes," Green said finally, and I let out my breath.

A few minutes later, eighteen dog cages tumbled through the wall like so much garbage, the dogs within bouncing off their bars and mesh tops, furious and noisy. Mangy jumped, curled more protectively around her oblivious larva, and added her weird, rock-scraping bark to the din. A cage grew up around her. When the cages had stopped bouncing, I walked among them like some kind of tattered lord, choosing.

"This dog, Green." It wasn't the smallest dog but it had stopped barking the soonest. I hoped that meant it wasn't a grudge holder. When I put one hand into its cage, it didn't bite me, also a good sign. The dog was phenomenally ugly, the jowls on its face drooping from small, rheumy eyes into a sort of folded ruff around its short neck. Its body that seemed to be all front, with stunted and short back legs. When it stood, I saw it was male.

"This dog? What to do now?"

"Send all the other dogs back."

The cages sank into the floor. I walked over to the feeding trough, scooped up handfuls of dog food, and put the pellets into my only pocket that didn't have holes. "Make all the rest of the dog food go away."

It vaporized.

"Make this dog's cage go away."

I braced myself as the cage dissolved. The dog stood uncertainly on the floor, gazing toward Mangy, who snarled at him. I said, as commandingly as possible, "Ruff!"

He looked at me.

"Ruff, come."

To my surprise, he did. Someone had trained this animal before. I gave him a pellet of dog food.

Green said, "This dog behaves correctly."

"Well, I'm really good," I told him, stupidly, while my chest tightened as I thought of Not-Too. The aliens, or their machines, did understand about anesthetic, didn't they? They wouldn't let her suffer too much? I would never know.

But now I *did* know something momentous. I had choices. I had chosen which room to train dogs in. I had chosen which dog to train. I had some control.

"Sit," I said to Ruff, who didn't, and I set to work.

Not-Too was returned to me three or four "days" later. She was gray and hairless, with an altered bark. A grub hung onto her elongated tail, undoubtedly the same one that had vanished from its cage while I was asleep. But unlike Mangy, who'd never liked either of us, Not-Too was ecstatic to see me. She wouldn't stay in her grub-cage against the wall but insisted on sleeping curled up next to me, grub and all. Green permitted this. I had become the alpha dog.

Not-Too liked Ruff, too. I caught him mounting her, her very long tail conveniently keeping her grub out of the way. Did Green understand the significance of this behavior? No way to tell.

We settled into a routine of training, sleeping, playing, eating. Ruff turned out to be sweet and playful but not very intelligent, and training took a long time. Mangy's grub grew very slowly, considering the large amount of glop it consumed. I grew, too; the waistband of my ragged pants got too tight and I discarded them, settling for a loin cloth, shirt, and my decaying boots. I talked to the dogs, who were much better conversationalists than Green since two of them at least pricked up their ears, made noises back at me, and wriggled joyfully at attention. Green would have been a dud at a cocktail party.

I don't know how long this all went on. Time began to lose meaning. I still dreamed of Zack and still woke in tears, but the dreams grew gentler and farther apart. When I cried, Not-Too crawled onto my lap, dragging her grub, and licked my chin. Her brown eyes shared my sorrow. I wondered how I had ever preferred the disdain of cats.

Not-Too got pregnant. I could feel the puppies growing inside her distended belly.

"Puppies will be easy to make behave correctly," I told Green, who said nothing. Probably he didn't understand. Some people need concrete visuals in order to learn.

Eventually, it seemed to me that Ruff was almost ready for his own grub. I mulled over how to mention this to Green but before I did, everything came to an end.

Clang! Clang! Clang!

I jerked awake and bolted upright. The alarm—a very human-sounding alarm—sounded all around me. Dogs barked and howled. Then I realized that it was a human alarm, coming from the Army camp outside the Dome, on the opposite side to the garbage dump. I could *see* the camp—in outline and faintly, as if through heavy gray fog. The Dome was dissolving.

"Green—what—no!"

Above me, transforming the whole top half of what had been the Dome, was the bottom of a solid saucer. Mangy, in her cage, floated upward and disappeared into a gap in the saucer's underside. The other grub cages had already disappeared. I glimpsed a flash of metallic color through the gap: Blue. Green was halfway to the opening, drifting lazily upward. Beside me, both Not-Too and Ruff began to rise.

"No! No!"

I hung onto Not-Too, who howled and barked. But then my body froze. I couldn't move anything. My hands opened and Not-Too rose, yowling piteously.

"No! No!" And then, before I knew I was going to say it, "Take me, too!"

Green paused in mid-air. I began babbling.

"Take me! Take me! I can make the dogs behave correctly—I can—you need me! Why are you going? Take me!"

"Take this human?"

Not Green but Blue, emerging from the gap. Around me the Dome walls thinned more. Soldiers rushed toward us. Guns fired.

"Yes! What to do? Take this human! The dogs want this human!"

Time stood still. Not-Too howled and tried to reach me. Maybe that's what did it. I rose into the air just as Blue said, "Why the hell not?"

Inside—inside *what?*—I was too stunned to do more than grab Not-Too, hang on, and gasp. The gap closed. The saucer rose.

After a few minutes, I sat up and looked around. Gray room, filled with dogs in their cages, with grubs in theirs, with noise and confusion and the two robots. The sensation of motion ceased. I gasped, "Where . . . where are we going?"

Blue answered. "Home."

"*Why?*"

"The humans do not behave correctly." And then, "What to do now?"

We were leaving Earth in a flying saucer, and it was asking *me?*

Over time—I have no idea how much time—I actually got some answers from Blue. The humans "not behaving correctly" had apparently succeeding in breaching one of the Domes somewhere. They must have used a nuclear bomb, but that I couldn't verify. Grubs and dogs had both died, and so the aliens had packed up and left Earth. Without, as far as I could tell, retaliating. Maybe.

If I had stayed, I told myself, the soldiers would have shot me. Or I would have returned to life in the camp, where I would have died of dysentery or violence or cholera or starvation. Or I would have been locked away by whatever government still existed in the cities, a freak who had lived with aliens, none of my story believed. I barely believed it myself.

I *am* a freak who lives with aliens. Furthermore, I live knowing that at any moment Blue or Green or their "masters" might decide to vaporize me. But that's really not much different from the uncertainty of life in the camp, and here I actually have some status. Blue produces whatever I ask for, once I get him to understand what that is. I have new clothes, good food, a bed, paper, a sort of pencil.

And I have the dogs. Mangy still doesn't like me. Her larva hasn't as yet done whatever it will do next. Not-Too's grub grows slowly, and now Ruff has one, too. Their three puppies are adorable and very trainable. I'm not so sure about the other seventeen dogs, some of whom look wilder than ever after their long confinement in small cages. Aliens are not, by definition, humane.

I don't know what it will take to survive when, and if, we reach "home" and I meet the alien adults. All I can do is rely on Jill's Five Laws of Survival:

1: Take what you can get.

2: Show no fear.

3: Never volunteer.

4: Notice everything.

But the Fifth Law has changed. As I lie beside Not-Too and Ruff, their sweet warmth and doggie-odor, I know that my first formulation was wrong. "Feel nothing"—that can take you some ways toward survival, but not very far. Not really.

Law #5: Take the risk. Love something.

The dogs whuff contentedly and we speed toward the stars.

SAFEGUARD

The uniformed military aide appeared at her elbow just as Katherine Taney rose from her gilded chair to enter the Oval Office. "The president will see you now," his secretary said simultaneously with the aide's statement, "Wait a moment, Katie."

She turned to stare at him. Keep the president *waiting? But his face told. For a moment vertigo nearly took her, a swooping blackness, but only for a moment. She said quietly to the aide, "Another one?"*

"Two more. Possibly three."

Dear God.

"Ma'am," chided the secretary, "the president is ready."

She straightened her aging back, thought a quick prayer, and went to brief the commander-in-chief. No, not really to brief—to plead, with the war-battered United States government, for compassion in the face of the unthinkable.

In the beginning, Li remembered, there had been big faceless people, white as cartoons. These memories were quick and slippery, like dreams. The other children didn't have them at all. Since that time, there had been only the real cartoons, the world, and Taney.

He had realized a long time ago that Taney was a person inside a white cartoon covering, and that he himself was a person inside the world, another covering. The world must also have an outside because when Taney left after each visit, she couldn't have stayed for days in the space behind the leaving door. The space was too small, not even room to lie down to sleep. And what would she eat or drink in there until she came back? And where did she get the fried cakes and other things she brought them?

"There's another door, isn't there, Taney?" he said yet again as the five of them sat around the feeder in the Grove. The feeder had just brought up bowls of food, but no one except Sudie was eating them because Taney had brought a lot of fried cakes in a white bag. Sudie, always greedy, had eaten three fried cakes and half a bowl of stew and now slumped happily against a palm tree, her naked belly round and her lips greasy. Jana sat with her knees drawn up to her chin, her thin arms clasped around her legs. Kim stared at nothing.

Li repeated, "Another door. You go out of the world through another door, don't you?"

"I can't answer that," Taney said, as always. The girls didn't even glance at her. Li didn't expect them to; he was the only one who ever questioned Taney.

But tonight Jana, still gazing over her clasped knees at the shadow of trees against the sky, said, "Why can't you answer, Taney?"

Taney's head swiveled toward Jana. It was hard to see Taney's eyes through the faceplate on her white covering; you had to get very close and squint. The cartoons covered like Taney didn't even have eyes, no matter how much you squinted at them.

There hadn't been any new cartoons for a long while.

Taney finally said, "I can't answer you, Jana, because the world keeps you safe."

The old answer, the one they'd heard all their lives from Taney, from the cartoons. For the first time, Li challenged it. "How, Taney? How does the world keep us safe? Sudie still fell over that stone and you had to come and fix her arm. Jana ate that flower and all her food came out of her mouth." The next day, all of that kind of flower, all over the world, had disappeared.

Taney merely repeated, "The world keeps you safe."

Sudie said suddenly from her place against the tree, "Your voice is sad, Taney."

Jana said, "When will we get new cartoons?"

But Taney was already getting to her feet, slow and heavy in her white covering. Even Kim knew what that meant. Kim climbed onto Taney's lap and started to lick frantically at Taney's face, and it took both Sudie and Li to pull her back. Kim was tall and strong. Taney said, as always, "Be well, dear hearts," and started away.

Li, clutching the screaming Kim, watched Taney walk the path between the trees until he couldn't see her anymore. The leaving door was in a big pink rock at the small end of the world, near the pond. Maybe tomorrow they would splash in the pond. That might be fun.

Except that nothing was as much fun as it used to be. Li didn't know why, but it was true.

Eventually Kim stopped screaming and they let her go. Jana folded and refolded the white paper bag Taney had left her, making pretty shapes. The sky overhead and beside the Grove darkened. The feeder with its three untouched bowls and one empty one sank into the ground. The blankets rose, clean even though last night Kim had shit hers again.

The four children wrapped themselves in blankets and lay down on the grass. Within minutes all were asleep in the circling grove of antiseptic palm trees that produced no fruit, and whose fronds never rustled in the motionless air.

"Two-and-a-half enclosed acres. Double-built dome construction, translucent and virtually impenetrable. Negative air pressure with triple filters. Inside, semi-tropical flora, no fauna, monitors throughout. Life-maintenance machinery to be concentrated by the east wall within a circle of trees, including the input screen. All instructional programs to feature only cartoon characters in biohazard suits, to minimize curiosity about other people."

Katherine said, "Two-and-a-half acres isn't sufficient for a self-sustaining biosphere."

"Of course not, ma'am," the high-clearance, DOD engineer said, barely concealing his impatience. "An outside computer will control all plant-maintenance and atmospheric functions."

"And personnel?"

"Once the biosphere is up and running, it will need little human oversight. Both functional and contact personnel will be your agency's responsibility. Our involvement extends only to the construction and maintenance of the cage."

"Don't call it that!"

The engineer, whom Katherine knew she should be thanking instead of reprimanding, merely shrugged. His blue eyes glittered with dislike. "Whatever you say, ma'am."

Three days later, Taney didn't come.

It was her *day*. But lunch came up on the feeder, and then dinner, and then the sky got dark, and the leaving door never opened. Kim sat staring at it the whole day, her mouth hanging open until Jana pressed it closed. Kim couldn't talk or do much of anything, but somehow she always knew when it was Taney's day. So she sat, while the others splashed in the pond and pretended to have fun.

All at once the water in the pond gave a small hiccup and sloshed gently onto the sandy beach.

"Did you feel that?" Sudie said. "The ground moved!"

"Ground can't move," Li said, because he was the leader. But it had. He waited for the ground to do something else but it just lay there, ground under water. Li got out of the pond.

"Where are you going?" Jana said.

"Feeder time," Li said, although it wasn't.

They pulled Kim to her feet and ran. By the time they reached the grove, their naked bodies were dry. Li could feel his hair, which Taney sometimes cut, curling wetly on the back of his neck. Jana's hair, shorter than his, stood up in yellow fluff that Li liked. Maybe Jana would want to play bodies with him tonight.

They sat in a circle under the trees, hungry and pleasantly tired from splashing in the pond. Sudie studied the keypad under the screen, each with a little picture on it, and chose the cartoon about four children helping each other to make sand paintings. Li was tired of that cartoon, although when it first appeared, they'd all loved it. Days and days had been spent making sand paintings with the many-colored sands on the beach by the pond.

The cartoon played, but only Kim really watched it. The feeder rose and—

"The bowls are empty!" Jana cried.

Li leaped up and examined the four wooden bowls. *Empty*. How could that be? Why would the feeder bring empty bowls?

The ground moved gently beneath them.

"The feeder is broken!" Sudie jumped up and ran to the keypad. Each of its buttons had a picture of a cartoon showing the right thing to do for eating, for playing, for cleaning themselves, for fixing bloody scratches if they fell, for not using up all their kindness if they got angry with each other. But nothing for a broken feeder, a thing that couldn't happen because the feeder was part of the world. But if there was an inside to the covering that was the world and therefore an outside then maybe—Li had never thought this before—maybe the feeder, like Taney, went outside and things *could* break there?

Cold slid along Li's neck. Kim started licking everyone's face, running from one to another. Li let her because Kim was stronger than he was and anyway he was used to it.

"I'm calling Taney," Sudie said, but she looked questioningly at Li. Calling Taney was, they had all been told over and over, very serious. The only times they'd ever called her was when Sudie broke her arm and when Jana ate the bad flower and all her food came back up through her mouth. Only twice.

"Do it," Li said, and Sudie pushed at the exact same time both buttons with Taney's picture.

Katherine sat very erect, the back of her best suit not touching the back of her chair, her face stone. A secret congressional hearing didn't scare her, veteran of far too many. But what this particular committee might decide, did.

"Dr. Taney, are they, in your expert opinion, the result of deliberate genetic experimentation?"

"Of course they are, Mr. Chairman."

"And intended by the enemy for use as a covert terrorist weapon against the United States?"

"The enemy does not inform me of its intentions."

"But if released, these things—"

"Children, Senator. And no one is suggesting releasing them."

"But—"

"They are children. Have you even seen them?" Katherine pressed the button on her purse. Equipment she should not have been able to get into the committee room suddenly flashed an image on the far wall. Four babies, three of them beautiful with skin pink or brown or golden, one of those with a shock of thick black hair and eyes already the color of coffee beans. They could have posed for a diversity poster. Smiling, plump-armed, adorable.

Lethal.

Li hadn't expected Taney to come right away, maybe not until morning. He couldn't sleep. He didn't want to play bodies with Jana or Sudie. All night, it seemed, he lay in his blanket, listening to Kim breathe heavily beside him, her mouth open. And in the morning, the world broke.

It began with a big shake of the ground, much harder than yesterday, that would have knocked them all down if anyone had been standing. Next came a terrible grinding noise like scraping rocks together but so loud that Kim clapped her hands over her ears. Sudie screamed. Then the ground shook even more, and the sky cracked, and pieces fell down on Li.

He rolled over and shut his eyes tight. The noise went on and on. A tree fell over—he knew it was a tree even without looking, and that made him jump up and shout, "Get away from the grove! Go! Go!"

No one moved. Another tree toppled and something went bang!

All at once, it was over.

Kim began licking Li's face, then Jana's. Sudie still screamed. Jana cried, "Stop that!" and hit her. Sudie stopped. Kim did not; she licked Sudie's face until Sudie shoved her away.

Silence.

"Children," Katherine said into the silence. "And I have more pictures. So do others, who know these babies' stories."

The chairman leaned forward, his face colder than the medals on the chest of the general beside him. "Dr. Taney, are you saying you have breached national security by leaking this information to others? And further, that you are attempting to blackmail—"

"I attempt nothing, Mr. Chairman. I don't have to. Secrets extend only so far, even secret terrorist weapons. Which these children are, in a long and shameful tradition. Children have been used to blow up American soldiers—and themselves—on four continents, to smuggle poisons into military camps, to deliver biological bombs. We all know that. Right now your impulse is to destroy these children as soon as researchers have taken enough blood and tissue samples. You want to destroy them partly because they are truly dangerous and partly to avoid widespread panic. With the war so recently ended, you don't want the populace to know what the enemy was—and may still be—capable of, both technically and morally. That's understandable. But—"

Katherine leaned forward, her gaze locked with the chairman's. "But I am telling you, Senator Blaine, that your information chain is not secure, and that if you destroy these children—these innocent and very photogenic babies—that fact will become known. This administration—and your political party—has worked very hard to position themselves as the new world force that acts compassionately, that does the right thing. You've had a hard row to hoe in that regard, given your predecessors' actions on the world stage. Do you really want to undo all that careful positioning by destroying four innocent children?"

The senator said angrily, "This is not a partisan—"

"Of course not," Katherine said wearily. "But you've already commissioned a feasibility study for a self-contained and completely secure dome to—"

"How do you know that, madam? How?"

She just stared at him. Then she said, in a different voice, "I was with the original team that extracted the children from behind enemy lines, and I just told you that your information chain is not secure. How would I not know?

"Senator—grow up."

Cautiously Li stamped one bare foot on the ground. It didn't move. He said, startled to hear his own voice so high, so squeaky, "Is anybody hurt?"

"No," Jana said. Sudie said, "Find the cartoon about the right thing to do if the world breaks."

"There's no cartoon for that," Jana said. She looked at Li. "What should we do?"

"I don't know," Li said, because he didn't. How could the world break?

"Let's go to the leaving door," Jana said. "Maybe Taney will come."

They wound their way to the far end of the world, Jana in the lead, Li lagging behind to look at everything. Trees fallen to the ground or leaning over. Big pieces of the sky on the ground—what if one of those had fallen on the Grove? And then, almost to the pond and the leaving door—

"Stop," Li said, and looked, and couldn't stop looking.

Sudie breathed, "What *is* it?"

Li took a long time to find the right words. "It's a crack in the world."

A narrow jagged break, just like when he cracked a stick on a hard stone. The break started at the ground and he could follow it with his eyes up the sky to a place where pieces of sky had fallen, making a white pile. Jana started toward the crack, stopped, started again. Li followed her. After a moment Kim darted after them both, frantically trying to lick their faces.

"Not now, Kim!" Li snapped. He stood beside Jana at the crack and they both peered through.

"What is it, Li?" Jana whispered?

"It's . . . it's another world. Where Taney goes when she leaves us."

Jana turned her thin body sideways and squeezed through. Li said, "No! You don't—"

"We need to find Taney, don't we?" Jana said.

Li didn't know. He didn't know anything anymore. The world on the other side of the crack looked so different . . . All at once he wanted to see more of it, see it all. He turned sideways and pushed himself through, scraping skin off his shoulders. Immediately Sudie and Kim began to howl.

"Stop that!" Jana said. "We're going to find Taney! Sudie, push Kim through."

Kim was the biggest but very strong and flexible; she wiggled herself through easily. Once out, she just stared from the tiny eyes in her broad, flat face. She didn't even try to lick anybody. For once Li knew how Kim felt. He had walked a few steps away from the old world and he couldn't stop staring.

Rocky, wrinkled ground stretched away on all sides—so much ground! Li's stomach flopped; this world was so *big*. But empty. He saw no palms, no bushes, no flowers, nothing but ground that was red and white and brown, endless ground, and far, far away the ground rose up high, blue with white on top, and above that—

The sky of this world was blue, not white, and it went on forever. Forever, so high above that Li's head wrinkled inside just like the ground. All this . . . and Taney had never told them. Why not?

"Li, Sudie won't fit," Jana said. "She's too fat for the break in the world."

Sudie had reached one arm through the crack and was frantically waving it and howling. Li wanted her to shut up; he wanted to go on looking and looking. The endless ground was covered with rocks, hundreds of rocks; for the first time, Li understood what the numbers cartoon meant by "hundreds." Rocks red and white and gray and black, all sizes and shapes, some tiny as a thumb and some bigger than Li, some—

"Li, she won't *fit*," Jana said. Sudie howled louder. Jana said, "Oh, be quiet, Sudie, we're not going to leave you. Li?"

"Tell her to go roll in the mud by the pond and get all wet and slippery."

Sudie did, and eventually they pulled her through, although not without making blood come out on her arms and shoulders and hips. Sudie didn't seem to mind the blood. But she took one look at the new world and promptly began howling again, plopping down onto the ground and covering her head with her bloody arms.

Something very bright came into the new sky over the top of the old world. Li tried to look at it and couldn't; it hurt his eyes too much. Fear filled him.

Jana gasped, "What's that? Sudie, shut up!" Kim began licking all their faces.

The bright thing didn't seem to be falling on them. Li said, "I think . . . I think it's morning."

"That's silly," Jana said. "Morning comes all over the whole sky at the same time."

"Not in this world," Li said. He felt a little dizzy, as if he'd been playing the spinning game. "Jana, this place is so *big*."

"Then how are we going to find Taney? I think we should walk on the path." She pointed.

Li had to turn his back on the morning and squint before he could see what she pointed at. A faint path, no more than a pressing down of rocks, led away from the real world. Closest to him, it had a broken pattern of triangles in the dust.

"Come on, Sudie," Jana said. "Get up. We're going to find Taney. Li, follow me and she'll come, too."

Li followed Jana, who didn't look around but just walked fast on her thin, long legs. Sudie and Kim stumbled after them, Sudie complaining that all the stones on the ground hurt her feet. Jana seemed to have become the leader now, but Li didn't care about that, or his feet. All he wanted to do was look and look.

Rocks, growing redder as the morning rose in the sky. The morning looked like a rock, too, brighter and brighter, so that looking at it for even a second hurt Li's eyes. And there, on that flat rock . . .

Sudie started to scream again. Jana, who had used up all her kindness, hit her. The thing on the rock scurried away, underneath more stones. Li said, "Don't hit Sudie, Jana!" at the same minute that Jana said, "I'm sorry. She won't—what was that, Li?"

"It was alive, I think," Li said uncertainly. "Like birds."

"Then why didn't it fly away?"

"I don't know." He had never seen anything alive except themselves, Taney, and the birds in the old world. A memory came, himself asking Taney, *"What do the birds eat?"* *"The world gives them food high up on the sky,"* she'd answered, *"just like the feeder gives you food. The world keeps you both safe."*

They weren't in that world anymore. Li said, "Watch out for other living things. Don't step on any because you might hurt them. You might even make them dead." They had all seen dead birds in the real world. Taney always took the bodies away with her.

They walked for a long time. The morning rock in the sky got brighter still. Something was wrong with the air; it got way too hot. Li was very thirsty but there was nothing to drink. They walked silently, even Sudie, and Li began to feel very afraid. The hard-to-see path didn't seem to go anywhere. Why would there be a path that didn't go anywhere? What if they couldn't find Taney?

"Look," Sudie said as they trudged over a low rise, "a big path!"

She was right, but this path was different: very wide and very straight and very hot. Putting a foot on the black stone, Li yelped and immediately pulled it back. But immediately he forgot about the pain. Something was coming very fast along the path.

Sudie screamed until Jana raised her hand and Sudie stopped. Li could feel Jana tremble beside him. All four children huddled into a knot. The thing made a lot of noise, growing bigger and bigger until it stopped with the loudest noise yet and a person jumped out.

A person who was not Taney, and not in a slippery white covering or a faceplate. Again Li's mind wrinkled and dizzied. Even Sudie was too scared to make noise. The only one who moved was Kim, licking everyone's faces.

"Oh my God, you kids caught in the earthquake? What in hell happened to you? Jack, one of 'em's bleeding!"

Another person got out of the moving thing. Now Li could see that the thing wasn't alive, like the not-bird had been, but it still made puffing noises. The second person had a lot of hair growing on his face, which looked silly and scary. But his voice was kind. "Where's your folks? And your clothes? Sally, they look damn near dehydrated. Get the water. Kids, what happened?"

Jana said, "We have to find Taney."

"Taney? Is that a town?"

Jana said, Li wondering at her bravery, "Taney's a person. The world broke and before that the feeders didn't give us any food and we have to find Taney!"

The person with the hair on his face looked away from Jana. His face above the hair looked very red. The other person came hurrying toward them with a white thing in her hand. "Here, drink first. Jack, go get some sheets or something from the trunk. Poor kids must have been asleep when the quake hit, you know these hippie tourists just let their kids sleep buck naked, it's a disgrace but even so—"

Li stopped listening to her words, which after all didn't even make sense. The white thing was sort of like a food bowl closed at the top and sort of like the spring faucet in the real world, giving out water. Li passed it first to Kim, as always, who drank greedily, the water dribbling down her chest. Then Jana, then Sudie, and by the time it got to Li, he felt he couldn't wait another moment. Nothing had ever tasted as good as that water, nothing.

The person called Sally handed a big thin blanket to Jana, who let it drop to the ground. "Put it on you, for God's sake," Sally said, and the kindness in her voice was getting used up.

Jack said, still not looking at them, said, "Sal, I think maybe they're in shock. Or maybe a little feeble-minded."

"Oh!" Sally said, and she looked at Kim, still trying to lick Sudie's face. "Oh, of course, poor things. Here, honey, let me help you." She picked up the blanket, tore it in half, and began to wrap Jana in it.

Jana pushed away. "It's not time to sleep!"

"Jana, let her," Li said. He didn't know what these people were doing, but the kindness had come back into Sally's voice, and they were going to need kindness, Li realized, to find Taney. This place was much different from the real world. Brighter and harder and hungrier and bigger.

From the corner of his eye he saw another of the not-birds watching him, stretched out on a flat gray rock. Its eyes were shiny and black as pebbles.

Sally tied blanket pieces around all of them and said, very slowly, "Now get out of this sun and into the car before you all broil. Honey, you're burning already, and bleeding, too. You get hit by debris in the quake?"

She was looking at Sudie, but Li answered. "She got scraped by the crack in the world."

"I knew it. Get in, get in!"

The "car" was just another covering, made of the same material as the place the sky met the ground in the real world. Inside the car, however, the air was more like the real world: cooler and not so bright. The four of them squeezed into a space in the back, and Sally and Jack climbed into the front space. Sally turned around.

"Now what all are your names?" She still spoke very slowly, making each word with her lips all pushed out.

Li said, "I'm Li. This is Jana and Sudie and Kim."

"Good," Sally said, smiling wide as a cartoon person. "Now tell Aunt Sally what happened. How you got all alone out on the desert."

Li said, "The ground shook last night and then this morning the world broke. We squeezed out through a crack in the sky and walked. We have to find Taney."

"Is Taney a town, son?" Jack said.

Li didn't know what a town was. "Taney's a person. She takes care of us."

"A foster mother?" Sally said.

Jack said, "I don't think a foster mother could handle four retards, Sal. More likely some sort of institution. Might be in East Lancaster."

"Doubt it," Sally said. "East Lancaster got hit pretty hard by the depression, only been minimal facilities there for fifteen years, and now with the quake and all. . . ."

"Well, them kids didn't walk very far buck-naked in the desert," Jack said. Li could hear that the kindness was getting used up in his voice. "Somebody must of took them camping or something. But I can't go racketing around looking for some institution when we need to see how badly our place got hit. Best bring them home with us tonight and check the Internet for this 'Taney.'"

"Right," Sally said. "Kids, don't worry, everything'll be all right."

Jack snorted.

The covering round them leapt forward and Sudie screamed. Jana pinched her hard and Sudie stopped, although she didn't look any more terrified. Kim began licking Sudie's face. Sally watched a minute and then turned away, the tips of her mouth turning down. Li didn't want Sally's kindness to get used up again. He leaned forward.

"Sally, thank you so much for the water. It was very good."

"Oh, God, you're welcome," Sally said.

"My name is Li. Not God."

Jack laughed. "He's not so dumb after all!"

The "car" walked a long way, and everywhere on the long way looked the same. Li watched everything, inside and outside the car, until despite himself, he fell asleep. He woke up when the car stopped at a big square thing which, Li realized when they went inside it, was another world, with its own ground and sky. How many worlds were there?

"Still standing, by the grace of God," Sally said. "We're damn lucky. Jack, you get on that computer and start searching. Li, what did you say your last name was?"

"My name is Li."

"No, honey, your *other* name."

Li just stared. He had no other name. Jack sighed and went around a part of this world's sky. The place the children stood in was cool and dim, with large, funny-shaped rocks covered in blankets to sit on, and a feeder. The children crowded near it, waiting.

"Y'all are hungry, right?" Sally said. "Can't say as I blame you. Well, go ahead sit at the table and I'll rustle up something. A lot of smashed crockery in the kitchen, but that can wait."

This feeder was broken, too; no bowls rose from it. But apparently Sally had saved food from before it broke because she brought out big bowls. The food looked strange but tasted wonderful, and Li ate until his belly felt full and round. Afterward sleepiness took him again, and he stretched out on the floor beside Jana, who was making strange sounds in her throat.

"You got allergies, hon?" Sally said. "Never mind, I don't expect you to know. Jack, you making any progress in there?"

"Just over a million hits on 'Taney,' is all," Jack said, which made no sense. Nobody was hitting anybody. "This ain't going to be easy."

Li's throat felt strange, and not in a good way. Jana kept making strange noises in her throat. Li must have slept, because when he woke it was night again, and very dark. Something glowed in a far corner of the room, and at first that scared Li. He lay on the ground, watching to see if the glowing thing moved. It didn't. Slowly he crawled toward it, until he could see that it was a tiny ball of morning, like the big one in the sky of the big world, but not so bright. Li touched it, and snatched back his finger. The tiny morning was hot.

Carefully he studied it. It was a made thing, like the pretty folded things Jana made from Taney's paper bags. Li's breath came faster. All these things were made: the feeder and the bowls and the blanket-covered rocks—"chairs" Sally had called them—to sit on, and maybe even the sky of this world.

Of any world.

Li's mind raced. He never got back to sleep. All the rest of the night he either crawled around, touching things and trying to figure out how they'd been made, or else lying still, thinking. His throat still hurt but he ignored it. *Made things.* Other people. Worlds within worlds.

When morning—the big morning—returned, the girls still lay sleeping on the ground. All of them breathed too heavily. Li stood, stretched, and went to look around the parts of sky that touched the ground for Jack and Sally.

Jack sat slumped over a small screen, which still glowed. Sally lay on the floor. Both of them were dead.

Not here.

Katherine made another, equally futile tour of the biosphere, stumping heavily, leaning on her cane. She'd fallen two days ago, twisting her knee, which had led her to put off her visit to the children. Then had come the first quake, which had made her fall again as she hobbled across her living room. No one had predicted the second, massive quake.

She called again, knowing it was pointless. She'd seen the blood on the crack in the supposedly shatter-proof dome. The children had squeezed themselves through and set off, probably looking for her. They wouldn't get far, naked in the desert, without water. There was, by design, nothing within fifty miles of the biosphere. Scavengers, of air or ground, would get the bodies.

Tears welled in her eyes, behind the faceplate. *Stupid.* This was one solution, maybe the only solution, to a problem that could only grow as years passed. Katherine was nearly seventy—what would have happened after she could no longer carry on this long, painful fight? Some days she felt ninety. Some days she felt already dead, even as the world slowly revived itself from the bad years of the war.

Li, with his dark expressive eyes and quick mind . . . delicate Jana, who in another world would have been a startling beauty . . . funny emotional Sudie . . . even Kim, afflicted with both Down's and autism . . . even Kim she would miss. Her children. She'd had no other.

Katherine put herself through detox, leaving her biohazard suit behind, even as she doubted that detox was any longer necessary. She hobbled toward her car. The AC felt blessedly cool. Fifty miles to the village of Las Verdes, where a group of Native American descendents eked out a subsistence existence, survivors of past injustices just as the children had been of a future one. A mile outside Las Verdes, Katherine had built a house, which was now a pile of debris. The Indians would rebuild it for her; they were good at starting over. Although now there was no reason for her to stay.

Li. Jana. Sudie. Kim.

She drove home through a desert wavery with heat and tears.

"Why don't the buttons have cartoon pictures on them?" Jana said.

"It isn't for cartoons," Li said slowly. They stood around the little screen where Jack had died. Li and Sudie had pulled him off the chair and laid him on the floor beside Sally, and Jana had covered the people with a blanket. Li didn't know why she'd done that, but it seemed a good thing to do.

The children had examined this world. It had four places, two with faucet springs. In those two places a lot of things were broken, and sharp pieces of clear sky had fallen down. Jana cut her foot on one piece, but it only bled a little. One of the places had more of the strange food, but not very much of it. They'd eaten it all.

"If the screen isn't for cartoons, what is it for?" Sudie said. She stood behind Li, breathing heavily into his neck, and her voice sounded . . . thick, somehow. Like food was stuck in her throat, although she said it wasn't.

"I don't know what it's for," Li said. "But we can't take it with us because it's tied to where this sky touches the ground."

"Take it with us? Where are we going?" Sudie sounded frightened and Kim began to lick her face.

Jana said, "We can't just walk like yesterday, Li."

"We're not going to walk. I watched Jack make the car go. I think I can do that."

"But where?"

"We'll go along the big path. There's no more food here, Jana. Maybe the path will take us to Taney."

Jana considered. "Okay. You're right, we can't stay here. We have to find Taney. But first fill those white bowls with water from the faucet spring."

They went out the leaving door and climbed into the car, lugging blankets and water. Sudie had untied the blanket from her body, but Li made her put it back on. "People here are different," he said. "They use up their kindness faster if you don't have blankets around you. Oh—wait!"

He went back inside and brought out a big armful of the blankets behind another leaving door in the biggest place. They were like the blankets around Jack and Sally, all shaped like bodies and fastened together with tiny little strings or hard bumps that Li had examined in great detail. "Put these coverings on you," he told the girls.

"Like Taney has," Sudie said happily, even though none of Jack's and Sally's coverings were slippery like Taney's. But some were white, and Sudie picked one of those.

Li turned the thing that Jack had turned to make the car go, and it started making noises. But it wouldn't go forward until he pushed down with his feet on the flat things on the car's ground. Then the car stopped.

"It's dead," Sudie said.

Li made it start again, and pushed the flat things. The car stopped. "maybe I should just push one."

The car raced away so fast that Sudie screamed, even Jana gasped, and Kim started licking everyone frantically. Li pushed on the other flat thing and the car stopped.

Eventually he figured out how to make it go-stop-go-stop-go-stop, and they started down the wide dusty path, under the hot ball of morning high in the sky, to look for Taney.

"—eight point one on the Richter scale, slightly higher than the San Francisco earthquake of 1906. The president has declared southern California a federal disaster area, and the Department of Domestic Rescue is mobilizing to—" Katherine turned off the car radio.

She drove past the village. Las Verdes—a bitter joke of a name, if there ever was one—had gotten off fairly lightly because when all buildings were one-story adobe brick, collapse was quick and clean. No fires, no burst gas mains, no floods. The underground spring, the only reason this village existed at all, was still there, although the well-house had crumbled. The wind mills and lone cell tower lay on their sides; TV satellite dishes littered the rubble; somewhere a woman wailed, a high keening borne on the thin wind.

Katherine's house was a pile of dirt, but the shed in the backyard still stood. Under its deceptive façade of cheap plastic was a reinforced steel frame, thief-proof and, unlike the biosphere dome, far too small to crack. She let herself inside with the key around her neck. A generator-powered computer running encrypted, military-grade software sat on a table that nearly filled the small space. It had a direct uplink to a military satellite.

TOP SECRET
CODE WORD ACCESS ONLY
NOT FOR DISTRIBUTION
CASE NO. 254987-A
CODE NAME: ACHILLES
DATE: 6/12/28
AGENT IN CHARGE: SIGMA INVESTIGATOR K. M. TANEY
SUBJECT: DEATH OF GM JUVENILE AGENTS

She typed swiftly, sent the report, and turned off the computer. With a second key, Katherine turned a small lock set into the machine's side. She closed the door, hobbled back to the car, and drove several hundred feet away. Five minutes later, the shed exploded.

Now there was nothing to keep her here at all.

Nonetheless, she drove toward Las Verdes. The village had regarded Katherine with neither kindness nor suspicion. Mostly it had let her be: one more crazy white inexplicably in love with the inhospitable desert, wasting her time making bad paintings of rocks and sunsets, supported by means beyond their world. Still, the trunk of her car held medical supplies, among other things; perhaps she could help.

The car stopped going and Li couldn't make it start again no matter what he did. "Is it broken?" Sudie said. "Like the feeder and the world?"

"Yes," Li said. He opened the door; it was getting very hot inside. It was hot outside, too. The four children got out and sat in the brief shade on one side of the dead car, trying to not touch its burning side.

Jana started to say something, stopped, took Li's hand.

He gazed out across the big world, glanced briefly at the hot ball of morning in the big sky, and anger grew in him. All this—all this had been out here all the time, and Taney had never let them have it. All this, and now that they had found it, they were going to die here. Li knew it, and he guessed that Jana knew it, too. Sudie and Kim did not. But Kim might have known something, deep in her different head, because she crawled over Sudie and began to lick Li's face.

He pushed her away and dropped Jana's hand. His kindness, he knew, was all used up. He didn't want to die.

"I'm so thirsty," Sudie said. No one answered.

A long time later Sudie said, "Look at those big birds up there. Flying around and around in circles. Why are they doing that, Li?"

"I don't know," Li said.

Jana said, "Something is coming on the big path. There." She pointed.

Li strained his eyes. Finally he saw a sort of wiggle in the air—how could Jana see so far?—with a black dot in it. The dot got bigger and bigger and then it turned into another "car" but big, enormous, so that Sudie whimpered and tried to hide behind Li. The car stopped and a person got out.

"What the . . . what happened here, son?"

"This car stopped," Li said. He stood. The man didn't have hair on his face like Jack, and his voice sounded more like Taney's.

"*You* were driving? Where's your folks?"

Li didn't know what "folks" might be; everything in this world was so strange. He said, "We have to find Taney."

"But your parents . . . hell, get out of the sun, first. We can help you, son. We're Department of Domestic Rescue. Climb in."

Inside the big car was another little world, with chairs and blankets and a feeder. A woman gave them water and said, "Baker, where did they come from?"

Baker sat at another of the little screens and did something to it. "They said 'Taney,' but GPS isn't giving me anything like that."

"Well, we're due in Las Verdes like, now. Shall I drive? And while you're online, is there any more email on why we're being diverted to an ass-end hole like Las Verdes when real population centers are screaming for help?"

"No. Presumably Las Verdes got an emergency situation."

"Two states have got an emergency situation, Baker. Why the priority-one diversion to Las Verdes?"

"Ann, 'ours is not to reason why—'"

"Oh, roast it. I'll drive."

Baker gave them all food, and Li fell asleep on the moving ground of the car. When he woke, Baker and Ann were leaving the big car. "You stay here, Li," Baker said. "Safest and coolest inside, and we've got work to do. We'll get you sorted out tonight, I promise. Okay, buddy?"

There was kindness in Baker's voice, so Li said, "Yes."

"You could maybe . . . I know! Here."

Baker did something to the car's sky, and all at once a screen came down, glowed, and made *cartoons*. Sudie squealed with joy. A cartoon bird—how could cartoons have birds, not just people?—flew toward the hot ball of morning in the sky, chased by a person. Sudie, Kim, and Jana crowded close.

Li watched through the clear place in the car's sky as Baker and Ann walked toward piles of dirt and crying people. He watched for a long time. The hot ball of morning sunk down into the ground (how did it do that?) and the sky turned wonderful colors, purple and red and yellow. Baker and Ann came in and out, carrying things out with them. On one coming in, Ann touched a place on the wall and morning came inside the car's world, although not in the big world outside. The girls watched the cartoons, too absorbed to even laugh. Li looked outside.

Figures moved in and out of houses made of blankets, some of which Ann had folded. Little bits of morning lighted the blanket houses. And by that light, as he peered out of the car with his nose pushed flat against it, Li saw her.

"Taney!"

Her back ached. She had moved too much, lifted too much, grown too old for this sort of field work. For any sort of field work. But everything was done that could be done tonight. Under the capable direction of the DDR agents, Ann Lionti and Baker Tully, the wounded had been treated, the homeless housed in evac inflatables, the spring water tested and found safe. Everyone had been fed. Tomorrow the dead would be buried. Katherine looked up and saw a ghost at the window of the DDR mobile.

No. Not possible.

But there he was.

Li waved his arms and Katherine, dazed, half lifted her hand before she let it drop. *How* . . . But it didn't matter how. What mattered was that Lionti and Tully, that everyone here, that Katherine herself, was already dead.

The leaving door wouldn't open. It wouldn't *open*, no matter how Li pushed it. He cried out in frustration and shoved Sudie, who was making everything harder by pushing the door in a different direction from Li. But then he got the door open and tumbled down the square rocks made of sky material and he was with Taney, throwing his arms around her waist, Sudie and Jana and Kim right behind him. Kim started licking Taney's face, jumping up in mute excitement.

"Taney! Taney!"

"You found us!"

"You lost your covering! I can touch you!"

"Taney, the world broke and we came out! It broke!"

"Taney! Taney!"

"You know these kids?" Baker said behind Taney. She turned, Li and Sudie still clinging to her, and Baker said in a different voice, "Doctor—what is it?"

"We . . . they . . . Kim, *stop!*"

They had never heard that voice from her before. Li, startled, stepped back. But then Taney's kindness was back, although she sounded very sad.

"Li, take the others back inside the trailer. I promise I'll come in just a little while, okay? Just everybody go inside."

They went, of course; this was *Taney*. Jana and Li stared at each other. Sudie went back to watching the cartoons still showing on the screen. Kim pressed her nose against the clear sky-metal to watch Taney, mutely following her every tiny movement in the gathering dark. Li joined Kim.

A woman ran up to Taney and Baker, waving her arms and shouting.

"Experiments?" Baker Tully said, bewildered and angry and, Katherine could see, terrified. As well he should be. "Bioweaponry experiments?"

"From the very end of the war," Katherine said. "Intelligence discovered the operation and we sent in two entire battle groups five days before the surrender."

"And Ann—" He couldn't say it. It had been hard to pull him away from Ann Lionti's body, lying crumpled between a DDR inflatable and the ruins of an adobe house. Beside her, incongruously, lay an unbroken planter filled with carefully watered dahlias. Now Katherine and Baker stood behind the huge mobile, away from the others. She looked at his young, suddenly ravaged face, dimly lit by a rising gibbous moon, and she thought, *I can't do this.*

He had courage. He got out, "How long? For me, I mean?"

"I don't know for sure. The only tests we could run, obviously, were on animals. When did you and Ann first pick up the children?"

"About six hours ago. Give it to me straight, doctor. *Please*. I have to know."

She saw what he was doing: looking desperately for a way out. All his training, like hers, had taught him that the way out of anything was information, knowledge, reasoning. But not this time.

I can't do this.

She said, "I have to sit down, I'm sorry . . . knee injury." She eased herself onto the ground, partly cutting off the illumination from the floodlamps, so that they sat in shadowed darkness. That should have made it easier, but didn't.

"A virus in their breath gets into the bloodstream from the victim's lungs and makes a targeted, cytopathic toxin. When the virus has replicated enough for the toxin to reach a critical level, it stops the heart. And the virus is highly contagious, passed from person to person."

"So everyone here—"

"Yes," Katherine said quietly.

"I don't understand!" All at once he sounded like a child, like Li. Simultaneously Katherine shuddered and put a hand on his arm. Baker shook it off. "I just don't understand. If that's all true, the virus would spread through the whole country, killing everybody—"

"The—"

"—and then the whole world! The enemy would have killed themselves, too!"

"No," Katherine said. Her knee began to throb painfully. "There are racial differences among genomes. Small differences, and not very many, but enough. Think of genetic diseases: Tay-Sachs among Jews, sickle-cell anemia among Blacks. We've found more, and much more subtle. This virus exploits a tiny difference in genetic structure, and so in cellular functioning, in anyone with certain Caucasian-heritage genes. Tully—"

"The Indians here . . ."

She peered at his face, shrouded in night, and loved him. She had just told him he was going to die, and he had a soul generous enough to think of others. She started to say, "Depends on whether any of their ancestors intermarried with—" when his rage overcame his generosity.

"You're a fucking geneticist! You and the entire United States government couldn't come up with an antidote or vaccine or something!"

"No. Do you think we didn't try?"

"Why didn't you kill them all as soon as you found them?"

Katherine didn't answer. Either he hadn't meant the question, or he had. If it had been just more terrified rage, she certainly didn't blame him. If he meant it, nothing she could say would make it clear to him.

He said bitterly, "There were political considerations, right? Ten years ago it was fucking President DuBois, working so hard to undo the wrongs of the previous screw-ups, ending the war with compassion, re-establishing our fucking position as the so-called moral leader of the world, and so now Ann is dead and I have to . . ." Abruptly his anger ran out.

She waited a long moment and then uttered what she knew to be, the moment she said it, the stupidest, most futile statement of her entire life. "I'm sorry."

He didn't hear it. She sat dreading his reply, and it was a full minute, more, before she realized there wouldn't ever be one. Tully Baker still sat with his head thrown back in fury and anguish against the mobile's rear wheel, but when she felt for his wrist, there was no pulse.

Six hours, then, from the time of initial exposure.

He was too heavy for her to move, but nobody would find him there before morning. She returned to the tent where the villagers had laid Ann Lionti's body and told everyone that Baker was mourning alone, in the trailer. Katherine checked on the patients in the medical tent, issued instructions, and drank coffee to stay awake for the few hours until everyone else slept. Then she removed the distributor caps from the three working vehicles in the small camp and carried them with her inside the DDR mobile, where the children waited.

"Why doesn't she come? Why doesn't she come? Why doesn't she come?" Sudie made the words into a song, and it made Li's face itch. But he didn't let his kindness get used up. Maybe the song helped Sudie wait.

Eventually, however, she fell asleep, and so did Kim. Jana and Li waited. In the light from the car's sky, Jana's hair looked yellow as the big morning. She smelled bad because none of them had splashed in a pool since the first world broke, but Li put his arms around her anyway, just to feel her warmth.

Finally—finally!—the door opened and Taney came in. This time Li really looked at her, at Taney without her covering. Her face was wrinkled. Her eyes sagged. She walked as if something was broken, pulling herself up the square sky-metal rocks by holding onto the edge of the leaving door. Slowly she sat on a chair. Li's heart filled with love.

"Taney," Jana said softly, breaking free of Li's arms and climbing onto Taney's lap. "I knew we'd find you."

"No, you didn't," Li said. He sat on the ground at Taney's feet. "Taney, I have a lot of questions."

"I'm sure you have, dear heart," Taney said, and there was something wrong with her voice. "So do I. Let me ask mine first."

So Li and Jana told them about the break in the world, and Jack and Sally, and sitting beside the broken car on the wide hot path when Ann and Baker came along. Sudie snored and Kim whuffled in her sleep.

"Taney, why were we in that world and not this one?" Li said.

"Tell you what, I'll answer all your questions in the morning," Taney said. "I'm very tired right now and so are you. Look, Jana's almost asleep! You lie down here and sleep. I'm going to see about the other people once more."

"Okay," Li said, because he *was* sleepy.

Taney kissed them all, covered them with blankets, and left. Li heard the leaving door make a noise behind her.

A voice in Katherine's head said, *Even the most passionate minds are capable of trivial thoughts during tragedy.*

Standing there in the dark, it took her a long moment to identify the speaker: Some professor back in college, droning on about some Shakespearian play. Why had that random memory come to her now? She even recalled the next thing he said: that only third-rate dramatists put children in peril to create emotion, which was one reason Shakespeare was infinitely superior to Thomas Hardy.

That professor had been an ass. Children were always the first ones put in peril by upheavals in the world. But not like this . . . not like this.

She unscrewed the gas cap of the DDR mobile and drew the lighter from her pocket. Used for starting campfires at the center of the kindling, it could flick out a long projection that generated a shower of sparks.

The village's distributor caps were inside the mobile. Baker's body lay beside it. Everybody else, marooned here, would be dead by morning, except those with no European ancestry in their genes. And although she'd spent the ten years in Las Verdes mostly keeping to herself, Katherine was pretty sure no such Indians existed in the small village. If they did, they might conceivably be turned into carriers, like Li and Jana and Kim and Sudie, but Katherine didn't think so. The children had been designed to be carriers. Their genomes showed many little-understood variations. The enemy, free from laws against genetic experimentation, had done so with vengeance.

When all hosts died, so did their viruses.

She clicked the lighter and the projection snaked out, already glowing. Her hand moved toward the fuel tank, then drew back.

I can't.

But what were the alternatives? Let the children, locked inside, die of starvation. Or, either if they were picked up by other people or if Li somehow learned to drive the mobile as he had Jack's car, to let them infect more people, who would infect still others, until the airborne virus with a 100 percent kill rate had, at a minimum, wiped out two continents. Who in hell could decide among those three choices?

Katherine had fought for these children's lives, had tended them for ten years, had loved them as her own. What mother would choose the deaths of her children over the fate of the world?

What rational human being would not?

Hail Mary, Mother of God . . . More useless words, rising out of her distant past like subterranean rocks in an earthquake. Her hand again moved toward the fuel tank, again drew back.

She couldn't do it. It was physically impossible, like suddenly flying up into the air. And in less than a few hours she, too, would be dead, and none of this would matter to her any longer. That, too, was a choice: to do nothing.

From beyond the ruined village came wailing, many voices at once. So everyone hadn't gone to sleep, after all. The Indians were holding a ritual mourning for the three dead in the quake. Sudden light flared in the darkess: a bonfire.

Katherine clicked off the lighter and sank hopelessly to the ground. In a moment she would do it, in just another moment. The explosion would be violent and instantaneous; the children would not suffer . . . in just a moment. There was no other choice. Light found its way to her eyes, and she closed them because in such a world there should not be even the flickering light of the bonfire, let alone the steady lying beauty of the silver moon in the wide desert sky.

She woke at dawn. Cold, stiff, shivering—but alive.

With enormous effort, Katherine got to her feet. Limping, she made her way to the medical tent. Everyone in it was dead. So were villagers in the emergency inflatables, and an old man lying beside the ashes of the bonfire. Only Katherine lived.

Trembling, she hobbled back to the mobile, climbed the steps, and unlocked the door. Only Kim was awake, tearing at a loaf of bread with her small sharp teeth. She took one look at Katherine, dropped the bread, and began to lick Katherine's face. Katherine, stretched almost to breaking, started to shove Kim away . . . and stopped.

No. Not possible.

Li woke. "Taney!" he said, rubbing his dark eyes. "I was sleeping."

"Yes." It was a croak. Li noticed . . . those dark eyes, that quick little mind, missed nothing.

"You said you will answer my questions today."

"Yes." Her arms were tight around Kim, so tight the child squirmed. When had Katherine put her arms around Kim, who usually had to be shoved away? She couldn't remember, couldn't think . . . She got out, "Li, when does Kim lick people's faces?"

"When she thinks they're sad or angry or hurt. Taney, you said it was *my* turn to ask questions today."

"Yes."

He crowded close to her, smelling terrible. "You said the first world was to keep us safe. But the feeder broke and we were hungry and then the first world broke, Taney, it *broke*, and all this other world was out here. Why did you say the first world would keep us safe?"

"A safeguard," Katherine said, and wasn't sure what she was saying. "Oh, the bastards—an antidotal safeguard for the first researchers. In her saliva."

"What?"

"Thousands of compounds in saliva. We couldn't possibly have tested them all."

"*What*—"

"Taney," Jana said sternly from the floor, "stop crying. There's nothing to cry about. We found you. . . . Stop it, please, Taney, stop it before my kindness gets all used up."

The real fight was just beginning, she knew that. It would rage on so many fronts: medical, military, political, even journalistic if they drove her to that. So much energy would be required, so much strategy. She had won ten years ago but she was older now, and much more tired.

Nonetheless, her mind was already marshalling arguments. The enemy's research division had been thoroughly destroyed, and so had its personnel. But there was no guarantee that the bombs had actually gotten them all; there had never been any guarantee. The enemy was supposedly our ally now, but if the world situation changed again . . . and things always changed. A biological antidote was the first step toward a vaccine . . . *No, Mr. President, tissue samples cannot provide the same mechanisms as a living organism* . . .

Katherine, driving the DDR mobile across the Mojave, glanced back over her shoulder at Kim, the only ugly and unappealing child of the four. Kim, erratic about controlling her bowels, screaming like a stuck siren, forever licking the faces of people she loved. A child no one would want, a child likely to have been stuck in the back ward of some institution somewhere, while the other three babies would have been adopted, cuddled, loved. Kim, now the most important child on the planet.

"It's my turn now!" Jana said.

"In a minute," Li answered, just as the computer said, "Cat. 'Cat' starts with 'c.' Say 'kuh' for 'c.'"

"Kuh," Li and Jana said simultaneously, and the computer broke into congratulatory song. Li and Jana laughed with excitement.

Sudie suddenly appeared beside the driver's seat. "Taney," she said seriously, "Now that the real world got broke, are you going to keep us safe?"

Medical fights, military fights, political fights, journalistic fights. Katherine's knee throbbed. The desert shimmered in front of her, murderous with heat, the earthquake disaster behind. Katherine was nearly seventy years old, and her knee hurt.

"Yes, dear heart, I am," she said, and drove on across the desert, toward the next world.

FOUNTAIN OF AGE

I had her in a ring. In those days, you carried around pieces of a person. Not like today.

A strand of hair, a drop of blood, a lipsticked kiss on paper—those things were *real*. You could put them in a locket or pocket case or ring, you could carry them around, you could fondle them. None of this hologram stuff. Who can treasure laser shadows? Or the nanotech "re-creations"— even worse. Fah. Did the Master of the Universe "re-create" the world after it got banged up a little? Never. He made do with the original, like a sensible person.

So I had her in a ring. And I had the ring for forty-two years before it was eaten by the modern world. Literally eaten, so tell me where is the justice in that?

And oh, she was so beautiful! Not genemod misshapen like these modern girls, with their waists so skinny and their behinds huge and those repulsive breasts. No, she was natural, a real woman, a goddess. Black hair wild as stormy water, olive skin, green eyes. I remember the exact shade of green. Not grass, not emerald, not moss. Her own shade. I remember. I—

"Grampops?"

—met her while I was on shore leave on Cyprus. The Mid-East war had just ended, one of the wars, who can keep them all straight? I met Daria in a *taverna* and we had a week together. Nobody will ever know what glory that week was. She was a nice girl, too, even if she was a . . . People do what they must to survive. Nobody knows that better than me. Daria—

"Grampops!"

—gave me a lock of hair and a kiss pressed on paper. Back then I kept them in a cheap plastolux bubble, all I could afford, but later I had the hair and tiny folded paper set into a ring. Much later, when I had money and Miriam had died and—

247

"Dad!"

And that's how it started up again. With my son, my grandchildren. Life just never knows when enough is enough.

"Dad, the kids spoke to you. Twice."

"So this creates an obligation for me to answer?"

My son Geoffrey sighs. The boys—six and eight, what business does a fifty-five-year-old man have with such young kids, but Gloria is his second wife—have vanished into the hall. They come, they go. We sit on a Sunday afternoon in my room—a nice room, it should be for what I pay—in the Silver Star Retirement Home. Every Sunday Geoff comes, we sit, we stare at each other. Sometimes Gloria comes, sometimes the boys, sometimes not. The whole thing is a strain.

Then the kids burst back through the doorway, and this time something follows them in.

"Reuven, what the shit is *that*?"

Geoffrey says, irritated, "Don't curse in front of the children, and—"

"'Shit' is cursing? Since when?"

"—and it's 'Bobby,' not 'Reuven.'"

"It's 'zaydeh,' not 'Grampops,' and I could show you what cursing is. Get that thing away from me!"

"Isn't it *astronomical*?" Reuven says. "I just got it!"

The thing is trying to climb onto my lap. It's not like their last pet, the pink cat that could jump to the ceiling. Kangaroo genes in it, such foolishness. This one isn't even real, it's a 'bot of some kind, like those retro metal dogs the Japanese were so fascinated with seventy years ago. Only this one just sort of *suggests* a dog, with sleek silver lines that sometimes seem to disappear.

"It's got stealth coating!" Eric shouts. "You can't see it!"

I can see it, but only in flashes when the light hits the right way. The thing leaps onto my lap and I flap my arms at it and try to push it off, except that by then it's not there. Maybe.

Reuven yells, like this is an explanation, "It's got microprocessors!"

Geoff says in his stiff way, "The 'bot takes digital images of whatever is behind it and continuously transmits them in holo to the front, so that at any distance greater than—"

"*This* is what you spend my money on?"

He says stiffly, "*My* money now. Some of it anyway."

"Not because you earned it, boychik."

Geoffrey's thin lips go thinner. He hates it when I remind him who made the money. I hate it when he forgets.

"Dad, why do you have to talk like that? All that affected folksy stuff—you never talked it when I was growing up, and it's hardly your actual background, is it? So why?"

For Geoffrey, this is a daring attack. I could tell him the reason, but he wouldn't like it, wouldn't understand. Not how this "folksy" speech started, or why, or what use it was to me. Not even how a habit can settle in after it's no use, and you cling to it because otherwise you might lose who you were, even if who you were wasn't so great. How could Geoff understand a thing like that? He's only fifty-five.

Suddenly Eric shouts, "Rex is gone!" Both boys barrel out the door of my room. I see Mrs. Petrillo inching down the hall beside her robo-walker. She shrieks as they run past her, but at least they don't knock her over.

"Go after them, Geoff, before somebody gets hurt!"

"They won't hurt anybody, and neither will Rex."

"And you know this *how*? A building full of old people, tottering around like cranes on extra stilts, and you think—"

"Calm down, Dad, Rex has built-in object avoidance and—"

"You're telling me about software? *Me*, boychik?"

Now he's really mad. I know because he goes quiet and stiff. Stiffer, if that's possible. The man is a carbon-fiber rod.

"It's not like you actually developed any software, Dad. You only stole it. It was I who took the company legitimate and furthermore—"

But that's when I notice that my ring is gone.

Daria was Persian, not Greek or Turk or Arab. If you think that made it any easier for me to look for her, you're crazy. I went back after my last tour of duty ended and I searched, how I searched. Nobody in Cyprus knew her, had ever seen her, would admit she existed. No records: "destroyed in the war."

Our last morning we'd gone down to a rocky little beach. We'd left Nicosia the day after we met to go to this tiny coastal town that the war hadn't ruined too much. On the beach we made love with the smooth pebbles pocking our tushes, first hers and then mine. Daria cut a lock of her wild hair and pressed a kiss onto paper. Little pink wildflowers grew in the scrub grass. We both cried. I swore I'd come back.

And I did, but I couldn't find her. One more prostitute on Cyprus— who tracked such people? Eventually I had to give up. I went back to Brooklyn, put the hair and kiss—such red lipstick, today they all wear gold, they look like flaking lamps—in the plastolux. Later, I hid the bubble with my Army uniform, where Miriam couldn't find it. Poor Miriam—by her own lights, she was a good wife, a good mother. It's not her fault she wasn't Daria. Nobody was Daria.

Until now, of course, when hundreds of people are, or at least partly her. Hundreds? Probably thousands. Anybody who can afford it.

"My ring! My ring is gone!"

"Your ring?

"My ring!" Surely even Geoffrey has noticed that I've worn a ring day and night for the last forty-two years?

He noticed. "It must have fallen off when you were flapping your arms at Rex."

This makes sense. I'm skinnier now, arms like coat hangers, and the ring is—was—loose. I feel around on my chair: nothing. Slowly I lower myself to the floor to search.

"Careful, Dad!" Geoffrey says and there's something bad in his voice. I peer up at him, and I know. I just *know*.

"It's that . . . that *dybbuk*! That 'bot!"

He says, "It vacuums up small objects. But don't worry, it keeps them in an internal depository . . . Dad, what is that ring? Why is it so important?"

Now his voice is suspicious. Forty-two years it takes for him to become suspicious, a good show of why he could never have succeeded in my business. But I knew that when he was seven. And why should I care now? I'm a very old man, I can do what I want.

I say, "Help me up . . . no, not like that, you want me to tear something? The ring is mine, is all. I want it back. *Now*, Geoffrey."

He sets me in my chair and leaves, shaking his head. It's a long time before he comes back. I watch Tony DiParia pass by in his powerchair. I wave at Jennifer Tamlin, who is waiting for a visit from her kids. They spare her twenty minutes every other month. I study Nurse Kate's ass, which is round and firm as a good pumpkin. When Geoffrey comes back with Eric and Reuven, I take one look at his face and I know.

"The boys found the incinerator chute," Geoffrey says, guilty and already resenting me for it, "and they thought it would be fun to empty Rex's depository in it . . . Eric! Bobby! Tell Grampops you're sorry!"

They both mumble something. Me, I'm devastated—and then I'm not.

"It's all right," I say to the boys, waving my hand like I'm Queen Monica of England. "Don't worry about it!"

They look confused. Geoffrey looks suddenly wary. Me, I feel like my heart might split down the seam. Because I know what I'm going to do. I'm going to get another lock of hair and another kiss from Daria. Because now, of course, I know where she is. The entire world knows where she is.

"Down, Rex!" Eric shouts, but I don't see the stupid 'bot. I'm not looking. I see just the past, and the future, and all at once and for the first time in decades, they even look like there's a tie, a bright cord, between them.

The Silver Star Retirement Home is for people who have given up. You want to go on actually living, you go to a renewal center. Or to Sequene. But if you've outlived everything and everybody that matters to you and you're ready to check out, or you don't have the money for a renewal center, you go to Silver Star and wait to die.

I'm there because I figured it's time for me to go, enough is enough already, only Geoffrey left for me and I never liked him all that much. But I have lots of money. Tons of money. So much money that the second I put one foot out the door of the Home, the day after Geoffrey's visit, the feds are on me like cold on space. Just like the old days, almost it makes me nostalgic.

"Max Feder," one says, and it isn't a question. He's built with serious augments, I haven't forgotten how to tell. Like he needs them against an old

man like me. "I'm Agent Joseph Alcozer and this is Agent Shawna Blair."
She would have been a beauty if she didn't have that deformed genemod
figure, like a wasp, and the wasp's sting in her eyes.

I breathe in the artificially sweet reconstituted air of a Brooklyn
Dome summer. Genemod flowers bloom sedately in manicured beds.
Well-behaved flowers, they remind me of Geoffrey. From my powerchair
I say, "What can I do for you, Agent Alcozer?" while Nurse Kate, who's
not the deepest carrot in the garden, looks baffled, glancing back and
forth from me to the fed.

"You can explain to us the recent large deposits of money from the
Feder Group into your personal account."

"And I should do this why?"

"Just to satisfy my curiosity," Alcozer says, and it's pretty much the
truth. They have the right to monitor all my finances in perpetuity as a
result of that unfortunate little misstep back in my forties. Six-to-ten, of
which I served not quite five in Themis Federal Justice Center. Also as a
result of the Economic Security Act, which kicked in even earlier, right
after the Change-Over. And I have the right to tell them to go to hell.

Almost I get a taste of the old thrill, the hunt-and-evade, but not
really. I'm too old, and I have something else on my mind. Besides, Alcozer
doesn't really expect answers. He just wants me to know they're looking
in my direction.

"Talk to my lawyer. I'm sure you know where to find him," I say and
power on down to the waiting car.

It takes me to the Brooklyn Renewal Center, right out at the edge of
the Brooklyn Dome, and I check into a suite. For the next month doctors
will gene-jolt a few of my organs, jazz up some hormones, step up the
firing of selected synapses. It won't be a super-effective job, nor last too
long, I know that. I'm an old man and there's only so much they can do.
But it'll be enough.

Scrupulous as a rabbi, the doctor asks if I don't want a D-treatment
instead. I tell her no, I don't. Yes, I'm sure. She smiles, relieved. For
D-treatment I'd go to Sequene, not here, and the renewal center would
lose its very expensive fees.

Then the doctor, who looks thirty-five and might even be that, tells
me I'll be out cold for the whole month, I won't even dream. She's wrong.

I dream about Daria, and while I do I'm young again and her red mouth is warm against mine in a sleazy *taverna*. The stinking streets of Nicosia smell of flowers and spices and whatever that spring smell is that makes you ache from wanting things you can't have. Then we're on the rocky little beach, our last morning together, and I want to never wake up.

But I do wake, and Geoffrey is sitting beside my bed.

"Dad, what are you doing?"

"Having renewal. What are you doing?"

"Why did you transfer three hundred fifty million from the Feder Group on the very *day* of our merger with Shanghai Winds Corporation? Don't you know how that made us look?"

"No," I say, even though I do know. I just don't care. Carefully I raise my right arm above my head, and it goes up so fast and so easy that I laugh out loud. There's no pressure on my bladder. I can feel the blood race in my veins.

"It made us look undercapitalized and shifty, and Shanghai Winds have postponed the entire—Why did you transfer the money? And why *now*? You ruined the whole merger!"

"You'll get lots of mergers, boychik. Now leave me alone." I sit up and swing my legs, a little too fast, over the side of the bed. I wait for my head to clear. "There's something I need to do."

"Dad. . . ." He says, and now I see real fear in his eyes, and so I relent. "It's all right, Geoffrey. Strictly legit. I'm not going back to my old ways."

"Then why do I have on my system six calls from three different federal agencies?"

"They like to stay in practice," I say, and lie down again. Maybe that'll make him go away.

"*Dad . . .*"

I close my eyes. Briefly I consider snoring, but that might be too much. You can overdo these things. Geoff waits five more minutes, then goes away.

Children. They tie you to the present, when sometimes all you want is the past.

After the war, after I failed to find Daria in Cyprus, I went home. For a while I just drifted. It was the Change-Over, and half the country was drifting: unemployed, rioting, getting used to living on the dole instead of

working. We weren't needed. The Domes were going up, the robots suddenly everywhere and doing more and more work, only so many knowledge workers needed, blah blah blah. I did a little of this, a little of that,
finally met and married Miriam, who made me pick one of the thats. So
I found work monitoring security systems, because back then I had such a
clean record. The Master of the Universe must love a good joke.

We lived in a rat-hole way outside the Brooklyn Dome, next door
to her mother. From the beginning, Miriam and I fought a lot. She was
desperate for a child, but she didn't like sex. She didn't like my friends.
I didn't like her mother. She didn't like my snoring. A small and stifling
life, and it just got worse and worse. I could feel something growing in
me, something dangerous, until it seemed I might burst apart with it
and splatter my anguished guts all over our lousy apartment. At night,
I walked. I walked through increasingly dangerous neighborhoods, and
sometimes I stood on the docks at three in the morning—how insane is
that?—and just stared out to sea until some robo-guard ejected me.

Then, although I'd failed to find Daria, history found her instead.

A Tuesday morning, August 24—you think I could forget the date?
Not a chance. Gray clouds, ninety-two degrees, sixty percent chance of
rain, air quality poor. On my way to work I passed a media kiosk in our
crummy neighborhood and there, on the outside screen for twenty seconds, was her face.

I don't remember going into the kiosk or sliding in my credit chip. I
do remember, for some reason, the poison green lettering on the choices,
each listed in six languages: PORN. LIBRARY. COMMLINK. FINANCIALS. NEWS.
My finger trembled as I pushed the last button, then STANDARD DELIVERY.
The kiosk smelled of urine and jism.

"Today speculation swirls around ViaHealth Hospital in the Manhattan Dome. Last week Daria Cleary, wife of British billionaire-financier
Peter Morton Cleary, underwent an operation to remove a brain tumor.
The operation, apparently successful, was followed by sudden dizzying
trading in ViaHealth stock and wild rumors, some apparently deliberately leaked, of strange properties associated with Mrs. Cleary's con-
dition. The Cleary establishment has refused to comment, but yesterday an unprecedented meeting was held at the Manhattan branch of
Cleary Enterprises, a meeting attended not only by the CEOs of several

American and British transnationals but also by high government offi-
cials, including Surgeon General Mary Grace Rogers and FDA chief
Jared Vanderhorn.

"Both Mr. and Mrs. Cleary have interesting histories. Peter Morton
Cleary, son of legendary 'Charging Chatsworth' Cleary, is known for personal eccentricity as well as very aggressive business practices. The third
Mrs. Cleary, whom he met and married in Cyprus six years ago, has long
been rumored to have been either a barmaid or paid escort. The—"

Daria. A brain tumor. Married to a big-shot Brit. Now in Manhattan. And I had never known.

The operation, apparently successful . . .

I paid to watch the news clip again. And again. The words welded
together and rasped, an iron drone. I simply stared at Daria's face, which
looked no older than when I had first seen her leaning on her elbows in
that *taverna*. Again and again.

Then I sat on the filthy curb like a drunk, a doper, a bum, and cried.

It was easier to get into Manhattan back then, with the Dome only half-
finished. Not so easy to get into ViaHealth Hospital. In fact, impossible
to get in legitimately, too many rich people in vulnerable states of illness.
It took me six weeks to find someone to bribe. The bribe consumed half
of our savings, Miriam's and mine. I got into the system as a cleaning-
bot supervisor, my retinal and voice scans flimsily on file. A system-wide
background check wouldn't hold but why should anyone do a system-
wide background check on a cleaning supervisor? The lowliest of the low.

Then I discovered that the person I bribed had diddled me. I was in
the hospital, but I didn't have clearance for Daria's floor.

Robocams everywhere. Voice- and thumbprint-controlled elevators. I couldn't get off my floor, couldn't get anywhere near her. I'd
bribed my way into the system for two days only. I had two days only
off from my job.

By the end of the second day, I was desperate. I ignored the whispered directions in my earcomm—"Send an F-3 'bot to disinfect Room
678"—and hung around near the elevators. Ten minutes later a woman
got on, an aging and overdressed and over-renewed woman in a crisp

white outfit and shoes with jeweled heels. She put her thumb to the security pad and said, "Surgical floor."

"Yes, ma'am," the elevator said. Just before the door closed, I dashed in.

"There is an unauthorized person on this elevator," the elevator said, somehow combining calmness with urgency. "Mrs. Holmason, please disembark immediately. Unauthorized person, remain motionless or you will be neutralized."

I remained motionless, looked at Mrs. Holmason, and said, "*Please*. I knew Daria Cleary long ago, on Cyprus, I just want to see her again for a minute, please ma'am, I don't mean anybody any harm, oh please . . ."

It was on the word "harm" that her face changed. A small and cruel smile appeared at the corners of her mouth. She wasn't afraid of me; I would have bet my eyes that she'd never been afraid of anything in her life. Cushioned by money, she'd never had to be.

"There is an unauthorized person on this elevator," the elevator repeated. "Mrs. Holmason, please disembark immediately. Unauthorized person, remain motionless or you—"

"This person is my guest," Mrs. Holmason said crisply. "Code 1693, elevator. Surgical floor, please."

A pause. The universe held its breath.

"I have no front-desk entry in my system for such a guest," the elevator said. "Please return to the front desk or else complete the verbal code for—"

Mrs. Holmason said to me, still with the same small smile, "So did you know Daria when she was a prostitute on Cyprus?"

This, then, was the price for letting me ride the elevator. But it's not like reporters wouldn't now ferret out everything about Daria, anyway.

"Yes," I said. "I did, and she was."

"Elevator, Code 1693 Abigail Louise. Surgical floor." And the elevator closed its doors and rose.

"And was she any good?" Mrs. Holmason said.

I wanted to punch her in her artificial face, to club her to the ground. The pampered lousy bitter bitch. I stared at her steadily and said, "Yes. Daria was good."

"Well, she would have to be, wouldn't she?" Sweetly. The elevator opened and Mrs. Holmason walked serenely down the corridor.

There were no names on the doors, but they all stood open. I didn't have much time. The bitch's secret code might have gotten me on this floor, but it wouldn't keep me there. Peter Morton Cleary unwillingly helped me, or at least his ego did. The roboguard outside the third doorway bore a flashy logo: CLEARY ENTERPRISES. I dashed forward and it caught me in a painful vise.

But Daria, lying on a white bed inside the room, was awake and had already seen me.

The Renewal Center keeps me for an extra week. I protest, but not too much. What good will it be if I leave early and fall down, an old man in the street? Okay, I could rent a roboguard—not a good idea to take one from the Feder Group, I don't want Geoffrey tracking me. It's not like I won't already have Agent Alcozer and the other Agent, the hard-eyed beauty, whose name I can't remember. Memory isn't what it used to be. Renewal only goes so far.

It's not, after all, D-treatment.

But I don't want a roboguard, so I spend the extra week. I refuse Geoffrey's calls. I do the physical therapy the doctors insist on. I worry the place on my bony finger where my ring used to be. I don't look at the news. There's going to be something, at my age, that I haven't seen before? Solomon was right. Nothing new under the sun, and the sun itself not all that interesting either. At least not to somebody who hasn't left the Brooklyn Dome in ten years.

Then, on my last day in the Center, the courier finally shows up. I say, "About time. Why so long?" He doesn't answer me. This is irritating, so I say, "*Katar aves*? Stevan?" Do you come from Stevan?

He scowls, hands me the package, and leaves.

This is not a good sign.

But the package is as requested. The commlink runs quantum-encrypted, military-grade software piggy-backing on satellites that have no idea they're being used. The satellites don't know, the countries owning them don't know, the federal tracking system—and the feds track *everything,* don't believe the civil-rights garbage you hear at kiosks—can't track this. I take the comm out into the garden, use it to sweep for bugs, jam two of them, and make some calls.

The next day I check myself out. I wave at the federal agent in undercover get-up as a nurse, get into the car that pulls up to the gate, and disappear.

"Max," Daria said from her hospital bed all those decades ago, in her voice a world of wonder. She snapped something in Farsi to the guard 'bot. It let me go and returned to its post by the door.

"Daria." I approached the bed slowly, my legs barely able to carry me. Half her head was shaved, the right half, while her wild black hair spilled down from the other side. There were angry red stitches on the bare scalp, dark splotches under her eyes, a med patch on her neck like a purple bruise. Her lips looked dry and cracked. I went weak—weaker—with desire.

"How . . . how you have . . ." Her English had improved in ten years, but her accent remained unchanged, and so did that adorable little catch in her low voice. To me that little catch was femininity, was Daria. No other woman ever had it. Her green eyes filled with water.

"Daria, are you all right?" The world's stupidest question—she lay in a hospital room, a tumor in her brain, looking like she'd seen a ghost. But was the ghost me, or her? I remembered Daria in so many moods, laughing and lusting and weeping and once throwing a vase at my head. But never with that trapped look, that bitterness in her green, green eyes. "Daria, I looked for you, I—"

She waved her hand, a sudden crackling gesture that brought back a second flood of memories. Nobody had ever had such expressive hands. And I knew instantly what she meant: the room was monitored. Of course it was.

I leaned close to her ear. She smelled faintly sour, of medicine and disinfectant, but the Daria smell was there, too. "I'll take you away. As soon as you're well. I'll—"

She pushed me off and stared incredulously at my face. And for a second the universe flipped and I saw what Daria saw: a raggedy unshaven *putz*, with a wedding ring on my left hand, whom she had not seen or heard from in eight years.

I let her go and backed away.

But she reached for me, one slim hand with the sleeve of the lace nightgown falling back from her delicate wrist, and the Daria I remembered was back, my Daria, crying on a rocky beach the morning my shore leave ended. "Oh, Max, stay!" she'd cried then, and I had said, "I'll be AWOL. I can't!"

"I can't," she whispered now. Is not possible . . . Max . . ." Then her eyes went wide as she gazed over my shoulder.

He looked older than his holograms, and bigger. Dressed in a high-fashion business suit, its diagonal sash an aggressive crimson, the clothes cut sleek because a man like this has no need to carry his own electronics, or ID, or credit chips. Brown hair, brown beard, but pale gray eyes, almost white. Like glaciers.

"Who is your guest, Daria?" Cleary said in that cool voice the Brits do better than anybody else. I served under enough of them in the war. Although not like this one; no one like this had crossed my path before.

She was afraid of him. I felt it rather than saw it. But her voice held steady when she said, "An old friend."

"I can imagine. I think it's time for your friend to leave." Within an hour, I was sure, he would know everything there was to know about me.

"Yes, Peter. After two more minutes. Alone, please."

They gazed at each other. She had always had courage, but that look chilled me down to my cells. Only years later did I know enough to recognize it, when the Feder Group was involved with hostile negotiations: *I offer you this for that, but I despise you for making me do it. Done?* The look stretched to a full minute, ninety seconds. There seemed to be no air left in the room.

Finally he said, "Of course, darling," and stepped out into the hall. *Done? Done!*

What had Daria become since that morning on the rocky Cyprus beach?

She pulled me close. "Nine tonight by Linn's in alley Amsterdam big street. Be careful you are not followed." It was breathed in my ear, so softly that erotic memories swamped me. And with them, anguish.

She was not my Daria. She had stolen *my* Daria, who might have sold her body but never her soul. My Daria was gone, taken over by this manipulating, lying bitch who belonged to Peter Morton Cleary, lived with him, *fucked* him. . . .

I hope I never know anger like that again. It isn't human, that anger.

I hit her. Not on her half-shaven scalp, and not hard. But I slapped her across her beautiful mouth and said, "Face it, Daria. You always were a whore." And I left.

May the Master of the Universe forgive me.

I have never been able to remember the hours between ViaHealth Hospital and the alley off Amsterdam Avenue. What did I do? I must have done something, a man has a physical body and that body must be in one place or another. I must have dodged and doubled back and done all those silly things they do in the holos to lose pursuers. I must have dumped my commlink; those things can be traced. Did I eat? Did I huddle somewhere behind trash cans? I remember nothing.

Memory snaps back in when I stand in the alley behind Linn's, a sleazy VR-parlor franchise. Then every detail is clear. Hazy figures passed me as they headed for the back door, customers maybe, going after fantasies pornographic or exciting or maybe just as sad as mine. A boy in one of the ridiculous caped-and-mirrored sweaters that were the newest fashion among the young. A woman in a long black coat, hands in her pocket. An old man with the bluest eyes I have ever seen. These are acid-etched in my memory. I could still draw any one of them today. The alley stunk of garbage cans and urine—how did Daria even know of such a place?

And what was I expecting? That she would come to me, sick and thin from illness, wobbling toward me in the fading light? Or that Peter Cleary would arrive with goons and guns? That these were my last minutes on Earth, here in a reeking alley under the shadow of the half-finished struts that would eventually support the Manhattan Dome?

I expected all of that. I expected nothing. I was out of my mind, as I have never been before or since. Not like that, not like that.

At nine o'clock a boy brushed past me and went into the V-R parlor. He kept his head down, like a teenager ashamed or embarrassed about going into Linn's, and so I only glimpsed his face. He might have been Greek, or Persian, or Turkish, or Arab. He might even have been a Jew. The package dropped into my pocket was so light that I didn't even feel it. Only his hand, light as a breeze.

It was a credit chip, tightly wrapped in a tiny bit of paper that brought to mind that other paper, with Daria's kiss. In ink that faded and disappeared even as I read it, childish block letters said LIFELONG, INC. MUST TO BUY TONIGHT!

The chip held a half million credits.

I hadn't even known that she could read and write.

The car that takes me from the Brooklyn Renewal Center is followed, of course. By the feds and maybe by Geoffrey, too, although I don't think he's that smart. But who knows? It's never good to underestimate people. Even a chicken can peck you to death.

The car disappears into the underground streets. Aboveground is for the parks and paths and tiny shops and everything else that lets Dome dwellers pretend they don't live in a desperate, angry, starving, too-hot world. I lean forward, toward the driver.

"Are you an Adams?" This is an important question.

He glances at me in his mirror; the car is not on auto. Good. Auto can be traced. But, then, Stevan knows his business.

The driver grins. "Nicklos Adams, *gajo*. Stevan's adopted grandson."

All at once I relax. Who knew, until that moment, that my renewed body was so tense? With reason: It had been ten years since I'd seen Stevan and things change, things change. But *"gajo,"* the Romanes term for unclean outsiders, was said lightly, and an adopted grandson held a position of honor among gypsies. Stevan was not doing this grudgingly. He had sent his adopted grandson. We were still *wortácha.*

Nicklos stays underground as we leave Brooklyn, but he doesn't take the Manhattan artery. Instead he pulls into a badly lit service bay. We move quickly—almost running, I have forgotten how good it feels to run—to a different level and get into a different car. This car goes into Manhattan, where we change again in another service bay. I don't question the jammers; I don't have to. Stevan and I are *wortácha*, partners in an economic enterprise. Once we each taught the other everything we both knew. Well, almost everything.

When the car emerges aboveground, we are in open country, heading toward the Catskills. We drive through the world I have only read about for ten years, since I went into the Silver Star Retirement Home. Farms guarded by e-fences or genemod dogs, irrigated with expensive water. Outside the farms, the ghost towns of the dead, the shanty towns of the barely living. Until the micro-climate changes again—give it a decade, maybe—this part of the country has drought. Elsewhere, sparse fields have become lush jungles, cities unlivable heat sinks or swarming warrens of the hopeless, but not here. A lone child, a starveling and unsmiling, waves at the car and I look away. It's not shame—I have not caused this misery. It's not distaste, either. I don't know what it is.

Nicklos says, "The car has stealth shields. Very new. You've never seen anything like it."

"Yes, I have," I say. Reuven's 'bot dog, a flash of nearly invisible light, my arms flailing at the stupid thing. My ring with Daria's hair, her kiss. All at once my elation at escaping Brooklyn vanishes. Such foolishness. I'm still an old man with a bare finger and an ache in his heart, doing something stupid. Most likely my last stupid act.

Nicklos watches me in the mirror. "Take heart, *gajo*. *So ci del o bers, del o caso.*"

I don't speak much Romanes, but I recognize the proverb. Stevan used it often. *What a year may not bring, an hour might.*

From your mouth to God's ears.

From the alley behind Linn's I went straight to a public kiosk. That was how little I knew in those days: no cover, no dummy corporation, no off-shore accounts. Also no time. I deposited the 500,000 credits in my and Miriam's account, thereby increasing it to a 500,016. Fortunately, the deposit proved untraceable because Daria knew more than me— how? How did she learn so much so fast? And what had such knowledge cost her?

But I didn't think those compassionate thoughts then. I didn't think at all, only felt. The credits were blood money, *owed* me for the loss of the other Daria, my Daria. The Daria who had loved me and could never have married Peter Morton Cleary. I screamed at the screen in the public kiosk, I punched the keys with a savagery that should have gotten me arrested. As soon as the deposit registered, I went to a trading site, read the directions through the red haze in my demented mind, and bought a half million worth of stock in LifeLong, Inc. I didn't even realize that it was among the lowest-rated, cheapest stock on the exchange. I wouldn't have cared. I was following Daria's instructions from some twisted idea that I was somehow crushing her by doing this, that I was polluting her world by entering it, that I was losing these bogus credits exactly as I had lost her. I was flinging the piece of her dirty world that she'd given me right back in her face. I was not sane.

Then I went and got drunk.

It was the only time in my life that I have ever been truly drunk. I don't know what happened, where I went, what I did. I woke in a doorway, my boots and credit chip with its sixteen credits stolen, someone's spittle on my shirt. If it had been winter, I would have frozen to death. It was not winter. I threw up on the sidewalk and staggered home.

Miriam screaming and crying. My head pounded and my hands shook, but I had thrown up the insanity with the vomit. I looked at this woman I did not love and I had my first clear thought in weeks: *We cannot go on like this.*

"Miriam—"

"Shut up! You shut up! Just tell me where you were, you don't come home, what am I supposed to think? You never come home, even when you're here you're not here, this is a life? You hide things from me—"

"I never—"

"No? What is that plastic bubble with your old uniform? Whose hair, whose kiss? I can't trust you, you're devious, you're cold, you—"

"You went through my Army uniform? My things?"

"I hate you! You're a no-good son-of-a-bitch, even my mother says so, *she* knew, she told me not to marry you find a real *mensch* she said, this one's not and if you think I ever really loved you, a stinking sex maniac like you but—" She stopped.

Miriam is not stupid. She saw my face. She knew I was going to leave her, that she had just said things that made it possible for me to leave her. She continued on, without drawing new breath or changing tone, but with a sudden twisted triumph that poisoned the rest of our decades together. Poisoned us more, as if "more" were even possible—but more is always possible. I learned as much that night. More is always possible. She said—

—and, everything closed in on me forever—

"—but I'm pregnant."

Technology has been good to the Rom.

They have always been coppersmiths, basket makers, auto-body repairers, fortune tellers, any occupation that uses light tools and can easily be moved from place to place. And thieves, of course, but only stealing from the *gaje*. It is shame to steal from other Romani, or even to work for other Romani, because it puts one person in a lower position than another. No, it is more honorable to form *wortácha*, share-and-share-alike economic partnerships to steal from the *gaje*, who after all have enslaved and tortured and ridiculed and whipped and romanticized and debased the Rom for eight centuries. Technology makes stealing both safer and more effective.

Nicklos drives along mountain roads so steep my heart is under my tongue. He says, "Opaque the windows if you're so squeamish," and I do. It does not help. When we finally stop, I gasp with relief.

Stevan yanks open the door. "Max!"

"Stevan!" We embrace, while curious children peep at us and Stevan's wife, Rosie, waits to one side. I turn to her and bow, knowing better than to touch her. Rosie is fierce and strong, as a Romani wife should be, and nobody crosses her, not even Stevan. He is the *rom baro*, the big man, in his *kumpania*, but it is Rom women who traditionally support their men and who are responsible for their all-important ritual cleanliness. If a man becomes *marimé*, unclean, the shame lies even more on his wife than on him. Nobody with any sense offends Rosie. I have sense. I bow.

She nods her head, gracious as a queen. Like Stevan, Rosie is old now—the Rom do no genemods of any kind, which are *marimé*. Rosie has a tooth missing on the left side, her hair is gray, her cheeks sag. But those cheeks glow with color, her black eyes snap, and she moves her considerable weight with the sure quickness of a girl. She wears much gold jewelry, long full skirts, and the traditional headscarf of a married woman. The harder the new century pulls on the Rom, the more they cling to the old ways, except for new ways to steal. This is how they stay a people. Who can say they're wrong?

"Come in, come in," Stevan says.

He leads me toward their house, one of a circle of cabins around a scuffed green. Mountain forest presses close to the houses. The inside of the Adams house looks like every other Rom house I have ever seen: inner walls pulled down to make a large room, which Rosie has lavished with thick Oriental carpets, thick dark red drapes, large overstuffed sofas. It's like entering an upholstered womb.

Children sit everywhere, giggling. From the kitchen comes the good smell of stuffed cabbage, along with the bickering of Rosie's daughters-in-law and unmarried granddaughters. Somewhere in the back of the house will be tiny, unimportant bedrooms, but here is where Rom life goes on, rich and fierce and free.

"Sit there, Max," Stevan says, pointing. The chair kept for *gaje* visitors. No Rom would ever sit in it, just as no Rom will ever eat from dishes I touch. Stevan and I are *wortácha*, but I have never kidded myself that I am not *marimé* to him.

And what is he to me?

Necessary. Now, more than ever.

"Not here, Stevan," I say. "We must talk business."

"As you wish." He leads me back outside. The men of the *kumpania* have gathered, and there are introductions in the circle among the cabins. Wary looks among the young, but I detect no real hostility. The older ones, of course, remember me. Stevan and I worked together for thirty years, right up until I retired and Geoffrey took over the Feder Group. Stevan, who is also old but still a decade younger than me and the smartest man I have ever met, made each other rich.

Richer.

Finally he leads me to a separate building, which my practiced eye recognizes for what it is: a super-reinforced, Faraday-cage-enclosed office. Undetectable unless emitting electronic signals, and I would bet the farm I never wanted that those signals were carried by underground cable until they left, heavily encrypted, for wherever Stevan and his sons want them to go. Probably through the same unaware satellites I had used to call him.

Here, too, one chair was *marimé*. Stevan points and I sit.

"I need help, Stevan. It will cost me, but will not make money for you. I tell you this honestly. I know you will not let me pay you, so I ask your help from history, as well as from our old *wortácha*. I ask as a friend."

He studies me from those dark eyes, sunken now but once those of the handsomest Rom in his nation. There are reasons that stupid novels romanticized gypsy lovers. Before he can speak, I hold up my hand. "I know I am *gajo*. Please don't insult me by reminding me of the obvious. And let me say this first—you will not like what I ask you to do. You will not approve. It involves a woman, someone I have never told you about, someone notorious. But I appeal to you anyway. As a friend. And from history."

Still Stevan studies me. Twice I've said "from history," not "from our history." Stevan knows what I mean. There has always been affinity between Rom and Jews: both outcasts, both wanderers, both blamed and flogged and hunted for sport by the *gaje*, the Gentiles. Enslaved together in Romania, driven together out of Spain, imprisoned and murdered together in Germany just 150 years ago. Stevan's great-great-great-grandfather died in Auschwitz, along with a million other of the Rom. They died with "Z," for *Zigeuner*, the Nazi word for "gypsy," branded on their arms. My great-great-grandfather was there, too, with a blue number on his arm. A hundred fifty years ago is nothing to Romani, to Jews. We neither of us forget.

Stevan does not want to do this for me, whatever it is. But although the Rom do not make family of *gaje*, they are fast and loyal friends. They do not count the cost of efforts, except in honor. Finally he says, "Tell me."

Two days after I bought the LifeLong stock, the news broke. Daria Cleary had had not only a brain tumor but another tumor on her spine, and both were like nothing the doctors had ever seen before.

I am no scientist, and back then I knew even less about genetics than I know now, which is not much. But the information was everywhere, kiosks and the Internet and street orators and the White House. Everybody talked about it. Everybody had an opinion. Daria Cleary was the next step in evolution, was the anti-Christ, was an inhuman monster, was the incarnation of a goddess, was—the only thing everybody agreed on—a lot of money on the hoof.

Both of her tumors produced proteins nobody had ever seen before, from some sort of genetic mutation. The proteins were, as close as I could understand it, capable of making something like a warehouse of spare stem cells. They renewed organs, blood, skin, everything in the adult person. Daria had looked still eighteen to me because her body *was* still eighteen. It might be eighteen forever. The fountain of youth, phoenix from the ashes, we are become as gods, blah blah blah. Her tumors might be able to be grown in a lab and transplanted into others, and then those others could also stay young forever.

Only, of course, it didn't work out that way.

But nobody knew that, then. LifeLong, the struggling biotech company that Peter Cleary secretly took over to set up commercial control of Daria's tumors, rocketed to the stratosphere. Almost you couldn't glimpse it way up there. My half-million credits became one million, three million, a hundred million. The entire global economy, already staggering from the Change-Over and the climate changes, tripped again like some crazy drunk. Then it got up again and lurched on, but changed for good.

No more changed than my life. Because of her.

Should I say the success of my new stock was ashes in my mouth? I would be lying. Who hates being rich? Should I say it was pure blessing, a gift from the Master of the Universe, something that made me happy? I would be lying.

"I don't understand," Miriam said, holding in her hands the e-key I had just handed her. "You bought a house? Under the Brooklyn Dome? How can we buy a house?"

Not "*we*," I thought. There was no more "*we*," and maybe there never had been. But she didn't need to know that. Miriam was my wife, carrying my child, and I was sick of our cruelty to each other. Enough is enough already. Besides, we would be away from her mother.

"I got a stock tip, never mind how. I bought—"

"A stock tip? Oh! When can I see the house?"

She never asked about my business again. Which was a good thing, because the money changed me. No, money doesn't change people, it only makes them more of whatever they were before. Somewhere inside me had always been this rage, this desperation, this contempt. Somewhere inside me I had always been a crook. I just hadn't known it.

I could have lived for the rest of my life on the money Daria gave me. Easy. Miriam and I could have had six children, more, another Jacob with my own personal twelve tribes. Well, maybe not—Miriam still hated sex. Also, I didn't want a dynasty. I never touched my wife again, and she never asked. I took prostitutes sometimes, when I needed to. I took business alliances with men, Italians and Jews and Russians and Turks, most of whom were well known to the feds. And this is when I took on a separate identity for these transactions, the folksy quaint Jew that later Geoffrey would hate, the colorful mumbling Shylock. I took on dubious construction contracts and, later, even more dubious Robin Hoods, those lost cyber-rats who rob from the rich and give to the pleasure-drug dealers.

But dubious to who? The Feder Group did very well. And why shouldn't I loot a world in which Daria—Daria, to whom I'd given my soul—could give me money instead of herself? Money for a soul, the old old bargain. A world rotten at the core. A world like this.

I regret none of it. Miriam was, in her own way, happy. Geoffrey had everything a child could want, except maybe respectability, and when I retired, he took the Feder Group legitimate and got that, too.

I put Daria's lock of hair and paper kiss in a bank deposit box, beyond the reach of Miriam and her new army of obsessive cleaners, human and 'bot. After she died in a car crash, when Geoff was thirteen, I had the hair and paper set inside my ring. By then LifeLong had "perfected" the technique for using Daria's tumor cells for tissue renewal. The process, what came to be called D-treatment, couldn't make you younger. Nothing can reverse time.

What D-treatment could do was "freeze" you at whatever age you had the operation done. Peter Cleary, among the first to be treated after FDA approval (the fastest FDA approval in history, mine wasn't the only soul for sale) would stay fifty-four years old forever.

Supermodel Kezia Dostie would stay nineteen. Singer Mbamba would stay thirty. First came Hollywood, then society, then politicians, and then everybody with enough money, which wasn't too many people because after all you don't want hoi polloi permanently cluttering up the planet. When King James III of England was D-treated, the whole thing had arrived. Respectable as organ transplants, safe as a haircut. Unless the king was hit by a bus, Princess Monica would never succeed to the throne, but she didn't seem to care. And England would forever have its beloved king, who had somehow become a symbol of the "British renewal" brought about by Daria's shaved head.

There were complications, of course. From day one, many people hated the whole idea of D-treatment. It was unnatural, monstrous, contrary to God's will, dangerous, premature, and unpatriotic. I never understood that last, but apparently D-treatment offended the patriotism of several different countries in several different parts of the world. Objectors wrote passionate letters. Objectors organized on the Internet and, later, on the Link. Objectors subpoenaed scientists to testify on their side, and some tried to subpoena God. A few were even sure they'd succeeded. And, inevitably, some objectors didn't wait for anything formal to develop: they just attacked.

I stay with Stevan two days. He houses me in a guest cottage, well away from the Rom women, which I find immensely flattering. I am eighty-six years old, and although renewal has made me feel good again, it isn't *that* good. Sap doesn't rise in my veins. I don't need sap; I just need to see Daria again.

"Why, Max?" Stevan asks, as of course he was bound to do. "What do you want from her?"

"Another lock of hair, another kiss on paper."

"And this makes sense to you?" He leans toward me, hands on his knees, two old men sitting on a fallen log in the mountain woods. There is a snake by the log, beyond Stevan. I watch it carefully. It watches me, too. We have mutual distaste, this snake and I. If man was meant to be in naked woods, we wouldn't have invented room service, let alone orbitals. Although in fact this woods is not so naked—the entire *kumpania* and its archaically lush land are encased under an invisible and very expensive mini-Dome and are nourished by underground irrigation. This is largely due to me, as Stevan knows. I don't have to issue any reminders.

I say, "What in this world makes sense? I need another lock of hair and a paper kiss, is all. I have to have them. Is this so hard to understand?"

"It's impossible to understand."

"Then is understanding necessary?"

He doesn't answer, and I see that I need to say more. Stevan has still not noticed the snake. He is ten years younger than I am, he still has much of the strength in his arms, he lives surrounded by his wife and family. What does he know from desperation?

"Stevan, it's like this: To be old, in the way I'm old, this is to live in a war zone. Zap zap zap—who falls next? You don't know, but you see them fall, the people all around you, the people you know. The bullets are going to keep coming, you know this, and the next one could just as well take you. Eventually it *will* take you. So you cherish any little thing you still care about, anything that says you're still among the living. Anything that matters to you."

I sound like a damn fool.

But Stevan lumbers to his feet and stretches, not looking at me. "Okay, Max."

"Okay? You can do it? You will?"

"I will."

We are still *wortácha*. We shake hands and my eyes fill, the easy tears of the old. Ridiculous. Stevan pretends not to notice. All at once I know that I will never see him again, that this completes anything I might be owed by the Rom. Whatever happens, they will not set a *pomona sinia*, a death-feast table, for me, the *gajo*. That is all right. You can't have everything. And anyway, the important thing is not to get, but to want.

After so long, I am grateful to want anything.

We walk out of the woods. And I am right, Stevan never notices the snake.

Nicklos drives me back to the Manhattan Dome. "*BaXt, gajo.*"

"Good-bye, Nicklos." The young—they believe that luck is what succeeds. I don't need luck, I have planning. Although this time I have planned only to a point, so maybe I will need luck after all. Yes, definitely.

"*BaXt*, Nicklos."

I climb out of the car at the Manhattan Space Port, and a 'bot appears to take my little overnight bag and lead me inside. It seats me in a small room. Almost immediately a woman enters, dressed in the black-and-green uniform of the Federal Space Authority. She's a *shicksa* beauty, tall and blonde, with violet eyes. Genemod, of course. I'm unmoved. Next to the Rom women, she looks sterile, a made thing. Next to Daria, she looks like a pale cartoon.

"Max Feder?"

"That's me."

"I'm Jennifer Kenyon, FSA. I'd like to talk to you about the trip you just booked up to Sequene."

"I bet you do."

Her face hardens, pastry dough left out too long. "We've notified Agent Alcozer of the CIB, who will be here shortly. Until then, you will wait here, please."

"I've notified my lawyer, who will holo here shortly. Until then, you will bring me a coffee, please. Something to eat would be nice, too." Rom food, although delicious, is very spicy for my old guts.

She scowls and leaves. A 'bot brings very good coffee and excellent doughnuts. Max Feder is a reprobate suddenly awakened from the safely dead, but money is still money.

Twenty minutes later Agent Alcozer shows up, no female sidekick. He, Ms. Kenyon, and I sit down, a cozy trio. Almost I'm looking forward to this. Josh holos in and stands in front of the wall screen, sighing. "Hello, Joe. Ms. Kenyon, I'm Josh Zyla, Max Feder's attorney of record. Is there a problem?"

She says, "Mr. Feder is not cleared for space travel. He has a criminal record."

"That's true," Josh agrees genially. He's even more genial than his father, who represented me for thirty years. "But if you'll check the Space Travel Security Act, Section 42, paragraph 13a, you'll see that the flight restrictions apply only to orbitals registered in countries signatory to the Land-Gonzalez Treaty and—"

"Sequene is registered in Bahrain, a sig—"

"—*and* which received global Expansion Act monies to subsidize some or all construction costs and—"

"Sequene received—"

"—*and* has not filed a full-responsibility liability acceptance form for a given prospective space-faring individual."

Ms. Kenyon is silent. Clearly she, or her system, has not checked to see if Sequene had filed a full-responsibility liability acceptance form to let me come aboard. At least, she hasn't checked in the last hour.

Alcozer frowns. "Why would Sequene file a flight acceptance for Max Feder?"

Why indeed? Full-liability acceptances were designed to allow diplomats from violent countries, who might violently object to exclusion, to attend international conferences. The acceptances are risky. If said diplomat blows up the place, no government is legally responsible and no insurance company has to pay. The demolition is then considered just one of those things. Full-liability acceptances are rare, and not designed for the likes of Max Feder.

Josh shrugs. "Sequene didn't tell me how it made its decisions." This is true, since Sequene doesn't know yet that I am coming upstairs. Money isn't the only thing that can be stolen. Every alteration of every record is a kind of theft. Stevan's people are very good thieves. They have had eight centuries to practice.

Jennifer Kenyon, that blonde buttress of bureaucracy, finishes examining her handheld and says, "It's true—the form is on file. I guess you can fly, Mr. Feder."

Alcozer, still frowning, says, "I don't think—"

Josh says, "Are you arresting my client, Agent Alcozer? If not, then this interview is over."

Alcozer leaves, unhappy. Josh shoots me a puzzled look before his holo vanishes. Jennifer Kenyon says stiffly, "I need to ask you some questions, Mr. Feder, prepatory to your retinal and security scans. Please be advised that you are being recorded. What is your full name and citizen ID?"

"Max Michael Feder, 03065932861."

"What is your flight number and destination this afternoon?"

"British Spaceways Flight 165, to Sequene Orbital."

"How long will you be staying?"

"Three days."

"And what is the purpose of your visit?"

Our eyes meet. I know what she sees: a very old man with the hectic and temporary glow of renewal artificially animating his sagging face, too-thin arms, weak legs. A man with how long to live—a year? Two?

Maybe five, if he's lucky and his mind doesn't go first. A dinosaur with the meteor already a foot above the ground, and a criminal dinosaur at that. One who should be getting ready to check out already, preferably without causing too much fuss to everybody staying longer at the party.

I say, "I'm going to Sequene to take D-treatment so I can stay eighty-six years old."

Fifteen years after I established the Feder Group, a girl stopped me as I left the office. A strange-looking girl, dressed in a shapeless long robe of some kind with her hair hidden under an orange cap with wings. I didn't remember her name. I had hired her reluctantly—the orange was some kind of reactionary cult and who needs the trouble—but Moshe Silverstein had insisted. Moshe was my—what? If we'd been Italian, he'd have been my "consigliere." We weren't Italian. He was my number-two until, I hoped, Geoffrey became old enough. It was not a robust hope. Geoffrey, now sixteen, was a prig.

The girl said, "Mr. Feder, could I talk to you a minute?"

"Certainly. Talk."

She grimaced. Under the silly hat, the skinned-back hair, she had a pretty face. She was the accountant for show, absolutely honest, in charge only of the books for the Feder Group, which was also honest. You have to present something to the IRS. "She's brilliant," Moshe had argued. I'd argued back that for this small part of our operations we didn't need brilliant, but here the girl was. I hardly ever saw her, since I was hardly ever in the Feder Group office. My real business all took place elsewhere.

"I've found an irregularity," the girl said, and all at once I remembered her name: Gwendolyn Jameson, and the cult with the modest dress and orange hats was the Daughters of Eve. Opposed to any kind of genetic engineering at all.

"What kind of irregularity, Gwendolyn?"

"An inexplicable and big one. Please come look at this screen of—"

"Screens I don't need. What's the problem?" I was already late to meet a man about a deal.

She said, "A quarter million credits have been moved from the Feder Group to an entity called Cypress, Ltd., that's registered in Hong Kong.

I can't trace them from there, and even though the authorization has your codes on it, and although I found your hand-written back-up order in the files, something just doesn't seem right."

I froze. I hadn't authorized any transfer, and nobody should have been able to connect Cypress, Ltd. with the Feder Group. Nobody.

"Let me see the hand-written order."

She brought it to me. It looked like my handwriting, but I had not written it. It was *inside* our paper files. And somebody had my personal codes.

"Freeze all accounts *now*. Nothing moves in, nothing moves out. You got that?"

"Yes, sir."

I called Moshe, who called his nephew Timothy, who was my real accountant. We went over everything. I paced around the secret office while Tim ran heavily encrypted software for which I'd paid half my fortune. I chewed my nails, I cursed, I pounded on the wall. Like such foolishness could help? It didn't help. Finally Tim looked up.

"Well?" My throat could barely get the syllable out.

"Two and a half million is missing. They've penetrated three accounts—Cypress, Mu-Nova, and the Aurora Group."

"Zurich?" I said. "Did they get into Zurich?"

"No."

Thank you, Master of the Universe. Also thank the Swiss. Zurich held the bulk of my credits.

"This guy's good," Tim said, and the professional admiration in his voice only made me madder.

"Find him," I said.

"I don't do that kind of—"

"I'll find him," Moshe said. "But it will cost. A lot."

"I don't care. Find him."

Two weeks later he said, "I have him. You won't believe this—it's a goddamn *gypsy*. The name he's using is Stevan Adams."

It's not that hard to kidnap a Rom. They rely on hiding, moving, stealth, gypsy-nation loyalty, not so much on pure muscle. What with one thing and another, drought and flooding and war and famine and bio-plagues, the population of the United States is half what it was a hundred years ago. The Romani population has doubled. They take care of their own, but in their own way. Four Rom in a beat-up truck, even an armed and armored truck, were no match for what I sent against them.

Moshe flew me to an abandoned house somewhere in the Pennsylvania mountains. It was old, this house, and peculiar. How did people manage to live here, sixty years ago? Miles from everything, perched on a mountainside, no wind or solar or geothermal energy, facing north with huge expanses of real glass, now shattered. A vacation home, Moshe said. Some vacation—all the place had was a view, which I didn't see because we were using only the basement.

"Where is he?"

"In there."

"Alone, Moshe?"

"Just as you said. The others are in that room over there, the laundry room, drugged. He's just tied up."

"Are you sure you got the right one? Gypsies switch identities, you know. More names for the same person than a Russian novel." I'd done research on the flight in.

Moshe looked insulted. "I have the right one."

I opened the door to what might have once been a wine cellar. Dank, moldy, spiders. Moshe's men had set up a floodlight. Stevan Adams sat bound to a chair, a big man dressed in rough work clothes, with short dark hair and a luxurious mustache. His eyes glittered with intelligence, with contempt. But controlled contempt, this was no cheap cyberthug. This was a man you'd have to kill to break. I didn't kill, not even when it lost me money. There was plenty to take from the world without blood on your hands.

I said, "I'm Max Feder."

He said, "Where are my son and nephews?"

"They're safe. I hurt no one."

"Where are they?"

"In the next room. Drugged but unharmed."

"Show me."

I said to Moshe, "Take the other side of that chair and help me pull it."

Moshe looked startled—this was not how we did things. But it was how I wanted them done now. What so many people never understand is that it's not enough to make money. It's not even enough to be handed money, like Daria (whom I was still, in those years, cursing) handed to me. You have to also be able to keep money, and for that you must be a good judge of people. No—a superb judge of people. This is more than watching them closely, reading body language, seeing when they blink, blah blah blah. It's a kind of smell, a tingling high in the nose that I never ignore. Never. The mind sees what it wants to see, but the body—the body knows.

This smell is a talent, my only one really. I'm not an accountant, not a software expert (as Geoffrey never tires of telling me), not even a particularly good thief when I'm alone. Always I needed Moshe and the Robin Hoods I used, those shadowy young men so adept at stealing from the rich and so bad, without me, at not dying violently. Me, I don't need violence. I can smell.

Moshe and I grabbed the chair and dragged it out of the fruit cellar and into a crumbling laundry room. We gasped and lurched; Stevan was heavy and we were not exactly athletes. Three young men, one scarcely older than Geoffrey, lay bound on the rotted floor, angelic smiles on their sleeping faces. Whatever Moshe had given them, it looked happy.

"See, Mr. Adams? They breathe, they'll be fine."

"Bring them awake so I can see."

Moshe said, "Who do you think you—"

Again I cut him off. "Bring them awake, Moshe."

He grimaced and called, "Dena!" His daughter, our doctor, came in from outside, carrying her weapon. Her face was masked; I don't risk anybody but Moshe and me. She slapped patches on the boys and they woke up, easily and profanely. Stevan and they conversed in Romanes and even though I didn't speak the language, I could see the moment he told them it was no good trying any kind of physical assault. The youngest spat at me, a theatrical bit of foolishness I forgave at once. They were good boys. And would Geoffrey have done as much for me? I doubted this.

We dragged Stevan back into the other room and locked in the bound boys, Dena on guard. Even if they got themselves loose—which, it eventually turned out, they did—she had knock-out gases and everything else she needed.

I said, "You took two and a half million credits from accounts belonging to me."

Stevan said, "So?"

How do I convey the attitude in that one word? Not just contempt but pleasure, pride, deliberate goad. Even if I killed him, he was not going to back down. A *mensch*.

"So you also took my authorization codes. *And* you slipped into my paper files a forged back-up authorization. How did you do that, Mr. Adams?"

Again just that look.

"I'm not going to harm you, or your relatives. Never. In fact, I want to hire you. My operation can use a man like you."

"I do not work for *gaje*."

"Right. I know. *Usually* you don't work for *gaje*. You people go free-lance, this is gutsy, more power to you. But together, you and me together, I can make you rich beyond anything you can imagine."

"I don't need more riches."

Astoundingly, I later found out this was true, and not just because Stevan now had my two and a half million credits. The Rom are not interested in owning very much. Not property: they prefer to rent, so as to move easily and quickly. Vehicles, yes, even planes and helicopters, but always old and beat-up, not conspicuous. Gold for their women but not jewels, and how much gold can one woman wear? Mostly they want to live together in their densely carpeted rooms, getting all they need from gossiping and fighting and loving each other while stealing from everybody else.

Stevan said, "You have nothing I want, *gajo*."

"I think I do. My holdings are big, vaster than anything you've penetrated." So far, anyway. "And I know people. I can offer you something you can't get anyplace else. Safety."

Moshe echoed blankly, "Safety?" I had not told him about this part.

"Yes," I said, addressing Stevan. "I have access to military hardware. Some, anyway. I can get smaller, movable versions of the force-fences that buttress domes. You could keep away anyone you didn't want from your communities, your children, without guns. More: I can do a lot toward keeping any of you that get caught out of jail, unless you commit murder or something."

For the first time, Stevan's expression shifted. Jail is the worst thing that can happen to a Rom. It means separation from the *kumpania*, it means associating with *gaje*, it means it's impossible to avoid *marimé*. Romani will spend any amount of money, go to any lengths to keep one of their own out of prison. Also to keep their children safe; nobody loves their kids like the Rom. And I already knew that gypsies did not commit murder. On this point, eight centuries of bad press was just plain wrong.

"And of course," I said craftily, "money—a very lot of money—can help with lawyers and such if one of your little operations does happen to go awry."

"I don't work for *gaje*."

"Give it up, Max," Moshe said, with disgust.

But I trusted my nose. I waited.

Stevan gazed at me.

Finally he said, "Have you ever heard of *wortácha*?"

Jennifer Kenyon and the FSA let me fly up to Sequene. They have no choice, really. My lawyer is prepared to make a big civil-rights stink if he has to. The current president, who has not had D-treatment, does not want a big civil-rights stink in her administration. She has enough Constitutional problems already. I used to know some of the people causing them.

Shuttle security takes everything but your soul, and that it maybe nibbles at. Every inch of me is stripped and examined by machines and 'bots and people. If I carried any passengers before—lice, tapeworm, non-human molecules—I don't have them after Security is finished with me. I can't bring my own commlink, I can't wear my own clothes, almost I can't use my own bones. Shuttles and orbitals are fragile environments, I'm told. Nobody seems to notice that I'm a pretty fragile environment, too. Finally, dressed in a coverall and flimsy disposable shoes, I'm allowed to stagger onto the shuttle and collapse into a recliner.

Then starts the real punishment.

Space is a game for the young. The flight is hard on my body despite my renewal, despite their gadgets, despite all the patches stuck on my skin like so much red, blue, green, and yellow confetti. I'm eighty-six years old, what do you want from me. Few people wait that long for D-treatment. The attendant doesn't knock me out because then he wouldn't know if anything vital ruptured. It feels like everything ruptures, but in fact I arrive in one unbroken piece. Still, it's a long time before I can walk off the shuttle.

"Mr. Feder, this way, please." A young man, strong. I refuse to lean on his arm. But I look at everything. I've never been on an orbital before, and please the Master of the Universe, I never will again. Fifty years they've been up here, some of these orbitals, but why should I go upstairs? Money and influence travel by quantum packets, not shuttles. And there's never been anything upstairs that I wanted. Until now.

The shuttle bay is disappointing, just another parking garage. My guide leads me through a door into a long corridor lined with doors. Other people walk here and there, but they are led by cute little gold-colored robots, not by a person. Well, this is no more than I expected.

My guard shows me into a small, bare, white room a lot like the one at the Manhattan Spaceport. These people all need a new interior designer.

A woman enters. "Mr. Feder, I'm Leila Cleary. How was your trip up?"

"Fine." This is Peter Cleary's daughter by one of his wives before Daria. She looks about thirty but of course would be much older. Red hair, blue eyes, at least at the moment, who knows. Eyes as hard as I've ever seen on a woman. She makes Alcozer's sidekick and Jennifer Kenyon both look like cuddly stuffed toys.

"We're so glad you chose to honor Sequene with a trip. And so surprised, especially when we discovered that Sequene had filed a full-responsibility liability acceptance form for you."

"Discovered? When, Ms. Cleary?"

"After you had taken off from Earth and before you landed here. How did that happen, Mr. Feder?"

"I have no idea, Ms. Cleary. I'm an old man, can't keep track of all these modern forms. Unfortunately my memory isn't what it was once." I make my voice quaver. She isn't fooled.

"I see. Well, now that you're here, what can we do for you?"

"I want a D-treatment. I know I don't have an appointment, but I'll stay at the hotel until you can fit me in. And, of course, I'll pay whatever premiums you ask for a rush job. Whatever."

"We don't do 'rush jobs,' Mr. Feder. Our medical procedures are meticulous and individually tailored."

"Of course, of course. Everybody knows that."

"You are not just 'everybody,' Mr. Feder. And Sequene is a private facility. We reserve the right to grant or deny treatment."

"Understood. But why would you want to deny it to me? My record? You've treated others with . . . shall we say, complicated backgrounds." I don't name names, although I could. Carmine Lucente. Raul Lopez-Reyes. Worst of all, Mikhail Balakov. But D-treatment is supposed to be a private thing.

"Mr. Feder, you are eighty-six. Are you sure you know what D-treatment can and cannot do? If you think—"

"I don't," I say harshly. Master of the Universe, nobody knows better than I what D-treatment can and cannot do. Nobody. "How about this, Ms. Cleary. I'll stay in the hotel, your best suite, and your people can confer, can run whatever tests you like. I'll wait as long as you like. Meanwhile, take all the blood you want, pretend Sequene is Transylvania, ha ha."

The joke falls flat. Her look could wither a cactus. How much does she know? I have never, in fifty-six years, found out what Daria told Peter Cleary about me. Nor if Peter ever knew that Daria had given me that first half-million credits, so long ago. My guess is no, she doesn't know this, but I can't be sure.

"All right, Mr. Feder. We'll do that. You stay in the hotel, and I'll confer with my staff. Meanwhile, the screen in your suite will inform you about the procedure and all necessary consent forms. You can also send them downstairs to lawyers and relatives. Have a pleasant stay in Sequene."

There is no reason to not have a pleasant stay in Sequene. Once I move—or am moved, my young unsolicited bodyguard at my side— out of the shuttle bay area, the place looks like a five-star hotel in the most tasteful British fashion. Not too new, not too glossy, none of that neo-Asian glitter. Comfort and quality over flash, although Reggie (the b-guard's name) tells me there is a casino "for your gambling pleasure."

Probably the rest of it, too: the call girls, pretty boys, and recreational drugs, all discreet and clean. I don't ask, despite some professional curiosity. I am eighty-six and here just for the D-treatment, a harmless old man trying a last end run around Death. I stay in character.

My suite is beautiful, if small. On an orbital, space costs. Off-white and pale green—green is supposed to be soothing—walls, antique armoire for the my clothes, which have arrived on a separate shuttle. State-of-the-art VR, full scent- and tingly-sprays. The bed does everything but take out the trash. One wall chats me up, very courteously giving instructions for "illuminating" the window. I follow them, and gasp.

Space. The suite abuts the orbital shell, and only a clear-to-the-disappearing-point hull separates me from blackness dotted with stars. Immediately I opaque the window. Who needs to see all that room, all that cold? To me it brings no sense of wonder, only a chill. Three, maybe four atoms per square liter—who wants that? We're meant for warmth and air and the packed molecules of living flesh.

Daria is up here. Somewhere, sequestered, reclusive. She's here. And I'm not going away until I find her.

Before Stevan and I became *wortácha*, he insisted that I meet Rosie. He did not have to do this. Romani men do not need their wives' cooperation to conduct their business affairs; they are not Episcopalians. But Rosie and Stevan did things their own way. He relied on her.

And she was really something back then. In her late thirties, curly black hair, snapping dark eyes beside swinging gold earrings, voluptuous breasts in her thin white blouse. A pagan queen. Not since Daria had I seen a woman I admired so much. She hated me on sight.

"*Gajo,*" she said, by way of acknowledgment. Her lips barely parted on the word.

"Mrs. Adams, thank you for having me here," I said. It came out too sarcastic. I was barely "here" at all; we stood outside the building that the *kumpania* was renting at the moment, a former dance club miles from the Philadelphia Dome. This neighborhood I never would have entered without Stevan and five of his seven brothers surrounding me. A few blocks away, something exploded. Rosie never flinched. She blocked the door to the building like a battalion defending a bridge.

"Rosie," Stevan said, somewhere between irritation and resignation.

"You make a *wortácha* with my husband?"

"Yes," Stevan said. Irritation had won. "Come in, Max."

Carefully I oozed past Rosie, entered directly into the large main room, and sat where Stevan pointed. No one else was present, but I didn't know then how significant this was. All doors from the dark, thickly curtained room stayed closed. The wall screen had been blanked, although a music cube played softly, something with a lot of bass. In one corner a very large holo of some saint raised his hands to heaven over and over, staring at me with reproachful eyes.

Stevan said, "Some coffee, Rosie."

She flounced off, returning too soon—tension had fallen like bricks the second she disappeared—with three coffees. Two in glasses rimmed with gold, one in the cheapest kind of disposable cup. I like sweetener in mine but I didn't ask for it. Nobody offered.

Stevan explained to Rosie the tentative plans that he and I had discussed. She wasn't listening. Finally she interrupted him to talk to me.

"You kidnap my husband, my son, my nephews, and now you want us to do business with you? To make a *wortácha*? With a *gajo*? Are you crazy?"

"Getting there fast," I said.

Stevan said, almost pleadingly, "He's a Jew, Rosie."

"Do I care? He's *marimé* and for you—Stevan!—for you to even—" Abruptly she switched into Romanes, which of course I didn't understand, but it no longer mattered because now *I* wasn't listening.

"—died early a.m. Family mouth only said—" The soft music had given way to news; it hadn't been a music cube, after all, but one of the staccato newslinks that shot out information like rapid-fire weapons. "—no accident. Repeat, Peter Morton Cleary dead—"

"Max?"

"—and *no accident!* So—failure of D-treatment? All die? To—"

"Max!"

"—see later! Fire in Manhattan Dome—"

Then Rosie was pouring water on my head and I was sputtering and gasping. A lot of water, much more water than necessary.

Stevan said, with a certain disgust, "You fainted. What is it? Are you sick?"

"It was the news," Rosie said. "About that *marimé gaji* with the tumors. Have you had D-treatment, *gajo*?"

"No!"

She studied me. I could have been something staked out in a vivisection lab. "Then did you know this Cleary big man?"

"No." And then I said—was it despair or cunning? who knows these things—"But once, long ago, I met his wife. Briefly. Before she was . . . when we were both kids."

Stevan was not interested in this. Rosie was. She gazed at me a long time. I remembered all the old stories about gypsy fortunetellers, seers, dark powers. Nobody had looked at me like that before and nobody has looked at me like that since, for which I am seriously grateful. Some things are not decent.

Stevan said, disgust still coloring his voice, "Max, if you're not well, maybe I—"

"No," Rosie said, and the President of the United States should have such authority in her voice. "It's all right. Set up your *wortácha*. It's all right."

She left the room, not flouncing this time, and I didn't see her again for twenty years. This was fine with both of us. She didn't need a *gajo* in her living room, and I didn't need a seer in my soul. Everybody has limits.

Peter Cleary's death set off world-wide panic. He'd had D-treatment and all his tissues were supposed to be constantly regenerating to the age at which he'd had it, which was fifty-four. He shouldn't have died unless a building fell on him. Never was an autopsy more anxiously awaited by the world. The dead Jesus didn't get such attention.

The press swarmed from the hive. Peter Cleary hadn't been the first to get D-treatment because somewhere there had to be anonymous beta-testers. Volunteers, LifeLong had said, and this turned out to be true. None of them stayed anonymous now. Prisoners on Death Row, heart-breaking children dying of diseases with no cure, a few very old and very rich people. Thirty-two people before Peter Cleary had received pieces of Daria's tumors, and all thirty-two of them were now dead.

Each one died exactly twenty years after receiving D-treatment.

Daria Cleary was still alive.

But was she? That's what a corporate spokesman said, but no one had seen her for years. She and Cleary lived in the London Dome. He went to meetings, to parties, to court. She did not. Rumors had flown for years: Daria was a prisoner, Daria had been crippled by her constantly harvested tumors, Daria had died and been replaced by a clone (never mind that no had ever succeeded in cloning humans). Every once in a while a robocam snapped a picture of her—if it was really her—in her garden. She still looked eighteen. But now even these illegal images stopped.

For two weeks I stayed home and watched the newsholos. Moshe handled my business. Stevan, my new partner, didn't contact me; maybe Rosie had something to do with that. More people who had received D-treatment died: a Japanese singer, a Greek scientist working on the new orbitals, a Chinese industrialist, an American actor. King James of England, perpetually thirty-nine, made a statement that said nothing, elegantly. Doctors spoke, speculating about delayed terminator genes and foreign hosts and massively triggered cell apoptosis and who knows what else. A woman standing in a museum talked about somebody named Dorian Gray.

I waited, knowing what must happen.

The mob appeared to start spontaneously, but nobody intelligent believed that. Cleary stock, not only LifeLong but all of it, had tumbled to nearly nothing. The wild trading that followed plunged three small countries into bankruptcy, more into recession. Court claims blossomed like mushrooms after rain. The attacks on the LifeLong facility and on the Clearys had never stopped, not for twenty years, but not like this. It might have been organized by any number of groups. Certainly the professional terrorists involved were not Dome citizens—at least, not all of them.

The London Dome police would have died to a soldier to stop terrorists, but firing on several thousand of their own citizens, mostly the idealistic young—this they couldn't bring themselves to do. And maybe the cops disapproved of D-treatment, too. A lot of class resentment came in here, and who can tell from the British class system? For whatever reason, the mob got through. The Cleary force fences went down—somebody somewhere knew what they were doing—and the compound went up in flame.

Press robocams zoomed in for close-ups of the mess. Each time they showed a body, my stomach turned to mush. But it was never her.

"Dad," Geoffrey said beside me. I hadn't even heard him come into my bedroom.

"Not now, Geoff."

He said nothing for so long that finally I had to look at him. Sixteen, taller than I ever thought of being, a nice-looking boy but with a kind of shrinking around him. Timid, even passive. Where does such a thing come from? Miriam hadn't exactly been a shy wren and me . . . well.

"Dad, have you had D-treatment? Are you going to die?"

I could see what it cost him. Even I, the worst father in the world, could see that. So I tore my eyes away from the news and said, "No. I haven't had D-treatment. I give you my word."

His expression didn't change but I felt the shift inside him. I could smell it, with that tingling high in the nose that I never ignore. I smelled it with horror but not, I realized, much surprise. Nor even with enough horror.

Geoff was disappointed.

"Don't worry, son," I said wryly, "you'll take over all this soon enough. Just not this week."

"I don't—"

"At least be honest, kid. At least that." And may the Master of the Universe forgive me for my tone. The cat-o'-nine-tails.

Geoff felt it. He hardened—maybe there was more in him than I thought. "All right, I will be honest. Are you what they say you are at school? Are you a crook?"

"Yes. Are you a *mensch*?"

"A what?"

"Never mind. Just drink it down. I'm a crook and you're the son of a crook who eats and lives because of what I do. Now what are you going to do about it?"

He looked at me. Not levelly—he was not one of Stevan's sons, he would never be that—but at least he didn't flinch. His voice wobbled, but it spoke. "What I'm going to do about it is shut down all your businesses.

Or make them honest. As soon as they're mine." He walked out of the room.

It was the proudest of him I had ever been. A fool but, in his own deluded way, himself. You have to give credit for that.

I went back to searching the news for Daria.

She appeared briefly the next day. Immediately the world doubted it was her: a holo, a pre-recording, blah blah blah. But I knew. She said only that she was alive and in hiding. That scientists now told her that only she could host the D-treatment tumors without eventually dying. That she deeply regretted the unintentional deaths. That the Cleary estate would compensate all D-treatment victims. A stiff little speech, written by lawyers. Only the tears, unshed but there, were her own.

I stared at her beautiful young face, listened to the catch in her low voice, and I didn't know what I felt. I felt everything. Anger, longing, contempt, misery, revenge, protection. Nobody can stand such feelings too long. I contacted Moshe and then Stevan, and I went back to work.

My first evening at Sequene I spend in bed. Nothing hurts, not with a pain patch on my neck, but I'm weaker than I expect. This is not the fault of Sequene. The gravity here, the wall screen cheerily informs me, is 95% of Earth's, "just slightly enough lower to put a spring in your step!" The air is healthier than anyplace on Earth has been for a long time. The water is pure, the food miraculous, the staffs "robotic and human" among the finest in the world. So enjoy your stay! Anything you need can be summoned by simply instructing the wallscreen aloud!

I need Daria, I don't say aloud. "So tell me about Sequene. Its history and layout and so forth." I've already memorized the building blueprints. Now I need current maps.

"Certainly!" the screen says, brightening like a girl drinking in boyish attention. "The name 'Sequene' derives from a fascinating European and American legend. In 1513—nearly six hundred years ago, imagine that!—an explorer from Spain, one Ponce de León, traveled to what is now part of the United States. To Florida."

Views of white sand beaches, nothing like the sodden, overgrown, bio-infested swamp that is Florida now.

"Of course, back then Florida was habitable, and so were various islands in the Caribbean Sea! They were inhabited by a tribe called the Arawak."

Images of Indians, looking noble.

"These people told the Spanish that one of their great chiefs, Sequene, had heard about a Fountain of Youth in a land to the north, called 'Biminy.' Sequene took a group of warriors, sailed for Biminy, and found the Fountain of Youth. Supposedly he and his tribesmen lived there happily forever.

"Of course, no one can actually live forever—"

Daria?

"—but here on Sequene we can guarantee you—yes, guarantee you!—twenty more years *without aging a day older than you are now*! Truly a miraculous 'fountain.' As you undergo this proven scientific procedure—"

Pictures of deliriously happy people, drunk on science.

"—we on Sequene want you to be as comfortable, amused, and satisfied as possible. To this end, Sequene contains luxurious accommodations, five-star dining room—"

I said, "Map?"

"Certainly!"

For the next half-hour I study maps of Sequene. I can't request too much, I have to look like just one more chump willing to gamble that twenty years of non-aging life is better than whatever I would have gotten otherwise. It's clear the hotel, the hospital, the casino and mini-golf course and other foolishness don't take up more than one-third of the orbital's usable space. Even allowing for storage and maintenance, there's still a hell of a lot going on up here that's officially unaccounted for. Including, somewhere, Daria.

But it's not going to be easy to find her.

I have dinner in my room, sleep with the help of yet another patch, and wake just as discouraged as last night. I can't communicate with Stevan, not without equipment they didn't let me bring upstairs. I can't do anything that will get me kicked out. All I have is my money—never negligible, granted—and my wits. This morning neither seems enough.

All I really have is an old man's stupid dream.

Eventually I slump into the dining room for breakfast. A waiter—human—rushes over to me. I barely glance at him. Across the room is

Agent Joseph Alcozer. And sitting at a table by herself, drinking orange juice or something that's supposed to be orange juice, is Rosie Adams.

A year and a half after Peter Cleary died, D-treatments resumed. And there were plenty of takers.

Does this make sense? Freeze yourself at one age for twenty years and then zap! you're dead. All right, so maybe it made sense for the old who didn't want more deterioration, the dying who weren't in too much pain. Although you couldn't be too far gone or you wouldn't have strength enough to stand the surgery that would save you. But younger people took D-treatments, too. Men and women who wanted to stay beautiful and didn't mind paying for that with their lives. Even some very young athletes who, I guess, couldn't imagine life without slamming at a ball. Dancers. Holo stars. Crazy.

LifeLong, Inc. reorganized financially, renamed itself Sequene, and moved out of London to a Greek island. The King of England died of his D-treatment, a famous actress died of hers, the sultan of Bahrain died. It made no difference. People kept coming to Sequene.

Other people kept attacking Sequene. By that time, force fences had replaced or reinforced domes; there should have been no attacks on the island. But this is a mathematical Law of the Universe: As fast as new defenses multiply, counterweapons will multiply faster. Nothing is ever safe enough.

So the Greek Island was blown up by devices that burrowed under the sea and into subterranean rock. Again Daria survived. Nine months later Sequene reopened on another island. Customers came.

That was the same year Geoffrey and I finally reconciled. Sort of.

For three years we'd lived in the same house, separate. I admit it—I was a terrible father. What kind of man ignores his sixteen-year-old son? His seventeen-, eighteen-, nineteen-year-old son? But this was mostly Geoff's choice. He wouldn't talk to me, wouldn't answer me, and what could I do? Shoot him? He went to school, had his meals in his room, studied hard. The school sent me his reports, all good. My office, the legitimate Feder Group, paid his bills. For a kid with a large amount of credit behind him, he didn't spend much. When he left high school and started college, I signed the papers. That was all. No discussion. Yes, I tried once or twice, but not very hard. I was busy.

My business had gotten bigger, more complicated, riskier. One thing led me to another, and then another. Stevan Adams and I made a good team. But I took all the risks, since the Rom would rather lose deals than end up in jail. Maybe I took too many risks—at least Moshe said so. He never liked Stevan. "Dirty gypsy keeps *his* hands clean," he said. Not a master of clear language, my Moshe. But the profits increased, and that he didn't complain about.

Federal surveillance increased as well.

Then one October night when the air smelled of apples, a rare night I was home early and watching some stupid holo about Luna City, Geoffrey came into the room. "Max?"

He was calling me "Max" now? I didn't protest—at least he was talking. "Geoff! Come in, sit down, you want a beer?"

"No. I don't drink. I want to tell you something, because you have a right to know."

"So tell me." My heart suddenly trembled. What has he done? He stood there leaning forward a little on the balls of his feet, like a fighter, which he is not. Thin, not tall, light brown hair falling over his eyes. Miriam's eyes, I saw with a sudden pain I never expected. Geoff didn't dress in the strange things that kids do. He looked, standing there, like an underage actor trying to play a New England accountant.

"I want to tell you that I'm getting married."

"Married?" He was nineteen, just starting his second year of college! This would be expensive, some little tart to be paid off, how did he even meet her . . .

"I'm marrying Gwendolyn Jameson. Next week."

I was speechless. Gwendolyn—the accountant Moshe had made me hire, the "brilliant" weird one that had first noticed Stevan's penetration of the Feder Group. Her cult dress and hat were gone, but she was still a mousy, skinny nothing, the kind of person you forget is even in the room. How did—

"I'm not asking your blessing or anything like that," Geoff said. "But if you want to come to the ceremony, you're welcome."

"When . . . where . . ."

"Tuesday evening at seven o'clock at Gwendolyn's mother's house on—"

"I mean, where did you meet her? When?"

He actually *blushed*. "At your office, of course. I went up with the papers for my college tuition. She was there, and I took one look at her and I knew."

He knew. One look. All at once I was back in a *taverna* on Cyprus, twenty again myself, and I take one look at Daria standing by the bar and that's it for me. But *Gwendolyn*? And this had been going on a whole year, over a year. A wedding next week.

Somehow I said, "I wouldn't miss it, Geoff." It was the only decent thing I'd ever done for my son.

"That's great," he said, suddenly looking much younger. "We thought that on the—"

A huge noise from the front of the house. Security alarms, the robo-butler, doors yanked open, shouting. The feds burst in with weapons drawn and warrants on handhelds. Even as I put my hands on top of my head, even as the house system automatically linked to my lawyer, I knew I wasn't going to make Geoff's wedding.

And I didn't. Held without bail: a flight risk. A plea bargain got me six-to-ten, which ended up as five after time off for good behavior. It wasn't too bad. My lawyers did what lawyers do and I got the new prison, Themis International Cooperative Justice Center, a floating island in the middle of Lake Ontario. American and Canadian prisoners and absolutely no chance of unassisted escape unless you could swim forty-two kilometers.

But islands aren't necessarily impregnable. While I was in prison, Sequene was attacked again. Its Greek island was force-fielded top, bottom, and sides, but you have to have air. The terrorists—the Sons of Godly Righteousness, this time—sent in bio-engineered pathogens on the west wind. Twenty-six people died. Daria wasn't one of them.

Sequene moved upstairs to one of the new orbitals. No wind. Two years later, they were back in business.

My third year in prison, Gwendolyn died. She was one of the victims, the many victims, of the Mesopotamian bio-virus. I couldn't comfort Geoff, and who says I would have even tried, or that he would have accepted comfort? An alien, my son. But there must have been something of me in him, because he didn't marry again for twenty-five years. Gwendolyn, that skinny bizarre prig, had imprinted herself on his Feder heart.

When the government got me, they got Moshe, too. Moshe fought and screamed and hollered, but what good did it do him? He also got six-to-ten. Me, I don't bear a grudge. I do my work and the feds do theirs, the *schmucks*.

They couldn't get close to Stevan. Never even got his name—any of his names. If they had, Stevan would have been gone anyway: different identity, different face. For all I know, different DNA. More likely, Stevan's DNA was never on file in the first place. The Rom give birth at home, don't register birth or death certificates, don't claim their children on whatever fraudulent taxes they might file, don't send them to school. Romani don't go on the dole, don't turn up on any records they can possibly avoid, move often and by night. As much as humanly possible in this century, they don't actually exist. And Rom women are even more invisible than the men.

Which was probably part of the reason that, forty years later, Rosie Adams could be sitting in the dining room of Sequene orbital, pretending she didn't know me, while I totter to a table and wonder what the hell she's doing here.

Alcozer ambles over, no sweat or haste, where can I go? Uninvited, he sits at my table. "Good morning, Max."

"Shalom, Agent Alcozer." For the feds I always lay it on especially thick.

"We were surprised to see you here."

The royal "we." Everybody in the fucking federal government thinks they're czars. I say, "Why is that? An old man, I shouldn't want to live longer?"

"It was our impression that you thought you were barely living at all."

How closely did they observe me in the Silver Star Home? I was there ten years, watching holos, playing cards, practically next door to drooling in a wheelchair. The government can spare money for all that surveillance?

"Have some orange juice," I say, pushing my untouched glass at him. Too bad it isn't cut with cyanide. Alcozer is the last thing I need. Over his shoulder I glance at Rosie, who frowns at the tablecloth, scratching at it with the nails of both hands.

She doesn't look good. At the *kumpania* less than a week ago, she looked old but still vital, despite the gray hair and wrinkles. Then her cheeks were rosy, her lips red with paint, her eyes bright under the color-ful headscarf. Now she sits slumped, scratching away—and what is *that* all about?—as pale and pasty as a very large maggot. No headscarf, no jewelry. Her gray hair has been cut and waved into some horrible old-lady shape, and she wears loose pants and tunic in dull brown. From women's fashions I don't know, but these clothes look expensive and boring.

Alcozer leans in very close to me and says, "Max, I'm going to be honest with you."

That'll be the day.

"We know you've been off the streets for ten years, and we know your son has taken the Feder Group legitimate. We have no reason to touch him, so your mind can be easy about that. But somebody's still run-ning at least a few of your old operations, and we don't know who."

Not Moshe. He died a week after his release from prison. Heart attack.

"Also, there are still old investigations on you that we could re-open. I don't want to do that, of course, but I *could*. I know and you know that the leads are pretty cold, and on most the statute of limitations is close to running out. But there could be . . . repercussions. Up here, I mean." He leans back away from me and looks solemn.

I say politely, "I'm sorry but I'm not following."

He says, "Durbin-Nacarro," and then I don't need him to chart me a flight path.

The Durbin-Nacarro Act severely limits the elective surgery avail-able to convicted felons. This is supposed to deter criminals and terrorists from changing their looks, finger prints, retinal patterns, voice scans, and anything else that "hinders identification." Did they think that someone who, say, blows up a spaceport in San Francisco or Dubai would then go to a registered hospital in any signatory country to request a new face? Ah, lawmakers.

Sequene is, of course, registered in a Durbin-Nacarro country, but nobody has ever applied D-treatment to Durbin-Nacarro. The treatment doesn't change anything that could be criminally misleading. In fact, the feds like it because it updates all their biological records on everybody who passes through Sequene. Plenty of criminals have had D-treatment: Carmine Lucente, Raul Lopez-Reyes, Surya Hasimo. But if Alcozer really wants to, he can find some federal judge somewhere to issue a dog-shit injunction and stop my D-treatment.

Of course, I have no intention of actually getting a D-treatment, but he doesn't know that. I put on panic.

"Agent . . . I'm an old man . . . and without this . . ."

"Just think about it, Max. We'll talk again." He puts his hand on mine—such a fucking *putz*—and squeezes it briefly. I look pathetic. Alcozer walks jauntily out.

Rosie is still scratching at the tablecloth. Now she starts to tear her bread into little pieces and fling them around. A young woman in the light blue Sequene uniform rushes over to Rosie's table and says in a strong British accent, "Is everything all right then, Mrs. Kowalski?"

Rosie looks up dimly and says nothing.

"I'll just help you to your room, dear." Gently the attendant guides her out. I catch her eye and look meaningfully upset, and in five minutes the girl is back at my table. "Are you all right then, Mr. Feder?"

Now I'm querulous and demanding, a very rich temperamental geezer. "No, I'm not all right, I'm upset. For what I pay here, that's not the sight I expect with my breakfast."

"Of course not. It won't happen again."

"What's her problem?"

The girl hesitates, then decides that my tip will justify a minor invasion of Rosie's privacy.

"Mrs. Kowalski has a bit of mental decay. Naturally she wants to get it sorted out before it can progress anymore, so she came to us. Now, would you like anything more to eat?"

"No, I'm done. I'll just maybe take a little walk before my first doctor's appointment."

She beams as if I've just declared that I'll just maybe bring peace to northern China. I nod and start a deliberately slow progress around

Sequene. This yields me nothing, which I should have known. I can't get into restricted areas because I couldn't carry even the simplest jammer through shuttle security, and even if I could, it would only call attention to myself, and that I don't need. There are jammers and weapons here somewhere, and from my study of the blueprints I can make a good guess where. I can even guess where Daria might be. But I can't get at them, or her, and it comes to me that the only way I am going to see Daria is to ask for her.

Which I'm afraid to do. When your entire life has narrowed to one insane desire, you live with fear: you breathe it, eat it, lie down with it, feel it slide along your skin like a woman's lost caress.

I was terrified that Daria would say no. And then I would have nothing left to desire. When that happens, you're already dead.

In the afternoon the doctors take blood, they take tissue, they put me in machines, they take me out again. Everyone is exquisitely polite. I talk to someone I suspect is a psychiatrist, although I'm told he's not. I sign a lot of papers. Everything is recorded.

Agent Alcozer waits for me outside my suite. "Max. Can I come in?"

"Why not?"

In my sitting room he ostentatiously takes a small green box from his pocket, presses a series of buttons, and sets the thing on the floor. A jammer. We are now encased in a Faraday cage: no electromagnetic wavelengths in and none out. An invisible privacy cloak.

Of course—Alcozer has jammers, has weapons, has anything I might need to get to Daria. Agent Alcozer.

Angel Alcozer.

He says, "Have you thought about my offer?"

"I don't remember an offer. An offer has numbers attached, like flies on fly paper. Flies I don't remember, Joe." I have never used his first name before. He's too good to look startled.

"Here are some flies, Max. You name three important things about the San Cristobel fraud of '89. The hacker's name, the Swiss account number, and the organization you worked with. Then we let you stay up here on Sequene without interference. Sound good?"

"San Cristobel, San Cristobel," I mutter. "Do I remember from San Cristobel?"

"I think you do."

"Maybe I do."

His eyes sharpen. They are no color at all, nondescript. Government-issue eyes. But eager.

"But I need something else, too," I say.

"Something else?"

"I want—"

All at once I stop. High in my nose, something tingles. This time there is even a distinct smell, like old fish. Something is wrong here, something connected to Alcozer, or to the San Cristobel deal—Moshe's deal, not Stevan's—or to this conversation.

"You want what?" Alcozer says.

"I want to think a little more." I never ignore that smell. The nose knows.

He shifts his weight, disappointed. "Not too much more, Max. Your treatment's scheduled for tomorrow."

How does he know that? I don't know that. Alcozer has access to information I do not. Probably he knows where Daria is. All I have to do is give him the San Cristobel flies, and who gets hurt? Moshe is dead, that particular Robin Hood is dead, the island where it all happened no longer even exists, lost to the rising sea. The money was long since moved from the Swiss to the Indonesians and on from there. Nobody gets hurt.

No. There was something else about San Cristobel. Old fish.

I say, "Let me think a few hours. It's a big step, this." I let my voice quaver. "A big change for me, this place. You know I never lived big on Earth. And for a kid from Brooklyn . . ."

Alcozer smiles. It's supposed to be a comradely smile. He looks like a vampire with a tooth job. "For a kid from Des Moines, too. All right, Max, you think. I'll come back right after dinner." He turns off the jammer, pockets it, stands. "Have another nice walk. By the way, there's no restricted areas on Sequene that you could possibly get into."

"You think maybe I don't know that?"

"I'm trying to find out what you know." Alcozer looks pleased with himself, like he's said something witty. I let him think this. Always good to encourage federal delusion.

Old fish. But whose?

I go to dinner. The second I sit at a table, Rosie totters in to the dining room, lights up like a rocket launch, and shouts, "Christopher!"

I look around. Two other diners in the room so far, and they're both women. Rosie lurches over, tears streaming down her cheeks, and throws her arms around me. "You came!"

"I—"

A harried-looking woman in the light blue uniform hurries through the doorway. "Oh, Mr. Feder, I'm so sorry, she—"

"It's Christopher!" Rosie cries. "Look, Anna, my brother Christopher! He came all the way from California to visit me!"

Rosie is clutching me like I'm a cliff she's about to go over. I don't have to play blank—I *am* blank. The attendant tries to detach her, but she only clutches harder.

"So sorry, Mr. Feder, she gets a little confused, she—Mrs. Kowalski!"

"Christopher! Christopher! I'm going to have dinner with my brother!"

"Mrs. Kowalski, really, you—"

"Would it help if I have dinner with her?" I say.

The attendant looks confused. But more people are coming into the dining room, very rich people, and it's clear she doesn't want a fuss. Her earcomm says something and she tries to smile at me. "Oh, that would be . . . if you don't mind . . ."

"Not at all. My aunt, in her last days. . . . I understand."

The young attendant is grateful, along with angry and embarrassed and a half dozen other things I don't care about. I reach out with my one free hand and pull out a chair for Rosie, who sits down, mumbling. A robo-waiter appears and order is restored to the universe.

Rosie mumbles to herself all through dinner, absolutely unintelligible mumbling. The attendant lurks unhappily in a corner. The set of her body says she's has been dealing with Rosie all day and is disgusted with this duty. Stevan must have created a hell of a credit history for Mrs. Kowalski. Rosie says nothing whatsoever to me, but occasionally she beams at me like a demented lighthouse. I say nothing to her, but I get worried. I don't know what's happening. Either she really has lost it—in less than a week? is this possible?—or she's a better actress than half of the holo stars on the Link.

She eats everything, but very slowly. Halfway through dessert, some kind of chocolate pastry, the dining room is full. The first shift, the old people who go to bed at ten o'clock (I know this, I'm one of them) have left and the second shift, the younger and more fashionably dressed, are eating and laughing and ordering expensive wine. I recognize a famous Japanese singer, an American ex-Senator who was once (although he didn't know it) on my payroll, and an Arab playboy. From Sequene's point of view, it is not a good place for a tawdry scene.

Rosie stands and cries, "Daria Cleary!"

My heart stops.

But of course Daria is not there. There's only Rosie, flailing her arms and crying, "I must thank Daria Cleary! For this gift of life! I must thank her!"

People stare. A few look amused, but most do not. They have the affronted look of sleek darlings forced to look at old age, senility, a badly dressed and stooped body that may smell bad—all the things they have come to Sequene to avoid experiencing. The attendant dashes over.

"Mrs. Kowalski!"

"Daria! I must thank her!"

The girl tugs on Rosie, who grabs at the tablecloth. Plates and wineglasses and expensive hydroponic flowers crash to the floor. Diners mutter, scowling. The girl says desperately, "Yes, of course, we'll go see Daria! Right now! Come with me, Mrs. Kowalski."

"Christopher, too!"

I say softly, conspiratorially, to the girl, "We need to get her out of here."

She says, "Yes, yes, of course, Christopher, too," and gives me a tight, grateful, furious smile.

Rosie trails happily after the attendant, holding my hand.

I think, *This cannot work.* Once we're out of the dining room, out of earshot, out of hypocrisy . . .

In the corridor outside the dining room Rosie halts, shouting again, "Daria!" People here, too, stop and stare. Rosie, suddenly not tottering, leads the way past them, down a side corridor, then another. Faster now, the attendant has to run to catch up. Me, too. So Rosie hits the force fence first, is knocked to the ground, and starts to cry.

"All right, you," the girl says, all pretense of sweetness gone. "That's enough!" She grabs Rosie's arm and tries to yank her upward. Rosie outweighs her by maybe twenty-five kilos. A service 'bot trundles towards us.

Rosie is calling, "Daria! Daria! Please, you don't know what this means to me! I'm an old woman but I was young once, I too lost the only man I ever loved—remember Cyprus? Do you—you do! Cyprus! Daria!"

The 'bot exudes a scoop and effortlessly shovels up Rosie like so much gravel. The girl says viciously, "I've had just about enough of—"

And stops. Her face changes. Something is coming over her earcomm.

Then there is an almost inaudible pop! as the force-fence shuts down. At the far end of the corridor, a door opens, a door that wasn't even there a moment ago. Stealth coating, I think, dazed. Reuven's robodog. My hand, unbidden, goes to my naked ring finger.

Standing in the doorway, backed by bodyguards both human and 'bot just as she was in the ViaHealth hospital fifty-five years ago, is Daria.

She still looks eighteen. As I stumble forward, too numb to feel my legs move, I see her in a Greek *taverna*, leaning against the bar; on a rocky beach, crying in early morning light; in a hospital bed, head half shaved. She doesn't see me at all, isn't looking, doesn't recognize me. She looks at Rosie.

Who has changed utterly. Rosie scrambles off the gravel scoop and pushes away the attendant, a push so strong the girl falls against the corridor wall. Rosie grabs my hand and drags me forward. At the doorway, both 'bot and human bodyguards block the way. Rosie submits to a body search that ordinarily would have brought death to any man who touched a Rom woman in those ways, possibly including her husband. Rosie endures it like a pagan queen disdaining unimportant Roman soldiers. Me, I hardly notice it. I can't stop looking at Daria.

Still eighteen, but utterly changed.

The wild black hair has been subdued into a fashionable, tame, ugly style. Her smooth brown skin has no color under its paint. Her eyes, still her own shade of green, bear in their depths a defeat and loneliness I can't imagine.

Yes. I can.

She says nothing, just stands aside to let us pass once the guards have finished. The human one says, "Mrs. Cleary—" but she silences him with a wave of her hand. We stand now in a sort of front hall. Maybe it's white or blue or gold, maybe there are flowers, maybe the flowers stand on an antique table—nothing really registers. All I see is Daria, who does not see me.

She says to Rosie, "What do you know of Cyprus? Were you there?"

She must think Rosie was a whore on Cyprus when Daria herself was—the ages would be about right. But Daria's question is detached, uninvolved, the way you might politely ask the age of an historical building. *Dating from 1649? Really. Well.*

Rosie doesn't answer. Instead she steps behind me. Rosie can't say my name, because of course we are all under surveillance. She must remain Mrs. Kowalski so that she can go home to Stevan. Rosie can say nothing.

So I do. I say, "Daria, it's Max."

Finally she looks at me, and she knows who I am.

The Rom have a word for ghosts: *mulé*. *Mulé* haunt the places they used to live for up to a year. They eat scraps, use the toilet, spend the money buried with them in their coffins. They trouble the living in dreams and visions. Wispy, insubstantial, they nonetheless exist. I could never find out if Stevan or Rosie actually believed in *mulé*. There are things the Rom never tell a *gajo*.

Daria has become a *muli*. There is no real interest in her eyes as she regards me. This woman, who once in a hospital room risked both our lives to bring me riches and atonement and shame, now has lived beyond all risk, all interest. Decades of being shut away by Peter Cleary, of being hated by people who make periodic and serious efforts to kill her, of being used as a biological supply station from which pieces are clipped to fuel others' vanity, have drained her of all vitality. She desires nothing, feels nothing, cares about nothing. Including me.

"Max," she says courteously. "Hello."

The throaty catch, the hesitation, is gone from her voice. For some reason, it is this which breaks me. Go figure. Her accent is still there, even her scent is still there, but not that catch in the voice, and not Daria. This is a shell. In her eyes, nothing.

Rosie takes my hand. It is the first time in forty years, except for when she was crazy Mrs. Kowalski, that Rosie Adams has ever touched me. In her clasp I feel all of the compassion, the life, that is missing from Daria. Nothing could have hurt me more.

I can't look anymore at Daria. How do you look at something that isn't there? I turn my head and see Agent Alcozer round the corner of the hallway outside the apartment, running toward us.

And then, at that moment and not a second before, I remember what stank about San Cristobel.

The scam went through fine. But afterward, Moshe came to me. *"They want to do it again, this time with a mole. They've actually got someone inside the feds, in the Central Investigative Bureau. It looks good."*

"Get me the details," I said. And when Moshe did, I rejected the deal.

"But why?" Anguished—Moshe hated to let a profitable thing go.

"Because," I said, and wouldn't say more. He argued, but I stood firm. The new deal involved another organization, the one the mole came from. The Pure of Heart and Planet. Eco-nuts, into a lot of things on both sides of the law, but I knew what Moshe did not and wouldn't have cared about if he had. The Pure of Heart and Planet were connected with the second big attack on LifeLong, on that Greek island. The Pure of Heart and Planet along with their mole in the feds, altered and augmented in sacrifice to the greater glory of biological purity, a guy from what used to be Des Moines.

Alcozer runs faster than humanly possible. He carries something in his hands, a thick rod with knobs that I don't recognize. Weapons change in ten years. Everything changes.

And Daria knows. She looks at Alcozer, and she doesn't move.

The bodyguards don't move, either, and I realize that of course they've reactivated the force fence around the apartment. It makes no difference. Alcozer barrels through it; whatever the military has developed for the Central Investigative Bureau, it trumps whatever Sequene has. It handles the guard 'bot, too, which just shuts down, erased by what must be the jammer of all jammers.

The human bodyguard isn't quite so easy. He fires at Alcozer, and the mole staggers. Blood howls out of him. As he goes down he throws something, so small you might not notice it if you didn't know what was happening. *I know*; this is the first weapon that I actually recognize, although undoubtedly it's been upgraded. Primitive. Contained. Lethal enough to do what it needs to without risking a hull breach, no matter where on an orbital or shuttle you set it off. An MPG, mini personal grenade, and all at once I'm back on Cyprus, in the Army, and training unused for sixty-five years surfaces in my muscles like blossoming spores.

I lurch forward. Not smooth, nothing my drill sergeant would be proud of. But I never hesitate, not for a nanosecond.

I can only save one of them. No time for anything else. Daria stand, beautiful as the moment I saw her in that *taverna*, in her green eyes a welcome for death. *Overdue, so what kept you already?* But those would be my words, not hers. Daria has no words, which are for the living.

I hit Rosie's solid flesh more like a dropped piano than a rescuing knight. We both go down—*whump!*—and I roll with her under the antique table, which is there after all, a heavy marble slab. My roll takes Rosie, the beloved of my faithful friend Stevan, against the wall, with me on the outside. I never hear the grenade; they *have* been upgraded. Electromagnetic waves, nothing as crude as fragments. Burns sluice across my back like burning oil. The table cracks and half falls.

Then darkness.

Romani have a saying: *Rom corel khajnja, Gadzo corel farma*. Gypsies steal the chicken, but it is the *gaje* who steal the whole farm. Yes.

Yes.

I wake in a white bed, in a white room, wearing white bandages under a white blanket. It's like doctors think that color hurts. Geoff sits beside my bed. When I stir, he leans forward.

"Dad?"

"I'm here."

"How do you feel?"

The inevitable, stupid question. I was MPG-fragged, a table fell on me, how should I feel? But Geoff realizes this. He says, quietly, "She's dead."

"Rosie?"

He looks blank—as well he might. "Who's Rosie?"

"What did I say? I don't feel . . . I can't . . ."

"Just rest, Dad. Don't try to talk. I just want you to know that Daria Cleary's dead."

"I know," I say. She's been dead a long time.

"So is that terrorist. Dead. It turns out he was actually a federal agent—can you believe it? But the woman you saved, Mrs. Kowalski, she's all right."

"Where is she?"

"She went back downstairs. Changed her mind about D-treatment. Now the newsholos want to interview her and they can't find her."

And they never will. I think about Stevan and Rosie . . . and Daria. It isn't pain I feel, although that might be because the doctors have stuck on my neck a patch the size of Rhode Island. Not pain, but hollowness. Emptiness. Cold winds blow right through me.

When there's nothing left to desire, you're finished.

In the hallway, 'bots roll softly past. Dishes clink. People murmur and someplace a bell chimes. Hollowness. Emptiness.

"Dad," Geoff says, and his tone changes. "You saved that woman's life. You didn't even know her, she was just some crazy woman you were being kind to, and you saved her life. You're a hero."

Slowly I turn my head to look at him. Geoff's eyes shine. His thin lips work up and down. "I'm so proud of you."

So it's a joke. All of it—a bad joke. You'd think the Master of the Universe could do better. I go on an insane quest for a ring eaten by a robotic dog, I assist in the mercy killing of the only woman I ever loved, I save the life of one of the best criminals on the planet—my own partner-in-law in so many grand larcenies that Geoff's head would spin—and the punch line is that my son is proud of me. *Proud.* This makes sense?

But a little of the hollowness fills. A little of the cold wind abates.

Geoff goes on, "I told Bobby and Eric what you did. They're proud of their grampops, too. So is Gloria. They all can't wait for you to come back home."

"That's nice," I say. *Grampops*—what a word. But the wind abates a little more.

"Sleep, now, Dad," Geoff says. He hesitates, then leans over and kisses my forehead.

I feel my son's kiss there long after he leaves.

So I don't tell him that I'm not going back home any time soon. I'm going to have the D-treatment, after all. When I do have to tell him, I'll say that I want to live to see my grandsons grow up. Maybe this is even true. Okay—it is true, but the idea is so new I need time to get used to it.

My other reason for getting D-treatment is stronger, fiercer. It's been there so much longer.

I want a piece of Daria with me. In the old days, I had her in a ring. But that was then, and this is now, and I'll take what I can get. It is, will have to be, enough.

Publication History

These stories were originally published as follows:

"By Fools Like Me," *Asimov's*, 2007
"End Game," *Asimov's*, 2007
"The Erdmann Nexus," *Asimov's*, 2008
"First Rites," *Jim Baen's Universe*, 2008
"The Fountain of Age," *Asimov's*, 2007
"Images of Anna," *Fantasy Magazine*, 2009
"The Kindness of Strangers," *Fast Forward 2*, 2008
"Laws of Survival," *Jim Baen's Universe*, 2007
"Safeguard," *Asimov's*, 2007

About the Author

Nancy Kress is the author of thirty books, including four collections of short stories, and three books on writing. For sixteen years she was the fiction columnist for *Writers Digest* magazine. She is perhaps best known for the "Sleepless" trilogy that began with *Beggars in Spain*. Her work has won four Nebulas, two Hugos, a Sturgeon, and the John W. Campbell Award. Most recent books are an SF novel, *Steal Across the Sky*; a YA fantasy written under the name Anna Kendall, *Crossing Over*; and a short novel of eco-terror, *Before the Fall, During the Fall, After the Fall*. Kress lives in Seattle with her husband, SF writer Jack Skillingstead, and Cosette, the world's most spoiled toy poodle.

Since 2001, Small Beer Press, an independent publishing house, has published satisfying and surreal novels and short story collections by award-winning writers and exciting talents whose names you may never have heard, but whose work you'll never be able to forget:

Joan Aiken, *The Monkey's Wedding and Other Stories*
Ted Chiang, *Stories of Your Life and Others*
Georges-Olivier Chateaureynaud, *A Life on Paper* (trans. Edward Gauvin)
John Crowley, *The Chemical Wedding**
Alan DeNiro, *Skinny Dipping in the Lake of the Dead*
Hal Duncan, *An A–Z of the Fantastic City**
Carol Emshwiller, *Carmen Dog; The Mount; Report to the Men's Club*
Karen Joy Fowler, *What I Didn't See and Other Stories*
Greer Gilman, *Cloud & Ashes: Three Winter's Tales*
Angélica Gorodischer, *Kalpa Imperial* (trans. Ursula K. Le Guin);
*Trafalgar** (trans. by Amalia Gladheart)
Alasdair Gray, *Old Men in Love: John Tunnock's Posthumous Papers*
Elizabeth Hand, *Errantry: Stories**; *Generation Loss; Mortal Love**
Kij Johnson, *At the Mouth of the River of Bees: Stories**
Kelly Link, *Magic for Beginners; Stranger Things Happen; Trampoline* (Editor)
Karen Lord, *Redemption in Indigo: a novel*
Maureen F. McHugh, *Mothers & Other Monsters; After the Apocalypse*
Naomi Mitchison, *Travel Light*
Benjamin Rosenbaum, *The Ant King and Other Stories*
Geoff Ryman, *The Child Garden; The King's Last Song; Paradise Tales; Was*
Sofia Samatar, *A Stranger in Olondria**
Delia Sherman & Christopher Barzak (Eds.), *Interfictions 2*
Ray Vukcevich, *Meet Me in the Moon Room*
Kate Wilhelm, *Storyteller*
Howard Waldrop, *Howard Who?*

Big Mouth House Titles for Readers of All Ages

Joan Aiken, *The Serial Garden: The Complete Armitage Family Stories*
Holly Black, *The Poison Eaters and Other Stories*
Lydia Millet, *The Fires Beneath the Sea: a novel; The Shimmers in the Night: a novel**
Delia Sherman, *The Freedom Maze: a novel*

Forthcoming
Our ebooks are available from our indie press ebooksite:

www.weightlessbooks.com

www.smallbeerpress.com